# The American Girl

Rachael English

W F HOWES LTD

This large print edition published in 2018 by
W F Howes Ltd
Unit 5, St George's House, Rearsby Business Park,
Gaddesby Lane, Rearsby, Leicester LE7 4YH

1 3 5 7 9 10 8 6 4 2

First published in Ireland in 2017
by Hachette Books Ireland



A CIP catalogue record for this book is available from the British Library

ISBN 978 1 51009 193 1

Typeset by Palimpsest Book Production Limited,
Falkirk, Stirlingshire

Printed and bound by
T J International in the UK
Printforce Nederland b.v. in the Netherlands

*For Jenny in Swayfield*

# CHAPTER 1

*Boston, 1968*

Rose Moroney twirled around the bedroom. Arms outstretched, long brown hair swishing, she felt impossibly light, like a dancer *en pointe* or a gymnast on a sprung floor.

'You're still seeing him, aren't you?' said Nancy.

'You know, Nance, what I do is none of your business. I'm seventeen, I don't need a chaperone.'

'Yeah, well, Mom and Dad don't agree. Before they left, they warned me. "Keep an eye on her," they said. "Heaven only knows what she's up to."'

Rose raised a shoulder, smiled, but said nothing.

How she hated sharing a room with her elder sister. Her prissy, prying elder sister. They'd moved all the way out here to Milton, to this huge house, and still she didn't have a room of her own. Being the youngest of six was a drag. Oh, other folks had this crazy idea about her having lots of freedom. 'Lucky you,' they'd say. 'The youngest is always spoilt.' That wasn't how Rose saw it. Not only did her parents insist on watching her every move, she had to put up with her sister and four brothers meddling in her life. You'd swear they had no lives of their own. Actually, in Nancy's case this was true. At nineteen, she was already a frump, and her boyfriend, Theo, was the most boring guy in Boston.

A quick stop in front of the mirror, and Rose smoothed the front of her new dress. If she said so herself, she looked good. The sky-blue cotton brought out the blue of her eyes, and the short skirt emphasised her legs. She decided to back-comb her roots just a teensy bit more. She'd seen a picture of the English model Jean Shrimpton in a magazine and that was the look she was aiming for: wide-eyed, willowy, sophisticated. Not that it was easy to achieve. Just applying her mascara – scraping the brush across the black block before coating each lash – took the best part of ten minutes.

When she'd finished her hair and make-up, she turned to Nancy, who remained spreadeagled across her own bed. 'How do I look?'

'Available.'

'That's the general idea.' Of course, Rose wasn't available – she was Joe's girl – but she liked to keep her sister guessing.

Nancy made a snorting sound and returned to her book. Although Rose was also a reader, Nancy was determined to be the high-minded sister. She was endlessly competitive, anxious to prove to their parents, Ed and Grace, that she was the brighter, more industrious daughter. Rose enjoyed playing up her ditsy side. At school, she'd act dim then confound everybody by scoring straight As. 'That's my Rosie,' her dad would say. 'She keeps those teachers on their toes.' Her mom would get all crabby and tell her she was too old for such silliness.

Rose reached into the back of the closet and plucked out her black spike heels. When her parents were around, her favourite shoes had to remain hidden. 'Inappropriate,' her mother called them. 'Inappropriate' was one of her catchwords, along with 'trashy', 'cheap' and 'coarse'. Sometimes it felt like everything that appealed to Rose fell under one of these headings. Her mom didn't approve of anything young or cool. If she had her way, Rose would be swaddled in a nun's habit, wimple and all. The thought made her smile. She sprayed a cloud of perfume into the air before stepping into it, the way they recommended in the magazines. Then she pulled on her coat and waved goodbye to Nancy. 'See you when I see you,' she said.

'If Mom and Dad ask—'

'If Mom and Dad ask, you know nothing.'

Joe was waiting two blocks away in his brother's car, a wheezy old Pontiac. Given that Rose's parents were away for the weekend, visiting friends in Holyoke, she was probably overdoing the secrecy. Still, since the fuss at Christmas, they'd had to be careful. Plus, there was something romantic about slinking around. It gave her a buzz, and what was life without a buzz?

'We-ell, don't you look fine,' he said, as she eased into the passenger seat.

Rose leaned in, and they enjoyed a smooch. This was one of the many things she liked about Joe Brennan. My, but he could kiss. By comparison, other boys just slobbered or pecked. They were so awkward, trying to touch her up while making the experience about as appealing as a two-hour math lesson. Joe, on the other hand, made her feel like her insides were rearranging themselves. In a good way. Even though he was barely a year older than her and hadn't yet finished high school, she thought of him as a man; a grown-up with ideas and plans and opinions. When she'd first met him, standing on a street corner in Southie, chatting with one of her cousins, she hadn't been swept away or anything. With his bony features, pale brown hair and sad grey eyes, he wasn't even the best-looking guy she'd dated. The more she got to know him, though, the more smitten she became. Some people just had this energy about them. When they talked, you had to listen. Joe was one of those people.

'I'd been hoping we might go to the movies,' he said, 'except I had to buy gas, and money's sort of tight, so is it okay if we hang out at Bree's place?'

'Sounds good to me,' she said, before moving in for another kiss.

Bree was Joe's sister, and the couple spent a

great deal of time in the apartment she shared with her two daughters. Occasionally her husband, Davey, was there too. More often, he was missing, busy with . . . Actually, Rose wasn't sure how he made his living. She'd learned not to ask too many questions. The last thing she wanted was to appear nosy – or uppity. Money, or the lack of it, was part of her family's problem with Joe. But only part of it. His folks weren't exactly model citizens. His father was a boozer and his mom was one of those women who thought nothing of wearing her housecoat in the street. He had an uncle in prison too. As Rose saw it, this made Joe all the more admirable. Any fool would prosper in a strait-laced home like hers, but to grow up with his family and still be such a stand-up guy? That took real character.

By now, they'd left Rose's world – the immaculate colonial houses, the orderly gardens, the children strolling with their mothers – and were motoring towards Joe's world: a world of projects, peeling three-deckers and men mooching outside bars. Well, obviously, it was much more than that. For Rose, Joe's neighbourhood was a welcoming place. She felt like everything, good and bad, was out in the open there. Once, it had been the Moroneys' neighbourhood too. Not that this was something Rose's parents liked to dwell on. An outsider would never guess that Grace and Ed had spent a large chunk of their lives in South Boston, or that they had family still living there.

Joe parked the car close to his family's apartment and returned the keys. Rose waited on the sidewalk. Some days it was best not to get involved in the Brennans' dramas. According to Joe, this was one of those days.

They decided to go for a walk before calling in on Bree.

'I want to show you off,' said Joe, with a wink. 'If that's not too offensive.'

Rose smiled. During one of their long conversations, she'd expressed support for women's liberation. 'So long as I can show you off too,' she said.

'Not only is she cute, she's funny with it,' he replied, pinching her cheek. She pinched him right back.

Just a week earlier, the weather had been squally and bleak, but that Saturday afternoon, while still cool, had the sparkle of spring about it. The streets teemed with people, all shucking off their winter gloom. Many had Irish faces. A couple of years back, Rose had discovered that she could spot an Irish person by the shape of their face or the colour of their eyes or the way they held themselves. Often, she wondered about their stories. What had brought them to America? What did they think of their new home? And whom had they left behind? From time to time, her parents received letters from Ireland. More often than not, they were sombre: one person was ill, another had died, somebody else was in need of money.

Mostly, her mom and dad shrugged and put the letter in the trash, burying the bad news beneath a mound of coffee grounds and eggshells.

'What's up at home?' asked Rose. 'Is your mom okay?'

'As okay as she's ever going to be while my old man's around.'

'What I don't get is why she doesn't boot him out.'

Joe rounded his eyes. 'Money, Rosie. He earns it. She doesn't. As long as that continues, the poor woman's stuck.'

Rose had done it again. When it came to Joe's family, she had this embarrassing ability to say the wrong thing. The harder she tried to show her understanding, the more she displayed her ignorance. Cursing her misstep, she attempted to make light of the situation. 'Do you know, Joseph Patrick Brennan, I think you're more of a women's rights supporter than me.'

She was relieved that when he spoke again his voice was sprinkled with humour. 'Hmm,' he said. 'I'll take that as a compliment. Just don't go telling anyone else about my feminist streak.'

Around them, the air hummed with gossip. Some people were on their way up; more were on their way out. One guy was in trouble with his wife; another was on the run from the cops. There was talk of the Celtics and the Red Sox. There were laments for Blinstrub's nightclub, gutted by fire the month before. Mostly, though, people were going about their business. They were battling on.

When the couple arrived at Bree's apartment, the bottom floor of a sagging three-decker, she was in the hall fixing her hair.

'What do you think, Rose?' asked Bree, as she scowled at the mirror. 'Up or down?'

'Down, I think, with a little more height at the crown, perhaps.'

'Mmm, I reckon you're right. So, JP, to what do I owe the pleasure?'

Joe gave a full-wattage smile. Oh, that smile! One part goofy, one part kind, one part pure sex. 'We figured your day might need brightening up.'

'Aw, how decent of you. You're too late, though. I'm heading over to Dolly's place. She's having a party for her eldest girl. The kids are already there. You could come too . . . I suppose.'

'We could . . .'

'Or you could be honest and admit you're in need of somewhere to make out.'

'Us?' they replied together, acting all offended. In actual fact, none of them was being honest. Joe and Rose did more than kiss and cuddle. For months, they'd been going all the way, exploring each other in ways Rose hadn't thought possible. Bree pretended not to notice.

'Go on, the place is yours for an hour or two,' she said, as she gave her hair a final fluff. 'Try to leave it in one piece.'

Joe knew where Davey kept his liquor, and while

Rose settled into the lumpy brown couch, he fixed two whiskeys. Bree's lounge smelt of cigarette smoke and small children, yet Rose had come to think of it as her second home.

'What would your dad say if he could see us now?' asked Joe, as they cosied in together.

'He'd be thrilled, I'm sure. I can hear him saying, "You go for it, Rosie."'

He gave a gurgling laugh and kissed her neck. 'And your mom?'

'She'd be on her knees saying the rosary.'

Truth to tell, the Moroney family weren't especially religious. Yet when trouble called, her mother sought refuge in rituals and pieties. She liked people to think that they were fervent Catholics too. At Mass, they always had to sit up front. Rose would far rather have been down the back with her friends. When faced with any sort of difficulty, her mom's other trick was to remind the family of her impoverished start. She loved to bore them with tales from her west of Ireland childhood. The suffering. The indignity. The damp. The last time she'd gone on a misery binge, Rose had made the mistake of interrupting. 'I think you'll find, Mom,' she'd said, 'that the awful weather in Rathkelly wasn't my fault.' Her mother's sulk had lasted for three whole days.

Now, as Mick Jagger snarled on Bree's radio, Rose swallowed a mouthful of Wild Turkey and moved in for another smooch. Although the taste was rank, she did love how the whiskey tingled and burned all the way down. It made her light-headed too, which was cool.

'I don't expect you to agree,' she said, as they disentangled, 'but my dad's not the worst guy in the world. He's . . . Well, it's like he has life all figured out for me, and he doesn't want anything – or anybody – to get in the way.'

'I understand,' said Joe. 'Only times are changing. It's not the nineteen fifties any more. Old Ed will have to realise that.'

On Christmas Day, Rose had escaped from home to meet up with Joe. The two had spent most of the day in Bree's apartment. There were swarms of people there, and she'd had more fun than she could ever remember, singing and telling stories and playing games. According to Joe, this was the Brennans' Christmas ceasefire. 'Hostilities restart at midnight,' he'd joked. For her, it was a magical day. Or, rather, it was until her dad had tracked them down. There was an almighty row. There might have been a fist fight, only her father wasn't a particularly big man and some of Joe's cousins were tough. Up until then, her parents had been sniffy about Joe. They'd discouraged her from meeting him. Now she was forbidden from seeing him, period.

This only strengthened his appeal. Nancy, her voice buckling with condescension, maintained Rose would grow out of her Romeo-and-Juliet phase. Rose was honest enough to admit that part of her did like playing the romantic heroine. There was more to their relationship than that, though. She was sure of it.

Sometimes Joe and Rose talked about all the places they'd like to see. What would it be like to camp in the Rockies, they wondered, or to swim off the Florida Keys where even in December the water was warm as soup? Was San Francisco as cool as everybody said? How wild was Las Vegas? More often, they talked about what they wanted to do with their lives. Rose kept changing her mind. For a while, she'd wanted to be a teacher. 'But you don't like being in a classroom now,' Joe had said. 'Why would it feel any different if you were standing up top?' He had a point. All she could say for sure was that she would like to go to college and she'd like to find a job where she could immerse herself in life. Where she could get involved. Sitting in a typing pool was not for her.

When it came to his own future, Joe had lots of ideas but wasn't sure how to put them into practice. Some of his schemes were more serious than others.

'I'm planning on starting a rock band,' he announced, as he played with Rose's hair. 'We'll all become millionaires. Then I'll move my entire family – aunts, uncles, everybody – into the same street as your parents. We'll arrive like the Clampetts in *The Beverly Hillbillies* and terrify the neighbourhood.'

Rose giggled. 'I'm not saying your plan won't work, but it might be good to have an alternative.'

'Wouldn't it just? The trouble is, I look at what's

on offer and I find myself thinking, *Is that as good as it gets?*'

'What do you mean?'

'Walk down any street, what do you see? Guys who do jobs they can't stand, boring, back-breaking jobs. Come the weekend, you'll see those same guys getting blitzed so they can forget about it all. Then on Monday morning, there they are, trudging off to work again. And on and on it goes. And, yeah, I know I'm not exactly the first person to talk like this, but it's so frustrating.'

'Some people like what they do. I'm pretty sure my dad does.'

'Your dad's the boss, Rose.'

'True, but he's had plenty of other jobs too.'

Rose reckoned that it was the desire to make good that bound her parents together. Both had left Ireland in their teens, and both had been determined to grasp whatever opportunity came their way. Her father had taken work wherever he'd found it, mostly on construction sites. Despite clocking up sixty or seventy hours a week, he'd managed to do a business course at night. Eventually he'd accumulated enough cash to start his own construction company. If anything, her mother was more obsessive about forging ahead. 'I didn't cross the Atlantic to live in poverty,' she liked to say.

'I suppose,' continued Joe, 'what I'm trying to find is something that feels like it's worth doing. Something that's not just about the money. Does that sound lame?'

'Nope, I can see where you're coming from.'

With any other guy, she would be sceptical. She'd accuse him of spinning a line to charm his way into her panties. Joe didn't need to do that. Oh, she was sure that an eavesdropper would dismiss them as naive kids, but she believed that Joe meant every word he said. He was different. They were different.

Rose rested one hand on his thigh and kissed the side of his face. He responded with enthusiasm and for a while they stayed on the couch, kissing and nuzzling and touching. Pleasure tickled her body.

'And you,' Joe said.

'Sorry?'

'I'd like you to be part of my life, I mean.'

'That's what I'd like too,' she said, as Joe's hand crept inside her pantyhose.

'You know,' he said, his voice little more than a whisper, 'there's nothing to stop us using the bed.'

'Bree and Davey's bed?'

'I don't see either of them here, do you?'

'Let's go,' said Rose, her head all woozy, partly from the whiskey, partly from Joe's touch. She kissed his forehead. Just in that moment, she was incredibly, deliriously, happy.

It was funny. For the longest time, Rose had been able to picture Nancy's future: marriage to Theo; a house not far from their parents; a family of dull, well-behaved children. The shape of her own future had remained a blur. That was beginning to change.

* * *

How soon did she know? When her period was more than a week overdue, she had a fairly solid idea. Rose lied to herself, though, told herself it didn't mean anything. She kept pretending she could feel her period's dull weight, that it would start at any minute. She was like a small animal, hunkering low, hoping the danger would pass.

Hiding was easy. Boston, like the rest of the country, was convulsed by the assassination of Robert Kennedy. Coming so soon after the murder of Martin Luther King, the death felt doubly shocking. At night, the Moroney family sat around the TV, monitoring the tumult, Grace muttering about the world going to hell in a handbasket, Ed complaining that America had become a very strange place indeed.

By the time Rose spoke to Joe, she'd missed two periods. She was bloated and achy – and sick. The previous day, she'd had to throw up at school. Halfway through English class, she'd bolted for the bathroom. 'Stomach flu,' she'd explained. Although the nurse had tried to send her home, she'd insisted on staying put. The last thing Rose wanted was to attract her mother's attention.

They were in Bree's apartment. Outside, the June heat scalded the sidewalks, melted the roads and left red weals on pale Irish skin. Inside was cooler but airless. Joe was babysitting. Thankfully, both of his nieces had gone for a nap. Rose's mom and dad thought she was with her cousin, Teresa. They thought she spent a lot of time with Teresa.

As the news sank in, Joe's face changed. First a tic appeared in his right cheek. Then his mouth tightened, like it was being pulled by a string. Finally his entire face went rigid with panic. 'Damn it, Rose,' he said. 'How did that happen?'

The words cut through her, like a switchblade. That wasn't the reaction she'd expected.

Immediately, he realised his mistake. 'Oh, God, honey, I'm sorry. I didn't mean that the way it must have sounded. I was taken aback, that's all.'

The need to weep had been welling up inside her, and finally she succumbed. One tear became twenty, and one tremble became a hundred shudders. She did her best not to make noise – she was anxious not to wake the children – but hiccups and sobs kept bursting out.

Joe wrapped himself around her, his palms running up and down her back. 'Please forgive me, Rosie,' he said, and 'Everything's going to be okay,' and 'Please stop crying.'

When finally the tears did stop and the shuddering had run its course, Joe lit them both a cigarette. They sat in silence, long curls of smoke drifting to the ceiling. 'What are we going to do?' he said eventually.

'I don't know.'

He exhaled a last whoosh of smoke and stubbed out his cigarette. 'Well, I do. We're going to be together . . . if that's what you want. You, me and the baby. Our baby.'

'Of course it's what I want,' said Rose. 'I just didn't expect it to happen like this, you know? Not to us . . . to people who have lives to live.'

That was the truth. She'd been stupid. Not controlled enough. Not careful enough. Too caught up in the pleasure and adventure of being with Joe. Too convinced of her own sophistication. Now that she thought about it, she didn't believe any of her high-school friends were having sex. Sure, they claimed they were. But they exaggerated. To listen to them you'd think every peck on the cheek was a passionate embrace; every bungling fumble a life-changing experience. No, Rose was the only one who'd been dumb enough to have sex – and to get caught.

Joe was talking. 'We can still live our lives, Rose,' he said, as he stroked her hand. 'Don't you worry.'

She knew he was trying to reassure her, but fear remained in his eyes.

'I do love you,' he said.

'And I love you.' Another tear slithered down her face.

'And, okay, this is all moving more quickly than we might have planned but, like my mom says, things happen for a reason.'

Rose was going through a muddle of emotions. Her mouth was paper dry, her limbs heavy. Even though she'd given voice to what was happening, it still felt unreal. She expected that at any moment she'd be back in her bedroom, teasing Nancy, barely a serious thought in her head.

Joe put an arm around her and pulled her in close. 'How far along are you?'

'A couple of months, I guess.'

'All right,' he said. She could almost hear his brain whirring. 'We've got a bit of time, then. Does anybody else—'

'Oh, no, nobody at home has any idea. Can you imagine if they did?'

He brushed his lips along her forehead. 'My poor Rosie, keeping this bottled up. What we need is a plan.'

'I'll have to tell my parents, only . . .' She started shaking again.

'First things first,' said Joe, as he rose from the couch. Before she appreciated what he was doing, he was on one knee, squeezing her hand. 'Rose Moroney, will you marry me?'

She smiled, and a tear slipped into her mouth. 'Yes,' she said. 'I will.'

# CHAPTER 2

It was Nancy who joined the dots. She could have done the decent thing and spoken to Rose first, but she had to go blabbing, telling their mom about her sister throwing up and looking all queer. Whatever else Grace was, she was no fool. She'd been through eight pregnancies – six children and two miscarriages – and she knew what her elder daughter was saying.

Rose was terrified. She wished she'd had more time to rehearse her lines but she also felt an instinctive need to tell the truth. What was the point in lying? Even if she wanted to, she couldn't wish her pregnancy away. As the days passed, she was coming to terms with her predicament. Like Joe said, everything was moving more quickly than they'd planned. But so what? The same thing had happened to thousands, millions, before her, and they had coped. She loved Joe. He loved her. That was what mattered.

So, sitting across from both parents in the family's icy lounge, she gave an honest answer. 'Yes,' she said, 'I believe I am.'

‘Oh, Rosie,’ said her father, his face wilting. ‘Are you sure?’

‘I—’

Her mother intervened: ‘I should have known that something like this would happen. How could you be so stupid?’

Again, Rose tried to reply, but her mom didn’t want an answer. She wanted to continue her tirade. When she got angry, she lost all subtlety. The world was black or white; dirty or clean; respectable or cheap. Oh, and she went back to her roots. As she shouted, her accent returned to County Mayo. No insult was too base, no language too strong. Rose was no better than a whore; her behaviour was sordid; she was damaged goods and would end up in the gutter.

Rose stayed quiet. Her eyes remained dry. She had expected something like this. She would have to ride it out.

After a while, her dad attempted to speak, but her mother hadn’t finished. She waved a hand as if to say, ‘Butt out.’ ‘And the father?’ she said, her voice confused, as though the baby’s dad might be some random guy Rose had met on the street.

‘Joe,’ Rose said quietly. ‘Joe Brennan. It’s okay, though. We’re going to get married.’

Her mom appeared to lift herself up by a few inches. ‘Be sensible, Rose. Do you really think you’re going to get married and raise a child in some cockroach-infested apartment? You and a gang of criminals? You're little more than a child yourself.'

'Joe's not a criminal.'

'Some of his family are,' said her dad. 'And, whether you like it or not, most people end up living the life their family lived before them.'

'You didn't.'

With that, her mother leaned forward and slapped her – *thwack* – across the face. 'You won't compare your father to the sort of people you've been hanging about with.'

Rose recoiled, her only sound a feeble *ow*. She expected her dad to step in, but while a frown rushed across his face, he said nothing.

'Of course,' continued her mother, 'we should have done more to stop you seeing this Joe Brennan fellow. What we—'

Finally, her dad cleared his throat. 'You've made a serious mistake, Rose, and we're very disappointed in you. Whatever you might think now, you don't want to marry that boy. You haven't finished school, and I doubt he has any means of supporting you and a baby.'

Although her face was stinging, Rose willed herself to sound strong and firm. 'You don't know Joe. I promise you he's a smart guy. Like, really, seriously smart. He's just finishing high school and he's going to get a job and . . .' She was on the brink of suggesting her dad could give him that job only she feared it would be a step too far.

Silent panic filled the room. Rose had the

feeling that her mother regretted the slap. Respectable women didn't slap their daughters. Respectable women were subtle.

When her mom spoke again, her tone was more measured, her Boston accent restored. She looked directly at Rose. 'Please can we stop this foolish talk about marriage?' Before Rose could reply, her mother lobbed in another question. 'Apart from Joe, does anybody know you're expecting?'

'Unless he's told somebody, no.'

'That's how it's going to stay. While we decide what to do, you're not to say anything. Do you hear?'

'But I need to talk to him. He's entitled to know what's going on.' She hesitated. 'Perhaps you could invite him over.'

Her mother gave a hurried shake of the head. 'That, Rose, is out of the question. You're not to talk to him – or to anybody else. The last thing we want is word of your situation getting around.'

'I don't understand. You can't keep me here like I'm a prisoner or something.'

'You'll stay here while we work out what to do.'

'I don't follow you.'

Her mother massaged her forehead with both hands. Some time passed before she spoke, and when she did, her voice was flat. 'There are ways of handling these things,' she said.

There was consternation in the house, all of them weighing in with opinions and suggestions.

Everybody was allowed to have a view – except Rose. Mostly, she was confined to her room. Her mother told her to stay there and reflect on the damage she'd done. Even school was off limits. Rose didn't hear everything her family said but she heard enough to know there was friction. Her dad suggested a trip to the doctor to confirm the pregnancy. Her mom said no, she didn't trust the man. 'The news will be all around the neighbourhood, and where will we be then?' she asked. The one person who was consulted was the parish priest. Once again, bad news had brought out Grace's religious streak. Candles were lit, and previously unknown saints were asked to intercede.

Nancy and two of Rose's brothers, Ed junior and Ray, acted all shocked and appalled. Rose suspected they were enjoying her shame. 'I always said she was spoiled,' said Ray, sounding closer to fifty-five than his actual twenty-five. Another brother, Gene, didn't seem overly bothered. Then again, Gene was rarely bothered by anything. He lived in his own world, his face suggesting his thoughts were on another plane, far away from the dreariness of Moroney family life.

Her fourth brother, Kevin, thought she should be allowed to marry Joe. 'Okay,' he said, 'the situation's not ideal, but it's obvious Rosie loves the guy. Why not invite him over and talk it through?'

'Please tell me you're joking,' said their mother. 'Or is that the type of liberal nonsense they're teaching at BC these days?'

The brightest of the family, Kevin was in his junior year at Boston College. He hoped to go to law school. 'Just so as we're clear,' he said, 'what is it that's upsetting you? The fact that Rose is pregnant or the fact that you don't like the baby's father? Not that you even know this Joe Brennan fellow. You've simply decided he's too low class for us.'

Her mom picked an imaginary speck from the skirt of her pale peach dress. 'You think you're so superior to the rest of us, don't you? Well, let me tell you, when it comes to the workings of the world, you've got a lot to learn.'

'Please,' said her dad. 'Please can we stop this? It's not helping.'

Rose watched them with a peculiar sense of detachment. They were her family. She loved them. Apart from Kevin and her dad, though, she didn't enjoy spending time with them. They were too competitive (Nancy) or too strange (Gene), too obnoxious (Ray and Ed junior) or just too much hard work (her mom). Deciding she'd listened to enough of their bickering, she left the room and went to bed. Life was simpler there. She was desperate to see Joe but, short of digging a tunnel, she couldn't see a way of escaping. They'd been due to meet the previous Saturday, and she hoped he understood her no-show. She needed to get a message to him, only that wasn't easy either.

As the days passed, Rose found herself seesawing from one extreme to the other. The mornings were her optimistic time. She believed that sooner or later her parents would see reason. It was 1968, for God's sake. They couldn't keep her cloistered at home for ever. She pictured herself, the young Mrs Brennan, pushing her baby in a carriage. Joe would get a job, and she would finish her education at night. But the evenings? Oh, the evenings were tough. By eight o'clock, she was miserable. What if her mother and father continued to stop her seeing Joe? Why had she been so reckless? Why hadn't she been more cautious? She felt guilty too. Her family were quarrelling like Friday-night drunks, and it was all her fault.

Being trapped at home presented many challenges, among them her mother's obsessive scrubbing and polishing. Rose had long been irritated by her mom's cleaning rituals. Now she was sure they'd tip her into insanity. The drone of the vacuum cleaner, the clatter of saucepans, the whirr of the washing machine: these became the soundtrack to her misery. At least her mother didn't ask for help. When it came to housekeeping, she had decided that her younger daughter was an incurable incompetent. Rose fantasised about taking a hammer to her mom's beloved Waterford crystal and running a large rusty nail along her precious mahogany table.

Although Milton was wealthier than the family's old neighbourhood, it, too, was home to legions of Irish people. The difference, according to Rose's mother, was that they were the right kind of Irish.

They owned businesses; they sent their children to private schools; if they drank, they drank at home. In one way, Rose felt sorry for her mom. She could clean herself into a frenzy, yet in the eyes of those she most wanted to impress – the truly well-to-do – her origins would always count against her. She was no better than women who spent their days sitting on the stoop, cackling and chain-smoking. Rose wondered if her mother knew she was fighting an unwinnable war.

It was hard to say when the atmosphere changed. But it did. Her mom abandoned talk of shame and damaged goods. Instead, she bobbed and wove, refusing to give a straight answer to any of her daughter's questions. Rose's dad brought home two books. Purchased, no doubt, by one of the ladies in his office, they were bland historical tales and not really to her taste, but the thought was a kind one. Maybe, just maybe, her parents were adjusting to the situation. In return, Rose tried not to antagonise them. She made no attempt to leave the house; she kept her head low; she said nothing out of place.

One afternoon, she was sitting on her bed, nose pressed against the window, when she saw her cousin, Teresa, striding up the path. It was through Teresa that Rose had met Joe, and the sight of her cousin gave her an instant lift. Thankfully, her mom was in good humour. Not only did she welcome Teresa in, she was molasses sweet.

It was while Grace was in the kitchen making

tea that Teresa gave Rose a white envelope. 'This is from Joe,' she said. 'I wish I knew what all the secrecy was about, but I've a feeling you're not going to tell me.'

Rose slipped the envelope into her purse. 'I will,' she whispered. 'I promise you, I will. Not today, though.'

While she couldn't wait for her cousin to leave, her mom was in no such hurry. She enquired after every possible friend and acquaintance. She sought Teresa's opinion on matters great and small. From the new drapes in the dining room to the plight of the Kennedys, Grace was keen to hear her niece's view. Rose could see that Teresa was confused by this unusual display of warmth. Every now and again, she shot Rose a look, as if to say, 'What madness is going on here?'

When finally Teresa broke free, Rose stayed calm. Although she was dying to read Joe's note, she didn't want to raise her mother's suspicions, so she slouched around the house for twenty minutes before declaring herself in need of a rest.

Joe was anxious to meet. He assumed their news hadn't gone down well and that getting out wasn't easy. *I'm guessing you might not want to come to my place, either*, he wrote. *I'll wait for you between six and eight every evening near the Foggy Dew. Please try and come soon, my love. I'm going crazy here.*

Rose felt a spurt of joy. She would leave right away. She'd have to claim she was going to the store or some such. By the time her mom realised the truth, Rose would be with Joe. They'd come up with a plan and . . .

The stairs creaked.

Quickly, she fitted the envelope back into her purse. Seconds later, her mom was at the door.

Grace looked at her with questioning eyebrows. 'Why was Teresa here?'

Caught off-guard, Rose burbled her answer. 'I don't know. I haven't seen her in a while. I guess she must have been wondering . . . wondering if I was all right.'

'Hand it over.'

'What do you mean?'

'I don't for one second believe that Teresa Corcoran came trailing over here to enquire after your health. She gave you something from him. Now hand it over.'

'There's nothing to hand over.'

With one lunge, Grace scooped up the purse. Then she swivelled on her heel and made for the door. Rose threw herself onto her mother's back.

'Give it back to me!' she roared. 'You can't take what's mine!'

Her mom shook herself, causing Rose to tumble to the floor.

'Oh, hell,' said her mother, her eyes wide, smudges of pink on her cheekbones. 'Are you okay?'

'Like you care.'

'I know you don't believe me, but I only want what's best for you. That's all any of us wants. You're planning on throwing your life away, and

I can't let that happen. You've no idea what it's like to be poor or how frightening it is when every day's a struggle. You may think you love this Joe – and perhaps you do. I swear to you, though, Rose, marry him and you'll be setting yourself up for a life of sorrow. Before you know it, you'll be hard-faced from poverty and worry. You'll regret you ever set eyes on the boy.'

Rose wanted to reply. She wanted to say, 'The only hard-faced person around here is you.' But if she spoke, she'd start to cry. She was determined not to cry. Crying was for kids, and she was an adult now.

Her mother, still clutching the purse, tried to help her up. Rose flinched.

Grace sighed. 'You can have a wonderful life, you know, with everything this country's got to offer. Look at you, you're beautiful and you're clever. When I was seventeen, I was living in a rundown cottage in a swampy field. I would've killed for all this.' She waved a hand towards Rose's vanity, as if a bottle of Je Reviens and a compact of pressed powder were all anybody could want from life. 'You've just got to get over this mistake.'

'My baby's not a mistake,' said Rose, her voice muffled.

For the rest of the day, she stayed in her room, hot tears of frustration gathering in her eyes. She told herself that right was on her side. True, she still had a way to go with her mother but, as always, her father would be easier to win over. She would get what she wanted in the end.

Right now, what she needed was to see Joe. She would have to find an escape route. It wouldn't be possible today, not with her mother prowling around, like a tom cat in search of a fight. Her chance would come, though. In her mind's eye, she saw Joe waiting for her outside the Foggy Dew.

The image gave her hope.

# CHAPTER 3

Rose's opportunity came the next afternoon in the form of Mrs Mamie Ledbetter. Mamie was a rail-thin woman who wore flowery shifts and smelt like the perfume counter in Filene's. She was also on a thousand committees where ladies drank iced tea, complained about their husbands and wallowed in the failures of others. Rose's mom was in thrall to her. No doubt she hoped the fragrant Mrs Ledbetter would give her an entry to those committees so she, too, could waft around like a character from a Doris Day movie.

Rose was upstairs when Mamie arrived and she reckoned that was where she'd stay. She had no interest in an hour of phoney chit-chat about people who bored her and places she had no desire to visit. All the same, she couldn't avoid their visitor's shrill voice. Mamie wanted to drink her lemonade outdoors.

'Your garden is simply heavenly,' Rose heard her say. 'C'mon, Grace, the worst of the heat has gone. Let's sit out back.'

She couldn't quite decipher what her mother

said in response, but it sounded less than enthusiastic. Which would worry her mom more, she wondered: the danger that a rogue weed had poked up or the possibility that Rose would escape? Mamie persisted, however, and before long, Rose heard their sandals click-clacking out the back door.

This was her chance. If she dithered, one of the others might return from work. Pausing only to take a few dollars from Nancy's secret stash, she put on her sandals, tiptoed down the stairs and edged out the front door. She was three blocks away before she risked a celebratory punch in the air. Adrenalin zoomed through her body. Joe was waiting.

Except he wasn't.

It wasn't yet seven o'clock when she arrived at the Foggy Dew, but the only people outside were a glassy-eyed old man and a girl in a short red dress. The Dew was a squat brownbrick place with mean slits for windows and an overpowering stench of beer and stronger liquor. In the sunlight, the bar looked grimy and unkempt. It was right in the heart of the neighbourhood, though. They couldn't miss each other there.

And so Rose waited. The elderly man and the long-legged girl moved on. Others came and went. Two drunks asked for a kiss. 'My brother's off to the war,' the taller one declared. 'He reckons the journey would be easier if he got a kiss from a pretty girl. Just to send him on his way, y'know.'

Thankfully, they were young and harmless, and she played dumb until they stumbled away. After more than an hour of pacing and fending off drunks, Rose had to accept that Joe wasn't going to show. She felt like wailing with disappointment. Just then, even ten minutes in his company would have been enough. She needed to hear his cheery voice and to inhale his soapy smell. And they needed to make plans. Pretty soon, other people would know she was pregnant. They couldn't allow the situation to drift.

For a little while, she sat on the sidewalk, breathing in the salty July air and thinking. She would have to go to Joe's apartment.

Joe Brennan senior looked her up and down and up again. 'What is it you want?'

He had retained his Irish accent, its gentle rhythms at odds with his grooved and grizzled face. His grey work shirt was torn and he smelt of fried onions. *Oh, stop it*, thought Rose. *You're behaving like your mother*. Whether she liked it or not, this man was her baby's grandfather. She would have to get to know him. First things first, though. She needed to find Joe. She decided to use her ditsy act.

'I was looking for Joe junior, please. I was supposed to meet him, but I was a teensy bit late, and he'd already left, so I looked around only I couldn't find him. And then I said, "Don't be silly, Rose. He's probably gone home."' She raised her palms to the sky and gave what she hoped was an appealing smile.

'You're the lassie who caused the rumpus last Christmas.'

Although this wasn't quite how Rose would have described it, she nodded. 'Uh-huh.'

Joe's father lifted both shoulders. 'I haven't an idea where the boy's got to. Why don't you ask his sister? As far as I can see, she's the only one who keeps tabs on him. Oh, and if you do find him, tell him his old man said he needs to get his head together. It's time he got himself a job and quit flitting around the neighbourhood doing the Lord knows what. He's no better than the rest of us, whatever he might think.' By now, Mr Brennan's face had turned the colour of undercooked beef. 'Will you tell him that?'

Rose gave another nod.

Bree. Of course. That was where she should have gone. Even if Joe wasn't in Bree's apartment, she would know where to find him. Thanking Mr Brennan, she headed on her way.

Her first few knocks were gentle; the kids might be asleep. After a minute or two, she tried a harsher volley, then an all-out hammering. The apartment remained dark and quiet. Aching with frustration, Rose decided to leave a note. All she could find in her purse was a flimsy scrap of paper and an eyebrow pencil. They would have to do. *Darling Joe*, she wrote, *I've looked but I can't find you. I promise I'll be back soon. I miss you so much. We both do! All my love, Rose.*

Flustered, she returned to the Foggy Dew. Night was falling, and the streets were losing their appeal. A series of shouts crashed through the still air. Two cops patrolled the sidewalk, like they were warning trouble to stay away. There was still no sign of Joe or of anybody who looked familiar. It occurred to her that something bad might have happened. Her head flooded with worries. That didn't make sense, though. Joe was a popular guy. He wouldn't get into trouble. No, for some reason he'd been called away. She considered calling in on Teresa, but that would be risky. Her aunt Ita was the sharpest woman in Boston and might guess that Rose was pregnant.

She would have to go home.

As she turned her key in the lock, Rose prepared herself for her parents' questions. She worried that one of them would be waiting by the door. Instead, it sounded like most of the family were in the lounge. To begin with, she caught only fragments of the conversation.

'I didn't ask you to do it,' her mother was saying. 'That's not what I intended at all.'

'All due respect,' said Ed junior, 'that's exactly what you wanted. Otherwise, why show us his pathetic little note?'

'How often do I have to tell you?' said Ed senior. 'Don't speak to your mother like that. And she's right. There was no call for what you did.'

'Yeah, well, at least he won't be bothering Rosie any more,' chipped in Ray.

'Did it occur to either of you that this guy's family are tough? You'll both need to watch your step.'

Rose couldn't believe what she was hearing. She paused for a moment. The quarrelling continued, her family spitting insults at each other. She had to go in there and confront them.

As soon as she entered the room, the voices stopped.

'Go to your room, Rose,' her mother said. 'I'll deal with you later.'

'I'm going nowhere until you tell me what's happening.' She looked from one to the other. There was Ray, the makings of a bruise on his acne-scarred face. Beside him, Ed junior was peering at his sneakers. Their mother appeared to be staring at a spot on the wall. Her bouffant hairstyle looked as if somebody had let all the air out. Their father opened his mouth then quickly closed it again.

It was Nancy who spoke. Leave it to Nancy to stick the knife in and twist good and hard.

'Your boyfriend was waiting for you outside some dive bar or other, but I guess you know that. Presumably, that's where you've just been.' She smiled, her plain features awash with smugness. 'You were too late. Ray and Junior got there first.'

Rose faced her dad. 'Is that true?'

'It is, I'm afraid. But—'

'Please tell me Joe's all right,' she said to Ray and Ed junior. 'Please tell me you didn't hurt him.'

She could almost hear the crunch of fist on bone. Joe was hardy, but her brothers were older, bigger, nastier.

Ray shrugged. Ed junior smirked.

Rose was screaming now, the words coming from deep within. 'I want you to tell me you didn't hurt him.'

'He's fine,' said Ed junior, something close to humour in his tone. 'Just not quite as handsome as he used to be.'

'Jeez,' added Ray. 'What's with the hysterics?'

Ed senior turned to Rose. 'Go to your room. We need to talk, but it can wait until you've calmed down.'

Rose was lying on her bed, staring at the ceiling, when Kevin tapped on the door.

'There's something you need to know,' he said. 'Mom and Dad are going to fill you in later, but I . . . I want you to know that I don't agree with what they're doing.' Over the next few minutes, he told her about their parents' plans. Rose had misread her mother and father. At no point had either of them softened. They'd been lurking in the long grass, planning and scheming.

'An aunt?' She'd hauled herself up and was sitting on the bed, her legs drawn in close to her chest. 'In Ireland?'

'A nun. Sister Agnes. She's Dad's sister. You must have heard him mention her.'

Rose's world turned all wobbly. She wasn't able

to absorb what Kevin was saying. 'I think so. It rings a bell, only . . .'

'You'll stay with her and the other nuns until you have the baby. Nobody here will know.'

'I don't get it. How did they arrange all this?'

'They have telephones in Ireland too, you know,' said Kevin.

'Yeah, but surely I would have heard them?'

'I guess Dad must have called from the office.'

'It all sounds crazy. They can't hide me away. People will wonder where I've got to. And what about school?'

'When people ask, they'll be told you're helping an elderly aunt, a relation of Dad's, back in Ireland.'

'But Mom and Dad . . . it's not like they have any great attachment to Ireland. Why would they send me there?'

'It's a convenient place to hide a pregnant daughter. You'll only be there for a few months. When you've had the baby, you'll be able to come home.'

'And when we come back to America, what then?'

Kevin looked away. 'You're not getting this, Rose, are you? Your baby won't be coming back to America. It'll stay in Ireland. He or she will be adopted there.'

'No,' she said, her voice strange, too high, too flimsy. Even the air felt fragile. 'No. They wouldn't do that. Why would they do that? Why?'

He didn't answer.

'When?' she asked.

'Tomorrow. They've got a passport and a ticket for you. Dad will accompany you to Ireland and come back later in the week. Everything's arranged.'

Rose let out a rasping moan. She hadn't known she possessed such a sound.

'I want you to understand,' her brother was saying, 'I think it's all wrong. I pleaded with them, but there's nothing more I can do.'

'Thanks for . . . thanks for speaking up for me.' While she thought, she rested her head in her palms. 'Do you think I could run away? I mean, if we left now, would you give me a ride over to Joe's place?' He might be back by now. If he wasn't, Rose would give Bree another try. Bree would give her shelter.

'They'd find you and drag you home again. You're only seventeen. They've got all the power here.'

'If Joe knew, he wouldn't allow them to send me away. I swear he wouldn't.'

'Ray and Ed roughed him up fairly badly. I doubt he's in any state to intervene.'

'What if I went and stayed with Teresa and her parents?' Rose had discounted this earlier, but she hadn't been in such a bind then.

'I know you've stayed there before, but any hint of trouble and they'd be straight on to Mom and Dad.'

Salty liquid seeped into her mouth. She swallowed. 'I'm trapped, aren't I?'

'Jesus, Rose, I'm sorry. I'm so, so sorry.'

Rose couldn't watch Kevin cry. She slid to the floor, her knees raised, her head bowed. She closed her eyes and rocked slowly, back and forth.

There was nothing she could do.

# CHAPTER 4

*County Clare, July 1968*

Sister Agnes was not a woman for small talk. 'So this is the famous Rose?' she said, as she met her brother and niece at Shannon Airport. 'Look at her, only a slip of a thing and already causing all this bother.'

'I'm seventeen,' said Rose, who had vowed not to be cowed or bossed around. 'I'm not a child.'

'It's a shame you've acted like one, then,' replied the nun. 'Allowing your worst instincts to get the better of you. No self-discipline, it's a modern curse.'

Rose had been sick on the plane, and the journey had left her feeling ragged. On the plus side, she'd had lots of time to think. While her parents were behaving like lunatics, they weren't evil people. Give them space to reflect, and they'd soften. Was it really likely that her mother, a woman who'd filled her house with babies, would spurn her first grandchild? No, Rose was convinced that, in a few months, she'd be returning to Boston with her little boy or girl. In the meantime, she'd have to put up with the nuns.

With everything happening so quickly, she hadn't been able to get a message to Joe. She was desperate to know how he was. She'd write to him as soon as she got the chance. Maybe even tonight. She had to let him know that she'd be back – and that she still wanted to marry him.

Sister Agnes and her father were disagreeing about how much time had passed since they'd last met.

'Thirty-five years,' her dad said. 'That's how long I've been in Boston.'

'But I didn't see you in 'thirty-three. I was only a few months in the convent, and they wouldn't let me out. I reckon the last time we saw each was in the spring of 'thirty two at—'

'Mam's funeral.' He let out a long breath. 'And the pity of it is, we're only meeting now because . . .'

Agnes shook her head. 'There was nothing stopping you coming back, Edward. You could've come visiting at any stage. But, no, you're like all the rest of them. You got a taste of the good life in America, and you forgot about home. I wonder if your children know the slightest thing about their heritage – or their faith.' She sent a sour look in her niece's direction.

Rose feared that all sorts of slights, real and imagined, were about to be dragged up. Her aunt's thin, snippy voice didn't match her appearance. She was a round, rosy-cheeked woman with metal-framed glasses and swollen ankles. She wore a thick black dress and a black veil. Rose ran her fingers through her hair. Imagine being a nun and having all your hair shorn off. The thought gave her goose-bumps.

'If only it was that simple,' her father was saying. 'Why, for years we didn't have two quarters to rub together. Bringing up six kids isn't easy, even in America.'

'So I see,' shot back Agnes. 'Anyway, you're here now. I take it you'll be going to see the family?'

'Ah, yeah, I was hoping to go to Killeniska tomorrow.' He lifted Rose's case. 'Shouldn't we be making tracks?'

'Rose can carry her own bag. She may as well get used to looking after herself. There'll be nobody fetching and carrying for her in Carrigbrack.'

The Boston they'd left behind had been sluggish with humidity, and the shards of icy rain that met them in Shannon had taken Rose by surprise. The rain had stopped now, but the day was blustery, and she shivered as she climbed into the car. A driver had been waiting for them. Save for a brief greeting, he said little.

Her parents' home country had always puzzled Rose. She'd seen some Irish people get all weepy with longing for their birthplace, but her mom wasn't alone in her scorn. Her dad was equally unsentimental. The picture they'd painted was one of drudgery and duty, too many children and too few opportunities. At first, what Rose saw didn't tally with her expectations. It was too orderly, too new. They sped past some apartments, a series of row houses and what looked like a cluster of factories. Before long, though, the road narrowed and there was nothing to see apart from fields and the occasional scrappy-looking village. Later, the landscape changed completely. The fields turned to stone. Sky, land, houses: everything was grey.

So this was Ireland.

Throughout the journey, Agnes spoke like a machine, delivering a rapid-fire sermon about the evils of modern society. Rose had to resist the temptation to reach over and tap her on the head. 'Knock, knock,' she wanted to say. 'Is there a real person in there?'

As the small car (all Irish cars appeared to be small) pulled into Carrigbrack, Rose saw three girls. They wore navy skirts and tops. Two were heavily pregnant. Naive as it might sound, it hadn't occurred to her that there would be others there. In the main building's wide front hall, they encountered another girl, on her hands and knees, polishing the wooden floor. Presently, three more appeared, all wearing the same hideous uniform, all pregnant. Not a word was spoken. The entire place was unnaturally quiet. The other thing that struck Rose was the smell: a stomach-churning mixture of disinfectant, floor wax and boiled vegetables.

She sent her father a look of distress.

'How many, um, young women are staying here?' he asked Sister Agnes.

'Currently? Forty-eight. Rose will bring the number to forty-nine and another girl is due to arrive tomorrow.' She lowered her voice. 'A sad case. The poor child is only thirteen, and her uncle is thought to have fathered the baby.'

'Jesus Christ,' said Rose.

Agnes's body stiffened, and the polishing girl dropped her cloth. 'You will not, under any circumstances, take the Lord's name in vain,' her aunt said. 'Do you understand?'

Rose found herself nodding.

'I had no idea,' said her father. 'No idea so many girls were living here, I mean.'

'This is a busy home,' replied his sister. 'Unfortunately, many modern girls have peculiar ideas. They think they can do whatever they like without suffering the consequences. And, of course, they never pause to consider the pain and shame they're visiting on their families. Some of them even insist they can raise a child on their own. "I'll get a job, Sister," they say. "I'll take care of him." Honestly, most of them are incapable of taking care of themselves, let alone an innocent child. If it wasn't for Carrigbrack, I dread to imagine what would become of them. They're a danger to themselves, those girls.'

By now, they were in a large wood-panelled office. It was a dark place, sombre as a child's funeral. Agnes sat at a heavy table and gestured to Rose and Ed to sit down. Everything about her suggested she was used to her orders being followed without question.

'We live frugal lives here,' she said, 'but Rose will receive everything she needs. Most importantly, she'll have an opportunity to reflect on her sins and atone for them. I want to make it clear to both of you that while Rose may come from a different background to our other penitents, this doesn't mean she's in any way special. In fact, a girl with her advantages should be doubly repentant. It saddens me to think of the distress she's caused her family. Not to mention the slur she's cast on the good name of Irish people in Boston.'

Rose leaned forward. 'You've got to be kidding me,' she said. 'You're acting like I killed someone. All I did was go to bed with a guy I love, a guy I'm going to marry.'

'Rose!' said her father.

'I'm sorry, Dad, I don't belong here. I know she's your sister and all, but this woman sounds like she's from another planet. I'm American. My baby's American. There's probably some sort of law against what's going on here.'

'I think you'll find,' said the nun, her voice flint-hard, 'that this is exactly where you belong, and the sooner you grasp that fact, the better.'

Rose turned to her father. 'Surely this isn't what you want. This place is no better than a prison. Did you see those girls in the driveway? They were wearing prison uniforms.'

Ed flicked his gaze from his sister to his daughter and back again. His blue eyes were fringed with pink. His normally ruddy skin was putty-grey. 'You won't be unkind to Rose, will you?' he said to Agnes. 'She's not a bad girl, just a touch misguided.'

For Rose, what she'd seen and heard in the past thirty minutes had changed everything. She couldn't believe her father would leave her there. She tried to say something. No words came. To her annoyance, a tear rolled down her right cheek.

'There'll be no unkindness in Carrigbrack,' said Agnes. 'Rose and her baby will be well looked after. In time, and with the help of God, she'll recover her self-respect. She will, of course, have to work for her keep. Many of our girls work in the nursery. Others look after the fruit and vegetable gardens or do the laundry. I was thinking that Rose might like to work in the kitchen.'

Recalling the stink of boiled cabbage in the hall, Rose knew this was not what she wanted. Even the thought of the kitchen made her feel ill. Agnes had moved on, however, and was talking about giving her a new name. The girls were given temporary names, she said, to protect their privacy.

'I wouldn't go worrying about that,' said Rose. 'I doubt there are too many folks from Boston hanging around. I'd say my privacy's pretty safe.'

The nun ignored her. 'I'm giving you a beautiful new name, the same name as the President's wife.'

'Lady Bird Johnson?'

'Of course not. You're in Ireland now. Mr de Valera's wife is called Sinéad.'

'Shin-Aid?' repeated Rose. For the first time, she glimpsed amusement in Agnes's eyes.

'Sinéad,' said her aunt, 'I can see you're going to be quite a challenge.'

Three days later, Rose's father returned to Boston. She wasn't allowed to accompany him to the airport.

Before he left Carrigbrack, he gripped her arms with both hands. 'I know you don't agree right now,' he said, 'but we're doing the right thing here. You'll see.'

Rose nodded, gave a half-smile.

'Remember I love you.' He paused. 'And your mother . . . she loves you too. You've got to remember that. And, yeah, I know that sometimes she can be a little demanding.' He mirrored Rose's smile. 'What you've got to understand is that she behaves like that because she's scared for you.'

There were so many things Rose would have liked to say. But what was the point?

Everything was different in Carrigbrack. Nothing made sense. Life was reduced to work and prayer. Happiness was treated with suspicion. What Rose found most unsettling was the lack of sound. Apart from the nursery, everywhere was quiet. For a large part of the day, speaking was forbidden. A stray word or giggle, and punishment loomed. Amid the silence, the ticking of a clock could sound like an explosion. One drip from a faucet could feel like a roaring wave. How Rose longed for noise: for the thrum of traffic, the chatter of a crowd, the clank and whine of a T train. 'Oh, Joe,' she said to herself, a hundred times a day. 'Do you have any idea where I am?'

She wasn't allowed to write to him, or to her cousin, or to anybody apart from her parents. In return, she received bland letters about life in Milton. Gene was thinking of moving to the west coast. Nancy and Theo were talking about getting engaged. Rose's pregnancy was never mentioned. Neither was Joe.

At the start, the other girls gazed at her like she was the Creature from the Black Lagoon. They knew a little about America, but in a Hollywood sort of way. When she admitted she'd never met any movie stars or famous people, they were disappointed. Occasionally, she mentioned some of the things that young people talked about in Boston, like hippies and flower children, Vietnam and civil rights. Mostly she was greeted by empty stares. The Kennedys were a separate matter. Her fellow prisoners knew *all* about the Kennedys. Rose must have met at least one of the family, they'd insist. Again, she had to disappoint them.

Sometimes she had to speak slowly so that people could understand her. Often she couldn't understand them. Even their words were strange. A closet was a press. Cute meant clever. Kissing was called shifting. And she was 'the Yank'.

It wasn't just the girls' way of speaking that was different. To Rose, many of them seemed incredibly sad or dull. Or both. A couple were out and out retards and clearly didn't know how they'd become pregnant. More had obviously been raped. Most were accepting of their fate. 'Sure where else would I go?' they'd say. A number were content to hand over their babies. Some genuinely didn't want a child. Others were so brainwashed they maintained they wouldn't be up to the task. 'What about your boyfriend?' Rose would ask. In many cases, the baby's father was gone or married or otherwise unavailable. The majority of the girls hoped to return home, but a good sprinkling planned on leaving the country. They asked Rose about America. She joked that, as long as they avoided her family, they'd probably be okay.

Almost without exception, the girls were beaten down by guilt. They looked at the world through wary eyes. At night Rose lay there, listening to their strangled sobs, until she wanted to take a knife to whoever was responsible for banishing them to Carrigbrack.

One evening, a man turned up to claim one of the mothers and her baby. Apparently, he and the girl had been dating – or 'doing a line' as they called it in Ireland – but when she had fallen pregnant, he had refused to believe the baby was his. He'd waited until she'd given birth so he could satisfy himself that he was indeed the little boy's father. The girl's parents were consulted, as was a priest. Finally, she was allowed to leave, although what sort of life she would have with such an oaf of a man, Rose couldn't imagine.

Rose cried her own tears quietly, dabbing her

eyes with the stiff bedsheet or the corner of her nightdress, praying no one would hear. She didn't want anyone to think she was weak. As the weeks passed, and she became more conscious of the small person inside her, she pined for Joe. There were days when she was sick with longing. They should be experiencing this together. She thought of the two of them in Bree's apartment, making love, dancing to some silly song on the radio, talking about life. In her fantasies, Joe would travel to Ireland, track her down and rescue her. Deep down, she knew this wasn't very likely, but as the nights drew in, she found solace in those fantasies.

One thing baffled her. Although most of the girls in Carrigbrack were pregnant, some had long since had their babies. Often their children were already gone, living with an unknown family in an unknown place. Yet they continued to toil away, scrubbing and digging and minding newborns, their blue uniforms fluttering around their thin bodies. Finally, Rose asked one of the girls why she was still there. A mousy little thing whom the nuns had renamed Florence, she covered her mouth when she spoke, as if she was embarrassed by her teeth. 'I'm still earning my way out,' she explained. 'My family didn't have the money to pay for my keep, so they say I'll have to work here for another year at least.' Petrified that this would happen to her, Rose sought out Sister Agnes. For days, her aunt strung her along. 'I don't know, Sinéad,' she'd say. 'Stop annoying me with silly questions.' In the end she told the truth: Rose's father had given the nuns one hundred pounds. 'When you hand over that baby,' she said, 'you'll be free to go.' Rose stayed quiet. She had no intention of giving up her child.

Although Agnes looked after the day-to-day running of Carrigbrack, she wasn't in charge. The actual boss was a woman called Mother Majella, a distant figure who looked as if she'd taken a bath in starch. The most loathed nun was Sister Sabina. She was a grade-A bitch. If there was punishment to be handed out, she was there. If there was an insult to be delivered, it was on her tongue. She referred to the girls as 'offenders' and told them they'd have to spend the rest of their lives atoning for their sins. Others weren't so bad. One or two, like Sister Eunice, were capable of kindness. 'Don't worry,' she'd say, a soft look on her young face, 'soon you'll be able to begin again.' Rose found this harder to take than a lecture from Sister Sabina. Eunice genuinely believed that right was on the nuns' side. Not only were they saving families from humiliation, they were saving souls. 'Why do you swallow all this holy-roller garbage? Why can't you think for yourself?' Rose asked. Eunice smiled and walked away.

The kitchen was as vile as Rose had feared. The smells and the heat brought bile to her throat. There were no easy jobs. According to the other girls, the laundry was hell and the fields were little better. Carrigbrack grew its own vegetables, and no matter the weather, girls were sent to pick potatoes or sow seeds. Unless you were in labour – or dead – you had to keep going.

She learned that her workplace had one advantage: the nun in charge, Sister Mary Gertrude, was a devoted radio listener. If Rose was lucky, she managed to catch some of the lunchtime news. In the main, the stories were Irish, but there was also news from the rest of the world. Sometimes there were reports from America. On Sister Mary Gertrude's radio, she heard about the Soviet Union invading Czechoslovakia, about riots at the Democratic Convention in Chicago and about Jackie Kennedy marrying a Greek billionaire. Events that would once have glided past her ears became fascinating. Even the darkest news was a reminder that life went on. Outside, it was still 1968. In Carrigbrack, life was stuck in the nineteenth century.

Occasionally she was able to leave the kitchen. She might be sent to the garden to check on supplies or to another part of the convent to pass on a message. From time to time, she pleaded to be allowed into the yard. 'I suppose if I don't agree, you'll have the ear worn off me with your cribbing and moaning,' Sister Mary Gertrude would say. Then Rose would slip out back and inhale huge lungfuls of air. She wished she could hoard air, like a camel storing water.

It was on one of these breaks that she spotted

a small gap in the hedge that ran around the back of the building. The first time she broke out, she didn't go far. The second time, she was a little braver. On the third occasion, she made it as far as the village of Carrigbrack. She hadn't a cent to her name and any idiot would have known where she'd come from. *Still*, she thought, *what the hell.* She would call into a store, just to hear what they'd say. To her great and pleasant surprise, the woman behind the counter gave her a red-and-white piece of candy with a lovely peppery taste. 'Clove rock,' she said.

They had a chat about this and that. Normal stuff, not Carrigbrack sin and misery talk. If the woman – Winnie Lafferty was her name – found her presence odd, she didn't say. Instead, she urged Rose to be careful.

'They'll miss you above in that place,' she said. 'And you're better off not vexing those nuns. A couple of them are no bargains.'

Rose thanked her and headed on her way. Two weeks passed before she had another opportunity to escape. This time she spent even longer talking to Winnie. By the time she started to skulk back to the convent, night was closing in. She was only a short distance from the hedge when a voice, like a foghorn in Boston harbour, rose up out of the mist.

'Where do you think you've been?' It was Sister Agnes.

* * *

She wasn't proud of herself but Rose howled like a wild animal while Agnes cut her hair. Oh, she knew it was only hair, and that far worse happened every day of the week, but there was something nasty about her aunt's choice of punishment.

'If you don't quieten down,' said Agnes, 'you'll be a sorry girl.'

Rose whimpered. 'Why? What more can you do? Wait until I tell my dad what a bitch you've been.'

The nun brought her scissors even closer to Rose's skull. 'I had planned on leaving you with a decent covering, but you've changed my mind for me.' She sighed. 'We're only trying to help you, Sinéad. Why do you have to be so difficult? Sister Mary Gertrude allowed you some freedom. And how did you thank her? You ran off to the Lord knows where.'

Thankfully, the nuns didn't know she'd been to the grocery store. Mind you, she had the feeling that Winnie would be a match for any of them.

'My name is Rose.' She sniffled.

'You see, that's more of it. Why do you have to rail against everything? If only you'd keep your head down and do what's expected of you, your life would be an awful lot easier.'

Agnes continued until the floor was covered with a carpet of brown hair. Finally, she declared her job done. 'Now get a brush and sweep up that mess,' she said to her niece.

Rose put a hand to her head to feel the damage.

She'd been left with an inch or two all round. Her hair lay in swirls at her feet.

A week later, she ran away again, this time through a different gap. She knew she was being foolish but she couldn't stop herself. When Winnie Lafferty saw her shorn head, her hand flew to her mouth. 'The Lord save us, Rose, what have they done to you?'

'Are you saying the new look doesn't suit me?' she replied, doing her best to smile.

Winnie came out from behind the counter and put both arms around her. For a minute or two, they embraced in silence. Months had passed since Rose had felt human contact. The shop-keeper's decency hit her like a battering ram, and she found it hard to breathe. Her eyes filled, and she had to blink hard to stop the tears rolling down her face.

'Please mind yourself, pet,' said Winnie, as they drew apart. 'This will end, you know. You'll go home and you'll forget all about Carrigbrack.'

And then Rose got tired. She was seven months pregnant. Her baby was jumping and kicking. Her bump was chafing against the rough cloth of her uniform. Every morning she was up at six for Mass. The rest of the day was filled with grinding hard work. The kitchen was too hot, and the nights were too cold. She'd lie in her narrow bed, contorting herself into awkward shapes in a fruitless attempt to stay comfortable and warm. Her body felt all wrong, like nothing quite slotted together any more.

One afternoon, she saw a baby being taken away. Even as she watched, she knew the scene would stay with her. A girl called Dolores was determined to keep her little boy. When the day came to hand him over, she barricaded herself and the baby into a closet. Of course, that was dumb. Of course, it was never going to work. But Dolores was distraught beyond reason. When she was wrenched out of her hiding place and her child was taken, she was inconsolable. She lay on the hall floor, spasms of misery passing through her body. Rose and some of the other girls tried to comfort her, but all she did was scream.

That night, Rose told herself to accept the truth. Joe wasn't coming to save her. Nobody was. She would have her baby in Carrigbrack and she would do everything within her power to hold onto him (she was convinced she was having a boy). She was desperate to meet the little person who had already caused so much bother. In the meantime, she would just have to do as she was told.

Rose's labour was long and hard. The nuns didn't approve of pain relief. They felt every girl should endure as much as possible because it would remind them of their sins. Even soothing words or gestures were frowned upon. Sister Agnes told her niece to stay quiet and to offer up her suffering for the poor souls trapped in Purgatory. She was wasting her breath. Rose called for Joe and for her parents. She swore at the nuns and the nurse. She shrieked in undiluted agony.

Baby Moroney arrived at ten o'clock that Sunday night, and she too had plenty to say for herself. Rose was exhausted – and confused. 'You were supposed to be a boy,' she said to the bundle in her arms.

To her amazement, Sister Agnes smiled. 'God obviously wanted to bring another beautiful little girl into the world.'

'But I'd already chosen his name.'

'You'll have to choose again.'

'Josephine, then. I'll call her Josephine Jeannie.'

'Well, at least Josephine's a good biblical name,' said Agnes.

Overwhelmed as she was by her daughter's birth, Rose was surprised by the nun's warmth. Even when Josephine began to fret, all Agnes did was remark about how lovely it was to hear such healthy cries.

It was the following morning before the truth emerged. An hour before Rose had given birth, another girl had lost her baby. A short while later, the mother, a delicate girl called Bridget, died too. Sadness hung over the hospital and the nursery, Josephine's safe delivery providing the only relief. The girls in Carrigbrack had always believed that more babies died there than in a proper hospital. After all, it wasn't as though many of the nuns had any medical expertise. If something went wrong, your chances weren't good.

A man, called an 'undertaker' by the nuns, arrived to return Bridget's body to her family. Her baby, a boy, was left behind. He was buried with the other dead infants in a plot at the back of the convent. In death, as in life, he wasn't wanted.

Feeling all the more blessed that her daughter had survived, Rose wanted to be with her all the time. Agnes said no: the newborn had to go to the nursery with the other children. Rose would be allowed to see her only when she needed to be fed or changed. While nursing, she was ordered to face the wall for fear another girl caught a glimpse of her breast. That would be immodest, and lack of modesty was one of the reasons for her downfall.

Joe was ever-present in her thoughts. What would he make of his baby daughter? Although she knew it was too early to tell, she was sure Josephine had inherited her dad's eyes. If only he could see her. Rose wondered what he was doing. Had he found a job? Did he enjoy it? Was he trying to track her down? She knew that even if he did learn about Carrigbrack, there was little he could do. His letters would be confiscated.

Her mother and father must have been informed of Josephine's birth because, a week later, Rose received a letter telling her that soon she'd be able to return to Boston. 'What do you think?' she whispered to the baby. 'I reckon that if they see you, they won't want to lose you.' With each day that passed she became more convinced of it. Josephine was such a happy baby. Everybody said so. 'There's hardly a peep out of that child,' one of the nuns said, approval dripping from her voice like butter from hot toast. Oh, and she was so kissable! Every time Rose breathed in her daughter's fresh baby smell, she told herself that if either of her parents could do the same, they'd be converted.

Christmas came and went, and Rose returned to work in the kitchen. In one way, time moved slowly – some days seemed to last a year. In another way, the weeks whipped past.

In mid-February, Sister Agnes summoned her to the office. As was her way, there was no small talk, no softening up. 'Josephine will be going to her new home this afternoon,' she said.

A trapdoor opened beneath Rose. She blinked rapidly. 'I'm sorry?'

'You knew the day would come, and I've decided it's best to get this over with now. You're becoming too fond of that baby. Don't worry, we've found a wonderful family for her.'

Rose took a step towards the desk. There was a horrible metallic taste in her mouth. Fear, she supposed.

'I promise you,' continued Agnes, 'Josephine will have everything she needs.'

'What about my parents?' said Rose, her heart speeding up. 'They haven't even seen her. If they could see her, they wouldn't want to give her away. I know they wouldn't.'

'The time has come to stop that talk. Your parents are firm in their view. They want the baby to be adopted.' Agnes produced a piece of paper. 'They say it again in this letter I received only the other day.' She put on her reading glasses. '"We get the impression from Rose's letters that she's becoming attached to this child. We want to make it clear: there is no question of her bringing the baby back to America."'

'But she's mine.' Rose's voice splintered.

'Please, dear, don't make this more difficult than it has to be. Josephine is going to a lovely couple. They've no children of their own and they're only delighted to get her. You're seventeen—'

'Almost eighteen. It's my birthday next week.'

'All right then, you're almost eighteen. You've got your whole life ahead of you. You'll get married, you'll have other children, and this baby will be just a distant memory.'

Rose noticed the hint of humanity she sometimes saw in her aunt's eyes. She found it unsettling. How much simpler would it be if she could dismiss her aunt as thoroughly evil? *How can you do this?* she thought. *How can you do this again and again?*

'Can I not have one more day with Josephine?' she asked.

Agnes looked away. 'That wouldn't be wise. You can bath her and dress her, if that's what you'd like.'

For some minutes, both were quiet.

Rose broke the silence. 'There's nothing I can do to stop this, is there?'

Agnes didn't reply, and, in truth, Rose hadn't expected an answer. She could scream until she was hoarse. She could lock herself into a closet like Dolores. She could try to run away. It would make no difference.

She spent the next hour with her daughter. She gave her a bath and changed her into a special white suit provided by one of the nuns. Then she fed her for the last time.

Presently, Sister Agnes arrived to take the baby to her new home.

Rose didn't cry. She knew that if she did it would upset Josephine. There would be plenty of time for crying. She could cry every day for the rest of her life if she liked.

'One more minute,' she said to her aunt.

Agnes nodded.

Rose kissed the little girl's head. 'I know you won't remember me, but I promise I'll never, ever forget you,' she said. 'Please stay happy.'

# CHAPTER 5

Three days later, Rose was hit by the full force of her loss.

Instead of going straight to her job in the kitchen, she went to the nursery to look at the babies. She'd expected that Josephine's crib would still be empty. Instead, she found a tiny boy, curled into a deep sleep. Why that should upset her more than an empty bed, it was impossible to say. But it did. Before she knew it, she had slumped to her knees.

'My girl slept here,' she said.

She kept on saying it until a nun told her to leave. When she refused, Sister Sabina – the dreaded Sister Sabina – arrived and dragged her out of the nursery.

'You're supposed to be in the kitchen,' she said. 'I want you to go there. Now.'

Rose said nothing. She sat on the hall floor, her hands clasped around her knees, rocking to and fro. Sabina towered over her, breathing fire. She fulminated about selfish and sinful behaviour and accused her of being influenced by the devil. Rose didn't care.

What a fool she'd been. From the very beginning,

she'd been stupid. She'd believed her parents would allow her to marry Joe. She'd thought her father would look after her. She'd imagined that Joe would find her. She'd been dumb enough to think that if she wanted something badly enough, it would happen. Every single time she'd been wrong. Wrong. Wrong. Wrong.

Sister Sabina was joined by Sister Agnes.

'Get off the floor, Sinéad,' her aunt said. 'You're upsetting the other girls.'

Rose peered up at them. Spittle had gathered at the corners of Sabina's mouth.

'If you get up now, you can go to your dormitory,' Agnes added. 'There's little point in sending you to work today. You wouldn't be of any use to anybody.'

The scowl on Sabina's face made it clear she didn't approve of this concession. In the end, though, Rose trudged back to bed. She wriggled under the covers and tried to sleep.

Sleep wouldn't come to her that week. Nor did she eat. The food simply wouldn't go down.

The next week was no better. Rose might sleep for an hour or two before waking in a panic. No matter how hard she tried, she couldn't drift off again. And never had she been so desperate for sleep. When she was asleep, she didn't think; she didn't worry; she was in a comforting place. What she wanted was permanent sleep. Perfect black oblivion.

When she was awake, she obsessed about Josephine. Had her new family changed her name? Did they know she was American? Did they know her mother still wanted her?

Once or twice, Rose contemplated running away. She would have liked to see Winnie Lafferty. She didn't think she'd be able to talk, though. Not without making a fool of herself. More than a few words, and her voice began to quiver. Sadness had wrapped itself around her like ivy. One day soon it might get so tight she wouldn't be able to breathe.

By day, Rose attempted to work. Starved of food and rest, however, her body and brain were out of kilter. While peeling potatoes, she sliced off a piece of her thumb. She only noticed when crimson drops started falling into the pot, turning the water – and the potatoes – a sickly pink.

When Sister Mary Gertrude saw what was happening, she rose up in her chair like a monster from the deep. 'For pity's sake, watch what you're doing,' she snapped. 'Nobody will want to eat those potatoes now.' Rose was wasting food, she said, and being wasteful was a sin.

'I'm sorry,' Rose replied. 'I'm sorry.' It was all she could say. She felt a pain she couldn't describe or explain.

Sister Mary Gertrude ordered her to go and see Sister Agnes.

'What would your father say if he saw the state you've got yourself in?' asked her aunt. 'This has got to stop.'

'I'm sorry.'

'You know he'll be here next week to take you back to America, so why are you behaving like this?'

Rose hadn't known. She'd received a letter from Boston the previous day, but hadn't opened it.

Agnes played with her crucifix. 'I told your family we'd look after you here in Carrigbrack and I've done my best to honour that pledge. But you seem determined to hurt yourself. As far as I can see, your upbringing has left you ill-equipped to cope with life. You've got to realise, it isn't always easy. You have to trust the Lord.'

*I don't have to trust anyone*, thought Rose. She clasped a handkerchief to her thumb to try to stop the bleeding. Her hand throbbed with pain.

'No good will come of this moping,' continued Agnes. 'None at all. The sooner you realise that, the sooner you'll recover.'

Rose was tired. And cold. Even in the kitchen, she was cold. So her father was returning next week. That was good news, wasn't it? Or was it? She didn't know any more. She had considered herself an outsider. She'd thought she was different from the others. Now she understood that they were all the same.

The nuns instructed Rose to pack her belongings and return her uniform. It would be washed, and another girl would wear it. For the first time in months, she put on her own clothes: a sludge green skirt and a black sweater. Both were too big, hanging off her body like rags. She looked in the dormitory mirror, a thin piece of glass dotted with brown spots. Mirrors weren't approved of in Carrigbrack. They encouraged vanity, and vanity was a sin. Five months had passed since her aunt had lopped off her hair, and it was growing back in uneven tufts and hanks. There were dark smudges beneath her eyes, and her cheeks had collapsed. A cold sore scarred her top lip. Still, what did it matter? Apart from her dad, who would be looking at her? The other girls hardly spoke to her any more. They skirted around her, as if her unhappiness might be contagious.

Rose waited in the nuns' parlour. She studied her hands. The potato knife had left a long purple gash. According to Agnes, her father had already been in Ireland for a day or two, visiting family. They'd be returning to America that afternoon.

The nuns had made Rose sign a form in which she promised never to track down her daughter or to interfere with her adoption. She hadn't wanted to sign. She'd sat there for an age, her arms folded, her eyes closed. Sister Sabina told her she could sit in the chair for a month if she liked, she couldn't leave until she'd done her duty. Several hours later, her back aching and her head swimming, Rose crumbled. Although she tried to convince herself that writing her name on a piece of paper meant nothing, she immediately regretted her lack of resolve. What sort of person was she?

When her father arrived, he was all energy. She

heard him from the hall. It was an act she knew. His business act. It was odd to hear an American accent again. She wondered if her own accent had changed.

'We'll get you some tea,' Sister Agnes said to her brother, 'and a nice piece of cake. Sister Mary Gertrude's fruit cake is legendary.'

'Where's Rose?' she heard him reply. 'I'd like to see her first.'

'Of course, of course. Now, I should let you know that she hasn't been well for the past day or two. It's the time of year, isn't it? One girl gets a chill, and everybody else seems to catch it.'

'Oh. Okay. Where is she?'

When he entered the room, Rose wasn't sure what she saw in her father's face. Was it irritation? Sympathy? Revulsion?

'What happened?' he said. 'What . . .?' He turned to Agnes.

The nun forced a sliver of a smile. 'As I said, Rose hasn't been well.'

'I'm fine,' Rose heard herself say. She didn't want any fuss. 'I'm sorry about how I look.'

Her father ushered Agnes out of the room. Rose listened as their footsteps retreated along the corridor. She could hear her dad's voice vibrating with anger, but she couldn't make out what he was saying.

Twenty minutes later, he returned on his own.

'I can't bring the baby back,' he said. He spoke slowly, as if she was feeble-minded. 'The forms have been signed, and she's in her new home. We can't undo what's been done. Do you understand?'

'Yes,' said Rose. Her own voice sounded distant, as though it was coming from outside her body. Would she ever feel normal again? Or was this normal now?

'But we can talk about her,' her father was saying. 'Would you like that?'

'Please,' she said.

# CHAPTER 6

*County Clare, November 1985*

It rarely took long for Miss Casey's class to slide into chaos. Usually, the disruption started with a scattering of whispers or some stifled giggles. Within minutes, they were shuffling, sniggering, exchanging insults. Somebody asked a silly question or gave a ridiculous answer. On it went, the decibels rising until noise swamped the room and it was impossible for anybody to learn anything.

In her favourite seat, at the back beside the radiator, Martha Sheeran felt a twinge of sympathy for Miss Casey. It wasn't like she was the worst teacher in St Ursula's Community School. That was Mr Lillis. The previous week, three second years had lit a fire at the back of his woodwork class. The flames were practically licking the ceiling before he noticed. No, Miss Casey's problem was that she taught religion. And she taught in the old-fashioned way. Not for her the new-fangled practice of sugar-coating the pill with lessons about Hinduism or liberation theology. In Miss Casey's opinion, there was no reason to deviate from the Bible. This devotion wasn't shared by her students. While a handful claimed to have principled objections to religion, most simply couldn't be bothered with such a fusty old subject. There wasn't even an exam, so how were they meant to take it seriously?

Ten minutes in, and the play-acting was at full tilt. Three girls tittered over a copy of *Cosmopolitan*; two boys flicked pellets of soggy paper at each other; another pair shaped up for an arm wrestle. The one person who appeared to be paying attention was Martha's best friend, Cat O'Dowd. Head down, copybook open, Cat was writing like a demon. Anybody taking a closer look would see she was copying Martha's maths homework.

Neither was Martha listening to Miss Casey. She was working on a plan, lining up her pleas and promises in the hope of getting to Friday night's disco. Martha's mother had a talent for worrying, and the Templemorris community hall disco was high on Delia Sheeran's list of dangerous places. 'I know what goes on over there,' she'd say. 'Drinking and all sorts.' Martha suspected that if her mam ever set foot in the hall, shining a torch into the corners like an old-style parish priest, she would find it disappointingly tame. Mostly, the boys shook their hair to AC/DC and pretended to be cool, while the girls sang along to Madonna and pretended to ignore the boys. If you wanted to do really wild stuff, like getting plastered on vodka or high on magic mushrooms or having actual sex, you went to the field at the back of the graveyard. Everybody knew that.

Still, Delia was firm in her view that too many nights at the disco would lead her sixteen-year-old daughter into 'trouble'. What that trouble might be, she didn't need to say. There was only one type of trouble that mattered. The last time she'd warned about this, Cat had been there, perching on the kitchen counter like she owned the house. 'Don't worry, Mrs S,' she'd said. 'I won't let Martha bring shame on the family.' Shrewd as Martha's mother was, she could never get a handle on Cat. She'd smiled one of her tight tooth-free smiles before making a comment about boys being tricky. Neither Cat nor Martha owned up to the truth. With one or two exceptions, they had no interest in the teenage boys of Templemorris, tricky or otherwise. They hankered after exotic men from Ennis or Limerick. Or, better still, Dublin.

Immersed in her thoughts, it took Martha a couple of seconds to realise that the buzz of conversation had faded and that the words lingering in the air were those of her own name.

'Martha Sheeran,' repeated Miss Casey, her voice crisp as a new pound note.

'Miss?'

'I think she asked you a question,' whispered Cat.

Sensing a row, the room remained silent. As long as it was aimed at someone else, a teacher's anger could brighten even the dreariest November day.

'Ah,' said Martha, her cheeks tingling. 'I didn't quite understand. Can you ask the question again?'

The teacher gave her an eyebrows-up stare.

'Please,' hissed Cat.

'Please,' said Martha, regretting she'd ever wasted as much as a millisecond of sympathy on Miss Casey. Her only crime was daydreaming. The rest of the class had been behaving like a pack of toddlers.

'As you may be aware,' said the teacher, 'we were discussing John the Baptist's mother and I asked for your views on the significance of Elizabeth's story.'

'I . . .' she started. She should remember this. The knowledge was nestling somewhere at the back of her head. Wasn't Elizabeth the old woman in the desert? Or was that somebody else?

Before she said anything, Paudie Carmody, one of the soggy-paper boys, piped up: 'You're wasting your time asking her, Miss.'

For some reason, this prompted a wave of sniggers from his friends, and for a brief moment Martha was glad of the distraction.

'Be quiet, Paudie,' said Miss Casey. 'You'll get your chance.'

Paudie was undeterred. 'I mean, what would Martha know about anyone's mam when she doesn't even have one of her own?'

The sniggering rippled across the room.

'That's not a very Christian remark,' said the teacher, shifting slightly in her clumpy brown shoes.

'It's true, though, Miss. No father either. Well, I suppose she must have had right back at the beginning, like. But he didn't hang around.'

Martha said nothing. The tingling in her face had been joined by a tight feeling at the bottom of her throat. Conscious that almost everybody was looking at her, she wasn't sure she'd be able to speak. Even if she did manage to squeeze out a few words, they would sound stupid.

'Huh,' said Cat. 'Would you listen to yourself, Carmody? Of course she has a mam and dad. The only difference is, Martha's parents chose her. Your folks had no choice. They have to put up with you.'

'Woooh,' went Paudie's gang, a sound more usually associated with the early stages of a fight at the back of the handball alley.

'Miaow,' added Tina Bennis, one of the *Cosmopolitan* girls. Her friends struggled to swallow their laughter, their faces as maroon as their school sweaters.

'Quieten down now, quieten down,' snapped Miss Casey. 'I've heard quite enough from all of you – except Martha. Let's return to the question I asked.'

But hers was a voice in the wilderness. The floor was Paudie's.

'Did they pick her at the orphanage?' he said to Cat, a smirk on his shiny face. 'You know, like in the film?'

'What are you on about?' asked Cat.

'Little Orphan Annie,' chipped in Tina Bennis as she gave Martha what might have been a pitying look. (Tina's eyes were very close together, making her expressions difficult to read. Cat claimed her parents were first cousins who'd needed special permission from the Pope to get married.)

On the other side of the room, someone began to sing about the sun coming out tomorrow. Within seconds most of the class had joined in, giving it socks about betting their bottom dollars and sticking out their chins and such. Trevor Hawes, who always smelt of spot cream, stood to conduct.

Martha knew that when madness took hold of the crowd, sense and reason evaporated. Later, they might regret their behaviour, a few might even mumble an apology, but in that moment there was no time to think of such things. The room became a blur. All the faces were hazy, Miss Casey a wobbly outline. Tears were pooling in her eyes, and she wasn't going to cry in front of the class. She couldn't hear properly either; the voices sounded like they'd been filtered through concrete. She had to get out of there. As she stood, she was vaguely aware of Cat pulling at her sleeve.

'Don't mind them,' said Cat. 'They're a shower of idiots.' She raised her voice. 'Just a shower of fucking idiots.'

'Caitriona O'Dowd!' said Miss Casey, at last riled into action. 'You won't speak like that in my class. And sit down, Martha. I don't know where you think you're going.'

'Sure in a way wasn't Jesus adopted, Miss?' said Paudie. 'Joseph wasn't his real father.'

'That's more than enough,' shouted the teacher, one hand slicing through the air, fingers splayed in anger.

What she did next, what Cat did, Martha didn't know. She was in the corridor, running through the smells of sour milk and cheap shoes and sweat, past the coat hooks where the older boys hung first-years by their underpants, past the photographs of victorious sports teams and drama groups, out the back door, across the yard and onto the sparse grass of the playing field. Only when she reached the far end and could shelter behind some trees, did she stop. She rested against the rough bark of a horse chestnut, her breath jagged, her lungs burning. The ground was smothered with leaves, their scarlet and gold decaying to a sludgy brown. In the distance, she could hear the rush of traffic. She closed her eyes and covered them with her hands, pressing hard so that little spiral shapes popped up against the darkness.

# CHAPTER 7

Cat splashed milk into their coffee. 'Say when,' she said to Martha, who just nodded. Beside them, the spiky-haired waitress muttered about two miserable customers buying one pathetic coffee. Despite pooling their change, one cup was all they could afford. The rest of their money had gone on two cigarettes, which they'd bought as soon as they were freed from school.

'You do know I shouldn't be doing this, girls?' said the shop owner, as he handed over the smokes. 'But seeing as it's yourselves . . .'

'They're medicinal,' said Cat, tipping her head in Martha's direction. 'She's been through an ordeal.'

The two spent a quarter of an hour at the back of the community hall, pacing the pock marked tarmac, sucking on their cigarettes and comparing notes on what had happened after Martha had run out. Following ten minutes on her own, the school secretary had found her and brought her to the headmaster's office. There, while she'd quivered and dabbed at her face, Mr Noonan had stared at her, his eyes as dead as a stuffed animal's.

'The rules aren't there for the fun of it,' he'd said. 'What sort of school would we have if every student sailed off whenever the whim took them?' At that point he must have feared she was on the verge of an all-out wail because he paused, then told her she was free to go. 'Miss Casey says you may have been provoked,' he mumbled.

Poor Cat hadn't been so lucky and would have to spend the evening writing an essay about the effects of coarse language on society. Martha felt she should help, but her friend batted away the offer. 'Honest to God,' she'd said, 'shouting at that lot was the most fun I've had in ages. Did you see the face on Casey? I thought she'd go into orbit.'

Now here they were, sitting in the café, sipping their shared coffee, putting off the moment when they would have to go home. Pat Benatar floated from a crackly transistor. Outside, evening colours gathered in the sky.

Martha played with her skirt, folding the polyester into narrow pleats. 'I only hope they haven't heard anything at home.'

'Do you think Una will go squealing?' asked Cat.

'Nah, she won't say anything. It's other people I worry about.'

Two years younger than Martha, Una was the surprise child, the child Delia and Clem Sheeran hadn't thought they could have. A stranger looking at the family would probably assume that Una, as tall and solid as her parents were small and spare-framed, was the adopted one. When the humour took her, she could break world records for being difficult, but she didn't tell tales.

'You know the thing that really annoys me?' said Cat. 'The thing that drives me crackers? Weasel-face Carmody didn't get as much as half an hour's detention. I mean, how unfair is that?'

'Who said the world was fair?' replied Martha. As well as excelling at every team sport, Paudie Carmody represented the county in athletics. He'd been to the Community Games national finals five years in a row. He was untouchable.

'True, only I hate the thought of him strutting around the place, acting like he owns the town – him and Trevor Hawes and Richie Lyons and all the other hangers-on.'

Although outsiders tended to describe it as a village, the people of Templemorris found this offensive. 'It's a *town*,' they'd insist, 'a small town.' It had a church, a ramshackle supermarket, a funeral home, a set of traffic lights and seventeen pubs. Neither Martha nor Cat knew exactly what they wanted to do with their lives, but they were certain of one thing: their need to escape from Templemorris. It was all very well for the old folks to enthuse about a 'close-knit community'. When you were sixteen, you wanted something – anything – to happen. And in Templemorris you could die waiting.

That the town was as dull as dust didn't prevent it being a cauldron of gossip. 'You can't get as much as a new pair of knickers without everybody knowing your business,' Cat would say, 'and it doesn't help when half of them come trailing through your house.' Cat's mother ran a hairdressing business from the front room of their three-bedroomed semi. Despite the constant smell of perming lotion, Martha loved her friend's house. The chaos and clutter – here a broken hairdryer, there an overflowing box of toys – were so different from her own home, which was as neat as a show house. Cat's dad, who played the keyboards in a country-and-western band, was on a perpetual nationwide tour and rarely troubled them with his presence. Truth to tell, as the middle child of seven, Cat was rarely troubled by either of her parents. There was always somebody older or younger for them to get worked up about.

How Martha envied that freedom. Her own mother stayed at home, and her dad's job as a TV and video repair man meant he never travelled far. She sighed. 'Another few months and we'll be free.'

'You'd better believe it,' said Cat.

The following summer, the two were due to finish school and they hoped to go to university in Dublin. Shortly, they would have to fill out their college application forms. Cat argued that it didn't matter what they studied. 'It's not like there are any jobs in anything,' she would point out, 'so we may as well have a good time and worry about the grown-up world later.' Martha was less relaxed. Her mam was sceptical about university education and distrustful of what students got up to in Dublin. 'In my day, we were content to learn shorthand and typing,' she'd say. 'I don't know where yourself and the O'Dowd girl get your ideas from.' In her parents' world, you were considered fortunate to have a job. Choice didn't come into it.

Martha did her best to dazzle them with talk of courses and colleges and the fabulous opportunities that awaited young women with degrees. She tried to convince them that nowadays lots of ordinary girls went to university; education wasn't just for the children of doctors and solicitors. When the subject of money came up, as it often did, she assured them that there'd be a grant to cover everything. At least Una, who was looking forward to a bedroom of her own, could be relied upon for support.

Cat caught her breath, as if she'd been about to say something else but had changed her mind.

'Go on,' said Martha. 'Spit it out.'

'I was wondering, after all that carry-on this afternoon, do you think about her much?'

'Do I think about who?'

'Ah, Martha, don't act all thick on me. Do you think about your real mam? And your real dad, for that matter? You hardly ever mention them.'

'Clem and Delia are my real mam and dad.'

'You know what I mean.'

For a second or two, Martha closed her eyes and inhaled the warm fug of the café. It smelt of chip fat and cigarette smoke and the waitress's musky perfume. She wasn't sure why it was so difficult to talk about the woman who had brought her into the world. Maybe it was because she knew so little about her. She had no image, nothing to hold on to or turn over in her mind. All that Clem and Delia had been told by the adoption society was that their baby's birth mother was in good health and came from a 'highly respectable' family.

'Of course I think about them,' she said. 'Mainly I think about her, about who she is and why she gave me away.'

Cat was tracing circles on the red Formica table. 'Who would you like her to be?'

'Oh, God, I'm not sure. Like, I've never had any notions about her being a princess in a castle or a famous rock star or anything. For a long time, I had this idea she might be some poor woman who had too many children – like the old woman in the shoe who had so many children she didn't know what to do.'

Cat smiled.

'I'm serious,' said Martha. 'That's how I used to think. But now I reckon she was probably a misfortunate girl whose boyfriend left her and whose family threw her out. And you know what? Chances are she's not too far away from here, married to a guy who doesn't know she has a teenage daughter.'

Lurking at the back of Martha's mind was the fear that she'd been abandoned because her original mother simply hadn't wanted her. She hadn't wanted a child, or she hadn't wanted a girl, or she hadn't wanted *this* girl. Voicing her fear would only make it more real, so she kept it to herself.

'Do you think you've got brothers and sisters?' asked Cat.

'I suppose.'

'Does not knowing bother you?'

'What's this? Twenty questions?'

Cat tilted her head to one side. 'Well, it would send me mental. There must be loads of things you've inherited from her – and him. I don't just mean the way you look. There's other stuff too, like the way you're into books. You've read every book in the library. Where did that come from? I doubt Clem and Delia have ever read anything beyond the *Clare Champion* and the parish newsletter.'

Martha laughed, but what Cat had said was true. For as long as she'd been able to read, books had been her joy. If she hadn't read every book in Templemorris's tiny library, she'd worked her way through many of them. She remembered as a child being bamboozled by all of the English books, with their strange rituals and funny names. Who in her world had ever played lacrosse or drunk ginger beer? Who knew that Amy wasn't pronounced Ah-my or that Imogen had a soft *g*? As she'd got older, the librarian had encouraged her, recommending authors and asking for her opinions on what she'd been reading. Most recently, she'd given her *Play It As It Lays* and *The Women's Room*. If Martha's mother had had any inkling of what went on in either book, the library would have replaced the disco at the top of her danger list.

The honest answer to Cat's question was yes: not knowing who she was and where she came from did bother her. But her curiosity came in waves. Sometimes it was so strong she could practically taste it. Then the real world – a failed chemistry exam, a spat with Una – would intervene, and her head would fill with more urgent concerns. There were other times, mad as it might sound, when she wondered if they'd already met. Perhaps they'd sat beside each other on the bus or waited in the same post office queue and not known.

Martha fingered a sachet of sugar. 'About a year ago I was in Limerick with Mam and Una and I saw this woman in one of those bargain shops on William Street. I remember she had a baby in a buggy and a little girl pulling out of her. Anyway, me and the woman, we looked so alike – the droopy eyes, the mousy hair, the bony face, everything. I almost went over and said something.'

'Why didn't you?'

'Because I was only codding myself. She was too young. Besides, what would I say? "Ah, hello there. By any chance, are you my mother?"'

'I can't believe you didn't mention it at the time,' said Cat. 'You're terrible for keeping things to yourself. Imagine if it was her, and you missed your chance.'

The waitress, who'd been hovering, chose that moment to reach in and remove the empty cup. 'Isn't it grand for the pair of you, sitting here gossiping?' she said. 'Have you not got homework to do?' Before either girl had the chance to reply, she bustled off again, clicking her tongue as she went.

Martha shook her head. 'This town.'

'Come on,' said Cat, who picked up her green canvas schoolbag then sent the waitress her most syrupy grin. 'Our friend over there is right. We'd better get moving. I need to have some thoughts about coarse language.'

As soon as Martha opened the front door, her mother's voice rang out.

'There you are,' she called. 'We were beginning to think you'd run off on us.' There was a strained quality to the greeting, as though she'd been practising. This was not a good sign.

'Uh, hi there. With you in a sec,' shouted Martha. Not that she needed to shout. The Sheeran home was so small that anything above a whisper reverberated around it. From upstairs, she could hear the boom of Una's radio. When Martha was fourteen, she'd spent the year listening to a badly dubbed New Order cassette. Her sister would be hard pressed to tell you who was in the Top Ten. Una loved news, hoovering up dispatches about wars and political back-stabbing with an enthusiasm that most girls reserved for shopping trips to Dublin or perfecting their French kissing.

Slowly, Martha peeled off her coat, unwound her scarf and removed her shoes. She hoped her mother wouldn't catch a whiff of Silk Cut.

In the kitchen, Delia was stirring a pot of beef stew. A pan of potatoes was coming to the boil. Clem was there too, sitting at the table, head swooping low while he polished his shoes.

'You're very late,' said her mam.

'Sorry. I went for a coffee with Cat, and we lost track of the time.'

Her dad looked up. 'If you bring me in your shoes, love, I'll give them a shine.'

Although her eyes flickered, Delia said nothing. When Martha returned, ugly school shoes in hand, her mother abandoned the shilly-shallying. 'I nipped out for some carrots earlier, and who did I bump into only Ethel Guilfoyle.' Ethel was a notorious gossip. Unfortunately, her daughter, Lillian, was in Martha's class.

'Really?'

'She said there was a right old ding-dong in Religion this afternoon, and you were in the middle of it.'

'Honestly, Mam, it was no big deal. You know what Mrs Guilfoyle's like. You can bet the story lost nothing in the telling.' While Martha spoke, she tried to avoid looking either parent in the eye. Instead, she focused on her mother's spider plant. It was a monster of a specimen, fresh plantlets exploding from its dangling stems.

'How come you were involved?'

'Paudie Carmody and his mates were giving me a hard time.'

'A hard time? About what?'

Martha shrugged. Fingers crossed, if she stayed calm and kept her answers brief, her mam would give up. 'Just some nonsense or other. They all act up in Religion because there's no exam, and because Miss Casey's soft in the head.'

'I'm sure she's nothing of the sort. Anyway, what type of nonsense? If boys were teasing you, it must have been about something.'

'Oh, this and that. You know the way.'

'If I knew the way I wouldn't be asking.'

And so it continued, mother and daughter batting words back and forth, neither making progress, both becoming exasperated. Realising her mam had no idea what had caused the commotion, Martha scrambled about for a believable lie. An outsider might question why she was reluctant to talk. After all, the row hadn't been of her making, and it was only when the banter became unbearable that she had run away. But experience had taught her that no good would come from a close examination of the afternoon's events. While her mam and dad had never hidden that she was adopted, it wasn't something they were fond of discussing. More often than not, it led to a cloud of awkwardness and an outbreak of carpet-gazing. They seemed to believe that, if they didn't mention it, it wasn't true.

She willed her dad to get involved, but he was

staring at the blasted shoes like they were about to reveal the Third Secret of Fatima. *Oh, please, let the phone ring*, she thought, *or the doorbell – or let the house be struck by lightning or* . . . To be honest, she didn't care what happened so long as it provided a few minutes' distraction.

Just as Martha was about to cave in, she heard the *thud thud thud* of Una galloping down the stairs. Seconds later, her sister careened into the room, long fair hair trailing like the veil of a runaway bride.

'Wait until you hear this evening's news,' she said.

'For pity's sake, Una,' said their mother, 'you'll do yourself an injury tearing around like that. And half the terrace must have heard you thundering down those stairs.'

'I'd say they'll live. What I was—'

'I'm talking to Martha.'

'Ah, Mam, can it not wait?' said Una, who then launched into a breathless gush of news-speak. 'It's all go this evening on the news. Ronald Reagan and Mikhail Gorbachev had a meeting in Switzerland, which, as you can imagine, is a pretty big deal and they were talking about nuclear weapons only according to all the men on the radio it didn't go too well but there's another session tonight.' At last, she paused. 'What language do they speak, do you think? Or is everything done through interpreters?'

'Tuh,' said their mother, as she gave the stew a furious stir. 'I wouldn't get your hopes up. You can be sure precious little will come of it.'

Martha's eyes slid sideways. Although nuclear war was one of her sister's obsessions, her face was blank, too blank. *Fair play, Una*, she thought. *You know exactly what you're doing*.

Their dad snapped shut his box of polishes and cloths. 'A big meeting in Switzerland, is that right?' he said. 'Set the table, like a good girl, and you can tell us all about it.'

It didn't end there.

Later, when Clem was out playing cards and Una was in the sitting room, transfixed by the television news, Delia returned to the fray. Martha was at the kitchen table, twirling a pen between her palms. She was attempting to write three hundred words about animal imagery in *Othello*, only her thoughts kept flitting away.

'Are you going to tell me?' said her mother, as she pulled out a blue-vinyl-seated chair and sat down.

Martha was trapped, her head as empty as the page in front of her. So, as rain pecked against the window, she told the full story. Well, almost the full story. She edited out Cat's contribution. Her mam had no time for girls who swore, declaring it 'low class'. 'Would you listen to the Queen of England?' her dad liked to say, but there was always humour in his voice.

Her mother's reaction was slower, more measured, than she'd expected. There was no high-pitched outrage. For a while she said nothing, just tutted and clicked.

'That's a terrible way for youngsters to be conducting themselves,' she said eventually. 'All the same, I wish you'd stood your ground. It wasn't a good idea to go charging out of the class. People might think you'd something to be ashamed of.'

Afraid she might cry, Martha gave a tiny nod. Up close, she saw how tired her mam looked. Her blue eyes were even more washed out than usual, and the lines at the top of her nose were as sharp as box pleats. Her home perm had wilted, leaving several inches of flat hair followed by a burst of frizz.

'I've seen that Paudie Carmody fellow down the town,' continued her mam. 'You can tell he has ideas about himself. Take it from me, his type never amount to much. Give him a couple of years, and he'll be hanging around outside the betting shop, grateful for a few overnight shifts in the chipboard factory.' She tutted again. 'I've a good mind to have a word with his parents.'

'Ah, Mam. You can't do that. He'd never leave me alone.' Martha was dismayed to hear a crack in her voice. A tear fell down her right cheek.

Delia reached over and clasped her daughter's hand. 'It's all right. If you don't want me to, I won't.' She squeezed, and her small hand felt as thin and dry as parchment. 'I don't mean to go on at you, love. If I do, it's only because I worry. We both worry. You do understand that, don't you?'

This time, Martha's nod was more vigorous,

causing tears to spill down her face. She squeaked something about there being no need to worry.

'How I wish that was true. Believe you me, there's an awful lot of danger out there.'

Despite herself, Martha's lips bent into a smile. Cat always claimed that the problem with Templemorris was that it wasn't dangerous enough.

If her mother thought there was anything odd about the smile, she didn't say. Instead she eased a handkerchief from the pocket of her navy cardigan. 'It's clean,' she said.

For a minute or two, they were quiet. Apart from the faint purr of the gas heater and the *rat-tat-tat* of the rain, the kitchen had been drained of noise. Martha couldn't hear the television, which made her suspect that Una was eavesdropping. If the delegations in Switzerland had any sense, they would employ her as a spy. The heater gave the room a drowsy air, and Martha assumed her mother had said all she was going to say. She was wrong.

'Do you ever wish . . .' Her mam hesitated. 'Do you ever wish you were with your other mother?'

'What gave you that idea? I never—'

'I know you never said anything. I was curious, that's all. Like, maybe you think she might live somewhere more exciting than here. I do understand, you know. If you don't have big ideas at sixteen, when are you going to have them?'

'True.' Martha hoped she would always have big ideas, but she stopped herself saying so. It would sound wrong. Cruel, almost.

'Mind you,' added her mother, 'you've got plenty of time. I know you're sick of hearing this, but you've got your whole life ahead of you.'

Silence settled around them once more.

Martha's brain was swooshing with too many thoughts and emotions. Confusion and curiosity, guilt and plain old sadness: they were all there. She tried to picture her mam at sixteen. Had she always been satisfied with her make-do-and-mend life, or had she been restless too? And what about her dad? It was funny: there Martha had been, rambling on about not knowing her birth mother when, in reality, she hardly knew the woman beside her.

It reminded her of how everybody thought they had Cat figured out. She was a feisty, devil-may-care young one with barely a sensible thought in her head. The well-concealed truth was that she spent half her time worrying that her mam was overworked and the other half fretting that her dad was having wild sex with girls he met on the road.

Martha remembered listening to a woman on Una's radio. 'There's a story behind every door,' she'd said. The line had lodged in her head.

When her mam spoke again, there was wariness in her voice. 'I should have asked this before . . . When you're older, do you think you'll try to find your natural parents?'

Martha patted her face with the sodden handkerchief. 'Would it upset you if I did?'

'It's you I'm thinking of, love. From everything I've heard, a lot of these reunions don't go well.' She paused. 'You've got to realise, children are rejected for loads of different reasons. Who's to say why your birth mother gave you away?'

*Rejected*. How Martha loathed that word. She felt it like a branding iron sizzling against her skin.

Oblivious to her daughter's reaction, Delia continued, 'Of course not every woman wants to dredge up old memories. And then . . . sometimes people pull at one thread, and other threads unravel. They end up being sorry they didn't leave well enough alone.' Another pause. 'But it's up to you. Obviously, it's up to you.'

'Thanks. I—'

'There's no need to say anything. I don't want you upsetting yourself again.' Her mother's tone had changed. It was more spirited now, more reassuring. She smiled and glanced at Martha's exercise book. 'You're not getting too far with that homework either. Why don't I write a note to say you weren't feeling well? Then we'll go in and have a look at the telly.'

'We'll have to elbow Una out of the way first.'

'If you ask me, we'll be doing her a favour. All that news can't be good for her.'

Normally Martha would have expected at least a token display of stroppiness from Una. Tonight her sister took one look at the mottled mess that was Martha's face and offered to make tea.

'What's seldom is wonderful,' said Delia, as she folded herself into her brown armchair.

Martha laughed. Una stuck her tongue out at both of them, but she was laughing too.

A few minutes later, in the blue glow of the television, Martha turned the mug of scalding tea in her hands. She realised how tired she was; so tired she could barely focus on the wide-shouldered, bouncy-haired women on her mam's favourite American soap. She felt raw too, as if a layer of skin had been peeled away. Oh, and that wasn't all. Her mother's words were a reminder that Martha's real family was right there in Templemorris. It was Clem, Delia and Una who mattered, not some vague figure who would probably die a thousand deaths if Martha turned up on her doorstep. When everything else – the classroom taunts, the silly rows, the fantasising – was stripped away, two facts remained.

Her birth mother hadn't wanted her. This was her home.

# CHAPTER 8

*Dublin, September 2013*

Why was it, Martha wondered, that when she was being told something important her thoughts insisted on rambling? And, on that ramble, why did they have to alight upon the most trivial subject possible? Here she was, slap-bang in the middle of a delicate conversation, and all she could focus on was the colour of the walls. They had definitely been painted since her last visit to Dermot's office. If you were being generous, you would describe the new colour as pistachio. If you were being snarky, you might say it was closer to something a little boy would pluck from his nose. For the life of her, she couldn't recall the old colour. One of those bland creamy shades, perhaps. And the desk – long, black, glossy – that was new too, she thought.

The sound of her name and the tetchy note in Dermot's voice made her snap back to attention.

'Aren't you going to congratulate me?' he was saying.

'Yes, yes, of course I am. Of course.' Martha

was, she realised, rubbing the place where her wedding ring used to be. 'That's brilliant, Dermot. Honestly. And Layla . . . she's pleased?'

'Obviously she's pleased.' Martha didn't think it was obvious at all but managed to stop herself saying so. 'It's early days,' continued Dermot, 'so we're not telling many people at the moment. Just family. For fear . . . well, you know.'

'A wise move,' she heard herself saying.

Relief passed across his face, and they exchanged uncomfortable my-aren't-we-civilised smiles. What had he expected? That she would break into tears or stomp out like the wronged woman in a daytime soap? They were no longer married. Not quite divorced either, but that was another day's work. This didn't mean she was unaffected by the news. Barely two years had passed since their separation. There were still moments when she forgot they were no longer together.

When Dermot had asked if she'd be able to drop into the office ('I don't like putting you out, but we're up to our tonsils here'), Martha had assumed he wanted to talk about Evanne. She was going through an awkward phase, prone to saying everything that came into her head, no matter how harsh. Then again, she was sixteen. Who wasn't awkward at sixteen? Martha's only other thought had been to speculate that Dermot and Layla had split up. *This* she hadn't seen coming. More fool her. At least she was hearing the news from Dermot rather than second-hand from a friend or, worse, a tabloid headline. The papers adored Layla, or 'Raven-haired TV beauty Layla Fogarty', as they referred to her, the article usually accompanied by a large photograph. Dermot's new partner was of a different generation from his ex-wife, a generation who knew how to have their photo taken without looking scared or simple or multi-chinned.

On the other side of the black desk, Dermot continued to chatter away. Martha wished he would stop so she could consider the implications of what she'd just heard. He was talking about names. She didn't want to hear about names.

'. . . or for a boy, Layla is keen on Fingal or Luán. Isn't it interesting how these old Irish names are making such a comeback?'

'Um, "Fingal Fogarty"? Is it not a bit *Darby O'Gill and the Little People*?'

'Aren't you the funny one? He, if it is a he, won't be Fingal Fogarty. He'll be Fingal Waters. Layla and I . . . we will be getting married. Not quite yet, obviously, the damn divorce laws being what they are. But in a couple of years' time when we're all free to get on with our lives . . .' He trailed off, as though it had suddenly occurred to him that he was veering into sensitive territory.

Martha instructed herself to take a deep breath and to be generous. 'Sorry, Dermot, you'll have to forgive my ignorance. Congratulations. Again. I had no idea you'd proposed to Layla. Why didn't you tell me before?'

'Because I haven't.' Dermot rubbed his upper

lip. 'I mean, this has all happened so quickly. Perhaps a little more quickly than I'd planned, if the truth be told. I haven't had the opportunity to ask properly. But I thought it went without saying. Now we're going to be a family, what else would we do?'

Her face burned. Embarrassment being as contagious as the hottest virus, Dermot looked uncomfortable too. All the same, she ploughed on, 'And is that what Layla wants?'

'What do you mean?'

'Nothing really, except – how do I put this? – her generation isn't as fixated on marriage as we were.'

'Her "generation"? Jesus, Martha, she's twenty-nine, not eighteen.'

And you're forty-seven, she almost replied.

Fortunately, the exchange was cut short by Dermot's PA, Isobel, who teetered in with two coffees; proper coffee in the type of white cups and saucers you might see in a high-end hairdresser's. Where Martha worked, you were lucky to get a stained mug of instant. In Dermot's business, the trappings were important. Isobel gave Martha a smile that could have doubled as a grimace. Like many of those who passed through the offices of Dermot Waters Talent Management ('Ireland's premier media talent agency'), she gleamed with ambition. You might be there to make the coffee or unblock the drains, but chances were that you dreamed of seeing your name in neon and your face on the cover of a weekly magazine.

Martha remonstrated with herself. *Here I am*, she thought, *doing it again. I should be concentrating on what Dermot is telling me, not fretting about the opinions of a wannabe TV presenter.*

Strange as it sounded now, when Martha had first met Dermot, she'd been attracted by how uncomplicated he seemed. 'About as complicated as a two-piece jigsaw', according to her friend Cat. Martha had been emerging from one of the bleakest times of her life when in he had walked: straightforward, hardworking. Oh, and handsome too, in a slightly old-fashioned way. (Not that back then she would have used a middle-aged word like 'handsome'.) If that made him sound boring, maybe he had been. But, still bruised from her last relationship, she had surprised herself and fallen in love. Besides, what had been the alternative? More of what she'd just been through?

Now, on her bad days, she was dogged by the feeling that her marriage had been a mistake. Then she would get annoyed with herself. Obviously, it hadn't been a mistake. It had given her, had given them, Evanne. As strained as their relationship had become, Martha would never claim that Dermot was anything but a good father. Although his office was decorated with pictures of the almost-rich and semi-famous, the most prominent photo was of their daughter. It had been taken on their last family holiday. She was thirteen then with the squinty, unselfconscious smile of a child.

The split continued to disappoint Martha's

parents. More than that, it baffled them. 'You can't just give up,' her mother liked to say. 'That's not how marriage works.' But Clem and Delia were of another era. When they were young, even the worst cruelty was borne with stoicism. A woman could spend her days picking her teeth up off the floor, yet still she wouldn't leave.

Dermot had started a new life with more haste than Martha had expected. Now he was telling her that this life was permanent. While Layla wasn't the shiniest star in his constellation, she was definitely on the up. With Dermot's assistance, she had manoeuvred her way from a slot doing Pilates on afternoon television to being the show's co-presenter. Cat had pounced upon her lithe, fresh-featured appearance. 'Central Casting's been busy,' she'd said. This time, though, her quip was off-target. It was too glib, too easy. Martha didn't know a lot about TV presenting, but she knew that Layla was talented. She could segue from vivacious to serious to humorous with almost unnatural ease. When empathy was called for, she had that too.

In the beginning, Evanne had been upset by how quickly her dad was moving on. She'd even questioned whether getting involved with a client was ethical. 'It's not like I'm a psychiatrist or anything,' a flustered Dermot had protested. Over the months, Evanne had warmed to her father's new partner, but Martha wasn't sure how she'd react to the arrival of a small sister or brother. In your teens, you felt everything so keenly. The world was filled with sharp edges, exhilarating highs, devastating lows. Age was like a mild antidepressant. It stripped away the drama and emotion. Life became fuzzier.

Evanne must have been playing on Dermot's mind too because, after a few minutes of coffee-sipping and stilted conversation, he asked if Martha would break the news.

'Are you sure?' she replied. 'Will she not feel more involved if you tell her?'

'Yeah, except I'm not much good at that sort of thing. You know me. I'll sit there squirming while Evanne stares at me like I'm not the brightest crayon in the box.'

'Says the man who negotiates for a living. You manage to find the right words then.'

'That's different. Talking to teenage daughters requires another level of skill entirely.'

Martha raised her eyes to the ceiling.

'Seriously,' said Dermot, 'if you talk to her, she can call me afterwards. And she can have a chat with Layla too, if that's what she'd like. Then we'll meet up next week, maybe go somewhere for dinner. What do you say?'

She threw up her hands in surrender. 'I'm being steamrollered here, that's what I say.'

'Martha, you're a star. I really do appreciate this.'

'I haven't said I'll do it.'

'But you will?'

'Go on, then. Anyway, it's not like it's bad news. She'll be thrilled for you, I'm sure.'

'Thanks a million. I owe you one.' Dermot paused, the pause a beat too long. 'And you'll do it today?'

'Does it matter?'

'I wouldn't leave it too long.'

'Oh?'

'There's going to be a piece, a nice little feature, in one of the Sunday papers. The *Herald*. So it's probably best if it's all sorted by then.'

'What do you mean by "a nice little feature"?'

'An article in the supplement, the cover story actually.' Martha detected a layer of pride in Dermot's voice. 'The usual formula: rising star, baby on the way, excitement all round, blah, blah, blah. A few tasteful photos of Layla. Not much about me, thankfully. Sorry, I tell a lie. There will be one picture of the two of us, taken at some charity do or other. I wasn't keen, but Layla said it was for the best. She doesn't want it to look like there's no father on the scene. Even in this day and age, people can be terribly judgemental.'

Martha's back stiffened. 'So much for just telling family. Just family and a million Sunday-paper readers, you mean.' For once, she didn't care that her voice was too loud. 'You can't behave like this, Dermot. You know my parents read the *Herald*. It's such a . . .' Words truly were failing her today. 'It's such a tacky thing to do. And what about Evanne? Have you thought how she'll feel? It's like you're deliberately setting out to humiliate us by flaunting your glossy new family in some rag of a paper.'

'Ah, now, Martha, you're not being fair. You know I wouldn't—'

'I know you didn't think of Evanne or me or Mam and Dad. That's what I know.'

'Listen, I'm sorry. I hear what you're saying and, okay, announcing your pregnancy in a magazine may be a bit showbiz for some, but television *is* showbiz – and it's tough out there. Layla's got to let her bosses know she's still serious about the show, that she's not going to go disappearing for months on end. If she puts that out in the public domain now, her position will be more secure. We're talking about her future here.'

Martha gave a silent scream of frustration. She could protest further, but what was the point? No doubt the damn magazine was already at the printer's. She regretted raising her voice. There was every danger that Isobel was listening, and she didn't want to be pigeon-holed as the bitter ex-wife. Increasingly, she felt as if the world operated by rules she didn't understand. She wondered if other people were the same, or were they all adapting, leaving her behind? She wondered, too, if Dermot's comment about it being 'tough out there' was another swipe at her job as a part-time librarian. In the depths of one of their nastier rows, he'd dismissed it as a job for those who weren't brave enough to do anything else.

'I genuinely am sorry,' he was saying. 'Maybe I didn't think it all through. Honest to God, though, I didn't expect you to get so rattled.'

*Then you really don't know me*, she thought. 'I'd better talk to Evanne this evening, so. And to my parents. I don't want Dad getting worked up over his Sunday fry.'

'Would seeing me and Layla in the paper upset him?'

'Of course it would. He still thinks of you as his son-in-law. "Any word from Dermot?" he says to me, like one day soon we'll see sense and get back together.'

For a moment, they were quiet. The window was ajar, allowing the rumble of city traffic to creep in. Martha reckoned she should go, let him get on with whatever it was that had him so busy. Half an hour of peace wouldn't do her any harm either.

Dermot ran a hand through the dark hair that was now stippled with grey. 'Otherwise everything's okay? With Evanne, I mean.'

'Oh, grand. Occasionally I'm the best mother in the world. More often I'm ruining her life.'

'Is she still giving you grief about the other business?'

'She is.' Martha bent down and scooped up her handbag.

'I'd give you my opinion only—'

'Only I've already heard it a thousand times?' She rose to go, then stopped before she got to the door. 'The walls?'

He gave a sheepish smile. 'Layla's choice of colour, I'm afraid. I wouldn't have picked it myself, but there you go. We've all got to move with the times. Or so she tells me.'

In Martha's view, people underestimated the joy of walking in the city, of seeing Dublin in all its colours and humours. Despite having spent most of her life in the capital, she hated driving in the city centre. Everybody was so aggressive, in such a ludicrous hurry to get to the next bottleneck. Early in their relationship, Dermot had dubbed her 'small-town girl', and she supposed that was what she was. Not that she ever regretted moving to Dublin. Her attitude towards Templemorris might have softened with the years, but distance made it easier to be fond of home.

Needing time to digest Dermot's revelations, she decided to walk to the Luas station in Charlemont and to get the tram from there. She meandered along Baggot Street, soaking up the energy: the women in click-clack heels, the men in grey suits, everybody clutching the twenty-first-century essentials – a takeaway coffee and a phone. A swarm of voices talked of business coups, incompetent colleagues, nights on the town. Although the sun shone, the high glare of summer had dimmed, the September light a reminder that the dank days of winter were approaching. She turned at the bridge, checking the trees along the Grand Canal for the first signs of autumn. The older Martha got, the more determined she became to make the most of fine weather. She insisted on opening windows, on eating outdoors, on wearing sandals until her feet were practically blue. She drove Evanne crazy.

As she walked, she thought about what Dermot had said, and about what they'd avoided saying. Martha continued to live in what had been the family home. A three-bedroomed semi-detached in a Milltown cul-de-sac, they'd bought it as newlyweds. At the time, it had seemed such a brave thing to do. She remembered the two of them beaming at each other like fools, stunned that they'd made this grown-up decision, nervous about meeting the mortgage payments. Nights out had been replaced by trips to DIY superstores in far-flung industrial estates. Invariably, they'd got lost and ended up bickering. Looking back, she was embarrassed by the eagerness with which they'd embraced the rituals of the first-time buyer.

When their marriage finally fell apart, they'd agreed to sell and split the proceeds. At the time, the economy was in freefall, so they'd reckoned it was best to wait. Dermot had moved to a rented apartment in Sandyford. According to Evanne, it was 'a-may-zing': all blond wood, smoky glass and shiny appliances. Call her old-fashioned, but Martha didn't believe that an apartment, no matter how swish, was any place for a romping toddler. Not if you had the money for a garden. That wasn't all: the property market was resurgent. As much as the prospect of selling up and moving on depressed her, she knew the time had come.

She also knew she wouldn't be able to afford

anything like their home in Dolmen Crescent. Working three days a week had made sense when Evanne was small, and she'd been lucky to have the choice. Now she would have loved to increase her hours, but with the library service short of cash, her chances of getting more work were slim. While Dermot provided for Evanne, Martha didn't want to rely on him.

The split had been instigated by Dermot but, ground down by non-stop sniping and squabbling, she had agreed. Mostly she was happy with their separation. No, that wasn't quite right: mostly she was fine with their separation. When acquaintances asked, she answered by rote: she was 'scratching along' and it was 'for the best' and a 'fresh start' awaited and . . . Really, her store of banalities was endless. Evanne was the main source of joy in her life, but she had trained herself to take pleasure in small things: a good night's sleep or a cloud-free day or the face of a contented reader. She reminded herself that her health was sound and her job was safe. Wasn't safety what most of the world wanted? What right had she to complain about anything when she was safe?

And then sometimes . . . sometimes she was heart-stoppingly lonely. Those were the days when she felt that even a marriage where irritating each other was viewed as a competitive sport was better than being on her own. She might be surrounded by people yet feel alone, as if she was stranded in the wilderness, arms outstretched, palms raised, asking, 'What do I do now?' In December, she would be forty-five. She was unlikely to meet anybody else. She knew this was bad thinking, of course she did. That didn't make the thought go away.

How simple would life be if she could say, 'That's it. Decision made, line drawn, time to move on'? But Martha wasn't good at moving on. She wasn't good at decisions. She didn't want to be married but she didn't want to be not-married either.

When she reached home, Evanne was sitting at the kitchen table, her navy blazer on the back of a chair, her hair freed from its school ponytail. Although text books were piled high in front of her, she was more interested in the contents of her phone.

'Hi, Mum,' she said, giving Martha the briefest of glances. '*Honestly*, some people are such *idiots*. You'll never guess what Amy Lenihan has gone and done.'

On her journey, Martha had decided not to delay in passing on the big news. She didn't want to get side-tracked by the latest school gossip. Neither did she want to be rude, so for a short while she stood and nodded. She was listening, but not taking anything in. Eventually she pulled out a chair and sat down. 'Can I talk to you about something?' she asked.

'Uh, okay.'

Although Evanne had been blessed with the best of both parents, she didn't really look like either of them. She'd inherited her father's long legs and her mother's thin-shouldered, narrow build.

Mother and daughter also had the same high cheekbones. There the physical similarities ended. Evanne's eyes were a clear pale blue, Martha's a nondescript grey (like the Irish Sea on a bad day, according to a former boyfriend). When it came to their hair, the difference was even more marked. Martha had been a counterfeit blonde for so long that she barely remembered her natural shade of mouse. Evanne's hair was a deep, lustrous brown. It hung in the sort of loose waves that no hairdresser could replicate. Rich woman's hair, Martha called it. Occasionally, she wondered where it had come from.

Evanne's first response to news of Layla's pregnancy was a crisp 'You are having me on,' the sentence enunciated like there was a full stop after every word. This was followed by a sarcastic 'Way to go, Dad. *How* old is he again?'

'I'm sure forty-seven seems ancient to you, love, but plenty of men have children in their forties. It's no big deal.'

'It's a big deal to me. Like, Layla's all right and everything, only . . .' Evanne's voice tapered off.

'Do you want to call your dad later on? You could congratulate the two of them. He'd like that. And if you have any questions—'

'Ha! Don't get me started. I can think of tons of questions – like "Had you not heard of contraception, then?"'

Even though she'd taken a solemn vow never to begin any sentence with 'When I was your age . . .'

Martha shuddered to think how her own mother would have reacted to this remark. She was pretty sure the punishment would have involved indefinite grounding. 'Perhaps that wouldn't be the best approach to take.'

'Chill, Mum, I'll behave. When's he or she due to arrive?'

'March.'

'And this newspaper article . . . I presume it'll be online and everything too. Like, there's a danger the girls at school will see it.'

'I suppose. It's a bit of a pain, I know.'

Evanne gave a theatrical wince. 'It's more than that. It's complete tack-er-ama.'

'I couldn't have put it better myself.' Martha noticed a flicker of mischief in Evanne's eyes. 'What?'

'Oh, nothing. Well, I was just thinking, at least this baby will know all its relations. It won't be going around wondering who it really is.'

'Please, Evanne. Not today.'

'I can't understand why you don't want to solve a mystery. That's all.'

For months, Evanne had been pestering Martha about tracking down her birth parents. 'What are you afraid of?' she'd ask.

'I'm not afraid of anything,' Martha would reply. 'I'm happy with things the way they are. Your nan and granddad are the only parents I've ever needed. Besides, it's not that easy to trace someone.'

Evanne usually countered with a line about it not being impossible either. 'People are successful all the time,' she'd say. 'I've heard them on the radio.'

That was true. Despite the obstacles placed in their path, many adopted people did find their birth mothers. Almost every week fresh stories emerged about the Ireland of the past, about Magdalen laundries and mother-and-baby homes, about casual cruelties and unexpected kindnesses. But Martha had heard enough of those tales to know that a sizeable number didn't end well. Too often, people jumped through bureaucratic hoops only to be disappointed. There was no joyful reunion, no welcoming family, just suspicion or, even worse, hostility. They were rejected all over again. She had said all this and more to Evanne. Yet, at the end of every row, it was Martha who ended up cloaked in guilt.

She understood her daughter's obsession. Throughout Evanne's childhood, the sins of the twentieth century had been a staple of the news. She had grown up with monochrome images of pregnant girls in austere convents and emaciated kids in reform-school dormitories. When she was nine or so, she'd fixed Martha with an earnest stare and asked, 'In the olden days, did they not like children?' Now she was a few years older, she had realised that those TV pictures weren't ancient history. She wanted to know if her own family was part of the story.

For the moment, at least, she seemed content to let the matter rest. Instead she asked about the baby, about when they'd know if it was a boy or a girl, and about whether she would be a godmother. Then, in a hesitant voice, she asked a question that gave the lie to all her poise and bravado. 'This is kind of it, isn't it? You're not going to get back together again now.'

'We weren't anyway, love. But we're okay, aren't we, the two of us?'

'I will get to see Dad, won't I?'

Martha swallowed hard. 'I don't follow you. Why wouldn't you see him?'

'It's . . . Well, he's so busy with work. And everybody says babies take up *loads* of time.'

She waited.

'So he mightn't have much time left for me.'

Martha did her best to sound emphatic. 'I promise you, the new baby won't make a jot of difference. Your dad will always have plenty of time for you. Always.'

Evanne nodded in a way that suggested she didn't share her mother's confidence. Martha rose and busied herself at the kitchen counter, wiping away imaginary crumbs and wringing out a dry cloth.

'You're not upset, are you, Mum?'

Thrown off balance, her answer came too quickly. 'Gosh, love, not at all. I'm the finest.' She opened the fridge and stared intently at the contents. 'Do you know what you'd like for your dinner?' she asked.

For a couple of minutes, she thought it best to avoid her daughter's scrutiny.

# CHAPTER 9

Cat's cheeks twitched with amusement. '"I'm determined not to get typecast,"' she read. '"Some people don't understand that you can have a pretty face without being dumb. What I'd love is to make hard-hitting documentaries about issues like homelessness. That's where my true passion lies."' She dropped the previous day's *Sunday Herald* onto her kitchen table. 'Oh, give us a break. Why do they all feel the need to come out with this I'm-a-serious-person-really guff? Why not be happy with what you've got? I wish somebody would pay me to sit on a sofa and flirt.'

'To be fair,' said Martha, 'I think there may be a wee bit more to the job than that.'

'But, as you'd say yourself, what's fairness got to do with anything?' Cat sipped her coffee. 'How's Dermot?'

'At his most Dermot-like.'

'Very pleased with himself, you mean?'

Martha laughed. She was in need of a laugh. At home, Evanne was asking a million questions a minute, while in Templemorris her parents had reacted to Dermot's news like there'd been a death in the family. Of course she was still angry about his newspaper stunt, but Martha had never been one for putting her struggles on public display. Instead she recited platitudes to herself. 'Bitterness is bad for the skin,' she'd say, and 'A well-lived life is the best revenge.' She was a walking, talking fridge magnet.

Sometimes she wondered if being adopted had made her more compliant, less willing to stamp her feet and create a fuss. She suspected it had.

The conversation moved on, and for the first time in days, Martha felt as if she could unwind. She had long viewed Cat's house, and her kitchen in particular, as sanctuary. At nine, eight and five, her children were still at the stage where they asked easy-to-answer questions, like 'Why is chewing-gum chewy?' or 'Can we get a kitten?' The kitchen was wonderfully higgledy-piggledy too, festooned with paintings and photos and notes about swimming lessons and drama classes. That her coffee cup was chipped and one of the blinds skew-whiff only added to the appeal. Martha wasn't sure that a room could be called optimistic, yet that was how she thought of it.

At university, Martha and Cat had studied communications, or, as Dermot liked to put it, they had a degree in watching the TV. 'Was there a course that was *less* likely to get you a job?' he used to say.

'Probably not, but we did have a fantastic time,' she would reply, before tormenting him with the story of how she'd once got a first for an essay on the representation of women in *Dynasty*. He had been an accountant when they'd first met, so she could never have imagined that he'd end up making his living from the media. Adept at kissing high and kicking low, he was able to handle both the egos and the suits.

For her, the degree had been a dead end, and she'd returned to college to become a librarian. Cat was different. After several years of larking about, she'd found her calling. With her sharp eye and sharper wit, she'd turned out to be a brilliant advertising copywriter. Cars, cereal, cat-litter: you name it, she sold it. Following the birth of her youngest child, she'd left her job, throwing herself into full-time motherhood with an enthusiasm she'd once reserved for pursuing men and depleting the world's tequila stocks. Five years on, Jake was at school, and Cat was getting antsy. She was tired of scrimping and making-do and wanted to return to work.

'Anyway,' she was saying, 'I met up with an old colleague last week. I called into the office and, I swear to you, Martha, I felt about a zillion years old. I was convinced they were going to offer me a chair or start calling me "Ma'am". They were oozing condescension. And they were all so bloody glamorous. When did Irish people acquire polish? What was wrong with being the least groomed people in Europe?'

'I'm puzzled by the grooming thing myself,'

replied Martha. 'The pedicures and manicures and shaped eyebrows and eyelash extensions. Eyelash extensions, I ask you.'

'Mark my words,' said Cat, 'it won't end well.'

'You know what else gets to me? Every time I open a magazine, I'm presented with some twenty-five-year-old wonder-girl or other and they're always described as the "voice of their generation". I can't remember our generation having a voice.'

'Oh, we did. It was the voice in our heads. The one that said, "Get a job. Get married. Have children. Don't make a show of yourself."' Cat sucked in air through her teeth. 'Lord, when did we get so *old*?'

'So, if you could choose,' asked Martha, 'what age would you be?'

'I don't know.' Cat paused. 'Come to think of it, if I did have one wish, I'd like Jake to stay the way he is.' She smiled. 'He came bombing in here the other day, wearing his little red anorak like it was Superman's cape. You should've seen the joy on his face. I had to stop myself saying to him, "Jake, pet, will you stay five? Just for me?" Richie took a picture. If you hang on a minute, I'll get my—' Cat punched her right cheek. 'Oh, will you listen to me? Sorry for the boring-mammy act.'

'Don't worry,' said Martha. 'We've all done it.' If the newspaper article was anything to go by, she could expect an outpouring of mammy-talk from Layla. She was preparing herself already.

Perhaps nothing in Cat's life had been as

surprising as her choice of partner. In her younger days, she'd pledged to avoid all men from Templemorris. 'Just imagine the dreariness,' she'd say to Martha. 'Even one slip and you have permission to shoot me.' When she was thirty-two, she'd married Richie Lyons. The same Richie Lyons who'd sat near them at school and who'd been best friends with the dreaded Paudie Carmody (Paudie had confounded Martha's mother and done well for himself too, but that was another story).

Cat smoothed out a copper-coloured curl, then let it spring back to its natural state. 'Dermot and Layla aside, how are things with you? Is Evanne still giving you a hard time?'

Martha recounted their most recent skirmishes. 'She keeps asking what I'm afraid of.'

For a minute or so, Cat said nothing. Then she blew across the surface of her coffee. 'So what *are* you afraid of?'

'How many times do I have to say it? I'm not . . .' One look at the face on the other side of the table, and Martha's voice stalled. Cat's expression said, 'You might fool a teenager but you don't fool me.'

She took a long breath. 'To be honest, I'm afraid of a million things. I'm afraid how Mam and Dad will react. I'm afraid I won't be able to trace her . . . my birth mother, I mean. I'm afraid she might be dead. But most of all I'm scared I will trace her, and she won't want to know me. Not only would I be upset, Evanne would be devastated.'

'Any of those things might happen,' said Cat. 'Or maybe she's out there right now looking for you.'
'Maybe,' replied Martha, her voice scarcely louder than a whisper. These days she thought about her natural parents more often than she would like to admit. Once, she'd gone as far as getting the name and address of the adoption society that had placed her with Clem and Delia. She'd never followed through, and the scrap of paper containing the details was turning to lint at the bottom of her handbag.
'Then again,' continued Cat, 'perhaps she's always wanted to find you, only she's been putting it off because she's scared.'
'Well, that would be silly. What's there for *her* to be afraid of? Like we've been saying, none of us is getting any younger. If she leaves it too much longer, she might run out of time.'
'My point exactly. We've been talking about this, on and off, for the best part of thirty years, and I've tried not to be too much of a bore.' Martha's eyebrows shot up. 'Okay, okay, sometimes I've been a little firm in my views, but I genuinely believe that if you don't make an effort, you'll regret it. Why not think of it as solving a mystery?'
'That's funny. Evanne said the same thing – about thinking of it as a mystery.'
'You see? There you go. Great minds and all of that.'
'First Dermot, then Evanne, and now you're having a go. I'm seriously outnumbered here.' It

struck Martha that Cat's talk about getting old had been merely a scene-setter, a ruse. She'd been softening her up for this. 'You're not in cahoots with Evanne, are you? I wouldn't put it past you.'

'I don't know what gave you that idea,' said Cat, putting on a display of mock innocence.

Martha rested her head in her hands. In the days since Dermot's surprise, her brain had been buzzing and fizzing. Among all the thoughts jostling for space, one kept pushing to the front: if she didn't start searching now, she never would.

When she looked up again, it felt like an age had passed. In reality, it had been less than five minutes. She gave Cat what she hoped was a disgruntled stare. 'I don't appreciate being ganged up on, you know.'

'Message received,' said Cat, who didn't have the decency to look even vaguely chastened. 'What do you say, though? Will you give it a go?'

Martha swallowed the dregs of her coffee and got to her feet. 'I'd better get moving,' she said. 'I've got phone calls to make.'

# CHAPTER 10

'I hope you're not expecting too much,' said Delia, as she lowered herself onto Martha's old bed. She removed the lid from a faded shoebox and sifted through its contents. 'We didn't get a lot of information. That's not how things worked back then.' She smiled. 'We were happy just to get you.'

Martha, perched inches away on what had been Una's bed, returned the smile. It was a relief to see some of the tension lift from her mother's face.

Six weeks had passed since she'd decided to track down her birth parents. During that time she'd been busy. She'd discovered that the agency responsible for her adoption – St Saviour's – had closed and passed its files to the health service. She'd written to the relevant office and filled out all the necessary forms. She'd written to the Adoption Authority and completed another raft of paperwork. Every day underlined how little she knew, not just about herself but about the entire process of tracing a parent. What amazed her was how quickly she'd become swept up in her task. With every form and phone call, she'd become more determined to succeed. She went about her work with a zeal she hadn't known she possessed. Dermot, Cat and Evanne were right. She should have started sooner. The questions looped around her brain. Where had she come from? What were her birth parents' stories? And where were they now?

If Martha was being honest, there was another reason to immerse herself in the search: it was a distraction from the rest of her life.

What she hadn't done, until now, was to take the most important step. She hadn't sought the blessing of her mother and father. Every day she would intend to, and every day she would abandon that intention. She had excuses by the score: she was tired or her mam wasn't well or her dad was upset about the death of a friend. Eventually the excuses ran dry. Besides, not telling them was stupid. There was every chance they'd be able to help. They might reveal a nugget of information, a seemingly unimportant name or detail that would help to unlock the door. So, while Evanne spent the weekend with Dermot and Layla, Martha drove to Templemorris.

It took her three hours and four cups of tea to broach the subject. When finally she gathered up the gumption, her dad reacted with his usual equanimity. Her mam was more . . . Actually, it was hard to come up with a precise description of Delia's reaction. Her face was opaque. In a brittle voice, she expressed surprise at Martha's decision. 'I would have thought you'd got more than enough on your plate already,' she said.

Still, she pledged to help.

That was where the shoebox (for a pair of blue 'Clarks Clippers', priced three pounds) came in. It contained a treasure trove of childhood memorabilia, from one of Martha's baby blonde curls to an early school report that warned of her tendency to daydream. Her adoption papers were there too. Many years before, Martha's dad had shown her the official certificate, but she'd been young then, her interest only fleeting. Now she hoped the box would yield a clue to her origins.

As was her way, Delia was more interested in reminiscing about a black-and-white Polaroid of a sleeping baby in a white suit and crocheted hat. 'Do you know,' she said, 'that was taken on the day we collected you. We went in with an empty carrycot and came out with a baby. Our little Martha. I can't tell you how excited we were.'

Martha hugged a pillow to her chest. 'Were you nervous?'

'Petrified. You were only two months old, and I was terrified I'd drop you or, worse, that some official would butt in and say they'd made a mistake and we had to give you back. We'd been waiting for such a long time. You had to have been married for at least three years before you could even apply to adopt, and I'm sure you can imagine all of the other rules and regulations, about Mass-going and the like.' She paused to take another photo from the box. 'There's your dad and me, taken on the very same day. Would you look at the pair of us?'

'The state of you,' said Martha, with a grin. The lapels on her father's jacket were so wide there was a danger he would set sail, while her mother was wearing a Crimplene mini-dress and block-heeled patent shoes. 'Where did you go to collect me? Was I in one of those mother-and-baby homes like you see on the news?'

Her mam pressed her lips together before replying. 'I wouldn't pay much mind to that. If you ask me, people are too quick to criticise. I'm not saying those homes were ideal, but if a girl got herself into trouble, where else was she meant to go? Would these do-gooders prefer it if girls had given birth by the side of the road?'

Thrown by this vehemence, Martha found herself giving a wishy-washy reply. 'I guess they think it would've been better if the girls' families had looked after them. Or what about the babies' fathers? Shouldn't they have been involved?'

'Those were different times, Martha. Different times.' As if to emphasise her daughter's naivety, Delia gave a hurried shake of the head. 'Anyway, to answer your question, we collected you from an office in Ennis. And then a man – I think it was a man, it's all such a long time ago – he gave us one final piece of paper to sign. And that was it.'

'Do you have the piece of paper?' asked Martha,

hoping her mother would take the hint and reveal the remainder of the box's contents.

'I'm sure we don't. You've got to understand, we were so thrilled to be bringing you home we didn't give a fig about the paperwork. I wanted to get you back here so everybody could see how lovely you were. I remember the neighbours trooping in. Of course, in those days Templemorris was a far more neighbourly town. And the presents they gave you – we were overwhelmed. People mightn't have had much back then, but what they did have they'd willingly give.'

'So there wasn't any – I'm not sure if this is the right word – any stigma attached to me being adopted? No nasty comments or anything?'

'Yes and no.' Her mam pulled at one earlobe. 'I remember one woman in particular being a bit sniffy. Sadie Enright was her name. She used to live on Clancy Street. Had a haughty head on her. "Do you not worry about her real mother having loose morals?" she said to me, all hoity-toity like. "It might be hereditary."'

'You're having me on.'

'Indeed and I'm not. You used to get the odd old one who thought like that. Most of them had more sense than to come out and say it.'

'What did you say to her?'

'May God forgive me, I told her she'd be better off looking after her own daughter who'd let half the town into her knickers.'

'Mam! You did not.'

'I did so. She never bothered me again.' Her mother placed the two photographs to one side, and patted the candlewick bedspread. 'When he's had his rest, I'll show these to Clem. They'll bring back a few memories, I can tell you.'

Martha had heard it said that as couples aged they became more alike. With her own parents, the opposite was true. Every year, their personalities and habits diverged further. While his wife had a compulsion to be out and about, gathering up the local news and involving herself in everything from the Musical Society to the St Vincent de Paul, Clem preferred a quiet life. He enjoyed a snooze in the afternoon too. 'I'll put the head down for half an hour,' he would say.

To begin with, Martha had fretted about that, but her mother insisted her concern was misplaced. 'He doesn't know how lucky he is, being able to sleep like that,' she said. 'I'd kill for a decent night's sleep.'

'So,' said Martha, keen to return to the matter at hand, 'what else have you got in there?'

'Like I've told you, not much. A few odds and ends.' With her steel-coloured head bent over the box, Delia removed and unfolded Martha's adoption certificate. 'You've seen this one before,' she said, as she handed it to her daughter. 'And then there's this.' She pulled out another piece of paper. 'These are your details.'

The details, such as they were, were typed on a fragile sheet of A4. Even by 1960s standards, the typewriter must have been primitive because some of the letters were barely legible. Martha gazed at the scrap of paper. A strange sensation took hold of her. She felt like a child rolling down a very steep hill.

'*Girl*,' she read. '*Born eighth of December (Feast of the Immaculate Conception).*' At this, she stopped and smiled. '*Seven pounds, nine ounces. Sturdy and feeding well. Mother calls her Josephine Jeannie. Mother in good health, if too thin. Will return to her home soon. Father unnamed.*'

As she read, there was a slight tremor in her hands. Although the note told her little that was new, she was taken aback by how moving she found it.

'Jeannie,' she said. 'Dad told me about the Josephine part, but not the Jeannie.'

'Would you have preferred that name?'

'Gosh, Mam, not at all. It's just . . . interesting, you know.' Sensing a need to lighten the atmosphere, she made fun of the note. 'Don't you love the way they emphasised my sturdiness? Back in those days, it must've been the height of praise. Do you remember when the best thing you could say about a child was to call them "placid"?'

'There was nothing wrong with that. Believe you me, I know plenty of children whose manners could do with a brush-up.' Martha reckoned the barb was aimed not at her but at Una, whose two boys were fabulously rowdy. Not that their grandmother saw very much of them. Una's teenage obsession with nuclear war had matured into a passion for science, and she now worked at CERN in Geneva. Her husband, a talkative Dutchman called Bram, worked there too. In Martha's view, Clem and Delia had never quite grasped their younger daughter's achievement. Others were fascinated. 'Does she work on the large whatsit collider?' they'd ask.

'Nope, they only let her play with the small hadrons,' she would reply. She feared most of them didn't get the joke. To be fair, she didn't understand Una's job either.

'What else is there?' she asked.

'I'm not with you,' replied her mam. 'What else would there be?'

'Well, did you not receive a letter to say your adoption application was successful?'

Her mother frowned. 'We must have thrown it out. Once you were here, it wasn't relevant.'

'Were you ever given any hint about my birth mother?' said Martha, digging her nails into the pillow. 'Any suggestion as to where she was from or what her circumstances were?'

'Are you joking me? That type of information was confidential. We were told nothing about her, and she was told nothing about us. If she knew where we lived, she might've come snooping. No, you've seen what there is to see.'

Martha said nothing. She felt powerless, like a teenager who knows that adult conversations are taking place down the hall. The room didn't help.

In thirty years, it had barely changed. If she narrowed her eyes, she imagined she could still see their old pictures Blu-tacked to the walls: Che Guevara and the poster for *The Breakfast Club* on Una's side of the room; Morrissey and Rob Lowe on hers. Other memories came marching back. She could see their school uniforms draped over the chair while Margaret Thatcher held forth on Una's radio, and the smells of patchouli oil and hairspray lingered in the air.

In this room, she would always be sixteen.

Her mother was speaking: 'Your old school report was spot on. You're a terror for the daydreaming.'

'Sorry?'

'I asked you to give me that scrap of paper. It's survived for more than forty years. I'd hate for it to get damaged now.'

Martha did as she was told. She sensed that her mother was holding something back. But if Delia did know anything else, Martha wouldn't prise it out of her today. That was for sure.

Later, as she diced a weary-looking carrot, Delia returned to one of her favourite topics: Dermot and Layla. On that subject, she had plenty to say. 'Oh, but she's a crafty woman, trapping him like that.'

'Now, now,' said Clem, from behind his *Clare Champion*, 'you can't say that about the girl.'

'Are you telling me I'm wrong?' replied his wife, laying into the poor carrot with ever-swifter strokes.

Martha, who was wandering between the kitchen and living room, intervened: 'Mam, I can assure you Layla hasn't "trapped" Dermot. He's a willing participant. They're both free to do as they please, and they've chosen to have a baby.'

'Hmmph,' said her mam. 'What age is she? Twenty-seven?'

'Twenty-nine.'

'They said twenty-seven in the paper.'

'They were wrong.'

'That, if you don't mind me saying so, proves my point. She's worried she's getting on a bit, and she's desperate for a husband.' Delia turned her attention to a gnarled parsnip, hacking at it like she was fending off a wild animal.

Martha sighed. 'Breaking news, as Evanne might say. Not all twenty-nine-year-olds feel under mad pressure to snare a man.'

Her mother replied with another dismissive snort.

'Seriously,' said Martha, 'I'm well aware that in your day twenty-nine was considered ancient, and that if a woman wasn't married by the time she hit thirty, her parents would be installing a shelf for her. But those days are gone.'

'Well, I think you're being too flippant. I was twenty-one when we got married, twenty-seven when you arrived, and twenty-nine when I had Una. Those are good ages to settle down and start a family.'

'You lived in Templemorris. There wasn't much else for you to do.'

Her dad, who'd been listening from behind the safety of his newspaper, began to laugh. 'She's got you there, Delia,' he said.

With a clatter, her mother put down the knife, squared her shoulders and stood back to admire her mountain of chopped vegetables. 'All I'm saying is, I'm wise to the girl's antics, even if you're not.'

Martha wondered why her mam was directing so much vitriol at a woman she'd never met. She supposed everybody had their own technique for handling things. 'I'm going for a walk,' she said. She was out the door and halfway down the street before her parents had the chance to reply.

# CHAPTER 11

Nobody would claim that Templemorris was a pretty town. But on a good day – a tingling winter morning or a velvety summer afternoon – it had a certain busy charm. This was not one of those days. The grubby lavender sky gave the buildings a bruised appearance while gusts of November wind sent abandoned crisps packets hurtling along the pavement. On Main Street, the old supermarket was closed, a victim of the brash German discounter on the outskirts of town. Every few months, there was a spurt of gossip about who or what would take over the building: 'Rumour has it McDonald's are moving in,' someone would say.

'No, I've heard it's a casino,' another would insist.

'You're both wide of the mark. I've been told we're getting a cinema,' a third would chip in.

Maybe one day a rumour would prove to be true, but two years after the supermarket had breathed its last, the premises remained vacant, its windows whitewashed, posters for a circus and a novena slapped on top.

Other shops had closed too, victims of changing

tastes as much as straitened times. The butcher was gone, as were the record shop and the shoe-mender. 'Nobody can be bothered to get things fixed any more,' Delia would complain. 'Everything has to be newer and flashier and more expensive.' Martha guessed she was really referring to Clem's business mending TVs and video recorders, a business that had gradually become obsolete.

What else had changed? There were fewer pubs and more betting shops. The café where she'd idled away the hours with Cat was now a *faux*-American diner. There was a shop where you could trade jewellery for cash, an e-cigarette seller and – oh, the horror! – a place where you could get your nails polished and eyebrows plucked. She'd have to break the news to Cat. Even Templemorris had succumbed to the onward march of grooming.

Despite the closures and the drabness of the day, the town felt more prosperous than it had in the 1980s. With hindsight, Martha appreciated how hard-up some of her schoolmates had been. Girls hadn't worn sandals in December for the fun of it. They'd worn them because they'd owned no other shoes. Boys hadn't hacked and spluttered their way through the winter because their mothers were too feckless to take them to the doctor. They'd suffered because of a lack of money. While the Sheerans hadn't been especially flush, they'd always got by. Sometimes Martha was dismayed by how much Evanne took for granted. Not that long ago, she'd brought her daughter to the library so she could see how many people relied on the computers there. 'You see, not every teenager has their own iPad,' she'd said.

'In my school they do,' Evanne had replied.

Back in 1986, Martha had been part of a great scattering. Some had left to go to university in Dublin, Cork or Galway. Others travelled in search of work. They went to London and Munich, New York and Sydney. The lucky ones returned at Christmas with engagement rings and leather jackets. They talked about the freedom of being abroad. They asked for a 'soda' so you'd know they lived in America, or a 'flat white' to prove they'd been to Australia. At some point, they began to trickle home. Occasionally she bumped into people from her year in St Ursula's. They tended to recite well-rehearsed lines about Templemorris being a fabulous place to bring up kids, like there was something shameful about returning. Then they'd launch into a requiem for the good old days, when they were young and thin and ambitious. It seemed to Martha that her parents – bona fide old people – spent less time living in the past than her contemporaries.

She was nearing the end of Main Street, quietly reciting, 'Josephine Jeannie, Josephine Jeannie,' when she heard a familiar voice.

'They say talking to yourself's the first sign of madness, you know.'

Martha attempted to mask her embarrassment by giving Tina Bennis, Tina Coote as she was now, an overly effusive greeting. 'Hi there, Tina. It's great to see you. You're looking well,' she said, managing to tell two lies in the space of five seconds.

One of a hard core who'd never left Templemorris, gravity hadn't been kind to Tina. Everything – from her eyes to her mouth to her shoulders – sagged. Cat maintained it was a crime against feminism to measure yourself against old classmates. Yet they all did it. Martha suspected that Facebook had been invented for that very purpose.

Tina was accompanied by a little girl. 'This is Holly,' she said. With vanilla curls peeping out from under a pink woollen cap and solemn brown eyes, Holly was outrageously cute. She was five, she told Martha, and in senior infants at school. In a ham-fisted attempt at finding common ground, Martha mentioned that Cat also had a five-year-old.

She wasn't prepared for Tina's rasping laugh. 'Ah, here, Martha, Holly's not *my* daughter. She belongs to my eldest girl, Georgina. I mind her while Gina's at work. She has a job above in the call centre.' She gave another rasp. 'I'm past all that carry-on, thank God.'

The call centre had replaced the chipboard factory as the town's biggest employer. Martha wasn't sure what the calls were about, but it was a seven-days-a-week concern. Mortified by her mistake, she said something about the woman in front of her looking *way* too young to be a grandmother.

Tina accepted the compliment with enthusiasm, then enquired after Cat and Richie – and Paudie

Carmody. 'Do any of you come across him?' she asked. 'Isn't it amazing how well he's done?'

'Amazing,' agreed Martha, who said she hadn't encountered him in quite a while.

Tina was warming to her theme. 'Between you, me and the wall, I saw him in Fennessy's Lounge a few months ago – he must have been home for a couple of days – and he stared straight through me. I was fairly pissed off, I can tell you. "I shifted you five times when we were in fourth year," I wanted to say, "so don't go thinking you're too good for me now."'

'It's a shame you didn't.'

'He never did get married, did he? Is he gay, do you think?'

Tina had never been one to shy away from a blunt question. Martha suppressed a giggle. 'Ahm, no. Well, obviously I can't say for sure, but I don't think so.'

'Hmm, I'll take your word for it.' Beside them, a restless Holly was shifting from one foot to the other. Her grandmother didn't appear to notice. 'As I think of it, didn't he have a child with that model? What's her name?'

'Venus Barrington.'

'The very woman. What a name. You can bet that's not on her birth cert.' Tina wrinkled her nose. 'It's hard to believe he was such a terror at school. A right scut. I remember him giving you stick over being adopted. How mad was that? Sure there were scores of adopted kids back then. What was the big deal?'

Martha chose not to remind Tina that she'd been at the centre of the action. 'I remember it, all right,' she said.

'Did you ever meet your natural mother?'

While Holly twirled around them, Martha explained the situation.

'Holly, stop that, or I'll tell your mammy,' said Tina, in a half-hearted voice. Her granddaughter flashed them a smile and continued. Tina reverted to ignoring her. 'You know who you should speak to? My sister-in-law, Pauline. Pauline Hehir, as was. She was two years ahead of us in St Ursula's. Do you remember her?'

Martha shook her head.

'My brother Junior landed on his feet there, I can tell you. She's as sharp as a tack. Anyway, she was adopted, and a few years back she got a notion to track down her natural mother. She did it too. She's very determined, is Pauline.'

'Did everything go okay?'

'Ah, yeah. The pair of them are big buddies.'

'Does Pauline live in Templemorris?'

'She does indeed. She's over in the John and Paul estate.' Tina looked at her watch. 'I've a feeling she might be at work, though. She's in the call centre too.'

'Do you think she'd have a word with me at some stage?'

'Why don't you give her a ring? Get out your phone there, and I'll give you the number.'

Martha did as she was told and tapped the

number into her phone. 'Thanks,' she said. 'I really appreciate this.'

Tina took Holly by the hand. 'Come on, Missy. We'd better get going before you make a complete show of me.'

The pair of them started towards home, the little girl taking ballerina-like steps, her granny trudging beside her. Martha was about to ring Pauline when Tina turned around. 'Oh, and one other thing,' she called.

'Uh-huh.'

'The next time you bump into Paudie Carmody, will you tell him I was asking after him?'

'St Saviour's,' said Pauline Bennis, with a small nod. 'I was with the same adoption agency. I know *all* about them.'

Pauline had a tiny fox-like face with foxy hair to match. She was also a complete dynamo. 'No time like the present,' she'd said, when Martha rang. An hour later the two were sitting in the call-centre canteen. As sterile a place as Martha had ever seen, it had the sort of fluorescent lighting that makes even the healthiest face look like it belongs in an Edvard Munch painting. Posters warned of the evils of smoking and the benefits of a healthy diet. Pauline was nibbling at a cheese sandwich and drinking coffee from a flask. 'The stuff they sell in here tastes like it came straight from a drainage ditch,' she explained.

'I tried to get in touch with St Saviour's,' said

Martha, 'but it seems they've shut up shop. All their files were given to the health service.'

'Huh,' said Pauline. 'All their files, my eye. I'd say most of them were thrown onto a bonfire years ago. When I was looking for my mother, they claimed the files were "missing".' She made air quotes with her fingers. 'Dear Lord, they gave me the run-around. Still, that didn't stop me, and it shouldn't stop you either. You know, there's every chance we were born in the same place – the mother-and-baby home in Carrigbrack.'

'Carrigbrack?' Martha felt a jolt and a whoosh, as if she'd accelerated over a hump-back bridge. 'I've never—'

'No, I hadn't heard of it either. Until a few years ago, nobody spoke about these places. Imagine, thousands and thousands of girls passing through them, thousands of babies being put up for adoption, and not a word.' She paused for another nibble. 'Carrigbrack's in north Clare, near the Burren. It was never as massive as some of the homes, but in the fifties and sixties it was sizeable enough. They sent a fair few kids to the States too. I'm sure you're familiar with the rigmarole. They'd say it was all voluntary and wasn't it wonderful that the babies were off to good Catholic homes in Chicago or wherever. But you can be sure the nuns got a hefty donation in return.

'According to Lily – that's my birth mother – Carrigbrack was fairly grim. I mean, she was never beaten or anything, but the regime was harsh. It drives me crackers when normally sensible people come out with this nonsense about life being harder for everybody back then. As though that excuses everything. It's pathetic.' Pauline came to a sudden halt. 'Sorry for ranting. It's just I feel so strongly, I can't help myself.'

'No, no, you're fine,' said Martha. 'What was it like to meet your birth mother?'

Pauline cocked her head to consider the question. 'I'll never forget the first day. We arranged to meet in a hotel, and I saw her straight away, sitting in the bar with a worried face on her.' She laughed. 'I didn't have to ask if she was Lily – we're the image of each other. It was fantastic. I grew up in a family of hulking, dark-haired people. Do you remember that song from *Sesame Street*, "One Of These Things (Is Not Like The Others)"? They used to sing it to me. In a good-natured way, of course, but still . . . And, finally, there I was, with someone who looked like me. The feeling was . . . incomparable.'

'Does Lily have a family?'

'She's been married for more than forty years. They've two sons and a daughter. To begin with, none of them knew about me, so that was kind of awkward. But eventually Lily told them, and they've been great. Really great. I've been incredibly lucky. It does upset me, though, her spending all those years keeping a secret when she didn't need to at all.'

Martha was divided. Part of her was drinking in

Pauline's story but another part longed to find somewhere quiet so she could run the day's discoveries around her head. Plus, she was dying to hear what Evanne would make of her news. The conversation moved on to Pauline's frustrations with the official tracing system.

'It's so damn slow,' she said. 'There's such a backlog of cases, it'll be months before they even open your file. And then it'll probably be another age before they actually get anywhere.'

'They did warn me to expect a lengthy wait.' Again, Martha was torn. It was unreasonable to expect the social workers to drop everything in favour of her case, especially when it had taken her so long to come forward. But now she'd begun her quest, she couldn't bear the thought of years in limbo.

Eyes shining, colour rising in her cheeks, Pauline leaned forward. 'If you ask me, you shouldn't wait. Nobody can stop you going to the records office and doing your own search. You know your date of birth and your first two names, so you should be able to find your birth cert. It'll give you your birth mother's name and – who knows? – maybe your birth father's too.'

Martha nodded.

'Then you can try to track down her records. With any luck, you'll find her birth cert – and perhaps her marriage documents. They'll set you on the right track. Or, at least, they did for me.'

Martha couldn't say how long they'd been sitting

there, but if the impatient stares from Pauline's colleagues were anything to go by, her allotted break had long since ended. 'I'd better let you get back to work,' she said. 'Thanks for all your help. You've been brilliant.'

Pauline parcelled up the remainder of her sandwich and got to her feet. 'Take my advice. Keep the official channels open. You never know, they may be of some help in the end. But if finding your birth parents is what you want, you'll have to do it yourself.'

# CHAPTER 12

No matter that the man in the records office was faultlessly polite, Martha couldn't shake the feeling that she was up to no good. She expected that at any moment a large hand would grasp her shoulder and a gruff voice would ask what she was doing. 'Oh, get a grip,' she said to herself. 'You're looking for the truth. That's all.'

The register of births for December 1968 looked like it had passed through a thousand anxious hands. Its spine had snapped; its cover was worn. Most of its entries were in the old-style looped handwriting she'd been taught at school, the sort of handwriting that calls for a fountain pen and a bottle of ink. Martha turned the pages slowly, scanning every line. She urged herself not to get her hopes up. *If I'm not here*, she thought, *I'll just have to try something else*. Before she focused on the page for 8 December, she shut her eyes. She wasn't saying a prayer. Not really. She was preparing herself.

She knew that all sorts of skulduggery had been used to obscure people's origins. In some cases, the names of a baby's adoptive parents had been put on the birth cert. In others, the incorrect date and place of birth had been given. Occasionally, there were no records at all. People were told that they didn't exist.

When she opened her eyes again, her name was the first thing she saw. It was all she saw.

*Josephine Jeannie Moroney*, the entry read, *born Carrigbrack, County Clare*. The column for her father's name was blank. But her mother's name? Her mother's name was Rose Annalisa Moroney.

'Rose Annalisa Moroney,' she said, unable to stop herself speaking out loud. 'Rose Annalisa Moroney.'

Back home, Martha did an internet search for Rose Moroney. She found several, but not the right one. They were too young – or they were long since dead.

The next chance she got, she returned to the records office. Assuming that Rose was somewhere between fifteen and thirty when she had given birth, Martha began with the records for 1953. Her every spare hour was spent in the office, scouring book after book, page after page. Her eyes grew scratchy, her shoulders hunched, but not one Rose Annalisa Moroney did she find. There was a Rose Ellen Moroney, a Rose Bridget and two Rose Marys. The problem was that middle name, Annalisa: it was too unusual, too pretty.

As her search intensified, Martha shunted

everything else aside. She neglected her work. She ignored her parents. And Evanne? For all she knew, Evanne could have left school and embarked on a career as a pole dancer. Okay, that was an exaggeration, but Martha knew she should be spending more time with her daughter. The trouble was, she had wasted so many years. Only now did she appreciate how dislocated she felt. How incomplete. One of her questions had been answered, but a hundred more were waiting. Where was Rose from? What had become of her? Did she have other children? Who was Martha's birth father? Why had he rejected her?

There were days when she despaired of ever tracing Rose. Then she gave herself a talking-to. After all, many people searched for years, decades even, before tracking down their birth mother or father.

Rose was out there somewhere. She had to be.

# CHAPTER 13

Evanne was squaring up to her chemistry homework. She hated chemistry. She blamed her father, who'd insisted she study a science subject for the Leaving Cert. 'You'll thank me in the long run,' he'd said. 'You don't want to end up like your mother with a collection of meaningless qualifications. Take a leaf out of Una's book and focus on science.' Patiently, she'd pointed out that Una wasn't an actual blood relative, so there was no chance she would inherit her talent. He harrumphed something about role models, as if being in the same room once or twice a year was enough. Perhaps he thought Evanne would pick up Le Châtelier's Principle or Hess's Law through a process of osmosis. Ha! So she did remember some chemistry, after all.

Her mum and dad didn't agree on much, but when it came to school and careers they were on the same page. They were happy for Evanne to do whatever she wanted. As long as it was what they wanted too. Her parents saw the world like this – any career involving monstrous amounts of study, a gazillion A grades and a boring life: good. Everything else: out of the question.

A thousand times, Evanne had said, 'It's my life, you know.' But they never listened.

This was one of her Dad-and-Layla weekends, and she was in her Sandyford bedroom. It was lots cooler than her other bedroom. For starters, she had a proper desk from Ikea. Then there was the e-normous wardrobe and the bouncy double bed with the perfect white linen. The walls were hidden by huge prints of New York, bought by Layla when she was going through her please-like-me phase. Unfortunately, Evanne was always leaving vital stuff – like her pyjamas or her hairdryer – in Milltown. She didn't like saying she was going home for half an hour because her dad got all awkward. 'This is your home too,' he'd say, 'and if you need something, I'll get it for you.'

She found this unbearably tedious, so eventually she'd looked him in the eye and said, 'Tampons.' The next time he hadn't interfered.

Evanne was thrilled that her mother was trying to find her natural parents. Strangely, the search had made her even more airy-fairy. She would get wistful about all sorts of odd things. Like she'd ramble on about the joys of Templemorris when for years all she'd done was tell jokes about the place. Now it was all 'my lovely childhood' and how good the people had been and how she wished she'd appreciated them. Evanne had said this to Cat (since their pincer operation on the adoption issue, they'd kept in touch). 'Don't pay any heed to her,' Cat had replied. 'She flew out of that town like a redshank.' Evanne wanted to ask what a redshank was, but thought better of it. Cat was like her mum: mostly she spoke like a normal person, but sometimes she lapsed into country-person speak. If you queried what she said, she only ramped up her act, and before you knew it she was completely incomprehensible.

Evanne had also consulted her best friend, Serena Montague, who'd given a thoughtful nod, before replying, 'Midlife crisis. My mum's even worse. She got a tattoo on her ankle *and* she went to a One Direction concert.'

'Tragic,' agreed Evanne, although she couldn't see that this was quite the same.

From the sitting room, she heard voices: first, her dad's baritone, then Layla's squeakier tones. There was a false hush to their conversation, like they were making sure she wouldn't hear. They'd never had an all-out row in front of her, but sometimes she felt like she was dodging tripwires. One misstep and – *kaboom* – the roof would blow off. Now that she was pregnant, Layla was forever getting hyper about stuff. Some days she was absolutely wired. Then Evanne's dad would adopt this annoying attitude, as though he was saying, 'I'm trying hard to be patient here.' He was so . . . What was the word? Supercilious. That was it. Her mum said that when Layla got moody, Evanne should be extra nice because her hormones were doing the talking. Cat agreed, saying that nobody would blame Layla for getting nervy. She said any sensible woman would be at home watching afternoon television rather than appearing on it.

Evanne didn't believe her mum actually felt quite so generous, but wearing a brave face was part of what she did. 'Nobody likes a whinger,' she'd say. There were days when the stoic act got on Evanne's nerves. Why couldn't she say what she thought? Evanne blamed her grandmother Delia, who was forever wittering on about people getting their reward 'in the next life'. 'What if there is no next life?' she'd asked. Her nan had given her a look that said, 'Error 404 File Not Found', before telling her to go outside and check on the washing.

If her mum could be a complete head-wrecker, she could be funny too. Even her old-fashioned habits were funny. Like the way she'd say, 'Turn on the radio there, love, so we can get the news.' A million times, Evanne had told her that if she would just get a better phone, she could watch the news whenever she liked. But, no, she insisted on behaving like a relic. She dressed like a relic too, with her denim jackets and hippie skirts. Not that long ago, she'd unearthed a purple floaty number, which she claimed to have bought in London's Camden Market in 1992. Like that was something to be proud of. Then there was the time she'd had a long fringe cut into her hair. She was 'channelling Kim Gordon', she'd said. Evanne had googled the Kim woman. She was no

Taylor Swift, but you could see why the oldies might like her.

This didn't mean the two always got on. There were days when they totally let rip. Then Evanne would end up feeling like a complete cow. No matter how much her mum pretended she was fine on her own, it was clear she was lonely. She'd sit there with her sad grey eyes, and Evanne would resolve never to be a bitch again (unfortunately, her resolve wasn't that strong). It seemed to her that some women – and her mother was a prime example – reached a point where they reverted to being as messed-up and unsure of themselves as any teenager.

The voices in the sitting room had risen by several notches. Layla and her hormones were giving Evanne's dad a haranguing about something. Work, probably. They were always talking about TV shows, about who was hot and who was headed for the scrapheap. From what Evanne could gather, some of her dad's other clients were put out because he spent too much time promoting Layla and not enough fretting about their precious careers. One, a children's TV presenter named Heidi O'Halloran, had flounced off to a rival agent. Her dad said she was no loss and that in five years' time she'd be lucky to get work reading the death notices on local radio. He claimed that what he needed were fewer showbiz presenters and more current-affairs types. 'Longer shelf-life,' he explained. 'Their jowls can be swinging in the breeze and still they get work. And that includes the women.' Layla had laughed at this. Evanne couldn't imagine her mother being so amused.

Since her mum had started searching for her birth parents, life at number six Dolmen Crescent had been turned upside down. Rather than foostering about the house, she spent hour after hour bent over her laptop, looking at adoption message boards and websites. Dinners were slapdash affairs with everything either incinerated or semi-raw. Ironing teetered over the edge of the laundry basket. The phone went unanswered. That wasn't all. A couple of weeks back, she'd bunked off work so she could spend the day in the records office. If Evanne missed as much as five minutes of school, her mother would have to be scraped off the ceiling.

Evanne had begun browsing some of the adoption websites too. They were really sad. Not sad as in pathetic. Sad as in, well, sad. There was one woman who'd been trying to find her son for fifteen years. An official had asked if she had 'imagined' giving birth. And there was this man who found his birth mother and became friends with her. She was too ashamed to tell her family, so when she died he went to her funeral and sat at the back on his own. That had made Evanne cry. Then her mother began to blub. 'If those websites upset you, you're not to look at them,' she said. 'Or look at the happy stories. There are lots of happy stories.'

The voices had become even louder. Evanne put down her pen. How was she supposed to do her homework with that racket in the background? She thought of how the papers had been monitoring Layla's pregnancy ('Like she's a rare panda', according to Cat). Numerous articles had appeared, including her 'baby exercise plan', her 'pregnancy glow', and her 'new perspective on what truly matters'. What, Evanne wondered, would the people who lapped up all this hearts-and-flowers crap make of the scene in the next room?

She tiptoed to the door.

'You're not being fair, Dermot,' she heard. 'Our son shouldn't be brought up in a poxy flat.' A son? This was news to Evanne. Her dad insisted they didn't know the sex of the baby, that it would be a 'wonderful surprise'.

'Jesus, Layla, dial down the decibels, would you?' he said.

'Evanne can't hear us. She'll have her headphones on. And I still say you're being unfair.' Layla didn't realise that, when she got rattled, her voice could saw through earwax. Even maximum-volume death metal wouldn't drown her out.

'I don't want Evanne's life upended while she's doing the Leaving Cert,' her dad was saying. 'When she's finished school, we'll sell the house in Milltown and get a proper place of our own. And another thing, this is hardly a "poxy flat". I don't know about you, but I haven't noticed any heroin dealers on the landing or stolen cars in the courtyard. It's a lovely apartment, and we'll be grand here for another while.'

'Upending her life? The only person doing that is Martha and her daft crusade to find a woman who didn't want her – and who probably died donkey's years ago. Besides, it'll be another eighteen months before Evanne finishes school. You can't expect us to stay here until then.'

Evanne's hand hovered over the door knob.

'Layla, please be reasonable,' he said.

'I'm going for a lie-down,' came the curt reply.

*No, you're not*, thought Evanne. The time had come to march on in there and put them straight about a few things.

# CHAPTER 14

The weeks whirled by, one sliding into another, one year giving way to the next, and still Martha hadn't heard from the social worker assigned to her case. She called the office but was told they'd get around to her 'in due course'. Would it be possible, she asked, to have a general chat with someone? No, the receptionist said, everybody was too busy right then, but if she left her name and number they'd get back to her . . . in due course.

Neither had she made any further progress on her own. How often had she read that, in the internet age, nobody could disappear? Well, if anybody was exercising their right to be forgotten, it was Rose. So effectively had she vanished, you'd swear she'd never existed. Martha stumbled across an online adoption register and considered adding her name. There was a chance Rose would see it, but what if somebody who knew her birth mother came across the posting? How much trouble might that cause? She decided she couldn't take the risk. Although she found it hard to read the site without her eyes filling, there was humour amid the anguish. She kept seeing references to a man called 'Mr Diagonal Line'. After a while, she realised that this was what some people called their natural father. (Her own birth cert contained just such a line in the box where her father's name should be.) She didn't find the jokes surprising. If you asked her, even the hardest of lives contained far more humour than history ever recorded.

In late January, Una and her sons – Cory and Lorcan – paid a visit to Templemorris. Martha and Evanne joined them, and on Saturday evening they all sat around the kitchen table eating bacon and cabbage. Thankfully, their mother didn't seem to notice that the dinner wasn't a success.

'A taste of home,' she said to Una, her face aglow with satisfaction.

'A reminder of why I left home, more like,' whispered Una to Martha, who had to swallow her laughter.

As was her way, Evanne stared at her plate as if she'd been served a portion of cigarette butts. Martha gave her several pokes in the side, after which she did make an effort. Cory and Lorcan were less susceptible to maternal pressure and ate only their boiled potatoes before scampering back to the television. It wasn't that there was anything wrong with Delia's cooking, it was just that bacon and cabbage was such an old-fashioned dinner. Asking a youngster to appreciate it was like asking them to recite a few decades of the rosary or drink a pint of buttermilk. Martha ate with uncharacteristic enthusiasm. This wasn't a time to go upsetting her mother. She knew her search for Rose and Mr Diagonal Line was creating waves. Mostly, her parents conveyed their unease without saying a word. Her mam's deflated tone and her dad's silences communicated their unhappiness.

After apple crumble and custard, Delia, Clem and Evanne retreated to the sitting room. A local woman was due to appear on the national lottery game show and there was high excitement in Templemorris. Martha and Una reverted to their teenage years and did the washing-up. (Despite repeated offers to buy their mother a dishwasher, Delia was holding firm. 'Don't go wasting your money on me,' she'd say. 'Those machines are just another excuse to be idle.')

For a minute or two, they set about their task – Una washing, Martha drying – in, what Martha thought was, easy silence. Then Una pounced.

'Listen,' she said, 'this is kind of difficult, but, ahm, Mam and Dad asked me to have a word. They're worried about you.'

'Why so?' asked Martha, deciding to play dumb.

Her sister placed two dinner plates on the draining board. 'They're worried that you're spending all your time looking for someone who probably doesn't want to be found.'

'With all due respect, they don't know how Rose feels about me. Maybe she's dying to be found.

Anyway, I've only just started looking. I've an awful lot of work ahead of me.'

Una gave a saucepan an energetic scrub. 'That's part of the problem. To be blunt about it, they're feeling neglected.'

Martha pulled open the cutlery drawer with so much force it almost went flying to the floor. 'Well, they've no reason to feel like that. And they've nothing to be scared of either. I've been doing my best to keep them on board, you know. It's just . . . this really matters to me. It matters to Evanne too.'

'That's another thing. Mam's worried your search is distracting Evanne from her schoolwork.'

'Oh, for God's sake.' Martha threw knives and forks into the drawer with clattering abandon. 'Why don't I wait until she's finished school, so? And university? And then why don't I hang around for another while, for fear she wants to do a PhD or something? Of course by that stage Rose will be dead and gone, but at least Evanne won't have had any distractions.'

'Ssh,' said Una.

'They won't hear me. They've the telly turned up so bloody loud they could broadcast to half the county.'

'I'm only passing on their concerns, that's all. Let's not fall out over this, huh?'

'Don't worry. I've no intention of falling out with you – or with Mam and Dad. But I've no intention of giving up my search either.'

Una tipped out the dishwater and peeled off

her rubber gloves. 'How's Dermot?' she asked, in a pretend-casual voice.

'Fine, as far as I know. We haven't seen much of him lately. He's very busy, apparently.'

'And you? How are you? I mean, it can't be easy. There he is starting over, and you're—'

'Walking around like a spare part.'

'Ah, here, Martha, that's not what I meant.'

'Sorry. I know you're not having a go at me. You don't need to fret, though. Honestly, you don't.'

Martha knew her sister was being supportive, but right then she didn't want to talk about her ex-husband. Truth to tell, Dermot and Layla were testing her sanity. Every time she opened a paper, there was Layla, smug as a swimwear model in a communal changing room. You'd think the woman had invented pregnancy. Martha told herself that none of this should matter. She instructed herself to ignore the interviews. Her instructions were futile. With every article, she felt like the happy couple were taking a chisel to her dignity. *Chip, chip, chip*. She tried not to badmouth them in front of Evanne, but her patience was worn to a very thin thread.

'Come on,' she said, as she hung up her tea-towel, 'we'd better go in and see if Kitty Shinnors gets to spin the big wheel.'

'All right,' replied Una. 'And, Martha?'

'Mmm?'

'I really do hope you find Rose, but go easy on Mam and Dad, will you?'

# CHAPTER 15

'So, we're not telling Nan and Granddad because . . .?' asked Evanne, from the passenger seat of Martha's car.

'We're not telling them because they'll expect a visit, and I'll be the worst daughter in the history of daughters for not taking a detour to Templemorris. But if we visit we'll have to tell them what we're doing. And, I guarantee you, they won't understand. I can hear your nan now.' Martha made an attempt at Delia's slightly nasal tones. 'What in the name of all that's good and holy are you traipsing over there for, Martha? The place has been closed this thirty years. That's just madness. I said it to Clem. "It's stranger she's getting," I said.'

Evanne honked with laughter.

'Poor Mam,' said Martha. 'I shouldn't make fun of her. She means well.' She glanced at her daughter. 'When I'm an old woman, you're not to be doing impressions of me.'

'*When* you're an old woman?' said Evanne.

Martha was on her way to Carrigbrack, her daughter a willing accomplice. They'd figured that in the absence of hard information it wouldn't do any harm to get a sense of the place. Well, it was more than that, wasn't it? For the first time, Martha felt a compulsion to see the home where she'd been born. They'd left Dublin early, the sky still a wash of lemon. As they drove west, Evanne chattered away, lamenting the idiocy of various girls all of whom were called either Sophie or Sorcha. Martha pretended to listen, but if put on the spot, she would be hard-pressed to say which Sophie had the bulimia and which the Isabel Marant boots. Why anybody should be nervous about going to see an abandoned building, she couldn't say. But she was. Gradually, she grew tense, her hands welded to the steering wheel, a knot of pain forming at the base of her skull. When they reached Birdhill, she turned off the motorway and drove across country. Although the main route would have been quicker, the morning felt too gentle for highways and tunnels. Plus, she liked travelling along the back roads of Clare, especially at this time of year when nature was shrugging off its winter colours and the hedgerows were coming to life again.

In Killaloe, they found a café and stopped for a late breakfast. Martha drank her coffee and attempted to read the paper. She watched Evanne, hair teased into a careful tangle, nose stuck in the fashion and beauty pages of a Saturday supplement, knee jiggling in time with the radio. Her daughter turned the page, and there he was, Paudie

Carmody, wearing a Tom Ford suit and his most sincere face.

Evanne flicked back her hair. 'When you were growing up in Templemorris, did you know this guy?'

'Um, yeah. We were in the same class, actually. Him, me, Cat and Richie.' Martha explained how the king of Saturday-night TV had once been best friends with Cat's husband. But, she said, their friendship had waned over the years.

'Did you always think he'd be a big success?'

'Not a bit of it. He took me by surprise. He took us all by surprise.' Actually, Martha reckoned the only person who hadn't been confounded by Paudie's glittering ascent was Paudie himself. He had managed to turn a slightly successful sporting career (a blink-and-you'll-miss-it stint representing Ireland at cross-country running) into a far shinier role as the presenter of a children's sports show. After that, he had assiduously climbed the television ladder. If he'd had to negotiate the occasional slippery rung (the less than successful years in London; that *awful* game show), he had done so with aplomb. At the age of forty-five, he was the country's preeminent chat show host.

He was also Dermot's most lucrative client. Martha could never decide whether she was amused or annoyed that Paudie Carmody's earnings helped pay her mortgage.

'Is that how Dad became his agent?' asked Evanne. 'Through you?'

‘Gosh, no. That was nothing to do with me. If memory serves, your father was his accountant before he became his agent.’

‘Even though he’s an old-timer, Serena thinks he’s hot. I’ll have to tell her you were at school with him. She’ll be *sooo* jealous. What was he like?’

‘To tell you the truth, he was a cocky so-and-so.’ Martha scratched her neck. ‘I don’t know what he’s like these days. Well, I know what he’s like on the telly, obviously. But otherwise . . .’

‘You’d think that when Dad still lived with us, he would’ve invited Paudie around some time.’

‘It’s such a long time since we met, I can’t imagine we’d have anything to say to each other now,’ replied Martha, her words coming out a touch too quickly. ‘Listen, we’d better get moving. I’ll settle the bill, and you can wait in the car.’

‘What’s the hurry?’ asked Evanne, with a twitch of her nose.

‘It might rain, and I don’t want to be stuck out in Carrigbrack in the rain.’

‘I’ve never seen it look less like rain.’

‘I know this part of the world. Take my word for it, a downpour’s never far away.’

Evanne gave her one of the funny looks in which she specialised. This one said, ‘I think you may be losing whatever sense you once had.’ All the same, she tucked the magazine into her bag and did as she was told.

⋆ ⋆ ⋆

The former mother-and-baby home was a mile or so from the village of Carrigbrack, on the fringes of the Burren. They arrived via one of those narrow strips of road you get in the west of Ireland, grass along its centre, high hedges on either side. Road was too grand a description, really. Anywhere else it would be called a lane. As they skirted past the fields of limestone, Martha couldn't help herself. She recited strings of facts from her schooldays. She told Evanne about the Burren being one of the most special places on earth; about Arctic, alpine and Mediterranean plants growing side by side; about the megalithic tombs, the dolmens, the high crosses and ring forts. She'd been brought here as a child, she said, to pick hazelnuts and look at the wild goats. She couldn't recall having seen the mother-and-baby home. Then again, she hadn't been looking.

They parked the car beside a farm gate, and walked the last short stretch. The air was perfumed with the scents of spring: the top notes from trees and bushes whose names Martha had forgotten, the base notes earthy and damp. By the time they reached the entrance to the old home, Evanne, gangly as a giraffe in her skinny jeans and hoodie, was practically running. Martha dawdled behind, absorbing every small detail. Although a tall iron gate remained in place, the padlock and chain looked to have been shattered years before. The only sound came from a pair of insistent crows, caw-cawing as if they had vital information to pass on.

Carrigbrack was made up of a series of grey buildings: some small and squat, others long and narrow. Martha had read that after the home closed, the buildings had housed a centre for people with disabilities. That too was gone, and now the dormitories, the hospital, the nursery and the church were empty. Bit by bit, they were succumbing to the elements. Weeds poked up through cracks in the path, while plastic sacks of litter were scattered around the grounds. The walled garden had grown into a jungle. In one corner, an abandoned washing machine was turning to rust. In another, a stack of chairs stood beside a weather-bleached chest of drawers. The main house, where Martha assumed the nuns had lived, appeared to sag. Its windows were boarded up; white paint peeled from the front door.

Evanne looped an arm around her mother. 'What are you thinking?'

'I'm thinking this is far too beautiful a place for such a monstrosity,' Martha replied.

As they explored the outbuildings, she was surprised by the strength of her feelings. What must it have been like when scores of girls were corralled here, when the nursery housed row after row of cots, and long-skirted nuns patrolled the corridors? What had Rose made of it? Had she been allowed any happiness, or had every day been dreary? A lot of what Martha had read about the mother-and-baby homes sounded as if it came from a dystopian novel. But Carrigbrack wasn't a fictional horror story. It was part of her birth mother's life. It was part of *her* life.

Evanne had pulled out her phone and was taking photos of the buildings. Martha watched her crouch to get a better shot of the slate-coloured church. It was funny, she thought, how small a part religion played in the lives of Evanne and her friends. For them, the Catholic Church was a source of indifference. Like thatched cottages, slow sets at the disco and black-and-white TV, it belonged to the past.

Her thoughts slipped back to her own teenage years. To the hapless Miss Casey and her attempts to teach the Bible, and to Father Smith, a mildly creepy figure who'd been the curate in Templemorris. In the confession box, amid the smell of candles and whiskey, he'd invariably guided the conversation towards boyfriends. Did you have one? And, if so, what did you do with him? Cat had delighted in goading him. When asked how far she allowed her boyfriend to go, she'd replied, 'All the way, Father.' Hearing the splutters from the other side of the grille, she'd qualified her answer. 'I mean, I let him walk me the whole way home. Isn't that what you wanted to know?' Later, they'd realised that Father Smith had probably got his thrills from their make-believe sins. Mind you, in those days, all sorts of sleazy behaviour was tolerated. Encouraged, even. When Martha was sixteen, she'd worked in a local restaurant. Getting groped by the head chef was part of the job, and any girl who grumbled was labelled frigid.

Martha and Evanne walked around to the very back of the site and to what, at first glance, looked like derelict ground. It was then that she noticed the single headstone. *In Memory of the Little Angels*, it said. Nearby was a dilapidated wall, dotted at irregular intervals with rusty nails. How many, it was impossible to tell because part of the wall was obscured by a thicket of brambles and nettles. She'd read about this: the nails marked the spots where babies had been buried. The records were scant, so a family's chances of finding a particular grave were slim. She explained what she'd read to Evanne, who thought for a minute then punched the wall in anger.

'So the girls whose babies died, they didn't have a grave to visit? They were supposed to say, "Oh dear, that's a shame," then forget about it all?'

Martha nodded.

'How could the nuns do that to them? How could their families let it happen? I mean, what was *wrong* with those people?'

'I don't know, love. I don't understand it either. I like to think they didn't realise how much damage they were doing. At least, I hope they didn't.'

Tears were running down Evanne's face. Martha stepped forward, reached out and held her daughter tight against her chest. She wanted to kiss her head like she always had in the past, but Evanne had grown too tall.

'I'd like to go now, please,' her daughter said, in a small, small voice.

Not for the first time, it struck Martha that, in some ways, Evanne was much more sophisticated than she had been at sixteen. And, in other ways, far more innocent.

Figuring that chocolate was needed, they drove back to the village. The grocery shop was one of a dying breed. There was no chain-store neon, no breakfast rolls or take-away coffees. Instead, it was all dark wood and lino, the shelves offering everything from cans of vegetables to spools of thread. It was, thought Martha, a place where every local was known and every stranger asked about their business.

'Not a bad day,' said the woman behind the counter. 'Are you visiting the Burren?'

Martha was about to say yes when she decided that nothing would be lost by telling the truth. Having initially pigeonholed the woman – mid-fifties, square jaw, blunt haircut – as a life-was-tough-but-it-did-us-no-harm type, she soon realised she was wrong.

As she listened to Martha's story, the woman shook her head and made small 'tsk' sounds. 'Born there? God love you. I don't care what anybody says, that was a shocking place.'

'Did you know it? Back when it was a mother-and-baby home, I mean?'

'Didn't everybody? When I was at school, we

were told that if we didn't respect ourselves, it was where we'd end up.' She shook her head again, then offered a large hand. 'Fidelma Lafferty's my name.'

Martha introduced herself. 'Did you ever get to meet any of the girls?'

'Yes and no. The shop's been in the family for more than sixty years, so we saw a lot of comings and goings. We delivered groceries up there too. Not many, mind you. The nuns liked to go further afield – for fear my mam or dad recognised any of the girls. Everything had to be top secret. "Fallen women", some people used to call them, but, honest to God, most of them were only kids themselves.'

'Were they allowed out?'

'Officially, no. But some of them used to sneak away. You couldn't miss them. They had to wear these ugly navy uniforms with real rough cloth. The thing is, even if they broke free for an hour or two there was nowhere for them to go. They could hardly go home. And it wasn't like any of them had any money. My mam was sympathetic to them, which wouldn't have been altogether common in those days. If a girl pitched up here, she might give her a handful of sweets or an apple. Not much, because business was tight, but just a little something. A treat, you might say. I'm sure there were precious few treats above in that home.' She paused. 'What year did you say your mother was there?'

'1968.'

Fidelma tugged at one earlobe while she thought. 'I would've been nine or ten. And she's called Rose, you say?'

'Rose Moroney.' Martha hoped that Fidelma might remember some small snippet from that time. Unfortunately, her face suggested the name meant nothing to her.

'Mam's the woman you want,' she said. 'Her memory isn't great. But you know the way it is, ask her what happened last week and she won't have the foggiest, ask her about something that happened fifty years ago, and she'll give you chapter and verse. I'm always amazed by what she forgets – and she's always amazed by what she remembers. Have you got a minute?'

Evanne was waiting in the car. Martha toyed with the idea of popping out and filling her in, then decided against. The chances of Fidelma's mother recalling anything were small. This wouldn't take long. 'Sure,' she replied.

The shopkeeper ushered Martha behind the counter and through an old wooden door. 'Mam,' she called. 'I've someone to see you – a woman who was born up in the home. She's trying to find her real mother.'

Winnie Lafferty was a small woman with a cap of snowy curls. She wore a deep green shirt waister dress that could have belonged to any era from the 1950s to the present day. Around her neck, bifocals hung on a length of red cord.

'Sit down, dear,' she said.

Martha did as she was bade and again she recounted her story.

For the most part, Winnie listened wordlessly. She sat bolt upright, only occasionally tilting her head to one side to indicate that she'd missed something.

'Of course,' she said eventually, 'you do know they were made to change their names?'

'So I've heard.'

'It was supposed to be for their own good, so they could have a different identity while they were in Carrigbrack. I must say, I never liked it. I thought it was just another way of making them ashamed of who they were.'

Winnie veered off on a tangent about the punishment meted out to a girl who'd refused to use an alias. All the while, Martha's spirits sank. She'd been foolish to expect an elderly woman to remember one girl out of many. Chances were they'd never even met. She smiled what she hoped was a polite smile but she felt herself growing fidgety.

Fidelma gave a gentle cough. 'So, Mam, do you remember anyone called Rose? Rose Moroney?'

'I'm getting to that,' she replied. 'As a matter of fact, I do remember a Rose. She called in here several times. She liked to have a chat. I'd say she wasn't much more than seventeen or eighteen, the poor thing. And she had this lovely long hair. Oh, you should have seen it. Anyway, didn't one of the nuns cut it off to punish her for escaping. Not that it stopped her running away again. She was back here in jig time. What she didn't call those nuns.'

'Could she have been Martha's mother, do you think?'

'I can't say. There must have been other Roses, but she stands out. What with her being so pretty and so far away from home. "Rose the Yank", I called her.'

'Why did you call her that?'

Winnie fixed her daughter with a puzzled gaze. 'Because that's what she was. She was from America.'

'What was an American doing in Carrigbrack?'

Before Winnie had the chance to answer, the door creaked open.

'There you are,' said Evanne, rubbing the knuckles she'd grazed on the graveyard wall. 'You've been gone since forever. Is something up?'

Martha noticed that her daughter's newly applied make-up didn't quite hide the blotches left by her tears.

'That's her,' said Winnie, in a high, slightly breathless voice.

'That's who?' asked Fidelma.

'Rose, of course. You asked me about her, and there she is. That's Rose.'

# CHAPTER 16

Alex Arthur Waters was born at three a.m. on 17 March. A photograph on his mother's Twitter page showed mum and baby doing well.

'When a child is born on St Patrick's Day, you'd think his parents would have the decency to name him Patrick or Pádraig or *something* Irish,' said Cat.

'That's what Mam said,' replied Martha. 'Dermot and Layla changed their minds about giving him an Irish-sounding name. Dermot's worried they're becoming common. Apparently, south Dublin is infested with Maolsheachlanns and Lasairfhíonas.'

'Did it not occur to him that he already has a child with an Irish name?'

'Not until Evanne pointed it out.'

'I'd say that was fun. Anyway, you know my motto. Keep it simple. One syllable if possible. Chances are they'll have to emigrate one day, so you may as well give them a name others can pronounce.' Given that Cat's children were called Jake, Tom and Hope, this wasn't idle posturing.

While Tom and Hope were still at school, Jake

was sitting beside his mum on a playground bench. Exhausted from half an hour of slides and swings, he was content to sip his juice and float off into his own little world. At least, Martha hoped that was what he was doing. She wanted to talk about her hunt for Rose, and she wasn't sure it was a topic for five-year-old ears. The encounter with Fidelma and Winnie had left her reeling. Every night without fail, she woke at four o'clock, questions about her natural mother swirling in her head. And that wasn't all. The search had brought Martha's own insecurities to the surface. Increasingly, she reflected on what Rose would think of the girl she'd called Josephine Jeannie. Would she have expected a more accomplished career? A more successful marriage? A bigger family? Martha would lie there, sifting through her thoughts and listening to the sounds of the night – the howling alarms and yelping foxes – until sleep overtook her again.

She wondered if this insecurity was common, but wasn't sure who or how to ask. A support group might help, she supposed, only the idea of going public with her private fears terrified her. At least she had Cat. She had her daughter too, except leaning on Evanne wouldn't be right, especially when she already had so much to negotiate; not just the regular teenage angst but also the more modern concerns that left Martha in a state of bewilderment. Hand on heart, she didn't envy Evanne's generation. Okay, they mightn't have to contend with quite the same level of knuckle-dragging sexism, but to Martha it felt as if they were at war with themselves. How much easier had life been before selfies and thigh gaps and video bloggers who used fifteen separate items of make-up to create an 'everyday look'?

And then there was her schoolwork. Martha tried not to nag, but if Evanne wanted to go to university (and who *didn't* want to go to university?), her grades needed to improve. A lot. It would help if she had a particular course in mind, a goal to work towards. The problem was, every time Martha asked, Evanne sidestepped the question.

'What does Evanne make of her brother?' asked Cat.

'She reckons he looks like an angry walnut.'

'He looks like every other baby, so. Apart from Jakey here, that is.' Cat fluffed her son's hair. 'He was a bobby-dazzler. The other mothers were in awe.' Jake ignored her. 'How's Layla doing? I saw the Twitter picture. She looked her usual glowing self.'

'Evanne says that's a total lie. She put some make-up on, and they used one of those fancy filters. She's as wrecked and dishevelled as the next woman.'

'That's a relief. And Dermot?'

'Pick your cliché – cock of the walk, king of the hill, lord of all he surveys . . .'

'Six months without sleep should sort him out.' Cat turned her head towards Martha, eyes ever so slightly narrowed, as if to say, 'We can have a serious conversation about this if you'd like. It doesn't have to be all giddiness and drollery.' But, right then, that wasn't what Martha wanted.

'So,' she said, 'what do you think? About Winnie Lafferty, I mean?'

For a moment or two, Cat stayed quiet. In front of them, children whooped and squealed, while mothers and nannies engaged in competitive small talk. Around here it was the mothers who wore a uniform. Almost without exception, they were dressed in shiny black leggings and neat neon runners, as though at any moment they might sprint off into the distance.

'What I think,' Cat said eventually, 'is that Winnie's an old woman whose mind may be wandering. I'll give you this, though: the Evanne business is spooky.'

'You should have seen her. She was genuinely stunned. Eyes wide, mouth swinging open, the whole lot. By the time she'd gathered her wits and realised she wasn't staring at some sort of apparition, she was adamant that this American Rose must be the woman we're looking for. And, needless to say, Evanne's convinced she's right.'

'Except,' said Cat, 'it's all topsy-turvy. Those homes were in the business of exporting babies to America, not importing women.'

Martha raised her face skywards. The March day was unusually mild, and the spring sunshine danced across her face. Cherry blossom petals from a nearby tree floated past. 'But if she is American it would explain a couple of things – like why I can't find her birth cert.'

'Have you told them at home?'

Martha lowered her face again. 'What's there to tell, apart from the reminiscences of an elderly woman? I need something concrete before I say any more to Mam and Dad.' She still had to move carefully with her parents. In a reversal of roles, Delia had taken to sounding weary while Clem was unexpectedly spiky. 'Take it handy with your mother,' he'd said. 'She's finding this difficult.'

At the end of the bench, Jake began to wriggle.

'We'll go home soon, sweetheart,' Cat said to her son. 'Martha and I need to talk about some grown-up stuff, but I promise we won't be long.'

'Okay,' he replied, in his best sing-song voice. 'But can it be proper soon, not make-believe soon?'

'Cross my heart.'

Say what you like about Cat, thought Martha, but nobody had a better grasp of family complexities. And nobody's insight was more hard won. In her late twenties, as her advertising career was gathering pace, Cat had received a phone call to say that her dad had been killed in a car crash. The family's shock turned to mystification when it emerged the accident had occurred in Macroom; the rest of his band were two hundred miles away in Strokestown. It turned out that Frankie O'Dowd had been visiting his other family. He had a girlfriend and two children – twin girls named Reba and Jolene – in County Cork. Cat's mam, Freda, was inconsolable. For years, her hairdressing salon had been the epicentre of local gossip. Every minor event and transgression had been dissected. Meanwhile, her own husband had been leading a double life. As Cat liked to remind people, this was the same man who'd voted against the introduction of divorce – twice. 'Perhaps if we'd had a referendum on polygamy,' she said, 'he might have been able to support it.'

After the funeral, Freda shut her business and retreated from the world. When Cat's brothers and sisters all proved to be too busy, too idle or too far away to help, Cat had given up her job and returned to Templemorris. It had taken the best part of a year for Freda to shake off her paralysis. It was during those months that Cat had met up again with Richie Lyons. He'd just returned from five years working as an engineer in Frankfurt and, like her, was at a loose end. She was amazed to find that the twenty-nine-year-old Richie was an altogether more appealing creature than the lank-haired boy who'd sat near them at school. When her mam finally reopened the hairdresser's, Cat and Richie moved to Dublin. Two years later, they were married. Nothing would do them but to set up home close to Martha and Dermot. Martha frequently invited the couple for dinner. Dermot complained that his house was turning into a support centre for exiled Templemorris-ites.

'It's a conundrum, right enough,' Cat was saying now. 'What are you going to do?'

'There's a chance Winnie may remember something else, so I gave my phone number to Fidelma. But I'm not holding out much hope.'

'Evanne called me, by the way. She thinks you're moving too slowly. I said you'd a lot going on at the minute, and to give you a few weeks.'

'Thanks. I'm thinking of her too, you know. She got very upset in Carrigbrack.'

Martha was genuinely torn between her desire to find Rose and her concerns about her mam and dad. Throw Evanne into the mix, and life was turning into a high-wire act.

They had started walking back towards Cat's house. Jake, exuberance restored, skipped ahead. Then, unsure of his independence, he sloped back towards his mum.

Martha had long believed that fine weather made her braver, and there was something about the freshness and brightness of that March Tuesday that prompted her to think, *What am I waiting for?* She was reluctant to claim that hunting for the truth about Rose was making her confront her own past. It sounded too simplistic. But, whatever its source, an idea had gripped her and wouldn't let go.

'Do you ever think back on stuff you did . . . in your twenties, say . . . and wonder if it's too late to revisit it . . . to try to put it right?'

'Not particularly,' replied Cat. 'Why do you ask?'

'I've been going back over some old decisions. Some regrets, I suppose you'd say. That's all.'

'You're not going to turn all "Ballad of Lucy Jordan" on me, are you?'

'If you remember the song correctly,' replied Martha, with a grin, 'Lucy was thirty-seven when she gave up on Paris and the sports car. She was only a kid. Seriously, I promise you I won't be taking that route. It's just I've been thinking about the . . .' She wavered. Oh, what the hell? She might as well come on out with it. 'I've been thinking about Paudie. I want to talk to him.'

Cat came to an abrupt halt. 'You're kidding me, right?'

'No. After all these years, I reckon I owe him the truth. I'm . . . I'm going to give him a call.'

Subtlety wasn't Cat's strong suit, and she remained in the centre of the path, as immovable as a mountain. Her chin jutted out, the way it usually did when she got worked up. Jake gazed at her in confusion. One of the black-leggings women, who was wheeling a buggy so large it probably needed a licence plate and a tax disc, veered into the road to avoid them.

'Would you mind not blocking the footpath?' she said. 'You'll cause an accident.'

'Why don't you f—' Cat glanced at Jake. 'Why don't you go home to your spiraliser and your kale smoothies . . . or whatever it is that you women drink?'

The woman opened her mouth to reply but

thought better of it. Instead she scurried on her way, mumbling about some people not being fit to have children.

Cat, insulated by a force field of indignation, didn't appear to care. She turned back towards Martha. 'Talking to Paudie,' she said, 'is what you'd do if you were stark staring mad. But you're not, so you won't. Isn't that right?'

'Consider me warned,' replied Martha. But she said no more.

Later that week, she received a surprise phone call.

'Well,' said Fidelma Lafferty, 'if you only knew what you'd started.'

It turned out that, since her encounter with Martha and Evanne, Winnie had obsessed about American Rose. 'If I could remember whereabouts in the States she came from,' she'd say, 'then I'd be able to guide those girls in the right direction. It's such a massive country, they'll never find her otherwise.'

Fidelma had pointed out that there were lots of ways of tracking people down, and she'd urged her mam not to worry. Her words had fallen on stony ground. Then, while listening to a discussion on the radio, Winnie had had an epiphany. 'Bobby Kennedy,' she said. 'That's who we talked about. Bobby Kennedy, God be good to him. The poor man wasn't long dead, and Rose said her family were heartbroken. On account of him being local.'

Martha's thoughts returned to her schooldays.

Whatever people said about the Kennedys now, they had been royalty when she was growing up. No, better than royalty. As Irish Catholics who had risen to the top in the most powerful country on earth, they were hovering close to sainthood. While her mam and dad hadn't gone so far as to put a picture of JFK over the mantelpiece, there was no doubting the reverence in which the Kennedy family had been held.

'So,' said Fidelma, 'if Rose considered Bobby Kennedy a local, she must be from Boston.'

'Boston,' repeated Martha, as if the name was new to her. In truth, she didn't know much about the place. The Kennedys aside, what came to mind? The marathon bombing, of course. Harvard. Clapboard houses. Snow; she had an image of heavy snow. The Pixies – weren't they from Boston? New Kids on the Block. Ben Affleck and Matt Damon. Sylvia Plath. Oh, and Irish Americans. Thousands upon thousands of Irish Americans.

'What do you think?' asked Fidelma.

'Gosh, I don't know. It's possible, I suppose. Odd, but possible. Mind you, it raises a whole new set of questions.'

'Doesn't it just? And it doesn't answer the biggest question of them all: where is she now?'

Martha thanked Fidelma. Then she ran 'Rose Moroney, Boston' through Google. A rush of anticipation quickly turned to disappointment. Once again, there were Roses, but not the right Rose. She turned off her laptop and collapsed onto the bed. Not a million miles from Carrigbrack, there was a hill – Corkscrew Hill – where every time you thought you'd reached the top, you discovered there was another ridge to climb. That was how this felt.

Evanne was made of tougher stuff than her mother. That was how she saw it, anyway. What a disappointment her mum was turning out to be. It had taken her almost thirty years to look for her birth parents, and as soon as the going got tricky, what did she do? She caved in and started boring on about 'breathing space'. And she did this even though a woman in Carrigbrack – a woman who should know – had said that Evanne was 'the living image' of Rose.

'I thought we were going to solve your mystery,' said Evanne.

'And we will,' replied her mother. 'I need to slow down, though. I feel bad about how much time it's taking up. We haven't been to see your nan and granddad in ages.'

Evanne assured her that she was okay with the cremated dinners and the general absent-mindedness. She didn't think there was much point in fretting about Clem and Delia either. If she knew her nan, there would be ten minutes of chuntering about daughters who didn't visit. Then she'd make a hundred cups of milky tea, they'd watch some old-timer schmaltz on the TV, and everything would be fine. A couple of days later, Evanne and her mum would return to Dublin with a loaf of brown bread, a pot of jam, a sponge cake and a bag of scones. Her nan always behaved as though Dublin was in danger of running low on carbohydrates.

Her friend Serena was fascinated by the American revelation. Before the recession her mother had been to Boston on a shopping trip. It was quieter than New York, she said, but very classy. She also wondered if Evanne would be entitled to a US passport. To be honest, Evanne wished they could spend more time talking about Carrigbrack. Serena didn't find this subject quite so enthralling. 'Why don't you do your Leaving Cert history project on those homes?' she said. 'You know so much, it'd be a shame to waste all that reading.' Evanne attempted to explain that what she'd learned would never be wasted. She couldn't think of it as history. It was too personal – and too recent. Just thinking about Carrigbrack made her angry. One look at Serena's blank face made it clear she didn't understand.

'Intriguing,' was her dad's verdict on the Boston information. Then he did the regulation parent thing of warning her not to get carried away. 'It might come to nothing,' he said. This didn't stop him telling a story about a guy he'd known at college called Shamie McGroarty. Shamie had gone to Boston on a temporary student visa and never come home again. What relevance this had to anything, Evanne couldn't say. They were in the sitting room of the Sandyford apartment. Layla was slumped on the sofa, not actually sleeping, but not engaging either. She looked dazed, like she'd climbed off a really wild roller-coaster. There was baby sick on the shoulder of her tracksuit top. Alex was asleep. Evanne didn't know if her brother was an especially noisy baby, but he certainly did his share of crying. There was something flat about the atmosphere, and her dad was talking too much, like he was afraid of silence. That explained the Shamie McGroarty story, she supposed.

'So, Evanne,' said Layla, as she wound a lock of hair around one finger, 'what do you think of Justine?' Justine Winstanley was Layla's temporary replacement on afternoon TV.

'Um, I haven't seen very much of her. She's, like, okay. Okay for an oldster, I mean.'

'Watch it,' chipped in her dad, too much jollity in his voice. 'She's the same age as your mother. I'm sure Martha wouldn't like to hear herself dismissed as an "oldster".'

Evanne knew what Layla was looking for. 'Obviously, she's not as good as you,' she said.

'Thank you, sweetie. That's not what your father thinks, though. He thinks she's wonderful.' Layla stretched out the word 'wonderful' so that it seemed to last for about ten seconds.

'Now, Layla, you know I never said any such thing. All I said was, I'm pleased to see her getting a break. She's had a rough time. Her marriage broke up, and she's got four kids to provide for.'

Layla leaned in towards Evanne. 'Justine's an

absolute superwoman, don't you know? What's the betting she takes in laundry in her spare time?'

Evanne willed the moment to pass. She had a good nose for arguments – let's face it, she'd had plenty of experience – and she knew what was serious and what was of no consequence. This she didn't like. Her dad laughed, but it was a phoney kind of laugh. 'I reckon Justine's an ideal stand-in. She's also my client, so the household benefits from the arrangement. What's not to love?'

'Huh,' said Layla. 'You should have seen her the other day, Evanne. The state of her – in leather trousers at her age. That's not what the audience expects. I'll bet there were complaints. Then she waltzes over here with a present for Alex, and she's practically eating birdseed out of your father's hand. "Yes, Dermot. No, Dermot. Oh, you're hilarious, Dermot."' Layla folded her arms, as if to say, 'Discussion terminated.'

The room fell into silence.

Evanne knew from snatches of overheard conversation that her father's company had lost two more clients, and that this time he was sorry to see them go. The celebrity gardener, Violet Wren, had defected to a rival agency. Her dad moaned that if it wasn't for him she would still be using her real name, Gobnait McCrudden. 'How much work would she be getting then?' he had asked Layla, who'd had the good sense not to answer. Meanwhile, the radio presenter Ulick Boyle was abandoning broadcasting to become an academic. Her dad claimed that Ulick 'could've had a cracking TV career if only he'd got his squint fixed'.

As they sat there, rain walloping against the window, Evanne fished around for something to say. Nothing helpful came to mind, and she found herself gibbering on about a girl at school who'd cut her arms so badly she'd ended up in hospital, and another girl who'd stolen and crashed her father's BMW. (Admittedly, these stories served a dual purpose. It was always good to remind her parents that there were far more screwed-up daughters out there.) She was almost relieved when a hiccuping noise erupted from the baby monitor. That was the sound Alex made before he started to cry. Sure enough, within seconds a jagged wail filled the room.

'Oh, please, Alex,' said Layla, as she hauled herself up from the sofa. 'Would you ever give it a rest?'

Twelve hours later, Evanne woke to the strange sense of knowing that someone else was up. You didn't have to see a light; you didn't have to hear anything; you just knew. She slipped out of bed and padded out to see what was happening.

Her dad was cradling Alex, who was sucking his bottle with gusto. Layla was exhausted, he said, then added something about breastfeeding not suiting her. Evanne closed her ears to that part. Her dad talking about breastfeeding was too, too weird. Anyway, why shouldn't he be the one to get up in the middle of the night? To be fair, he looked wiped out. His hair was standing up in wiry tufts, and his eyes were swollen with sleep. Alex, on the other hand, was improving by the day. He'd lost his raw look and was turning into a real cutie. Evanne was mesmerised by his minuscule nose and the way he clenched his teeny-tiny hands into fists. She'd even put a picture of him on her Instagram. She told herself that babies were no different from kittens or lambs; that they were programmed to be lovable so that someone would look after them. Still, she was surprised by how appealing she found her little brother. It was a shame her mother wouldn't come and see him.

'Imagine,' she found herself saying, 'when Mum was a few weeks older than Alex, she was taken away from Rose and given to her new parents.'

'I hadn't thought of it like that,' said her dad.

Somehow, the muted light made talking easier. The absence of both her mother and Layla helped too, and for a while they chatted about Carrigbrack and the search for Rose. Their voices were low. Evanne wasn't sure whether this was for the benefit of Layla or Alex or both, but it felt nice.

'Don't be too hard on your mother,' said her dad. 'I know you feel she's hanging back, but this is a delicate time. She's probably nervous about what will happen if and when she finds Rose.'

Evanne knew he was right. All the same, her parents' hypocrisy amazed her. Her life consisted of one parent telling her to be kind to the other even though they'd no intention of following their own instructions.

'Do you think we'll find her?' she asked.

'It's hard to say. According to the piece of paper Delia showed your mum, Rose was going to return to her family, right?'

'Uh-huh.'

'Well, if she *is* American, and if she *did* go back home, she'll be easier to track down. In my experience, when it comes to records and information, America's completely different from here. They're not so hell-bent on keeping everything hidden.' He paused to give Alex a couple of gentle taps on the back. 'I presume she got married at some stage and changed her name, so Martha needs to find her marriage certificate. It may even be available online.' He paused again. 'And then the hard part begins.'

Evanne was about to ask what he meant, but opted instead to ask about something else that was bothering her. 'Now that you have Alex, will you and Layla be getting married?'

Her father responded with two more taps to the baby's back. Alex burped. 'Haven't we enough to be getting on with?' he said, as he smiled at his son. 'Don't worry, Evanne. We won't do anything without telling you.'

She wasn't sure that this could be called an answer, but her dad's fussing over Alex made it clear he wasn't going to say any more. 'Does he need changing?' she asked.

He replied, with a wink, 'No, we're all right. He's fine at the minute. I reckon we'll leave that job to Layla.'

The following morning, Evanne was all primed to ask about American marriage certificates. Perhaps her dad could help find Rose's records. But Alex was out of sorts and Layla was tired, so her plans came to nothing. Finding the atmosphere in the apartment too tense, she packed up her belongings and headed back to Milltown.

She searched for an age before unearthing what she was looking for: an email address for the public records office in Boston. Realising that nobody would take a sixteen-year-old seriously, she pretended that Rose was *her* natural mother. Within minutes, she received an insanely polite reply. She needed to post any available details to an address in a place called Dorchester. If there was a birth or marriage certificate that matched her query, the office would send it on. The fee was thirty-two dollars.

Delighted with this development, she raided her savings, which were stuffed into a sock at the back of her underwear drawer. She had planned on buying new make-up, but this was far more important. She practically skipped to the bank where, after filling in about a thousand forms, she sorted out the payment. She continued on to the post office where she fitted everything into an envelope. At the last minute, a thought struck her:

using her home address would be a mistake. What if her mum got to the post first and deprived Evanne of her *ta-dah* moment? Despite her dad's pleas, she remained annoyed with her mum. By rights, *she* should be doing this work.

In the end, Evanne decided to use Serena's address. She posted the letter, then called her friend to explain. Buzzing with anticipation, she kept her fingers crossed all the way home.

# CHAPTER 17

This was madness. A forty-five-year-old woman should not be lying to her sixteen-year-old daughter about where she was going and whom she was meeting. It was wrong, all kinds of wrong. The problem was, if Evanne had any idea that Martha was going for a drink with Paudie Carmody, her eyes would be out on stalks. Not only that, she'd start asking questions. Questions Martha couldn't answer.

She hadn't spoken to Cat either. The set-to near the playground had made her friend's feelings clear. Raising the matter again would lead only to more of the same. Martha was well aware that she was replacing one secret with another, but so be it.

'It's only a quick drink with an old friend,' she said to Evanne. 'I won't be long. If there's an emergency, give me a call.'

Her daughter gave her a bored look. 'Yeah, yeah, if the house goes up in flames or George Clooney turns up, I'll let you know.' Then she crinkled her brow. 'Is this "old friend" by any chance a man?'

'It's not that sort of drink. I'm meeting someone from school.'

'I hope she appreciates the effort you've made.'

'You know how it is. I don't want to appear old before my time.' And wasn't that the truth? According to the immutable law of ex-boyfriends, no matter how acrimonious the split or how little you cared for him, you never wanted an old partner to consider you dried up and past it.

'Fine, so,' replied Evanne. 'If George does drop by, I'll let him know you're available.'

'Good woman,' said Martha, as she closed the door.

April had always been her favourite month. The days lengthened. The gloom lifted. She treasured the first chimes of the ice-cream van and the smell of clothes plucked from the back of the wardrobe. And she loved the sense of promise: promise that the summer might yet be a hot one, a full-throttle 1976 or 1995 or 2003. One of those summers people talked about for decades to come. The evening didn't disappoint. A low sun glinted off the windows. Birds whistled and swooped. The smells of lilac and tom cat hung in the air.

It was an evening for being brave.

Although they'd arranged to meet in a bar not far from where he worked, Paudie was late. When had he ever been anything else? The bar was what Evanne would call 'a bit throwback Thursday', the walls dotted with photos of defunct football teams, the carpet patterned with brown and orange whorls. A strong smell of cigarette smoke wafted in from the beer garden.

While Martha ordered a glass of white wine, a text arrived: *Got held up. Promise I won't be too much longer.*

She sat down, stuffed the phone into her coat pocket, swallowed a large mouthful of Sauvignon and allowed her thoughts to drift back to the summer of 1991.

'The holiday of a lifetime,' Cat had called it. It was also their first foreign holiday. True, they'd spent the summer of 1988 in Ocean City, New Jersey. They'd had to work, though, so both Cat and Martha claimed it didn't count. This was different. They were going to Kenya to see zebras and lions and giraffes, and all of the other animals that had captured their imagination during childhood episodes of *Born Free*.

Two years had passed since their graduation from college. Cat had spent them in an assortment of jobs. She'd been a nightclub hostess, a hair-dresser's receptionist and an assistant in a tattoo parlour. While she'd yet to find a 'career' (in those days, they always put air quotes around the word, as if it was something that existed solely in theory), she had managed to put some cash aside. Martha worked in public relations. As much as she loathed the job, she needed the money. Both were single. Martha had recently finished a six-month stretch with a philosophy graduate called Ross Lowry. Ross, with his swirling black coat and cherry-red Doc Martens, was the kind of fellow who worked hard at being depressed. He spoke a lot about writing, but rarely wrote. Although she'd been fond of him, she shed no tears when he moved to London. Cat's list of ex-boyfriends was almost as long as her list of former jobs.

They were flying to Kenya with the cheapest option, Aeroflot, the Soviet airline. The route involved several stopovers, including a lengthy one in Moscow. But when you're twenty-two and setting off on an adventure, who cares about a bit of inconvenience?

In Moscow, their attempts to leave the terminal building were rebuffed. A grey-uniformed official scrutinised their passports, scowled at the lack of Soviet visas and shooed them back to the departure gates. They had no option but to sit and watch the comings and goings. What they saw was spellbinding. Martha remembered a group of white-robed men with prayer mats kneeling to face Mecca. Passengers shuttled by in traditional African dress, in hijabs, in a variety of uniforms. The sounds, too, were extraordinary. Here, a knot of youngsters spoke in high-speed Russian; there, a group of women chatted in an unknown African language.

There were other wonders besides. For an hour or more, they sat rapt in front of the mammoth departures board. The first flight to capture Martha's attention was to Ho Chi Minh City via Tashkent. Her eyes scanned the board, past flights to Bamako, Tegucigalpa and Sharjah. Beyond these there was a clutch of unfamiliar destinations with enticing names: Khabarovsk, Abakan, Raebareli. She felt like the world was unfolding in front of her.

And then the most bizarre thing happened. From behind them, a familiar voice asked, 'Is this place a bit livelier than Templemorris or what?' It was Paudie Carmody, accompanied by two friends, both called Noel. They'd been on the same flight from Shannon and were also on their way to Nairobi. 'I saw the pair of you on the plane,' said Paudie, buoyant as ever, 'but I thought I'd wait until we got this far to say hello. I wanted to give you a real fright.'

For the duration of the journey, they had to be friendly. The five of them ganged together when the plane stopped in Cyprus, and again in Yemen. It didn't take Cat long to begin flirting with one of the Noels. On the final stretch into Nairobi, Martha had a stern word with her friend.

'We're not spending two weeks with Paudie Carmody and his goons.'

'We'll shake them off when we get there,' was Cat's airy reply. 'Don't you worry.'

Two days later, they clambered into a white jeep and set off for the Maasai Mara. There were seven of them: Martha, Cat, Moses the driver, Paudie, Noel, Noel and Flynn, an Australian they'd collected along the way.

'It's better to travel with people you know,' insisted Cat. 'There'll be loads of others at the campsite. We won't be stuck with these lads.'

By that stage, Martha was softening towards Paudie. She'd expected that, after a year working in television, he'd be even more unbearable. Instead, the experience had blunted his edges. Although he had reams of anecdotes, he'd learned that not every conversation needed to have him at its centre. If she really couldn't stand her job, he said, she had to be brave enough to leave. She would find something else; he was sure of it. Oh, and he was sorry for the carry-on at school. 'The business about your mother?' he said. 'That was stupid. Did you ever try to find her?' No, she replied. It would be such a lot of hassle. And wasn't one set of parents bad enough? What would she want another pair for? He laughed, and they never spoke about it again.

On their last night at the campsite, they sat around a crackling fire, drinking Tusker beer and contemplating the sky. They argued over whether the stars were genuinely brighter and more numerous here than they were at home or whether it just seemed that way. They sang songs and told stories and drank more Tusker. Cat had abandoned her flirtation with Noel and was pursuing Flynn, like a cheetah zoning in on a wildebeest. One of the young Maasai who guarded the site was competing for her attention. Red hair was a novelty, and he was transfixed by Cat's curls.

At some point, Paudie and Martha went for a walk. They didn't go far. Only a fool would venture into the wild unknown. The night had a soft, fragrant warmth unlike anything she'd known at home, and she was just the right side of drunk. Guessing Paudie's intentions, her first response was amusement. Kissing him, having any involvement with him, would be madness. But they were four and a half thousand miles from Ireland. Cat aside, no one need ever know. A moment later, she was in his arms.

The next morning they drove to Lake Nakuru to see the flamingos. Then they headed for Mombasa, where they stayed in a cottage beside the Indian Ocean. They sprawled on the porch drinking dark coffee and tins of gin and tonic, and eating unfamiliar fruit. Paudie had a Walkman with two small speakers, and they played the REM album *Out of Time* over and over again. Sometimes they listened to the waves. The ocean was warm, the sand a creamy white, and if you forgot your sandals, it scorched your feet. By then, Cat and Flynn were together, and the two Noels had faded into the background.

In their schooldays, Martha had never stopped to consider what Paudie looked like. At twenty-two, she could see why he'd been a magnet for Tina Bennis and her gang. His brown eyes sloped at the corners, like he was always on the verge of laughter, and his dark hair was in the sort of floppy cut that was trendy at the time. His sporting career might have petered out, but he still did enough running to maintain a lean, hard look.

Their being from the same town was a bonus.

Martha could make a reference to somebody or something from her childhood without Paudie staring at her, like she was a hick from the back end of nowhere. And how refreshing was it, after months of Ross and his artistic pretensions, to talk to a man with a bit of old-fashioned Templemorris common sense? Once, when filleting a TV colleague, Paudie suggested, 'A week or two in the chipboard factory would do the guy no harm.' Even though this sounded like something her mam would say, Martha had to stop herself applauding. Another night they told stories about St Ursula's. Mostly they focused on silly stuff, like the day Cat's brother, Flan, had let a ferret loose in the woodwork room, or the time Trevor Hawes had taken magic mushrooms and hallucinated all the way through double physics. Their raucous laughter must have travelled for miles.

Flynn intended to spend several months travelling around Africa. Up next on his itinerary was Mount Kilimanjaro. He spoke about Uganda and Tanzania, Rwanda and South Africa. Fleetingly, Cat contemplated going with him. Martha remembered the two of them lazing on the beach, discussing what to do.

'It must be great to be Australian,' said Cat, as she dismembered a star fruit. 'They've got a licence to see the world. When we were sitting in the airport in Moscow, watching those flights take off, all I could think of was how amazing it would be to travel.'

‘Why don’t you stay on the road, then?’

‘For one thing, I don’t have the money. For another, I don’t have any of the right visas. And most importantly—’

‘They’d go mental at home.’

‘Got it in one,’ said Cat.

With hindsight, Martha thought that that conversation encapsulated their lives. Both had been wary of causing upset. If they’d rebelled, it had been in short spurts. They’d been back on the straight and narrow before anybody noticed. Now that she thought about it, perhaps the most rebellious act either had committed was going to university. The world was constantly telling Martha not to have regrets, but she did regret how obedient she’d been. If she had her time again, she’d be more daring. She’d be bolder.

When they had returned to Ireland, Martha had continued seeing Paudie. They told few people in Dublin and nobody in Templemorris. ‘You know what that town’s like,’ he’d say. ‘We’d get no peace.’ Cat disapproved of their secrecy. Still, she played along.

How would Martha describe their relationship? Given how it ended, she was tempted to focus on the darkness and the uncertainty. In its best moments, though, she experienced an exhilaration she hadn’t known before. Entire days were lost to sex and sleep and more sex. Martha was living in a rented house in Harold’s Cross with Cat and two other girls, and frequently Paudie spent the night there. She'd decorated her room with great care, filling it with film posters, photographs and other mementos, as if to say, 'This is who I am.' Paudie shared an apartment with the two Noels. His room was a more Spartan affair, like he was just passing through.

Now, when Martha thought of those times, she thought of dancing – dancing in bars, at gigs and in nightclubs. She thought of bombing around the country to festivals, sessions and twenty-first birthday parties. She thought of singing and laughing and staying up half the night debating subjects that didn't matter in the morning. They were at that stage in life where every experience felt important. They had nobody to worry about but themselves. Paudie's blossoming fame meant every door was open to them. Occasionally, she would call in sick to work so they could embark on some wild jaunt or other. Was it, to use the latter-day term, 'an exclusive relationship'? It was for her.

As the weeks whirred by, Paudie landed more and more work. A newspaper called him TV's new golden boy. Another said that London or even New York beckoned. According to that article, a 'telly insider' reckoned he'd be perfect for *The Word* or 'one of those late-night shows loved by drunks'. Martha got an attack of the giggles. Paudie sulked.

She stayed with the PR company but started saving so she could return to college.

Truth to tell, she wasn't always happy. Sometimes

she was very unhappy. Paudie became increasingly distracted and unreliable. They'd have plans for the weekend, then the phone would ring and in a finger click he'd be gone. She'd spend the evening sitting in the semi-dark, drinking mugs of whiskey and red lemonade, trying to figure it all out. A couple of drinks in, she'd round on herself for being dictated to and messed around. It flew against everything she believed in. What sort of feminist was she?

Cat was typically blunt. 'If he's making you this miserable,' she'd say, 'you've got to move on. Or, at the very least, you've got to talk to him.' She was right. Of course.

By early 1992, they'd been seeing each other for six months. Martha knew she liked Paudie too much. She treasured the physicality, the conversations, the fun. She was desperate to hear him say, 'I love you.' But he never did.

The end was almost comically predictable. One March Friday night, while Paudie was on location in County Kerry, she went for a drink with some colleagues from the office. One drink led to another and then to another, and they wound up at the Rock Garden in Temple Bar. As she adjusted her eyes to the gloom, Paudie was the first person she saw, squashed into a corner with a tall blonde. Briefly, a group of lads blocked her view, and she wondered if she'd imagined the scene. Music with a heavy bass line pounded from the speakers, and swirls of cigarette smoke stung her eyes. When the lads wove out of her way again, there he was. There the two of them were. Paudie leaned in to kiss his companion.

Now, as she recalled the scene, Martha tried to remember the girl's name. Oh, what was it? Nadia? Natalie? Nadine? She was a model/TV presenter/whatever who went to London and got gobbled up by the big city. What Martha did remember was every minute detail of her appearance. The starved-to-perfection body in the black Lycra dress. The wristful of silver bangles. The curtain of hair that had never been cut with nail scissors, much less bleached with Sun-In.

If she had one thing to be thankful for, it was that none of her work crowd had met Paudie. They didn't know that Martha's boyfriend was slouched in front of them swapping saliva with another woman. Her first impulse was to walk out, but with the stubbornness of the drunk, she decided, no: she would stand her ground. With exaggerated nonchalance, she stalked over to the bar and ordered a round of drinks. All the while, the music went *doof, doof, doof.* On her return, she caught his eye. She smiled a tart smile but said nothing. She rejoined her friends and tried to look like she was having the best night of her life. When next she risked a glance towards the corner, Paudie and the girl were gone.

The following afternoon, he turned up at her house. Cat was in Templemorris for the weekend. Otherwise, he would have been lucky to escape intact. The bravado of the night before was gone, and Martha's self-esteem was in flitters. Paudie looked rough: bleary-eyed and grey-skinned. He was sorry she'd bumped into them like that, he said. This half-arsed apology was accompanied by a share of shrugging and a collection of lines like 'You know what I am' and 'We're too young to get serious.' She should have called him out on his hackneyed excuses, then sent him on his way. Instead they had sex. Lacklustre, hungover sex. An hour later, she woke up in a lather of self-loathing and asked him to go. How she would love to say he put up a fight, but he left with hardly a murmur. 'I reckon it's for the best,' he said. 'There's been some interest from London, so I'll be heading over that way soon.' He wished her luck with everything. And then he was gone.

For two, three, four hours, Martha lay on the bed, curled into a comma, crying quietly. Then she got up and went about her business. She instructed herself not to look back. Only losers looked back. Oh, the innocence of her.

Over the years Martha and Paudie's paths did cross. Six months after the split, she bumped into him on another night out. He was off his head on something. Ecstasy, she presumed. Back then, everybody was doing E. She saw him in Fennessy's Lounge in Templemorris one Christmas but, at Cat's insistence, said little. On another occasion, she spotted his familiar strut and ducked into a shop.

London never really worked out, and by the late nineties Paudie was back in Dublin hosting a so-so TV quiz show and a not-so-bad-at-all radio programme. Martha was married to Dermot, who was working for a large accountancy firm. Just before the tax deadline, Paudie arrived with a plastic bag. When he turned it upside down, a year's worth of receipts and invoices spilled onto Dermot's desk. 'I think I'm in trouble,' he told the bemused accountant. 'None of it adds up.'

Having gone through all of the figures, Dermot decided that Paudie wasn't being paid enough. 'What you need is an agent,' he said. Somehow, he ended up with the job. Martha's husband quickly discovered that his media scepticism was a godsend. Management types could talk all they liked about artistic vision, Dermot's sole aim was to gather as much cash as possible for his clients.

Despite what Martha had told her daughter, Paudie *had* been to their house in Dolmen Crescent. Evanne had been only three or four at the time. Dermot knew that his wife and his top earner had been to school together, but little more. Their relationship remained a secret. As she poured the wine and carved the chicken, it hit her: despite everything, she still felt about Paudie in *that* way. She realised then that the person who affects you most may not be the one you end up with. Appalled by herself, she overcompensated, barely looking at him for most of the evening. The meal became so awkward that even now the memory made her cringe. Afterwards, Dermot rounded on her. 'Would it have killed you to be friendly?' he said.

'You know I didn't like him at school,' she replied, 'so why should I like him now?'

The last time she'd seen Paudie was three or four years previously at the funeral of a classmate. They'd exchanged nods, the way you do at funerals.

And now, here he was, walking into the bar, neck slightly bent, like he was conscious of people's stares. On cue, a group of women cocked their heads and swapped sideways glances. A barman winked. Although he had to be curious about why she'd contacted him, he was skilful enough not to let it show. After all this time, it was strange to see him up close. He seemed a shade older than he did on the TV, his eyes more tired, his lines more pronounced. He did look successful, though. Well put together, she supposed you'd call it. Like an American news anchor or a Spanish football manager. What, she wondered, did he see when he looked at her?

Paudie ordered a pint of Guinness, a toasted sandwich and another white wine for Martha. For some minutes they danced around each other, awkward as two strangers in a hotel lift.

'Tina Coote was asking after you,' she said.

'Who?'

'You must remember Tina. Tina Bennis, as she was in our day. She married a fellow from O'Rahilly's Cross called Senan Coote.'

Paudie shook his head. 'Not coming to me, I'm afraid.'

'Ah, come on. She was the founding member of your fan club. I can't believe . . .' His left cheek gave a tell-tale twitch. 'You're an awful messer,' she said.

He laughed. 'How could I forget the legendary Tina Bennis? She was the star attraction of the field behind the graveyard.'

'I'm sure she'd love to hear that. She's a grandmother now, you know.'

They spoke about Martha's search for her birth mother. She told him how she lurched between excitement and apprehension. He was fascinated by the American possibility. She promised to let him know how it all worked out. If it worked out.

Paudie talked about the son, Ruán, he'd had with Venus Barrington. Venus had married a businessman – 'something big in pensions' – and moved to Surrey. Paudie didn't see as much of his boy as he would like. 'He's completely English now,' he said. 'Not a trace of Templemorris in him. Mam's not impressed.'

Martha sipped her wine. 'What he needs is an instruction manual – *The Ways and Customs of the Small Irish Town* – so he'll know how to blend in.'

Again he laughed. 'Poor Ruán has a lot to learn, like what to do at Mass, for starters.'

'And how to duck out early without being seen,' said Martha. 'That's a pretty important skill. Oh, and what sort of language to use. That matters too. Even Dubliners can be hopeless. Like, Dermot is forever using that awful phrase "down the country", as if everywhere beyond Newlands Cross is one great boggy mass.'

'Dubliners? They think we're all "mucksavages" and "culchies" and "bog warriors" . . .'

'. . . when anybody with any sense knows we're from the *town*. We're sophisticates.'

'But,' added Paudie, with a good-humoured wheeze, 'looking down on people from the surrounding villages is perfectly acceptable.'

'Too right it is. That's what they're there for – to make us feel superior.'

'Oh, and to be a true son of Templemorris, Ruán would have to talk incessantly about the people who've left.'

'And he'd have to say things like "I don't know where she got her fancy notions from. She was no great shakes at school."'

'And he'd know what everybody was going to say . . .'

'. . . before they said it. I reckon these rules could be adapted for international use: *Small Towns and How to Survive Them*. What do you think?'

'I think that if they heard us in Templemorris we'd be excommunicated. Another drink?'

'Sure why not?' While Martha wouldn't go so far as to say she was relaxed, she was enjoying the conversation. She was indulging in her old weakness too, avoiding what she'd come to say. She realised that a nearby couple were listening in.

Paudie gave the couple his most brilliant smile and they turned away. 'Don't worry,' he said to Martha. 'I'm used to it.'

She wasn't, though, and she tried to lower her voice. Paudie asked about the library; about her mam, dad and Una; about Cat, Richie and the kids – and about Evanne. She told him that Evanne's best friend reckoned he was 'hot'. As soon as the word left her mouth she shuddered.

Thankfully, he found it amusing. 'Christ,' he said, 'your daughter has some screwed-up friends.'

It occurred to Martha that, aside from the story about his son, he'd said almost nothing about himself. Out of the corner of her eye, she spotted the eavesdropping couple tiptoeing away. This, she decided, was a signal. She couldn't put it off any longer. Rolling her shoulders, she plunged on in. 'So, you're probably wondering why I got in touch.'

Paudie cupped his hands around his glass. 'After more than twenty years? I've been wondering all right.'

'It's . . .' Martha had prepared a speech – God knew she'd had enough time – but the words ran away from her. 'It's something I should have told you a long time ago, only the more I put it off, the more difficult it became.'

'That doesn't sound good.'

'It's not a big deal. Well, that's not true. Some would say it's a huge deal. But at the time it felt like I was doing the right thing.'

'You've lost me, Martha.'

The noise around them receded, and everything became still. Martha paused to get her thoughts in order. She pushed her hair back from her face. 'After we split up, a few weeks later I discovered I was pregnant.'

'Mine?' he asked, then quickly thought better of it. 'Mine.'

She nodded.

# CHAPTER 18

Evanne was intrigued by her mother's behaviour. She'd been all tarted up like a woman on a date. But her mum had given up on men, so that didn't make sense. How did you even find a date when you were on the crumbling side of forty? Perhaps you went online – only those sites were full of weird guys who might take advantage of her.

At least her mum didn't pretend she was still young. Some women were terrible for that. Take Serena's mother: Tilly Montague had a head of extensions, like a Disney princess, and a weakness for beads and bangles. On a bad day, she looked like an explosion in Claire's Accessories. Poor Serena never said anything, but Evanne was mortified for her.

That wasn't the worst of it. Tilly also had the knack of asking *the* most embarrassing questions about boyfriends and such. Lots of the girls in Evanne's class claimed to be having sex. Actually, it was more complicated than that. With their arched eyebrows and affected giggles, they didn't say it as much as imply it. She would bet her

Michael Kors bag (a please-be-happy-about-the-baby bribe from her dad) that half of them were virgins. Serena was going out with a guy called Josh Bailey. They'd had proper full-on sex four times. She'd also done it with her last boyfriend, a complete user called Dylan Gilsenan.

Evanne had never had sex. Not that she would publicly admit it. She could arch her brows with the best of them. The problem was, the only guys who fancied her were boring rugby-playing types who spent hours styling their hair so they could look like toddlers woken from a nap. They liked to boast about how wasted they got and how they were going to leave home and live in Australia or Thailand or wherever. As if. Give them two years, and they'd be doing commerce at UCD. Give them ten, and they'd be working in a big accountancy firm and engaged to some insipid girl, who'd been planning her wedding since she was seven.

It wasn't just the actual sex that presented a problem (although she was a bit squeamish about all that poking and panting). When to have it and what to say about it were tricky too. Do it too soon, like Celestine Foster Walsh, who'd gone all the way with Cillian Cullinane when she was thirteen, and people thought you were damaged. Leave it too long, and the same people dismissed you as frigid or afraid to come out. Conscious that time was ticking by, Evanne resolved to accept the next decent advance. Just to get the whole virginity thing out of the way. Plus she could do with the excitement. Right then, the most exciting thing in her life was trying to find Rose.

She looked at her phone. Seven thirty: time to psych herself up for another attempt at her maths homework. She was in full psyching mode when Serena rang.

'Guess what?'

'For real?' Evanne's question came out as a squeak.

'Yep. I'm holding a big brown envelope with a lovely Boston postmark.'

'Uh, hello? Have you seen the time, Serena? Why didn't you call earlier?'

'We were at my nan's for dinner. I told you that this afternoon. And it was only when we got into the car to come home that my mum mentioned it. "Why are we getting post for Evanne Waters?" she said.'

'Did you say what we agreed?'

'Duh, obviously. "It's a present for her mum," I said. "A gift voucher or something. It's meant to be a surprise, so she gave our address." Then my mum started giving it loads about what a lovely girl you are.'

'Isn't she right?' said Evanne, with a laugh. She told herself not to get hysterical. 'Can you bring the envelope over?'

'Are you serious? I've got all my homework to do. Why don't I open it?'

'No!'

'Chill, would you? I'll give it to you in the morning.'

Evanne looked at the hieroglyphics in front of her. If she played around with the figures and letters for the next six months, she wouldn't understand them. 'I'm on my own,' she said, 'so I can come over to yours to collect it. Give me twenty minutes.'

In less than a quarter of an hour, Evanne was standing on the Montagues' doorstep, leaning on the bell like a mad thing.

'Homework issue,' Serena said to her mum, as she ushered Evanne in. Tilly, who reeked of headachy perfume, went to say something. Evanne just smiled and zoomed up the stairs. She was too excited to speak.

For a minute or so, she stood there, passing the envelope from one hand to the other, back and forth, back and forth, like she was holding her exam results. She wished Serena would leave. She wanted to do this on her own. But her friend was sitting on the bed, wringing her hands in a way that suggested she was almost as nervous as Evanne. Occasionally she made a *squeeee* sort of noise. Excluding her would be mean. Evanne took a deep breath and, gently, she opened the envelope.

It contained three pieces of paper. The first was a letter. The writer, who by wonderful coincidence was called Alex, said the files contained both a birth certificate and a marriage certificate for Rose Annalisa Moroney. Any more than that was impossible to read. The words were a jumble. Not because there was a problem with the letter, but because Evanne was intoxicated with excitement.

'Go on,' said Serena. 'Spill.'

'Give me a second, would you?' she snapped, before adding, 'Sorry, sorry. I'm going kind of crazy here.'

According to the birth cert, Rose had been born in Boston on 20 February 1951. Her father was called Edward, her mother Grace. Evanne paused to consider this before switching her attention to the third piece of paper. It told her that on 14 June 1973 in Milton, Massachusetts, Rose had married Mitchell Collins. She was described as an office worker. He was a businessman.

Realising that tears were creeping from the corners of her eyes, Evanne turned towards Serena and smiled. 'Oh, my God, it's her,' she said. 'It's definitely her.'

Serena leaped from the bed and hugged her. The two of them jumped and whooped and squealed and generally behaved like a pair of five-year-olds until Tilly appeared, wondering what in the name of God was going on.

Evanne could barely remember returning to Dolmen Crescent. She might have levitated. No sooner was she in the door than she was sitting with her iPad on her knee. *Rose Collins*, *Boston* she tapped. A site that specialised in finding people revealed that there were twenty-four matches for that name in Massachusetts. Two were described as being in their sixties. One lived in Milton. Hands trembling, she tapped for more information. Within seconds, there it was. There *she* was. Rose Annalisa Collins, 64 Amber Street, Milton, MA 02186. A map showed that Milton was on the outskirts of Boston. Also listed at the Amber Street address were Mitchell J. Collins, Robert F. Collins and Brooke M. Collins. So she was still married to Mitchell. That was good. After the grimness of Carrigbrack, Evanne hoped she was having a happy life. Robert and Brooke must be her children. Her other children.

The whys and what-abouts, the mad illogicality of it all, didn't matter. She had found her mother's mother. She had found her mother's brother and sister. She wanted to do more searching. She wanted to dance around the room. What were the chances that Brooke – such an American name! – and Robert were on Facebook or Twitter or Instagram or *something*? Before she did anything else, though, Evanne picked up her phone and called her mother. This totally counted as an emergency.

# CHAPTER 19

Voice low, muscles taut, ears closed to distractions, Martha began her story. Beside her, Paudie appeared impassive but engaged. Another glass of wine had appeared, and while it was probably one more than was sensible, she was reassured by its presence. Besides, it was a bit late in the day to start worrying about what was sensible. She was glad they'd arranged to meet in a pub. She couldn't get emotional here.

'I suppose,' she said, 'it took me a couple of months to face up to the truth. I'd missed two periods, and for a while I kidded myself it was because I was upset. Upset about us splitting up, you know? "You're all over the place," I said. "Of course your body is playing up." Anyway, Cat twigged that something was wrong. As soon as I told her, she was out the door and off to the chemist's. Ten minutes later, she was standing in front of me waving a pregnancy test. Actually, she bought two or three of the things. "To be sure, to be sure," as she said herself. Needless to say, the tests were positive.' Martha took a mouthful of wine. 'Cat was amazing. If it was up to me, I would've stayed in bed, sobbing and being useless. Right from the off, she was on my case. "You've got to decide what you want to do, and then you've got to do it," she said. "If you're going to have an abortion, there's no time for messing about."'

Paudie traced a finger down the side of his pint glass. 'Why didn't you ring me?'

'I thought about it. Well, I did more than think about it. Several times, I lifted the phone. Once, I followed through and dialled the number. One of the Noels answered. He said you were in Cork or somewhere. I was going to try again, but something always held me back. I was fairly sure you wouldn't see it as good news. You'd just walked away. You were talking about London. The whole world was coming alive for you.'

'Yeah, only—'

'Believe me, Paudie, I weighed it all up. A small part of me thought, *You never know* . . . But a far bigger part said, *Don't involve him. It's your mess, deal with it.*'

'It was my mess too. I won't pretend I would've danced down O'Connell Street with delight, but I would have coped. I would have helped you.'

'I hear you. Just say, though . . . Just say you'd decided to do the "decent thing" and we'd stayed together. Would either of us have been happy? I don't think so. I would have felt guilty. You would have felt tied down. It would never have worked. The problem was . . .' She hesitated. Strangely, the words on her tongue were the hardest to say.

'The problem was, Paudie, I was in love with you. And you weren't in love with me. What a terrible situation it would've been, for you, for me and for the baby.'

Momentarily he closed his eyes. 'You never said that back then. The love part, I mean.'

'Did I need to? Wasn't it obvious? I presumed that was one of the reasons you broke up with me. It had become more than a bit of a laugh. It had for me, at any rate. You weren't interested in that sort of commitment. And I don't blame you.'

'I wish you'd told me about being pregnant, though.' Paudie looked at Martha, his brown gaze unwavering. 'I wouldn't have stopped you having an abortion, but I was entitled to know what was happening.'

'Yes, you were. I'm sorry. And I'm sorry it's taken me this long to talk to you. At the time I was all over the place. I was overwhelmed. And I told myself I was saving you from a difficult decision. Later, I convinced myself that you were better off not knowing. It's only in recent months that I've come to realise I was wrong.'

'You never considered keeping the baby? Bringing it up on your own? Or—'

'Or putting the child up for adoption? I know, I know, given my own story, you'd think it would've been the logical choice. But the truth was, I wanted everything to go away. I was disgusted with myself for letting my life become so messy. Pregnancy was meant to be this magical, romantic state, but what

I felt most was panic. I wanted to start afresh. I remember, and no doubt this sounds insane, I remember doing a deal with God. "Get me through this," I said, "and I'll be a different person, a good person." At the time, I thought a lot about my birth mother. I presumed she was caught in a similar situation. But at least I had choices. I made my own decision. I doubt she was so fortunate.'

Paudie took a mouthful of his pint. 'I take it you didn't tell your parents?'

'No, not then and not since. Can you imagine? Back in 'ninety-two there would've been ructions about me being pregnant. Mam probably thinks I was a virgin on my wedding day.' Paudie raised an eyebrow. 'Okay, I'm exaggerating, but not much. She certainly wouldn't have approved of any involvement with you. No matter that you're on the telly, in her book you'll always be the little pup who teased me at school. And never in a million years could I have told her I'd had an abortion. She'd have been devastated.'

'I understand. What I don't get is why you didn't tell Dermot. I mean, obviously he doesn't know about the two of us. But you were married for – what? – fourteen or fifteen years? Were you never tempted to tell him you'd had an abortion?'

'Dermot hasn't a clue, and that's the way I'd like it to stay. Not, I suppose, that it matters much any more.'

He gave a small nod. 'Did you go to London?'

'Mmm.'

For as long as Martha could remember, Irish people had been shouting at each other about abortion. When she was a child, listening to the news had been like taking a course in advanced gynaecology. She recalled eating her dinner while a fractious discussion about fallopian tubes, ovaries and zygotes played out in the background. Finally, her mam had decided she'd had enough. 'There's no need for that sort of thing, not at this hour of the day,' she'd declared, as she turned off the radio.

'Did Cat go to London with you?' asked Paudie.

'She offered, but I said I'd be okay. I got the ferry to Holyhead, then the train into Euston and made my way from there. The clinic was up around Finsbury Park, I remember. I stayed the night in a guest house and . . . and the next day I came home again.'

For a moment, they were distracted by a small florid-faced man, who bounced over to their table with advice for Paudie. 'If you don't mind me saying so, what you need are bigger guests. Like that Graham Norton. His show gets great guests. The fellow's had half of Hollywood on his sofa.' Paudie put on a polite face. Unfortunately, the man spoke in the sort of run-on sentences that make it impossible to interject. Martha came to the rescue.

'Do you mind?' she said, as she gave him her best squinty-eyed stare. 'My friend is too polite to tell you to go away and leave us alone, but I'm not.'

Paudie sent her a look that was one part embarrassment to three parts relief, and the man stumbled off, no doubt to tell his friends that Paudie Carmody had very unusual taste in women.

'You mightn't like this question,' he said, 'but have you ever regretted the abortion?'

Sometimes Martha feared she'd spent so many years listening to people on the radio telling her how she ought to feel that her actual feelings had got lost. She tried to give an honest answer. 'In the immediate aftermath of it all, I was a wreck. I felt like such a failure, like I'd let everybody down. I used to sit in the dark, listening to music . . . the same tapes over and over again. There's a Joan Armatrading song, "The Weakness In Me" – Cat says that if she ever hears it again, she'll know she's died and gone to Hell. And now . . . it's like part of me says, no, no regrets. But at the same time, I find it difficult to talk about it all without getting upset.' Martha's eyes were watering and she willed the tears to stop. 'Do I believe the fires of Hell are waiting for me? No. But I can't say I never think about the baby either. He, or she, would be twenty-one now.'

'Not much younger than we were back then.'

'Mad, huh? I suppose the straightest answer is, no, I don't regret having an abortion, but I do regret not telling you.' A tear dribbled down her face and she reached into her bag for a tissue. 'Sorry, I swore I wouldn't do this. I don't want to embarrass you.' The memory of those months remained vivid. Despite Cat's support, what Martha remembered most was the loneliness. The constant, stinging loneliness.

Paudie stared at his pint, and for a short time they said nothing. Other conversations crept back into focus. Two men discussed the situation in the Middle East. 'Honest to God,' one said, 'there's some nights when watching the news is like watching the Old Testament.'

Two women, their speech thick with alcohol, argued about a man: 'Don't get ratty with me, Sandra. I don't like the guy and you won't change my mind.'

Martha could only hope that nobody had been listening to her. She was also struck by a sensation of something being slightly off beam. Oh, it was hard to be precise . . . but shouldn't Paudie be more worked up about what he'd just heard? Sure, he had questioned her, tested her, but she'd anticipated a more impassioned response. She blotted away another tear and scrunched the tissue into her jacket pocket. 'So—'

Paudie reached over and tapped her wrist. 'Listen, Martha, I wasn't going to tell you this. I'm still not sure that I should. But, to use the modern phrase, in the interests of full disclosure . . .'

'Go on.'

'I already knew about the abortion. I've known for years.'

An electric current went skittering down Martha's back. Or, at least, that was what it felt like. 'I'm sorry?'

'Richie Lyons told me. God, it must be a decade ago now. I bumped into him at something or other, and we went for a drink. I hadn't seen the lad in for ever, so we got trashed. Absolutely twisted. Pints, shots, kebabs, the whole lot. At some point, he blurted it out.'

Martha waited for Paudie to elaborate.

'Cat had told him. She'd sworn him to secrecy, only you know what Richie's like. He always was a blabber.'

'I didn't know Cat had told him.' Martha's words were all strange and disconnected. 'She never said.'

'I can see how taken aback you are. There was nothing malicious about it, though. He just figured I should know. He's a grand fellow, Richie. I'm only sorry I don't see more of him.'

'Why didn't you tell me you already knew?'

'Tonight? I'd half an idea you were going to talk about it. When it turned out I was right, I wanted to hear your explanation.'

'And before? I can't understand why you didn't confront me years ago.'

'I considered it, you can be sure I did. For a while, I was raging.' Paudie ran his tongue around his teeth. 'But what would've been the point in creating a fuss? Would it have made me feel better? Hardly. There you were with Dermot and your little girl, perfectly happy as far as I knew. Oh, and Venus was pregnant at the time. Things between us were never that smooth, so the last thing my life needed was more hassle. And then . . . well, anger dims, doesn't it?'

A flurry of thoughts hit Martha. Some women told their husbands everything, but for Cat to have told Richie about the abortion wasn't right. No wonder she hadn't wanted Martha to speak to Paudie. She'd known she'd be rumbled. Just as Martha was about to ask another question, she heard her phone jingle-jangling in her coat pocket.

'I'd better check that,' she said, with an apologetic shrug, 'for fear anything's wrong at home.'

'Fire ahead.'

'Hi, love, is everything all right?' she asked.

Evanne squealed down the phone. A rush of words followed. She'd solved the mystery, she said. She'd found Rose. She was in some place near Boston and she was married with two children and wasn't it amazing and why hadn't her mum answered the phone earlier because this was the third time Evanne had called and what if there'd been a genuine emergency and—

'Whoa,' said Martha. 'Calm down, Evanne. I'll be home soon.'

'You've got to come home now. Like, it's still early in America. You can call her.'

'No, Evanne. I can't. That's the last thing I'm going to do. I'll be with you shortly, okay?'

'Why don't you care that I've found her? What's wrong with you?'

'Nothing's wrong with me, and of course I care. Like I—' She realised her daughter had hung up.

Paudie gave her a look, as if to say, 'What was that all about?' When she told him, he said simply, 'Time to go home.'

'But—'

He handed Martha her coat. 'We can talk again. I'll call you.'

# CHAPTER 20

In the taxi, Martha attempted to compose herself. As excited as she was about Evanne's news, she was also annoyed that her daughter had gone ahead and traced Rose on her own. Alongside this, she was grappling with the evening's other revelation: Cat had betrayed her. Was that too strong a word? No, she decided, it wasn't. Her oldest friend had betrayed her. She tried to focus on Evanne and on Rose, but her thoughts kept switching back to Paudie and the calm way he'd handled the situation. She'd thought her confession would make her feel better, but now she didn't know what to think or how to behave. She wished she hadn't cried. Crying never achieved anything. Four glasses of wine hadn't helped. Dear God, four glasses of wine. Or had it been five? What had possessed her? It occurred to Martha that she must be drunk. Not room-spinning drunk, but drunk all the same. She gave the taxi driver too much money and darted up the path.

'Glad you were able to make it,' said Evanne.

'I'll put the kettle on,' said Martha, 'and you can tell me all about your discovery.' She hoped she sounded bright and unfazed. 'Why didn't you tell me what you were doing?'

'I thought you'd lost interest.'

'No, love, we talked about this. I explained to you that I needed more time. I was neglecting everything else . . . in the same way that, maybe, you've been neglecting your homework.'

Immediately, Martha knew she'd made a mistake. Evanne, who'd been lolling against the kitchen door, snapped to attention. 'Give me a break, would you?' she said. 'How can you think that writing down a load of old guff – guff I'm never going to use – is more important than finding our own flesh and blood?'

'That wasn't what I said.' Already Martha's head was thudding. She reached for the teabags. Her daughter began patrolling the room, up and down, round and about, in figures of eight, until Martha was dizzy. She wasn't able for a show of teenage pyrotechnics.

'This was meant to be a present for you, a distraction from Dad and Layla and Alex, a reason to get excited. You know the day we went to Carrigbrack? That was the best day ever. I'm sorry I got all teary and everything, but shit happens. And when we were reading the adoption websites? That was cool too. It felt like what we were doing actually mattered. But, hey, what do I know? Because, by the look of you, you don't give a rat's ass. You go out drinking. You can't be bothered to answer your phone. And when you do come home you nag me about my fucking homework. You totally know how to suck the magic out of things.'

Martha slammed the mugs against the counter. 'That's enough, Evanne. I know you're upset, but you're not being fair.'

'Yeah, right. You want to know what's not fair? I went to loads of trouble to give you a fantastic surprise, and you don't even care. This should've been a brilliant day, and you've gone and ruined it.'

Martha saw tears in her daughter's eyes. 'I'm sorry,' she said. 'I'm sorry.' How many times had she used that word tonight?

'Honestly,' said Evanne, her face wet now, her voice shrill. 'Honestly, I never want to get old if it means being like you.'

'Please, love. I really am sorry and I really do want to hear about Rose.'

'Whatever.' The word was accompanied by a *glug*, indicating that Evanne was on the brink of a full-blown wail.

Martha tried to embrace her. At first she resisted but eventually she succumbed, whimpering and weeping and hiccuping until all of her anger and emotion was spent. For five, ten minutes, there they stood, in the middle of the kitchen, one sobbing and shaking, the other urging her to stop.

'Come on,' said Martha, 'we'll sit down and talk about it.'

'Sorry,' started Evanne. There was still a catch in her voice. 'I didn't mean what I said about not wanting to be like you. I got all upset and—'

'Ssh. There's no need for an apology. I should've been here earlier, and I shouldn't have prattled on about your homework. There I am, the woman who hates nagging, and I end up sounding like my own mother.'

Evanne gave a tiny smile of acknowledgement.

'And for fear I didn't say it, well done you. Where would I be without you spurring me on, huh? Will you tell me everything?'

'Of course I will.'

Martha squeezed her daughter's hand. 'I was wondering . . . I'm not working tomorrow. What if I wrote you a note for school and you stayed at home so we can write to Rose?'

'For real?'

'Like you say, it's very important.'

'Thanks, Mum,' said Evanne, a proper smile breaking across her beautiful face, the face she might have inherited from a woman in America. 'You won't regret it. I promise.'

In the morning, Martha settled on a career for her daughter. 'A private detective,' she said. 'That's what you ought to be. You're my own Nancy Drew.'

Evanne tapped the side of her head. 'I'm not a complete airhead, you know.'

'Tuh. Who said you were? No child of mine could be anything other than smart.'

The two were back at the kitchen table, laptop open, paper and pen at the ready. Evanne had already been through Facebook. She'd found two people she reckoned were the right Brooke and Robert Collins. If she was correct, Brooke was married with two children and worked in public relations. Given her own unhappy flirtation with PR, this made Martha smile. Robert, or Bobby as he appeared to be known, was a teacher. Nowhere on either page could they find a photo of Rose. Both Martha and Evanne kept returning to the pictures of Brooke and Bobby. Was there a family likeness? Evanne insisted there was. Her mother wasn't so sure.

Martha remained frayed from the night before but was doing her best to hide it. She would have to talk to Cat. Not today, though. Today was a day for letter-writing.

Although she'd read about contacting a birth parent for the first time, actually doing it turned out to be quite a challenge. She wanted to be subtle yet clear; friendly but not needy.

Evanne thought she should be upfront. 'Why not tell the truth?' she asked.

'Because her husband might see the letter.'

'So?'

'What if she's never told him about me?'

'That's a massive secret. How would she be able to keep it to herself?'

'If you think about it, Cat's father managed to hide a girlfriend and two children. Compared to that . . .'

'. . . staying quiet about something that happened before you were married must be simple.'

'Besides, we're not a hundred per cent sure we've found the right woman.'

Evanne bristled. 'Are you doubting my fine detective work?'

*Damn*, thought Martha, who was desperate to avoid another scene. 'No, love. Of—'

'Chill, Mum. I'm only messing with you. Obviously, we're not a hundred per cent sure, but I reckon we've found our Rose. And when you think about it, there's a chance that Mitchell's your birth father. I mean, on the websites there are quite a few stories about people whose birth parents got married in the end.'

'It's funny, I was just wondering about that. With any luck, we're about to find out.'

For an hour or more, the two played around with words and phrases until finally they were both happy. They'd decided to keep it simple.

> Dear Rose,
>
> I hope this letter finds you well.
>
> This is your old friend, Josephine. Although we haven't seen each other in more than forty years, I often think about you, and I decided the time was right to get in touch. It would be great if we could write and catch up on old times.
>
> I'd love to hear how life has been treating you. I'm well, as is my daughter Evanne. I've told her about you and she says she'd really like to meet you. If that's not possible, a letter would be great.

I live in Dublin, these days. If you would like to contact me, this is my address:

6, Dolmen Crescent,

Milltown,

Dublin 6.

All my love,

Josephine

PS I'm now known as Martha Sheeran, so if you do decide to write, that's the name to use.

'What now?' asked Evanne.

'Now we do some more waiting.'

'Do we have to? Like, what if I went back onto Facebook and asked Brooke and Bobby to be my friends?'

'You'll do no such thing.'

Evanne patted Martha's shoulder and laughed. 'It's okay, I'm only joking. You're easy to wind up today.'

'Actually, I'll tell you what we'll have to do. We'll have to pay a visit to Mam and Dad.'

'I've got exams next week.'

'Grand, but as soon as you're finished, we'll go to Templemorris for a couple of days. I don't want them thinking we're hiding something.'

# CHAPTER 21

'You're very quiet,' said Cat.

'I'm a quiet person.'

'Nah, something's up. Why don't you come on out with it?'

For several days, Martha had avoided Cat. She wanted to tell her friend about tracking down Rose but knew she'd also have to tackle her about Paudie and the abortion. She decided she needed time to calm down. Unfortunately, with every day that passed, her anger grew. Finally, she called, and they arranged to meet in a Ranelagh café.

That was where they were now, cappuccinos in front of them, awkwardness in the air.

Cat was delighted to hear about Rose. She was fascinated by the news about Brooke and Bobby. She had countless questions too. Would Martha go to America? Would Evanne go with her? And what would she say to Clem and Delia? Clearly, something about Martha's answers revealed she had more on her mind.

'Okay,' Martha said eventually. 'You're right. There is something else I need to say.'

To be fair to Cat, she made no attempt to dodge

the question. Yes, she said, she did confide in Richie. And, yes, he did tell Paudie. And, yes, Cat had been aware of this for the past ten years. She didn't, however, seem overly apologetic. 'I screwed up,' she said. 'Or, rather, Richie screwed up. He always says too much when he's drunk. But he didn't mean any harm.'

'Why didn't you talk to me?' asked Martha.

'I thought you were better off not knowing. I can't believe you went and met up with Paudie. That was dumb.'

'I don't think you're in any position to tell me what I should or shouldn't be doing.' She paused while a waitress swivelled past. 'You lied to me.'

'No, I didn't. I just didn't see any reason to go stirring up the past. I still don't.'

'You must have known the truth would surface eventually.'

'Sometimes it's best to move on. Let the past stay in the past.'

'You've changed your tune. How many times have you complained that I keep too much to myself? Not to mind all those speeches urging me to find my birth mother.'

'That's different. If you hadn't looked for her, you'd always have been wondering. But some information does more harm than good. Do you think Mam is better off for knowing about my dad's other family? Well, let me tell you, she's not. For her, ignorance was definitely bliss. All of her happy memories were wiped out.' Cat tucked her hair behind her ears. 'Answer me this: are you planning on seeing Paudie again?'

'As a matter of fact, he did say he'd call me.'

'I used to think the worst thing you could do was get back together with Dermot, but now that option's off the table, you're determined to find trouble elsewhere.'

Something within Martha stiffened. 'Oh, for God's sake, Cat. That's not what this is about. I've no interest in Paudie, and you can be damn sure he has no interest in me. I'm still amazed he was so calm about everything.'

'You must know he's single again. It's been all over the papers.'

'I don't read the sort of papers that waste ink on Paudie Carmody's love life.' That wasn't true. In the library, Martha often had a sneaky peek at the red tops, and she was usually up to date with Paudie's affairs. Somehow she'd missed the latest break-up. No wonder he'd been so reluctant to talk about himself.

'So you will be seeing him?'

'You know what? I don't think that's any of your business.'

'Yeah, but it will be when you turn up in a crumpled heap after he's let you down again.'

'Now you really are being stupid.'

Cat reached into her bag, took out a five-euro note and placed it on the table. 'There's no point in me sitting here if you won't listen to reason. I hope you hear from Rose soon.' With a loud scrape of her chair, she stood up. Aware that people were looking at them, Martha watched her go.

For another ten minutes, she stared into her empty cup. She was the one with the legitimate grievance. If anybody had had cause to stomp out, it was her. As soon as Cat calmed down, she'd understand this.

Wouldn't she?

Delia was wearing her wounded look. It was a look that made Martha squirm with guilt. Her dad's face was harder to read, but he was likely to be at one with her mam. *I should be wearing penitential purple*, she thought, *and a crown of thorns*. In the front room, the television glowed silently. Outside, children played football, the game punctuated by shrieks and roars. When Evanne was younger, she'd been left wide-eyed by the droves of boisterous boys and girls who congregated on the green patch near the Sheerans' house. In Dublin, childhood had become an organised affair, dominated by play-dates, classes and schemes. In Templemorris, youngsters were still free to play their own games.

Martha realised her mother was talking again. 'Sorry, Mam,' she said. 'I missed that. What did you say?'

'I said I don't know why you didn't tell us sooner.'

She had a point. Not only had Martha already told Cat, Dermot, Una and Paudie about her breakthrough, she'd also called the Laffertys and Pauline Bennis. She should have broken the news to her parents first. Not that she had any intention of admitting this. 'I promise you,' she said, 'I haven't been ignoring you. It all got so complicated that I didn't want to tell you over the phone. I wanted to wait until the two of us were able to come down and give you our news.'

'That's right, Nan,' said Evanne. 'We were dying to fill you in, only my exams got in the way. Isn't it fantastic that we've found Rose and written to her and everything?'

Delia, who seemed determined to nit-pick, shook her head. 'I have to say, it sounds like a funny story. What would an American woman have been doing around here in 1968? In those days, it was rare enough to meet someone from Dublin, not to mind the United States.'

'But isn't it exciting?' continued her granddaughter.

'If you ask me, Evanne, you're in danger of getting distracted from what matters – your schoolwork. I keep reading in the papers about the big demand for university places. You've a very important year ahead of you and you don't want to get left behind.'

Remembering how, thirty years earlier, she'd sat in the very same chair and listened to her mother pour cold water on the notion of girls going to college, Martha smiled. Her mam's anger had no walls. She was annoyed with Martha so she had to be annoyed with everybody. If there was fault to be found, she'd find it.

'And those jeans,' Delia was saying now, as she cast a narrow eye over Evanne's carefully shredded black denims, 'I take it they were like that when you bought them?'

'Cool, aren't they?' replied Evanne.

'Your mother used to wear something similar. They looked ridiculous back in those days too.'

'Actually,' said Martha, 'mine were second-hand Levis 501s, and I ripped them myself. I've a feeling I still have them somewhere.'

Evanne gave her a funny look, like she wasn't sure whether to be impressed or appalled.

'Anyway, Mam,' continued Martha, 'don't you worry about Evanne's exams. She'll be fine. And in future I'll do a better job of keeping you informed about our search for Rose.'

'What I don't understand,' said Clem, 'is how you heard about this Rose lady to begin with.'

'We met this a-may-zing old woman, and she told us about her,' replied Evanne. 'You see we went to Carrigbrack and—'

'Hold on a minute,' said Delia. 'What were you doing above in Carrigbrack?'

While the question was directed at Martha, it was Evanne who replied. She explained how they'd travelled to north Clare because they'd wanted to see where Martha was born. 'It was terrible, Nan. Shameful. What went on in those homes was barbaric.'

The lines at the corner of Delia's mouth deepened. 'Listen, pet, I'm not saying I approve of everything the nuns did, but they weren't all bad. A lot of them meant well, and they did good work too.'

'Ah, Mam,' said Martha.

'Don't "Ah, Mam" me. You're putting modern-day values on a different time.'

'We're not talking about the Middle Ages. We're talking about forty years ago.'

Her mother sniffed. 'To listen to the pair of you, you'd think shameful behaviour was confined to the nineteen fifties and sixties. There's plenty of it now – cruelty to children and drug-taking and shootings and stabbings and the Lord knows what else. Not to mention all those girls going to England for abortions when there are thousands of couples who'd do anything for a child.' Martha twitched, but her mam was in full flow and didn't appear to notice. 'You should've had more sense than to take Evanne to Carrigbrack. I don't know what you were thinking of.'

'I'm glad we went,' said Evanne. 'You've got to remember, Nan, when Rose was locked up she was only a few months older than me.'

Clem cleared his throat. 'So by now Rose should have your letter?'

'I think so,' replied Martha.

'We'll have to wait and see what happens, then.'

'Thanks, Dad.'

'By the way,' he said, 'how's Dermot getting on?'

# CHAPTER 22

*Boston, May 2014*

Rose told herself she was being foolish. She told herself she was inviting trouble. But from the moment she saw the letter, she wanted to reply. First, she needed to think. She also needed to come up with an argument. So for several days it rested at the back of a drawer. No, that wasn't quite true. On numerous occasions, she removed it and re-read the looping script. She kept seeing new things, like the way her daughter had underlined her adoptive name and the way she had put a circle rather than a dot over the letter *i*.

For years, Rose had tried not to think about her elder daughter. She'd kidded herself that if she kept busy she might not feel the loss. She had focused on her other children, and then on her grandchildren. She cooked and polished, weeded and pruned. Not that her efforts were always successful. Frequently, she woke up thinking about Josephine. Where was she now? What did she look like? How had life turned out for her? Did she have children of her own? And would she understand why her mother had let her go? Rose could have found out about her daughter. There were ways and means. But she'd agreed with Mitch that she wouldn't go picking at the sores of the past.

If asked about her children, she said what she needed to say. 'I have two,' she would reply, 'one boy, one girl.' Behind her back, she kept her fingers crossed.

In Boston it was hard to avoid references to Ireland; in Milton it was impossible. This was a suburb where the coffee shops sold Barry's tea and the bars served Jameson; where the devout placed statues of the Virgin Mary in the yard and everybody celebrated St Patrick's Day. Yet, for decades, Rose had tried to distance herself from the country where she'd spent the most wretched months of her life. If it popped up on the news – and back in the seventies and eighties Ireland was *always* on the news – she left the room. If a well-meaning acquaintance suggested a trip, she had a hundred excuses. 'Ireland?' she'd say. 'Oh, we don't have the money right now. Besides, I don't think the kids would like it there.' Somewhere along the line, however, her fear had burned out. She could hear about the place without feeling like the air had been squeezed from her lungs.

These days, it felt like every time she turned on the TV, a pop-psychologist was pontificating about 'living in the now' and 'seizing the day'. 'Never look back,' they said. God love their innocence.

Did they not realise that sometimes life forced you to look back?

As she considered the letter, Rose wondered why Josephine, or Martha as she must learn to call her, had chosen to write now. She hoped it wasn't because her daughter was ill or facing some sort of crisis. But what if that was the case? Then, it was doubly important that they make contact. Rose knew that the laws in Ireland remained strict and that adopted children had few entitlements. Somebody somewhere must have spoken out of turn. Still, as she ran a finger over Martha's words, she was hit by an almost forgotten sensation. It was excitement, she guessed.

Convincing Mitch she should reply was another matter. Eventually, on Wednesday evening, one of those perfect May evenings when the magnolias are in bloom and it feels like winter has finally given up, she told him. They were in the lounge. Rose was perched at the edge of the pale blue couch. Her husband was in his leather armchair, a tumbler of whiskey and that day's *Globe* at his side.

Despite the letter's cryptic nature, he immediately grasped its significance. He was a clever man, was Mitch. And, in many ways, a kind one. How often had Rose told herself that he was better than she deserved?

'I take it you're not going to do anything about this,' he said.

'Actually, no,' she replied. 'I think I am.'

Mitch straightened his spine. 'I don't understand. I thought we had an agreement.'

'We agreed I wouldn't seek her out. This is different.'

He said nothing, and Rose had to resist the urge to fill the silence. To start wheedling. *Give him time*, she thought.

'I don't know that you've thought this through,' he said eventually.

She couldn't tell him that she'd thought about little else for days. 'I'd like to see her. Or, if that's not possible, to talk to her. I want to know something about her.'

'If you wait a little while, you might change your mind.'

'I'm pretty sure I won't,' she said, her voice low.

'What'll you tell Brooke and Bobby?'

'The truth. Well, not the whole truth. Obviously, not the whole truth.'

'And Josephine or . . .?'

'Martha.' Rose liked saying the name. *Martha. Martha. Martha.* Somehow, it made her feel closer to her daughter. 'I'll tell her something similar.'

Rose had learned to think of the truth as layered. At the very bottom, there was the full unvarnished version. Overlying it were different portrayals of events she could recite when required. For more than forty years, she had lived in a world of concoctions and evasions, of slight obfuscations and outright lies. Sometimes she suspected that the real and the imaginary had fused in her brain. Perhaps that explained her faulty memory. Her memories of Ireland were particularly unreliable. Something small, like the piercing voice of a nun or the colour of the nursery floor, would come back to her with complete clarity. Then she'd try to recall something momentous, like her last day in Carrigbrack, and the memory would be cloudy and indistinct.

Mitch was asking a question. 'Are you sure?' he was saying. 'Are you completely sure?'

'I am.'

Mitch ran both hands through his thick fair hair. Whatever else had changed about him, Rose's husband still had the hair of a young man. 'Are you not worried how Brooke and Bobby will react?'

'Yes,' she said. 'The same way I once worried how you would react. But we got through it.'

'That was a very long time ago, Rose.'

'I never thought I'd want to tell them. It's just . . . It feels like the right thing to do, you know? Carrigbrack, and everything afterwards . . . Well, like you say, it was a long time ago.' She rubbed her neck. 'It'll all be easier to handle now.'

'I'm not sure you appreciate how difficult this might get,' said Mitch.

Later, Rose called Brooke and Bobby. She'd considered waiting, mulling over the situation for another day or two, but she feared her resolve would falter. Both were puzzled by her request to see them.

'Saturday?' said Bobby. 'Like, three days from now?'

'Yes,' said Rose. 'You will be there, won't you?'

'Sure. You're okay, aren't you?'

'I'm fine. I'll explain when I see you.'

Brooke, too, asked if she was ill.

'No, don't worry,' Rose replied. 'Something has come up, and I'd like to talk to you about it. That's all.'

She knew her daughter was dissatisfied with her vague response. So be it. Telling Brooke and Bobby together would be easier. As would talking to them without their partners. Just the thought of Chris's questions and Ashley's uncomprehending stare made her shiver.

Was Martha like Bobby or Brooke? she wondered. Did she retain any trace of her mother – or her father – or had she been remoulded by her upbringing? Rose couldn't help but notice that while the letter referred to a daughter, there was no mention of a husband. Nor did she mention a job. Rose hoped Martha had received a decent education. Ireland hadn't struck her as a place where the schooling of girls was a high priority. According to the newspapers, everything had changed. Ireland was different now, they said, the Catholic Church as troubled there as it was in Boston. She had read some of the reports about abuse in religious institutions, about cruelty and deprivation, about how the authorities had manipulated and minimised, ducked and deflected. She wasn't surprised. How could she be?

As much as she wanted to talk to Martha, there

were parts of her life Rose didn't wish to discuss. Over the decades, she had honed her act. If you asked neighbours or acquaintances, no doubt they'd describe her as solid, capable, respectable. Good Lord, how she hated that word. It was strange, really: respect was such a powerful word. It suggested esteem, dignity, honour. But respectable? It implied something more supine. Something unpleasant. It described a family who thought nothing of banishing their daughter to another country and stealing her child. If you probed a little more, those same neighbours might say that sometimes she was too brusque; that she didn't always make eye contact; that she could be diffident, distracted.

In many ways, Rose had the perfect life. The Collins family lived in a large colonial house with a flower-filled garden in a suburb of tree-lined streets. Every year, one magazine or other put Milton on its list of best places to live in America. She had two loving, accomplished children and a husband for whom she cared a great deal. And yet she always felt she was just a slide or a stumble away from losing it all. There were times when sadness hovered over her, like birds over landfill; when she believed she might be overwhelmed by darkness; when her head went places where others couldn't follow. Dank, distressing places.

Following her phone calls to Bobby and Brooke, she spoke again to Mitch. He had misgivings, he said. Many misgivings. She assured him that she was in control.

'If you're determined to put yourself through this,' he said, 'then I can't stop you. But please be careful.'

For the next two days, she scuttled about the house, desperate to keep herself occupied. She polished the silver; she washed the windows; she folded and refolded every towel and sheet in the closet. Every so often, she stopped to re-read Martha's letter.

On Saturday morning, she went to her local salon for a blow-out. Call her vain, but good hair gave her a feeling of control. Afterwards she strolled back to Amber Street, her brain taking off in a hundred different directions.

While the beauty of Rose's youth had faded, she remained elegant. She didn't want to end up like her sister, Nancy, a woman with a chin for every day of the week and a spare one for Sunday. Neither did she want to look like those waxy, perma-shocked women who spent their lives flicking through the rails in Barneys and Neiman Marcus. To her, that was just a different kind of ugly.

Joe Brennan was prominent in her thoughts. Many years had passed since she'd been able to talk about him. Sometimes she doubted her memories of their days together. Had they really been that golden? Had she honestly been that ambitious, that *happy*? Or was her brain playing tricks on her?

Still, this wasn't the time to obsess about such things. She would talk to Brooke and Bobby, and she would write to Martha. The time had come for Rose to open up about her past. Or part of it, at least.

# CHAPTER 23

*Limerick and Dublin, May 2014*

The first thing Martha noticed about Malachy McCracken was that he was horrifyingly young. The second was his air of enthusiasm. Maybe she was being unfair, but she'd expected him to be less animated, dour even.

'Why wouldn't I be enthusiastic?' said the social worker, as he gestured to her to sit down. 'I've the best job in the place. I love reunions. Okay, not everything works out well. It's not all hugs and tears, like you see on the telly. But before this I was working with neglected children. Which job would you prefer?'

Malachy's office was like a scene from another television programme: the one about compulsive hoarders. Everywhere Martha looked, there were files, mountains of files. Some appeared to be in imminent danger of toppling over. His desk was strewn with scraps of paper, Post-it notes and yet more files.

The office was in Limerick, and Martha had left a disgruntled Evanne in Dublin. 'You can't come with me all the time,' she'd said. 'You've got school, and you can spend a couple of hours with your dad, Layla and Alex. They'd like that.' Evanne had muttered something about Alex being the only person who was happy to see her. Martha had pretended not to hear. 'You'll be the first to know what happens,' she'd promised.

'Right then,' said Malachy. 'Obviously we would prefer if you'd waited and conducted your search through the official channels. However, I can tell you . . .' He paused as though waiting for a drum roll. 'I can tell you that you've found the right woman.'

Martha threw back her head and clapped with delight. 'Seriously?'

'Seriously. According to the paperwork, your birth mother is listed as Rose Annalisa Moroney of Milton, Massachusetts. We didn't have an up-to-date address for her, but the address you've given me tallies with the one we unearthed.'

'Thank you,' she said. 'Thank you. Thank you. Thank you.' She was beginning to see why Malachy liked his job. She was also surprised to discover that she was tingling with excitement. Thinking she had found her biological mother was pleasing. Knowing was another matter entirely. For the first time it really, truly hit her: her birth mother was American.

Across the desk, Malachy looked amused by her giddy response. 'You do know the road ahead could be a rough one,' he said. Martha listened while he warned that it might take Rose a long time to respond. That was if she did respond. He spoke about not all reunions ending happily, and about the need for support from family and close friends.

Her spirits dipped. She wished Cat was there. Or at the other end of a phone line. Three weeks had passed since their argument in the café. The thing was, although she longed to pass on her news, Martha wasn't prepared to make the first move. She had no intention of grovelling. Not when she was in the right. She consoled herself with the knowledge that they'd fallen out before. Once, in their mid-twenties, they'd gone for more than a month without speaking. And at least they'd had the decency to argue about something of significance. Her mother and a neighbour, Mona Killeen, had ignored each other for eighteen months following a row about the correct way to trim a hedge.

As she tuned back in, Malachy was talking about people's differing attitudes to the past. Sometimes, he said, people were plain confused. One lie had spawned another until the truth had got lost. Others were anxious to talk; they found it cathartic. More would rather forget. 'Even now,' he said, 'I meet men and women who don't want to admit that their family behaved badly or that anybody got hurt.'

'My mam's like that. Not, obviously, that she behaved badly, but she gets defensive about the way things worked back then.'

'She's not alone. And, in my experience, nothing is too strange or unlikely. You wouldn't believe some of the stuff that went on.'

'Just one other question,' said Martha. 'I was wondering if you'd found out anything about . . .'

'Your birth father?'

'Yes.'

Malachy rubbed his beard. 'I'm sorry,' he said. 'There's nothing. Not a word.'

When Evanne arrived at her dad's apartment, it looked as though a small tornado had passed through. A sour smell drifted from the kitchen and, on the baby monitor, Alex was grizzling. Layla was flat out on the sofa.

'Will I . . .?' asked Evanne.

'Whatever you like,' she said. 'You're very good with him. Don't worry, though, I'm sure he's fine. Believe me, if there was anything wrong, he'd let rip. He howled like something possessed last night. I was in and out to his room half a dozen times, and I couldn't figure out what was wrong. It's so frustrating when they can't tell you. That's why I'm lying here now. I didn't get a wink of sleep.'

Alex wasn't exactly smelly but he was a little damp, so Evanne changed him and put him down for a nap. Then she tidied up. If her mum could have seen her, she'd have corpsed with laughter. Housework was not Evanne's thing. While she worked, Layla lay there, throwing shade at Justine Winstanley. Evanne didn't know if the barbs were meant to be funny, but more than once she had to stop herself giggling.

'I bet the wizened old cow is sleeping with someone powerful,' Layla declared, 'and I'm going to find out who.'

In the autumn, Justine would continue to present *Live at Four* full time. Layla had been offered her old slot doing Pilates. Actually, it was worse than that. She'd been asked if she would do a spot of yoga instead because it was more fashionable nowadays. Evanne's dad wanted her to accept. Layla said she'd rather work on the back of a bin lorry.

'Justine suits the *Live at Four* demographic, apparently,' she continued. 'No wonder half of the people at work refer to it as *Dead by Five*.'

'Can't Dad do something about it?'

'You're assuming he cares.' Evanne must have looked taken aback because Layla quickly added, 'I was on a short-term contract, so the bosses can do whatever they like. If they want a new presenter, be it Justine Winstanley or Francis the Talking Mule, that's their right.'

Evanne had always reckoned that Layla had a streak of madness. She'd said as much to her mother, who'd laughed and said, 'Don't we all?' At the moment, though, her behaviour was especially odd. One minute she was angry, the next all squashed and silent.

In Evanne's experience, most women were total bores about their babies. Layla, on the other hand, seemed frightened of Alex. When she did talk about him, it was to ask a question. Is he hungry? Is he sick? Why won't he stop crying? Evanne wondered if she was suffering from post-natal depression. But, if that was the case, wouldn't she be tearful? Also, if there was anything seriously wrong, her dad would be on the case, surely.

Whatever was going on with his mother, Alex was thriving. He was still fond of a good wail but he'd also picked up a couple of new sounds, including a lovely gurgle. He was more alert too. Evanne was convinced he recognised her, which was pretty cool.

When she'd finished tidying, she offered to do Layla's make-up. Nothing sparkly or sexy, just a nice natural look. Although she said so herself, Evanne was good at hair and make-up. And Layla was an ideal model. She had a few wrinkles around her eyes, but they were only teeny things, not like her mother's lines, which spread halfway across her face when she smiled.

Thankfully, Layla accepted her offer. If she looked more like her real self, maybe she might act that way too. It was beyond strange to see her in a crumpled hoodie and bootleg jeans. The last time bootlegs were fashionable, Evanne was sitting in a high chair, eating puréed carrot and drinking from a sippy cup. Honestly, Layla was one step away from going to the shops in her pyjamas. Even her voice was slipping. When she was on the telly, she was all 'How now brown cow'. In real life her voice was more – how should Evanne put this? – rural. Evanne's dad claimed that Layla's home town was so tiny it made Templemorris look like Las Vegas. As she ripped into Justine Winstanley, she sounded like a complete mucksavage. On top of that, she never bothered to update her Instagram or Twitter or Facebook. Even if she didn't want to post pictures of herself, there was no reason why she couldn't put up some photos of Alex. How else would people know she was still alive?

A couple of the magazines had wanted to do a mother-and-baby photo-shoot, but Layla said they'd only ask her about *Live at Four* and she didn't want the hassle. Evanne had seen lots of these features. Invariably, the new mother gushed about being 'the luckiest woman alive' and 'truly blessed'. Right then, it was difficult to imagine Layla coming out with the appropriate lines.

Evanne should have been doing her schoolwork, but, with so much else happening, she didn't have the headspace. Her mum had called from Limerick to say they'd found the right Rose. Fizzing with excitement, she considered telling Layla. Then she remembered her snarky comments about their search. She decided that just having the information, hugging it to herself, was enough.

She had a bad feeling about her exams. Serena said that if she wasn't careful she'd end up in a class with the thicks. There weren't many thicks in St Attracta's. According to Evanne's father, the fees were so expensive that unless you aced all your exams there was no point in going there. 'You'd be as well off in a community school, learning how to roll joints and fill out social welfare forms,' he said. Evanne knew he was joking, but it wasn't one of his better efforts. After all, her mum, Una and Cat had gone to a community school. As had Cat's husband, Richie – and Paudie Carmody.

Some days, Evanne felt like she could do anything. Like she had endless choices. Like she was soaring. Others, she was grounded by fear. Worried that Serena, who was friendly with everybody, would ditch her for one of the *über*-popular girls, like Sorcha McWilliams or Sophie Cooper. Frightened she'd be a big ugly failure with a wage-slave job. Terrified that nobody sexy or interesting would like her and that she'd end up on her own or with some loser who was nasty and abusive. Or – and, yes, she did feel bad about this – she worried she'd wind up like her mother, with a so-so job, a barren social life (there'd been no repeat of the 'old friend' date) and a general sense that life hadn't worked out as planned. Still, she guessed Layla didn't want to hear any of that. Not right now.

While Evanne patted on foundation and concealer, Layla revealed that her thirtieth birthday was only a month away.

'And I'll be seventeen,' she replied. It was not a smart move.

'You don't know how lucky you are,' said Layla.

'Make the most of the next few years because after that it's all downhill. Everything gets out of control.'

Evanne hated to hear older people drone on about life being tough. She was sure they could still have adventures if that was what they wanted. Instead, they chose to let their lives become dull; to do what they thought was expected of them. 'You don't mean that,' she said, 'not when you've got Alex and my dad and everything. And you'll get a new job soon. Everybody knows you're brilliant.'

'Thanks, sweetie.' Layla patted her hand. 'Listen, don't pay any heed to anything I've said, especially the stuff about Justine. I needed to let off steam. Alex's conversation skills aren't great, and your dad's hardly ever here. I promise you, everything's fine.'

Evanne wished she believed her.

It was early evening by the time Martha got back to Dublin. The house was quiet. For a while, she sat on the stairs and thought. When Evanne left, this was what it would be like all the time. As usual, flyers for gyms and takeaways were puddled beside the door. She bent to pick them up. Underneath there were two white envelopes, one a bank statement, the other an electricity bill. At the very bottom there was a smaller white envelope. The name and address were in unfamiliar handwriting. The stamps were American.

Was it physically possible for the heart to skip a beat? Martha wasn't sure, but that was exactly how it felt. Carefully, she tore the top of the envelope. Then she sat down again and read.

My dear Martha,
Thank you for your letter. You have no idea how delighted I was to hear from you and to learn something about your life. I don't know how you found me, but I'm very glad you did.

Writing this letter is hard, not because I don't know what to say to you, but because there's so much I want to say. I find it impossible to know what to include and what to leave for another day. Until I started to write, I didn't appreciate how difficult it is to put emotions into words. The most important thing is this: I have never forgotten you. In more than forty-five years – how can it be so long? – there hasn't been one day when you weren't in my thoughts.

In many ways, life has been kind to me. I've been married to Mitch for just over forty years. We have two grown children, Brooke and Bobby, and Brooke has two sons, Daniel and Matt. It's fantastic to hear that I also have a granddaughter! Please give my love to Evanne. Please also give my love and thanks to your adoptive parents. It's a source of solace to me that you found a good and loving home.

I should let you know that while I told Mitch about you a long time ago, we decided not to tell Brooke and Bobby. To be honest, I never imagined you would come back into my life, and it seemed simpler not to say anything. With hindsight, this is something I regret. I told them about you today. As you might expect, they were surprised – and curious.

You must be wondering how a girl from Boston came to be in Ireland. The short answer is that when my parents discovered I was pregnant, they sent me there. Both my mom and dad were originally from Ireland. My dad was from County Clare, my mom from County Mayo. It's hard to imagine anybody doing such a thing today but, even in America, those were different times. I want you to understand that I would never have chosen to give you away. I was given no option. I know every mom says her baby is beautiful, but you truly, truly were. Saying goodbye to you broke my heart.

You probably have a thousand questions, and I hope that over time I can answer them. I would very much like to talk to you and Evanne. I'm including my telephone number at the bottom of this letter. If you would like to talk, please call at any time. I also hope that despite the miles between us we will be able to meet.

I'm enclosing two photographs, one from when I was younger, the other taken more recently.

Once again, Martha, I want to say how much your letter meant to me. I do hope I hear from you soon.

With all my love,

Rose

It took a couple of minutes for what she had read to register fully. Then Martha was struck by a series of emotions. Relief came first. She remembered how scared she'd been that Rose would spurn her approach. Instead she wanted to meet her. She felt exhilarated, thrilled that she'd finally get to hear something about her other family. And she felt sad. *I want you to understand that I would never have chosen to give you away*. Martha couldn't imagine a more poignant line. She tried to picture what it must have been like for a seventeen-year-old American to be wrenched from her home and sent to a bleak institution in the west of Ireland. It was true: other people's experiences might affect you, but nothing tore at the heart like your own story.

As she sat on the step, she realised that something was bothering her. Something struck her as not quite right, only she couldn't put her finger on it.

If the letter prompted a jumble of sensations, Rose's photograph hit Martha like a jab to the stomach. She saw why Winnie Lafferty had mistaken

Evanne for her grandmother. The intense blue eyes, the twists of brown hair, the wide smile: they were as familiar to Martha as her own face. The second photo was a family shot: an older Rose with a man who must be Mitch and two others she recognised as Brooke and Bobby. Now she saw some similarity between herself and her sister. She wouldn't claim the resemblance was overpowering. If anything, her half-brother and -sister, with their thin noses, cautious smiles and wheat-coloured hair, took after their father. It occurred to her that she must take after her own birth father, Mr Diagonal Line.

# CHAPTER 24

The instant Evanne read the letter, she wanted to call Rose. Martha managed to persuade her that this would be a poor idea.

'You saw how upset your nan was when she thought we were ignoring her,' she said. 'Before we do anything, we'll have to talk to her.'

After some minutes of sighing and hair-swishing, Evanne agreed.

Martha was relieved when her dad answered the phone. Her relief heightened when he told her that Delia was at a St Vincent de Paul committee meeting.

She told him everything she knew, which was relatively little.

There was a long pause while he considered his answer. Martha was about to ask if he was all right when finally he replied. 'Well, doesn't that beat all out?' he said, in his telephone voice, which was like his usual voice only much, much louder. (When he spoke to his brother in Liverpool, he practically roared the house down.) 'When are you going to talk to her?'

'Soon, I think. Don't worry, I promise we'll let you know what happens.'

It was the following evening before mother and daughter sat down to call America. After complex negotiations, they'd agreed that Martha would talk first. Later, she would hand the phone to Evanne, who had pledged to keep her questions to a minimum.

Tapping out the number, Martha was simultaneously terrified and excited. The phone rang once, twice, three times and then a woman's voice, a clear, firm voice, said, 'Hello.'

Martha was so overwhelmed she almost hung up. 'Is that Rose?' she asked. 'This is Martha.'

'Hello, Martha.' There was a pause, as if Rose was collecting herself. Then she said, 'I've been waiting a long time to talk to you. And now that I can, I don't know what to say. Could you speak so I can listen to your voice?'

'That's what I was going to say to you.'

Their words came in fits and starts. Occasionally they fell into silence, then they'd both speak together. It was slightly awkward. It was surreal. It was wonderful.

Martha told Rose that she wished she'd started searching years ago. She told her about Clem, Delia, Una and Evanne. She mentioned Dermot but didn't dwell on him. Of course she had questions of her own. Slowly, carefully, she brought up the question of her father. She learned that his name was Joe. Joe Brennan.

'A good Irish name,' said Rose, 'for a good Irish-American boy. Not that he was good enough for my parents.'

'Is that the reason you called me—'

'Josephine? Yes, it is. But, you know, I prefer Martha. It's such a sweet name. And Evanne? Why, that's lovely. Is it Irish?'

'Mmm, the Irish word is *aoibhinn*. It means "beautiful" or "delightful".' Martha longed to hear more about her birth father. Rose had moved on, however. She was talking about Mitch, Brooke and Bobby. Martha sensed that Joe was a sensitive subject. Best to leave it for now, she decided. They had plenty of time.

They shared morsels of information. Martha spoke about her job. Rose revealed that she had one sister and four brothers, two of whom were dead. One had passed away recently, the other in the 1970s. Both her parents were dead too. She'd once worked in an office, but ever since Brooke's birth she'd been a full-time homemaker. Mitch owned an insurance business. He, too, was Irish but his roots went further back. As far as they knew, his people were from Limerick.

Martha tried to guide the conversation towards Rose's months in Carrigbrack.

'Do you mind if we don't speak about it today, dear? Those were . . . those were not happy times, and I want this to be a happy day.'

Martha realised that Rose was crying, and her own eyes filled with tears. 'That's no problem,' she said. 'No problem at all. In fact, I have someone here who's going to combust if she doesn't get to speak to you soon.'

Evanne seized the phone and launched into a cheery monologue about how she'd been instrumental in finding Rose. 'Everybody reckons we're the living image of each other,' she said, before breezing through her life story. She spoke about school: 'Art and French are fine. The other subjects not so much.' Then she moved on to Templemorris: 'Compared to Dublin, it's kind of backward, but Nan and Granddad are happy there.' Another quick gear change and she was telling Rose about her parents: 'Even though they aren't together any more, they're fairly civilised. Dad and his new partner have a *gorgeous* baby boy called Alex. She's called Layla. Her parents named her after some old song.' A pause. 'Really? You know it?'

It struck Martha that Evanne had been practising, something she found so touching that her tears turned from a trickle to a flood.

'So,' continued Evanne, 'what I was thinking was, if you give me your email address, I'll send you some photos. I'm on Instagram and Facebook and Twitter, too, so you can find tons of pictures there. Mum's, like, pretty useless, I'm afraid. But I'll put some photos of her on my Instagram, and you can see her tonight. She looks like a refugee from the mid-1990s, but she's still pretty. Oh, and are you on Skype or FaceTime or anything? That way we could have a long talk – and see each other at the same time.'

Fearing that Rose might have heard enough for one day, Martha signalled to her daughter to hand back the phone. Evanne pulled a face and said a lengthy goodbye.

When Martha picked up the receiver, Rose was asking a question.

Her answer was immediate. 'Yes,' she said. 'Oh, yes. Of course we'll come and see you.'

# CHAPTER 25

Life became a blur of activity. Every day was spent consulting, planning and organising. Oh, and paying bills. So ecstatic was Martha to receive Rose's invitation that she hadn't stopped to consider how much a trip to the United States would cost. Still, cost be damned: Martha and Evanne were going to America. Her mam and dad were surprised by her plans, as was Una. 'What's the rush?' her sister said.

'Una, I'm forty-five,' she replied. 'I've spent most of my life wavering and dithering. Why would I wait any longer?'

Dermot was more enthusiastic. 'Didn't I always say it would work out?' he asked.

There was one thing troubling Martha. A month had passed since her quarrel with Cat. She remained adamant that right was on her side. It was Cat who'd behaved badly; Cat who'd betrayed a confidence. And yet it was Martha who was finding the schism unbearable. She'd love to hear what her friend would say about Rose. She needed advice too. How should she go about reaching out to Brooke and Bobby? How could she ensure that her mam and dad didn't feel abandoned? And, given Rose's reluctance to talk about him, should she try to make contact with her birth father? (She'd googled 'Joe Brennan, Boston'. The search yielded 809,000 results. Needles and haystacks didn't come close.) She longed to know what had happened to him. When Evanne had noticed Cat's absence, Martha had fobbed her off with some flim-flam about Cat being busy because she'd secured freelance advertising work.

'Too busy to make a phone call?' her daughter replied.

Martha yammered on about the children and Richie, and Cat's widowed mother in Templemorris, until Evanne gave up and returned to updating her Facebook page.

Their contact with Rose continued, fresh information emerging in dribs and drabs. Rose had been given the second name Annalisa because of an Italian friend of her mother's. Martha's original second name was inspired by a singer called Jeannie C. Riley, who'd been popular the year she was born. Yes, Rose was a reader. Her favourite authors were Anne Tyler and Wally Lamb, although she also loved Dennis Lehane and Michael Connelly. Yes, she remembered the Laffertys' shop and Winnie's kindness. No, she'd never returned to Ireland, but her sister had visited more than once. As much as Martha relished her birth mother's emails, there was a cautious quality to their communication, as if they were just paddling in the shallows. She hoped that when they met, this would change.

She attempted to find out more about Irish Americans, especially those in Boston. She discovered that Milton had more people of Irish heritage than any other place in America. Yet the internet also told her that it was a prosperous, desirable area. She tried to square this with her own prejudices. In Martha's head, Irish Americans were vaguely embarrassing people who dreamed of a place of half-doors, set-dancing and daily rosaries. They wore bulky Aran sweaters and got sentimental about a country that had forced their families into exile. That was the benign stereotype. In the darker version, they were all gangsters and psychopaths, like Whitey Bulger and his henchmen. She guessed her stereotypes must be out of date.

She told Paudie about her plans to visit Rose. He was friendly, he was warm, yet she sensed his thoughts were elsewhere. They must meet up again, he said. He was run off his feet at the moment, though. 'Me too,' she replied. 'Me too.' Neither mentioned the abortion. She started to wonder whether talking to him had been a wise move. She might have quenched her desire to tell the truth, but in the process she'd alienated her best friend.

The library was entering its quiet period. With most students away for the summer, Martha was no longer tripping over earnest youngsters. As much as she grumbled about them, she missed their carefully tatty clothes and the way they posed with their volumes of Adorno and Foucault, probability theory and quantum physics. For the next couple of months, she would see only the hardcore clientele: the people who simply adored reading, the people who wanted to use a computer, and the people who craved company. And then there was George, an elderly homeless man, who liked to pass a few hours in the library. Not, God love him, that he ever did any harm. Sometimes, though, he shouted in his sleep, and then the children would get the giggles and somebody would complain about there being 'better places for people like him', so it was best to be vigilant.

The newspaper rack was in its usual state of chaos. The *Racing Post* (minus two torn-out pages) was on the floor; the *Irish Times* was bedraggled; the *Sunday Herald* had been turned into origami. It was while she de-wrinkled the *Herald* that Martha spotted Paudie. He was on the gossip page – where else? – an arm draped around a blonde: a young, lightly tanned blonde, showing off her young toned arms and her young white teeth.

**Let's Chat About Paudie's New Girl**

He's always walked between the raindrops, and Paudie Carmody hasn't wasted any time mourning the end of his relationship with TV cutie, Thalia Treacy. Yes, Mr Saturday Night TV has already welcomed another young lovely onto his couch. And this time we think he's met his match. Friends say the forty-five-year-old chat show king is well and truly smitten with twenty-six-year-old stunner Sara Richardson.

Trinity graduate Sara is best known for her *Sunday Herald* column where she talks about her hectic life as a girl about town. With her trademark effortless style, some say she's the voice of her generation. The Dalkey beauty has also been known to tread the catwalk for the Prestige Modelling Agency. As if that wasn't enough, pals say Sara is penning her first novel, a coming-of-age tale about a Dublin girl who takes on New York. Phew! We only hope Paudie can keep up.

We hear the loved-up pair are jetting off for a romantic break in the sun-kissed South of France. Stay tuned for developments.

'Oh, puke,' said Martha, her words loud enough to stir George, who woke with a splutter. He blinked several times before peering at her with rheumy eyes.

'You know what, George?' she said. 'The old saying is true. There's no fool like an old fool.'

Martha wasn't sure whether she was talking about herself or Paudie.

'What I can't understand,' said Dermot, 'is how such a bright girl who goes to such an excellent school – such an *expensive* bloody school – can do so badly. One B, one C, two Ds and three Es. And the B is in art. Art! Oh, and she managed to fail geography. It takes a special talent to fail geography. What's she been up to?'

'What's that supposed to mean?' replied Martha, pacing the kitchen, fingernails digging into her palms.

'You know what I mean. Did she do any studying, or has she been larking about the place?'

'I thought it would be my fault.'

'That's not what I said.'

'It's what you meant, though. I know the way your mind works. All I can say is, Evanne does plenty of homework while she's here. When she's at your place all she does is look after Alex.'

'That's not fair,' said Dermot, slapping his fingers against the table. 'It's not true, either. She helps out occasionally but only when she wants to. Most of the time she's in her room. Mind you, if you ask me, she spends far too much time fiddling with her phone and listening to music.'

'Ah, Dermot, you sound about five hundred years old. And, by the way, there's nothing wrong with being good at art.'

'Yeah, because there are so many jobs for artists. The paper's full of them, all offering six-figure salaries too.'

Martha was on the verge of shouting something caustic, but stopped herself in time. They could spend the rest of the afternoon like this. Lobbing and volleying. Achieving nothing. He'd marched in twenty minutes before, pouring scorn on everything and everybody. It was a reminder of how, late on in their marriage, he'd developed a habit of walking in and finding fault. 'It's too hot in here,' he'd say. 'I'll turn off the heating.' Or 'It's too cold, I'll turn on the heating.' Or 'Look at all those crumbs under the table. How did you not notice them?'

Martha would stand there, looking at the ceiling, thinking, *Christ, is this what we've been reduced to?* With Dermot everything had to be neat and in its place, and while this was hardly a heinous offence, it had driven her insane. He could have done something really dreadful – like gambling away the house or having a noisy affair with a neighbour – and she would have been better able to cope.

She pinched the bridge of her nose. 'Will you listen to the pair of us, squabbling like kids? This won't help Evanne.'

'I know, I know,' he said. 'It's just so disappointing to see her throwing her chances away. This time next year she'll be doing the Leaving Cert. If she doesn't get her act together, God only knows where she'll end up.'

Martha pulled out a chair and sat down. 'Maybe it *is* my fault.'

'That's not what I—'

'I mean, we spent so much time arguing. And then there was the separation. We upended her life. We shouldn't be surprised she's had difficulty adjusting.'

'She's had almost three years.'

'Please, Dermot, be reasonable.'

He tilted his plate, watching the crumbs, the remains of the cheese and ham sandwich he'd wolfed down on arrival, fall to the front. 'I suppose Alex's arrival hasn't helped. He's been quite a distraction.'

'Perhaps I chose the wrong time to go looking for Rose.'

'Yeah, but leaving it any longer would have been risky. There was never going to be an ideal—'

Dermot's phone sprang to life. He glanced at the screen, pressed the off button and shook his head. 'The dreaded Manus Lally. The fucker would crawl naked over broken glass for five minutes' air time. Go away,' he said to the silent phone. 'You have no talent, except for being a fucking nuisance.' He looked at Martha. 'Sorry, I'm worn out from dealing with over-ambitious mediocrities.' He paused. 'So what are we going to do about Evanne?'

'You wouldn't believe what some parents are up to,' said Martha. She dipped into her bag and pulled out a newspaper cutting. 'This was in the paper the other day.' She read, '"This year, exam coaches are *de rigueur* in some circles, and have been rushed off their feet coping with demand from students needing help in planning their study, diet and exercise regimens."'

'Exam coaches?' said Dermot. 'You're having me on.'

'Wait – it gets better.' Martha returned to her clipping. '"One mother is putting her daughter's flawless results down to the masseuse who came to her house after each paper to help the girl de-stress."'

'Sweet Jesus, there's a place for those people – in a large hospital with high walls.'

She smiled. 'I remember Cat and me de-stressing by smoking cigarettes at the back of the community hall.'

'I may have done something similar myself,' he said, wistfulness in his voice.

If marriage had taught Martha nothing else, it had taught her how to be devious. She knew that if she suggested extra tuition for Evanne, Dermot would moan about the cost of her school fees. But if he heard about the extreme measures other parents were adopting . . . well, he wouldn't want his daughter to be left behind.

'Anyway,' she said, 'I'm not saying Evanne needs an exam coach, but she could do with some extra help in a couple of subjects, like maths and chemistry.'

He thought for a moment. 'I suppose.'

'I reckon we should both talk to her – in a calm, friendly way. She's almost seventeen. We should be able to sit down together, like adults, and discuss her future.'

'Fair enough. When you get back from America, why don't we all have a chat?'

'That sounds good. How's Layla?'

'Why do you ask?'

Something about Dermot's tone told her to proceed with caution. 'Gosh, no particular reason.'

'She's got a new job, anyway. She's going to be a reporter on an evening magazine programme, a new show starting in the autumn. She'll be doing lifestyle features – stories about plucky kids, talented dogs, that class of thing.'

'That's great. Isn't it?'

'I think so. Layla's not convinced. She wanted to be the presenter. She tends to forget she's not the only television presenter in the world.' Dermot straightened his back and squared his shoulders, a sure sign he was warming to his argument. 'I know she's had a setback. And she's right, she wasn't treated fairly. But, like I keep saying to her, life's not fair. The sooner she grasps that the better. She doesn't seem to appreciate that I've already spent a huge amount of time on her career, so much time that some of my other clients were fairly pissed off.'

'Oh.'

'They wanted more hand-holding. Four left me. Two were dead wood, but the other two were solid earners.'

'Oh. And Alex, he's well?'

'Ah, Martha, give it a rest, would you?'

'What's wrong? I'm only being polite.'

'No, you're not. You're pussyfooting around, looking for information. No doubt Evanne has told you that things aren't good, and she's right.

Alex does nothing but gurn and bawl, and Layla isn't much better.'

'She said nothing of the sort. She may have hinted that Layla's finding motherhood a bit testing, but I didn't read too much into that. Sure weren't we all the same? When Evanne was Alex's age, there were days I would gladly have paid somebody to take her away. But these things pass.'

What Martha didn't say was that she would never have coped without her mother. Delia had been brilliant. When she'd realised that Martha was struggling, she'd turned up in Dolmen Crescent with an overnight bag and a limitless supply of energy. She'd stayed for six weeks. Not only had she cared for Evanne, she'd shopped, cooked and cleaned. She'd even befriended the neighbours. Now, if her mam was being crabby or demanding, Martha reminded herself of those weeks. 'Besides,' she said, 'the summer's here, so Evanne can spend some more time looking after her brother. It's not as though it'll be any trial to her. She's mad about him. And it'll give Layla a bit more space.'

Martha hadn't heard any wedding talk lately. Then again, a couple with a new baby didn't have much time for talking. The following year Martha and Dermot would be able to divorce, and she assumed that soon he would set the process in motion.

'I'm sure Layla will appreciate the help.' Dermot hesitated. 'It's more than that, though. Some days I feel like Alex cries so much because he knows he's surrounded by tension. It's like he can tell that things aren't working out.'

*Please, Dermot*, she thought, *don't do this*. 'You're under pressure,' she said. 'Everything appears off key. You'll be away on your holidays soon. It'll give you a chance to forget about the likes of Manus Lally for a week or two. Layla will get used to her new job. Evanne will find her equilibrium. Everything will be grand again, you'll see.'

'I don't know that it will.' He stared at his empty plate. 'It's not as though everything is Layla's fault. I say the wrong things. I get hostile when I've nothing to get hostile about. It's like an auto-immune disease. I'm determined to sabotage my best interests.' Again, he hesitated. 'Like I did with you.'

'There were two of us in it, Dermot. We were the unhappiest couple in Ireland. Were you listening to us ten minutes ago, ripping each other apart? That's what we were like.'

'At the end.' He brushed her forearm. 'But for a long time we were happy, weren't we?'

Head swirling, Martha floundered for a response. 'We were,' she said.

# CHAPTER 26

Rose might have forgotten some things about Carrigbrack, but her memories of the day she'd lost her baby had never dimmed. She could still see the nursery. She could picture the determined look on Sister Agnes's face, and the way Sister Sabina had moved her weight from one foot to another. 'Stay happy': that was what she'd said to Josephine, as the nuns took her away. A pointless wish, yet at the time it had felt important.

Now she wondered how much happiness life had given Martha. As upbeat as she was in their phone calls and emails, Rose had detected a certain sadness about her. No, sadness was overstating it. Disappointment was closer to the mark, like she'd expected life to be more of an adventure. 'Quit being silly,' she said to herself. 'You've never even met the woman. You've no idea how she feels about her life.'

Rose was in the garden, weeding and dead-heading. Her rhododendrons were in blossom, the garden a mosaic of colour. Dew clung to the lawn, a sure sign of another fine day to come. Occasionally, she raked one hand along a lavender bush, then paused to inhale the scent. Bliss.

A while back, Mitch had asked if the work was becoming too much for her. 'Wouldn't you like some help?' he'd said.

'Oh, no,' she'd insisted. She thought of the garden as part of her therapy.

Rose and Mitch had met two years after her return from Carrigbrack when she'd been working for an office supplies company. While the job hadn't been particularly interesting, it had provided a salary. It had also filled her days. When she had time on her hands, she did too much thinking. Thinking led to trouble. Her hopes of going to college had been snuffed out. According to her mother, university would only pull Rose back into harm's way.

Although she'd tried to push aside her memories, Joe was still in her head. Every time she thought she was over him, up he'd pop. She'd hear one of his favourite songs or he'd drift through one of her dreams or she'd see a guy who looked like him. His memory lay in wait, taunting her, teasing her. She hadn't believed anybody could fill his space.

And then Mitch had arrived. He'd been to school with one of her bosses, and it was pretty clear the Collins family were everything the Brennans weren't. They were sober, prosperous – and respectable. Achingly respectable. They were Irish but not too Irish; wealthy but not vulgarly so.

Mitch worked for his dad's insurance company. One day he hoped to take over.

To begin with, Rose had tried to ignore him but he wooed and cajoled until finally she agreed to a date. One date became two, the movies became dinner, and soon they were an item. All the while, her mother reminded her that she was fortunate to have caught the eye of such a decent, successful man. Although some of Rose's prettiness had been restored, Ireland had stripped away her lustre. Mentally, she was a dullard, trying to make it through the day without screwing up or breaking down. That wasn't all: no matter how hard she tried, she couldn't relax. She was distant, aloof. She'd learned that the best way to avoid extreme lows was to eschew extreme highs. It wasn't just physical intimacy that scared her. She worried that if anybody got close, her secrets would tumble out. Now, it struck her as immensely sad that a twenty-year-old should feel so inhibited. At that age, life should still be filled with frivolity. With risks. With passion. At the time, her reserved behaviour had simply felt sensible.

After a couple of months of sterile kisses and tepid fumblings, Mitch questioned why she was so uptight. They'd been to the movies to see *Klute*. They'd enjoyed it, her more than him. Afterwards, he'd moved a hand up her thigh. She'd slapped it away.

'Seriously, Rose,' he said, his voice heavy with frustration, 'I feel like I'm dating a robot. What's wrong with you?'

Her first response was to try to end the relationship, but Mitch wasn't easily deterred. 'What aren't you telling me?' he asked.

They were sitting in his car, the only illumination from the dashboard light. Something about the set of his face told Rose that if she was ever going to trust anybody, this was the man.

'I have a daughter,' she said. 'In Ireland.'

Immediately, she regretted her candour. She wasn't supposed to breathe a word. She expected him to walk away. That was what any sane man would do. Instead he listened. For all that she gave him an edited version of her story, Rose revealed more than she'd revealed to anybody – before or since. Mitch told her that, while he understood, others within their circle might take a different view. His family weren't as conservative as the Moroneys, but neither were they especially liberal. He relied on his job with the family firm and couldn't afford to alienate his father. Rose pledged to keep quiet about her past and to abandon any notions of finding her daughter. Two years later, on a sun-bleached June day, they were married. The bride wore high-necked white silk and carried a bouquet of apricot roses. Her parents were delighted with the match.

Now, as Rose snipped a dead bloom and added it to her pile, she thought about their son and daughter. Since she'd told Brooke and Bobby about Martha's existence, relations had been tense. They wanted to meet their sister, but they were angry about being kept in the dark. They were wary too. 'Why's she going to all this bother now?' asked Brooke. The unspoken suggestion was that Martha wanted something. Money, presumably.

Rose was amazed that her children could be so similar and yet so different. They certainly looked alike. Both were tall and fair with the sort of angular frame that owes as much to genetics as to exercise and diet. Plainly she was biased, but Rose believed both were good company. Brooke, in particular, with her waspish tongue and laconic delivery, had always been able to make her laugh. And while neither had been Ivy League material, they weren't dumb either.

In other ways, they were north and south, fire and water. With his enthusiasm and his genial temperament, Bobby was easy to love. Even his high-school scrapes had been harmless. Rose knew that their son's indifference towards the business, his insistence on becoming a teacher, had disappointed Mitch. It had never bothered her. She just wished he would settle down. Not with Ashley, mind. She was far too insubstantial. (Rose was well aware that she, above all people, should know better than to meddle in her son's relationships. Still, she was entitled to her opinion.)

Brooke was a different proposition. Outwardly as graceful as falling snow, she seemed to exist in a constant state of inner turmoil. And, oh, but she was demanding. If she wanted something, be it a ride home or a new job, she wanted it now. She wasn't helped by her compulsion to do it all – to be a good wife, a perfect mother and a model employee. Even her appearance had to be just so: her hair permanently sleek, her make-up fresh, her body sculpted. No wonder she was always tired. Irrational as it might be, Brooke's prickliness made Rose love her all the more.

Rose was also conscious that in her desire not to follow her mother, she'd given the teenaged Brooke too much freedom. She'd indulged her whims, ignored her misdemeanours. But, honestly, would anybody blame Rose for trying to distance herself from Grace?

Out of courtesy, she'd called her sister and brothers and told them about her contact with Martha. As expected, each of them questioned her decision. Any breach of their code of silence was unwelcome. Nancy actually scolded her. 'Why do you want to go dredging up the past?' she said. 'That's all forgotten about now.'

'Not by me, it isn't,' replied Rose.

It hadn't been forgotten by Kevin either, and the death of her favourite brother from throat cancer had hit Rose hard. She didn't know how her brother Gene had felt about what happened. By the time she'd returned from Carrigbrack, he was in California. That was where he died six years later, in a San Francisco dosshouse, a needle in his arm. Of course, the wider world thought he'd been killed in a car wreck. Of course.

Rose guessed that her remaining siblings –

Nancy, Ray and Ed junior – saw the events of 1968 as a small bump on a long road. They cleaved to the view that their parents had been right to send her away. They didn't understand that she continued to live in Carrigbrack's long shadow. She reassured herself that she'd done her best to bring everybody on board. All the same, she worried that in her efforts to explain herself to Brooke and Bobby, she had said too much.

Martha had ten days to remake herself. That was appallingly superficial, she knew. Yet every time she looked at the photos of her American family, she was taken aback by their beauty. Both Rose and Brooke were elegant and well put together. (She didn't want to use the word 'groomed'. It reminded her of Cat.) By contrast, she was so . . . ordinary. True, she wasn't hideous or anything, but she wasn't especially memorable either. Her face, which had always been a little bony, was growing even thinner with age. Her grey eyes, once her best feature, were heavy-lidded, and her teeth belonged to the time before orthodontics had arrived in Ireland.

Ever since her teens, when she'd been impressed by the line in *The Women's Room* about silly women running to the mirror to see who they were, Martha had tried not to judge people by their appearance and not to be defined by her own. She hadn't always lived up to her ideals. At university, she'd been envious of the cool girls and awestruck by the genuinely beautiful. Her time with Paudie was proof of her weakness for good-looking men. Yet she'd never felt that her own shortcomings had held her back. Like many young women of her era, she'd worn a uniform: black leggings, black boots, a second-hand black blazer from the Eager Beaver in Temple Bar. Occasional variations were allowed: a well-faded denim jacket, a black micro-mini or a cotton tea-dress.

As she grew older, the going had got tougher. The first time Martha discovered it was possible to speak through gritted teeth was on her wedding day. One of Dermot's aunts had given her a cool appraisal before remarking that she'd always pictured him with somebody more glamorous. Since then, hundreds of trends had come and gone without impinging on Martha's life. Now that she thought about it, it wasn't that she didn't care about her appearance, more that she didn't have the energy or the know-how to make changes. Here she was, marooned between playsuits and polyester slacks, ill-equipped to deal with a world in which women had their skin lasered and their teeth bleached.

Be that as it may, she didn't want to turn up on Rose's doorstep looking like the plain relation. The time had come for an overhaul. Luckily, she knew the woman for the job.

'By rights,' said Evanne, as she gave her mother's face an exploratory poke, 'you should visit a clinic. They can do wonders these days with injections and peels and whatnot. Serena's mum has regular appointments.'

'Thanks, love, that's exactly what I wanted to hear. My daughter reckons I need surgical intervention.'

'Now, Mum, don't twist my words. Anyhow, I'm guessing you're not going to go for Botox or anything.'

'You're guessing correctly.'

'I'll have to see what I can do, then.' Evanne lifted up a hank of Martha's hair. 'You should try a warmer blonde.'

'I'm sure that can be arranged.'

'And your eyebrows are *all* wrong.'

'Oh.'

'Show me your legs.'

Martha pulled up the hem of her jeans. 'Here you go.'

'What do you shave them with – a hedge trimmer? You wouldn't, by any chance, consider having them properly waxed?'

'All right,' said Martha, 'if it's not too expensive.'

'And your feet. You ought to do something about your feet. Like, a pedicure, maybe.'

Martha looked down. 'There's a first time for everything, I suppose.'

'Hello? You've never had a pedicure?' Evanne gazed at her mother as if she'd admitted to killing a basketful of kittens. '*Eeeew*, what have you been doing all these years?'

'Not caring for my feet, obviously.'

'And perhaps we could do a small bit of shopping?'

'I've already told you I don't have a lot to spend.'

'I'll have to go bargain-hunting, so.'

Martha found herself wishing that Evanne had the same enthusiasm for her schoolwork. Her post-exam sheepishness had faded, helped on its way by the excitement surrounding their Boston trip and by her seventeenth-birthday celebrations. Along with Serena and a gaggle of other girls, she'd spent the evening in the city centre, eating pizza and drinking far too much wine. Not that Martha was one to talk. She'd spent her own seventeenth in Fennessy's Lounge, getting drunk on Pernod and blackcurrant. Almost thirty years later, the memory still made her queasy. 'Fair enough,' she said. 'We'll go into town on Saturday.'

'Cool. Now can we go through your make-up?'

'You know where it is.'

The two went upstairs to Martha's room. Evanne poured the contents of her mother's make-up drawer onto the cream quilt. She raised a well-shaped eyebrow. 'This, if you don't mind me saying so, is a pathetic haul. Like, I own better stuff.'

'I know. I paid for most of it. When I was your age—'

'I thought you'd promised never to use that phrase.'

'Okay,' said Martha. 'When I was at school, I owned three items of make-up: a mascara, a sky-blue eyeliner and a metallic purple lipstick.'

'Yee-uch. It's a miracle you ever had a boyfriend.'

'You're probably right. Mind you, wearing too

much make-up was considered naff. There was this poor girl – Breda Arkins – who always wore a thick coat of dark foundation, and when she walked down the corridor, the boys used to sing "Caribbean Queen".'

'That's terrible,' said Evanne. 'Nowadays you'd get into major grief for bullying like that.'

'In our day it was dismissed as "messing". Unless blood was spilled, everything was seen as harmless.'

'It's a good job times have changed. Anyway, are you willing to try a couple of new things?'

It occurred to Martha that her daughter's generation had myriad ways of inflicting cruelty on their peers, most of them far more harmful than a burst of 'Caribbean Queen'. She passed an ageing bronzer from one hand to the other and nodded. 'Once you don't buy anything too garish.'

'Says the woman who wore purple lipstick. My taste is impeccable.'

'I'll have to put you to the test.'

Evanne grinned and tossed an ancient lipstick into the bin. 'Can I ask another question?'

'Go on.'

'Where's Cat?'

'Like I told you before, she's got a lot on at the minute.'

Evanne scooped up two eyeshadows and a grubby sponge. They also went sailing into the bin. 'I mightn't be too hot at chemistry and maths, but I'm not a complete fool either. You've fallen out, haven't you?'

'Yes, but it's not the first time and these things—'

'Spill.'

Martha ran a hand along one sandpaper shin. 'Can we talk about it another time?'

The night before their departure, when her entire body was fluttering with anticipation, Martha decided she couldn't go to America without talking to Cat. They had known each other for the best part of forty years. Other friendships had burned bright, then flickered out, but Cat had always been there, as integral to Martha's life as her parents, sister and daughter. Martha had rarely had to second-guess their friendship. For years, her only concern had been that she received more than she gave. Sometimes they didn't talk so much as bat comments back and forth, but that was okay. Every conversation didn't have to be a heart-to-heart, any more than every song had to be a classic or every book a life-changer.

She rehearsed what she would say. A quick chat would do. The rights and wrongs of their row could be thrashed out later. The first time she called, the phone went unanswered. This was no surprise. Cat was likely to be busy. Twenty minutes later, she tried again. No answer. She waited a further twenty minutes. Still no answer. The fourth time the phone clicked through to voicemail, she left a message.

'Hi,' she said. 'It's me. I just wanted to talk to you for a minute or two. I, ahm, I'm not sure if you know this, but we're flying to America tomorrow – Evanne and me. To see Rose, of course. She sounds great, really great. I'm fairly nervous. Evanne's up to ninety. So I . . . I wanted to let you know and to thank you for encouraging me to find her. I hope things are good with you and Richie and the kids. I don't know, maybe you're away? Whatever . . . if you get this, will you call me? Please?'

At midnight, when it was clear that Cat wasn't going to return her call, Martha went to bed. Somehow, the sheets were too rumpled, the pillows too floppy. The room was airless. Then it was too cold. For what felt like for ever, she writhed and turned. At last, with the blackbirds in full song and the first light seeping through the curtains, she fell asleep. In her dreams, she was imprisoned in Carrigbrack; Evanne was dressed as a nun; Rose had no hair; Dermot and Cat were peering through the window. Nobody would help her to escape.

Dublin Airport was thronged, mammoth queues zigzagging around the departures hall. Martha watched as a clutch of girls in crop tops and shorts lined up beside a harassed mother and a tantrum-throwing toddler. Next to them a tattooed young fellow played with the pockets of his rucksack while a woman in a magenta kaftan shifted from one foot to the other. A luggage-free man, his suit shiny from too many pressings, flicked an eye over his fellow travellers, as if to say, 'Amateurs.'

'We should have been here half an hour ago,' she said, as they joined the queue for Boston.

'Hmm,' replied Evanne, who was unusually ill at ease. One moment she was fidgeting with her bag, the next checking her phone.

'Are you all right, love?'

'Not a bother,' said Evanne, her tone at odds with her words.

They shuffled forward. Martha heard her phone. It had to be Cat.

It was her mother. In a wobbly voice, she wished them the best of luck. 'Safe travelling,' she said, 'and tell her . . . tell Rose . . . I said thanks. Will you do that?'

'Cross my heart, Mam. And you'll be the first to know how we get on.'

Another shuffle and the phone rang again. Dermot said he was thinking of them both, and that Alex and Layla sent their love. The improbability of this made Martha smile. 'Thanks,' she said. 'We'll be in touch.'

No sooner was Dermot gone than Martha heard the ping of a text. This must be Cat, surely. It was Paudie. *Is today the big day? Good luck with Rose. Thinking of you.*

Fortunately, Evanne was too preoccupied to ask who the message was from.

While Martha prodded out a reply, she heard a kerfuffle from the back of the queue. 'There's always one,' said a man.

'Typical,' added a woman. 'Some people just

aren't capable of waiting their turn.' Martha craned her neck to get a better view.

And there she was, in her favourite bottle-green jacket, negotiating her way along the line, red curls bouncing all the while.

'Thanks a million,' said Cat, to a scowling man. 'I need to talk to my friend, you see.'

Martha looked at Evanne, who was smiling so broadly that every last tooth was on display. She shoved the phone back into her bag. 'Can you make way, please?' she said to the granite-faced couple beside her.

Finally, Cat was at the top of the queue.

'A phone call would have done, you know,' said Martha, laughter in her voice. 'You didn't have to traipse all the way out to the airport.'

'Traipse all the way out to the airport? Did you not notice the suitcase? I'm coming with you.'

Later, after they'd cleared security, Martha heard the full story. Worried about their falling-out, Evanne had contacted Cat. What was happening? she wanted to know. Cat said they'd had a disagreement over something that had occurred many years ago. 'It's best we don't go into it,' she insisted. Evanne agreed to let the matter drop, but not before she'd told Cat all about Rose and their visit to Boston.

'Well, that was it,' said Cat. 'For thirty years, I'd been urging you to track down your birth parents, and now the action was about to unfold without me. I couldn't be having that. So I bought a plane ticket. Then I called your hotel and – what do you know? – they were able to get us a triple room.'

'But why didn't you answer your phone last night?' asked Martha.

'We both reckoned Cat coming to Boston should be a surprise,' said Evanne.

'And judging by the look on your face when I produced my suitcase, I think I can say "mission accomplished",' added Cat. She brought her hands together and clapped the tips of her fingers. 'On my way in here, I met a group of Americans – you know the type, heading off in search of their roots. They got me thinking, what's the betting you're the first Irish person in history to go to America to trace yours?'

Martha couldn't stop smiling; it was like she'd lost control of the muscles at the corner of her mouth. 'Do you know?' she said. 'You might be right.'

While Evanne fetched coffee, Martha and Cat agreed that this wasn't the time to rake over their differences. There would be another day for that.

'I still can't believe you're doing this,' said Martha. 'It isn't a cheap trip.'

'Thanks, Missus. You make it sound like we're destitute.'

'Don't be daft. Seriously, though, coming to Boston must be costing you a fortune.'

'I had a little bit put away, and Richie agreed that this was the right time to spend it. Seventeen-year-olds have their uses, but I thought you might need some adult support. Besides, I could do with the break.'

'I hate to ask, but who's minding the kids?'

'I gave them a strong dose of sedatives and locked them in their rooms. Richie's going to stick his head around the door every so often to make sure they're still breathing.' She winked. 'They're staying with Mam. She's only thrilled to have them. They can experience the delights of Templemorris for a week.'

'Lucky them,' said Martha, stretching out a leg to admire her sea-green toenails.

Evanne returned with a tray of coffees and a bag of muffins.

'So here we are,' said Cat, as she gave her coffee a vigorous stir. 'Thelma and Louise – plus sidekick.'

'Without the guns, I hope,' said Martha.

'Although if we did come across Brad Pitt in a cowboy hat . . .'

'He'd definitely be allowed to tag along.'

Evanne's eyes slid from her mother to Cat and back again. 'What *are* you on about?'

Cat's lips curled into a smile. 'An important cultural reference from before your time.'

'Sad,' said Evanne.

# CHAPTER 27

'You're not going to eat that, are you?' said Cat, as she leaned over and took a pancake from Martha's plate. She cut it in two and gave half to Evanne.

'Sorry?' replied Martha. 'I was—'

'Miles away, I know. We've been talking about you for the past five minutes, saying all sorts, and there hasn't been a word out of you.'

'Oh?' said Martha, as she put down her knife and fork, the tremor in her hands causing them to clatter against the table. She contemplated picking up her coffee cup, but decided against. Her grip was too unsteady, and her throat had closed. The only thing she could compare this to, this feeling that eating was physically impossible, was the early stages of falling in love.

Evanne laughed. 'We haven't really been talking about you. We've been talking about Boston and about what Cat's going to do while we go to see Rose.'

'The Freedom Trail, I think,' said Cat, 'although I could leave that until tomorrow. You might be able to come with me then.'

Martha noticed how their table was illuminated by a shaft of sunlight. It glanced against the coffee pot and highlighted their pale Irish skin. 'You'll have to humour me,' she said. 'I'm a bit preoccupied and a bit—'

'Nervous,' said Cat, who seemed determined to finish Martha's sentences as well as her food.

All around them, people were eating, reading newspapers, laughing, jabbering about the day ahead. Martha was in an alternate world, a world where she was cocooned with her own thoughts and concerns.

'What are you thinking?' asked Evanne.

'I'm wondering if it's too early for a brandy,' she said.

Amber Street was long and tree-lined and, on that July morning, it shimmered in the heat. Apart from some spirited birdsong and the distant buzz of a lawnmower, it was quiet. Martha and Evanne walked slowly. Despite the pools of shade provided by the trees, sweat gathered along Martha's spine and at the back of her neck. She was glad she'd decided against the brandy. Although it was just thirty minutes from downtown Boston, Milton felt completely different. At first glance, it looked more like small-town America. A second glance revealed its Irishness. They passed businesses with Irish names and shamrock motifs; a woman wore a Dublin GAA jersey; a poster advertised Irish-dancing classes.

'I think it's this next house,' Martha said.

'The big one?' asked Evanne.

Rose's house wasn't just big, it was magnificent: two storeys of cream clapboard, a midnight blue door and a porch with wicker chairs. All that was missing was a white picket fence. Instead, the lawn was bordered by rhododendrons and azaleas.

'It's like something from a magazine,' whispered Evanne.

Martha couldn't help but make the most basic, the most unfair, comparison. 'We're a long way from Templemorris,' she whispered back.

'I'm pleased we didn't bring flowers. It's like the Botanic Gardens here already.'

'Mam would definitely approve.'

'Are you ready?' asked Evanne, her voice still low.

'As I'll ever be. Do you want to go first?'

'Okey-doke,' Evanne replied, with the youthful nonchalance that Martha envied. A nonchalance she didn't think she'd ever possessed.

'Good luck to us,' she said.

Martha had read dozens of accounts in which people spoke about meeting their birth mother for the first time. She'd spoken at length to Pauline Bennis. She'd seen photos of Rose. They'd spoken on the phone. Yet when the door opened, and Rose was standing in front of her, she felt totally unprepared. One of her knees gave an abrupt wobble and her immediate instinct was to do an about-turn and run away.

Thankfully, she didn't have to speak. Rose stepped forward, and they merged into a hug.

'Look at you both,' Rose said, as they pulled apart. 'I'm . . . Well, I don't even know the word. I'm spellbound, I guess.'

By now, she was ushering them into the hall. Rose was smaller than Martha had expected. More fragile too. But her eyes were as clear and her smile as wide as the photos had suggested. Her bobbed hair was freshly coloured, her navy summer dress elegant. It would be wrong to describe her as glamorous. That was too tacky a word. She was still beautiful.

The women embraced again, first one by one, then all three together. When eventually they disentangled, they stood and gazed at each other. Rose, her eyes gleaming, ran a finger along Martha's cheek before doing the same to Evanne.

It was Evanne who broke the silence. 'Here we are at last,' she said. 'Three generations of us.'

'That's right,' replied Martha, not trusting herself to say much more. Her breath was coming in short puffs, her heart thud-thudding in her ears. The one other thing she could say for sure was that all of her thoughts were in the present. She was conscious that this was a once-in-a-lifetime moment.

'Where are my manners?' said Rose. 'Let's go into the lounge. It must be a relief to get out of the heat. They say it could reach ninety degrees today. Would you both like a drink?' Her speech was slightly stilted, but why would it be any other way? No doubt, her head was also a tangle of thoughts and emotions.

Nodding, Martha and Evanne accompanied her into a large room with cream walls and a Persian carpet. It was gloriously cool. They sat side by side on a blue sofa while Rose fetched three glasses of lemonade. The room contained a few silver-framed photos – Bobby and Brooke's graduations; Brooke's wedding; Brooke, Chris and their sons – but not as many as Martha had expected.

She was calmer now, and as much as she wanted Rose to open up, she also told herself that it didn't matter. This was a first meeting. If they confined themselves to the weather and bland chit-chat, that was fine. There would be other days to talk about the Moroney family, about Carrigbrack – and about Joe Brennan.

When Rose returned, they lapsed into small talk. 'If we got a day like this in Ireland, it'd be the main story on the news,' said Martha. Evanne agreed. Rose spoke about the impossibility of keeping the garden looking well. Martha said she'd never seen such a gorgeous display of flowers and that she must take some photos to show her mam and dad. Evanne admired the house. Rose told her it was built in 1890 for a doctor and his family. 'Sometimes I think it's too big for us,' she said. 'But it's been our home for so long, I can't imagine living anywhere else.' She promised to give them a full tour.

Slowly, the conversation moved to more personal matters.

'I know we've told each other quite a bit in our emails and on the phone,' said Rose, 'but you must have other questions. So I'm going to try and tell you about my life and my family. I've been thinking about this a little. Well, that's not true. I've been thinking about it a *lot*. But you've got to understand that some episodes are hard to talk about. And, then, there are other things that I'm not sure I remember correctly. It's not as though I'm in the habit of talking about the past. So I hope that you, both of you, will forgive me if I get things mixed up.'

'Please don't feel under any pressure,' said Martha. 'That's the last thing we'd want. Isn't that right, Evanne?'

'Yes,' she said, her small face a study in concentration. She was drinking in every word Rose said.

Martha found she couldn't stop staring at the woman sitting across from her. She was fascinated by every last detail. Like her legs. Martha had the same narrow ankles. And her long-lobed ears. Martha had those too. Back in college, she'd had them pierced four times; she had plenty of ear to spare. What gave her most delight, though, was Rose's obvious joy at their visit. She had one of those smiles that was impossible to fake.

'When I was thinking about what I wanted to tell you,' said Rose, 'I realised I couldn't just start in Carrigbrack. I needed to go back a bit, so for a few minutes, I'm going to ask that you indulge me.' She took a long breath. 'I was in my early teens when our family moved here to Milton. Now, don't get me wrong, our house wasn't as lovely as this. But, for the Moroney family, it was a definite step up in the world. Up until then, we'd lived in an old-style blue-collar neighbourhood where lots of people were just getting by and some . . . some were struggling.'

'Like in the films?' said Evanne. 'I've been watching some of them – like the one with Leonardo DiCaprio and the other one with Ben Affleck and—'

'You've got it,' said Rose, with an encouraging smile. 'We seem to be popular with Hollywood these days.'

Evanne's Boston education hadn't been confined to films and TV programmes. She'd absorbed every word of the books Martha brought home from the library. Detective novels, guidebooks, local histories: she'd read them all. If Boston was a subject in the Leaving Cert, she'd be assured of an A1 in the honours paper.

'They give you some idea of what our old neighbourhood looked like,' continued Rose. 'Not that it was filled with gangsters. It most certainly wasn't. But it could be a rough and ready place, with everybody living on top of everybody else. There were scores of bars where guys drank away their pay cheques, that's if they had a pay cheque. And some of the kids were wild. My family, though, were what you'd call "lace curtain". Does the phrase mean anything to you?'

'Yes,' said Martha. 'You sometimes hear it used at home to describe people who have aspirations, people who want to get on in the world, especially if they think they're better than the neighbours.' It struck her that Rose had rehearsed her story. She was like a teacher, coaxing them along, making certain they understood.

Another smile passed across Rose's face. 'You've described my parents, Ed and Grace Moroney. I don't think any teenager likes moving. When you're fourteen or fifteen, you have your girlfriends, you know the boys you're sweet on – and the boys to avoid. You've got to remember too that we're talking about the nineteen sixties. What a fabulous time to be a teenager in America. There was the music and the clothes and, as silly as it sounds, there was this sense that . . . that anything was possible. Later life became darker, what with Vietnam and everything, but when I was a kid, life was great.'

'It must have been amazing,' said Martha. 'In Ireland, people like to joke that the nineteen sixties didn't arrive until the seventies.'

'That doesn't surprise me,' said Rose, a caustic note hitting her voice. 'Anyway, in Boston it was a time to rebel, and every chance I got I was back in the old neighbourhood, bunking down with my cousin.' She hesitated. 'That's how I met Joe Brennan. I was sixteen. He was a year older. And I was crazy about him. Actually, I think it's safe to say we were crazy about each other. He was smart and kind and tender and funny. A good guy.' Rose tipped her head towards Martha. 'You do look like him, you know. He had light brown hair and grey eyes. "Sad Eyes", I called him. Which is not to say there was anything sad about him. I've never met anybody so full of life.'

At last Martha knew: she did take after Joe. She considered asking if Rose had a photo from those days, but decided against. She might only break her flow.

Rose told them about discovering she was pregnant, about the hellish situation at home – and about being shipped off to Carrigbrack. While she explained how one of the nuns, Sister Agnes, was her own aunt, her voice broke. She shut her eyes tightly, as if she was forcing back tears. 'I'm sorry,' she said. 'You'll have to give me a minute.'

'If this is too difficult, you don't have to continue,' said Martha. 'We didn't come here to upset you.'

'No, I swore I'd tell you about it and I will. The thing is, I'm not accustomed to talking about those months, or about my parents. So you'll have to bear with me.'

'You take your time. Maybe we could get you a glass of water or a cup of tea.'

Rose opened her eyes. 'I'll be fine. Don't you worry. We can have some lunch in a little while.' She paused, then resumed her story. 'I guess you're wondering about Joe. He knew I was in Ireland, but that's about all. I discovered later that while I was away my mother told him I'd lost the baby. She said I'd gone to an aunt's house to recuperate.'

Evanne gasped. 'What a scummy thing to do.'

'You said it. My mom had a masterplan for me, and Joe was never going to feature. I remember her saying he was no better than a tinker. I didn't even know what a tinker was.'

'When you were in Carrigbrack, was there no way you could have written to Joe . . . to let him know what was happening?' The question was out of Martha's mouth before she appreciated how naive it was. Silently, she cursed her stupidity.

'Martha, honey, there was no way on earth Agnes would have allowed me to do that. And even if I'd been able to get to the post office, the folks there would've given the letter to the nuns. Afterwards, I realised I could have asked the woman you met, Mrs Lafferty, to post something for me. But at the time . . . well, I was young and I didn't think.'

Rose told them about life in the convent and about the day her baby was born. By now, she was speaking carefully, like every word was painful. Conscious that even an ill-timed breath would feel like an intrusion, Martha stayed quiet.

'At the very end,' said Rose, 'everything moved so quickly I . . . I had no time to fight. One day you were there, the next I was saying goodbye. A hasty goodbye. "It's for the best," Sister Agnes said.' She stopped and swallowed. 'I'm sorry. I wish I'd tried harder.'

Before Martha could say anything, Evanne was

on her feet. She went over to Rose and wrapped her arms around her. 'It's all right,' she said. 'I understand, and Mum does too. There was nothing you could do.'

Evanne's words made Martha's eyes fill. She questioned whether her tears were appropriate. For once in her life, though, she wasn't crying for herself. For all her grousing about Delia, Martha couldn't have wished for a better adoptive family. Neither had she ever been in any doubt about their love for her. It was Rose who had suffered, who was still suffering.

'Oh, my,' Rose said eventually, flapping her hands in front of her eyes. 'I swore to myself I wouldn't start weeping, and now we're all at it. There's a box of tissues over there, Evanne, honey.' She gestured towards a corner table. 'If you wouldn't mind.'

Evanne fetched the tissues and returned to the sofa. Martha smoothed a hand over her daughter's head. Then the three dried their faces.

After a minute of silence, Rose completed her story. All the while, she looked at the floor. 'I didn't see who took you away. I signed a form pledging never to interfere with your adoption or to make any attempt to contact you. Three weeks later, my father arrived to take me back to Boston. He said that when we got home, I wasn't to tell a soul where I'd been. "If the truth got out, it would kill your mother," he said. By that point, I was as meek as a lamb. My baby was gone. I didn't see much point in protesting.

'Afterwards, my pregnancy was rarely mentioned. It was like my parents and my brothers and sister believed their own lies. I was expected to get on with my life. And that's what I tried to do. I never thought I'd see you again.' She reached for another tissue. 'I still can't quite believe you're here.'

Martha was reluctant to probe further, this wasn't a time for poking and prying, but there was one question she had to ask. When she spoke, she was taken aback by how reedy her voice sounded. 'And Joe? Did you speak to Joe?' Seeing Rose flinch, she immediately regretted her question. 'I'm sorry, I didn't—'

'No. It's all right,' said Rose. 'Joe was gone, dear. Joe was dead.'

# CHAPTER 28

'A car crash,' said Martha, 'while Rose was in Carrigbrack.'

'Sheesh,' said Cat, 'what an awful story.'

'The entire tale was so terrible, I was desperate for a happy ending. Foolish, I know, but there you go.'

'But you knew they didn't end up together, so—'

'I suppose I was holding out hope that they'd met up again, and that there was some sort of bond there. I pictured Joe living a regular suburban life with his wife and family. Nothing flash, but a contented existence, you know. Only the way it turned out, he died thinking Rose had lost their baby. There were four of them in the car, apparently – young lads on a night out. No doubt they were going too quickly. Or maybe they'd been drinking. Rose didn't say. She told me where he's buried, so I can visit his grave if I want. But . . .'

'Are you very disappointed?'

'I'd be lying if I said I wasn't, only meeting Rose was so brilliant that wanting any more seems unreasonable. Even asking too much about Joe felt wrong. You should have seen her. After she'd told us about Carrigbrack, she was completely drained.'

And that was the truth. Yes, Martha was disappointed by the news about Joe, but her sadness was tempered by the joy of meeting Rose and the knowledge that her birth mother was now part of her life. As she sat in the hotel bar, a glass of white wine in front of her, the hum of conversation all around, she was grappling with everything she'd learned. How was it possible for an afternoon to have been uplifting and depressing, fascinating and upsetting all at the one time? She'd spent much of the day in a state of fear: scared she would ask the wrong question or make a crass remark. But she also had a feeling of fulfilment. She'd solved her personal mystery.

'When you think about it,' said Cat, 'what Rose's family did was insane. Shipping her off to some obscure home in the west of Ireland and telling her boyfriend she'd lost their baby? It's a funny take on Christianity.'

Martha sipped her wine. 'I know similar stuff used to happen at home, but, in my innocence, I'd expected a big American city to be different.'

'In fairness, poor old Templemorris doesn't have a monopoly on snobbery.' Cat lifted her glass. 'One more?'

'Ah, sure why not? Evanne could be a while talking to Dermot, and then she wants to call Serena. We've plenty of time.'

While Cat went to the bar, Martha examined

her surroundings. The round-backed leather chairs, the tinkling middle-of-the-road soundtrack, the dark carpet (so useful for hiding stains) were identical to those in countless hotel bars in Ireland. America didn't feel as different as it had back in the eighties when they'd spent their summer in New Jersey. As Evanne had pointed out, with a blend of surprise and disappointment, there weren't even that many fat people in Boston. A quick look, and you could have been in Dublin. The clothes were similar; the food was similar. The cinemas were showing the same films; the drug stores stocked the same brands. It was a long way from Ocean City, 1988, when, bewildered by the differences, Cat and Martha had compiled an inventory of the unexpected and exotic. Recalling some of the items on their list – bagels, coffee in takeaway cups, condoms in the supermarket – made her smile. Since then, she'd been to the US just once: five days in New York before Evanne was born. Never much of a television-watcher, much of Martha's knowledge came from books, but the ones she chose always seemed to feature either over-privileged east-coasters or worn-down Midwesterners. Her grasp of modern-day America was weak. She assumed the differences were still there. They were just more subtle now.

The more she thought about it, the more Martha understood that meeting Rose hadn't brought her quest for knowledge to an end. She wanted to delve into her Boston backstory. She longed to walk the streets where Joe and Rose had met and fallen in love. It was invigorating, the sense that there was more to learn.

'What was Mitch like?' asked Cat, as she sat down again.

'He was . . . interesting.'

'Good or bad interesting?'

'It's hard to say. Don't get me wrong, he was perfectly amiable. But I couldn't avoid the feeling that he was there under sufferance, and that he views Evanne and me as a bit of an intrusion.'

'That's a shame. Mind you, I can't imagine how Richie would react if I suddenly went, "*Et voilà*, here's a daughter I made earlier."'

'But Mitch has known about me for ages, since before they got married, apparently.'

'Ah,' said Cat. 'I didn't know that.'

Because of their prolonged silence, there were gaps in Cat's knowledge. Several times, Martha had said something about Rose only to find that Cat didn't know what she was talking about. Oh, and she was still being careful about what she revealed, especially where Paudie was concerned. An hour earlier she'd received another text from him: *Hope all went well. Give me a shout when you get back*. It occurred to Martha that he felt sorry for her. Poor rudderless, husbandless Martha going around apologising for things she'd done twenty years ago. The last thing she wanted was his pity. Then again, perhaps these were stupid, corrosive thoughts. Perhaps he was simply being friendly. She would have liked to talk through all of this with Cat.

But she couldn't.

Neither did she tell Cat about her bizarre conversation with Dermot. With hindsight, she was sure he hadn't meant what he'd said. Didn't tiredness get the better of everybody at some stage? When she was tired, the world could be a very bleak place indeed. No, his complaints, his insinuations, were best forgotten.

'Will you try to find out more about Joe?' Cat was asking now.

'I will. There's no rush, though. To be blunt, he's not going anywhere. We're meeting Brooke and Bobby tomorrow evening, and as keen as I am to see them, it might be tricky.'

'When Evanne's finished talking to Dermot, will we go and find somewhere to eat?'

'I'd better phone Mam and Dad first,' said Martha, who couldn't decide how much or how little to tell Delia and Clem. She had another balancing act to perform.

Mesmerised. Rose knew she was using the word too much, yet that was what she'd been in their company. It was the word she'd chosen when telling Brooke and Bobby about the experience. She used it again with Mitch.

'It's hard to describe,' she said. 'Normally you watch your family grow and change, day by day, year by year. To meet two fully formed human beings, and to know that they're part of you, is remarkable.'

'I'll say one thing,' replied Mitch, 'they're definitely not imposters. Evanne gets her looks from you. And Martha . . .'

'Looks like him.'

'Yeah, she looks just like him.'

If Rose had to use one other word to describe herself, it was elated. It had taken forty-five years, but finally she'd met Josephine again. She tried to imagine what her parents would have said about the afternoon's gathering. *What would you have done if you were here, Mom? Would you still have been ashamed? Would you still have been scared?* But it was too late for that now.

Martha and Evanne had been taken aback by what she'd told them about Joe. That was hardly surprising. For Martha, the news must have been especially disappointing.

She'd been right about her daughter. Despite her obvious joy at their reunion, there was a slight weariness about her. There'd been no mention of a partner either. Not that every woman needed a man. But from Rose's vantage point, forty-five was young. Too young to be on your own. *Oh, what am I doing?* she thought. *I've only met Martha once and already I'm worrying about her.*

Rose finished wiping the kitchen counter and turned to face her husband. 'I did do the right thing, you know.'

'Did I say otherwise?'

'You didn't have to. Your voice gave you away.'

'You have a lot of balls in the air,' said Mitch. 'I hope you can catch them all.'

Evanne reckoned that her dad looked like a hostage. His face was grey and distorted, and there were sagging folds beneath his eyes. To be fair, he wasn't alone: Skype tended to do that to people.

There was so much to say, she didn't know where to begin. Unfortunately, her father was distracted, and she figured most of her news would have to wait for another day. She decided to home in on the most important bits, like how Rose had been trapped in Carrigbrack, and how she'd lost both her baby and the baby's father.

Her father shook his head, his movements all jerky on her screen. 'That's terrible, pet,' he said. 'I hope you didn't find it too upsetting.'

'It *was* upsetting,' she replied, 'and that was how it should be. What happened was shocking.'

Right then, every problem Evanne had ever experienced seemed embarrassingly trivial. She knew that feeling wouldn't last. Give it a couple of days, and she'd be stressing about random nonsense again. She wished she was good at writing. That way she could write down everything she'd heard and describe how she felt. She said this to her dad.

'Don't get worked up about things you can't change,' he replied. 'Just enjoy your holiday.'

Before Evanne had the chance to point out how patronising he was being, he'd moved on. 'How's your mother?' he asked. 'Is she there?'

'No, she's in the bar with Cat. I'm up in the bedroom.'

He frowned. 'Cat? Why's Cat in Boston?'

'It's a long story. You see—'

'What are they doing in the bar?'

'Ahm, they're doing what people usually do in bars. Having a drink.' Her dad really was being very difficult. There were times when Evanne could *totally* understand why her parents were no longer together.

'She said she'd call me,' said her father, who promptly dissolved into a mess of pixels.

'I'm sure she will. It's not long since we got back from Rose's place.'

Her dad was back again. 'Is she okay?' he was asking. 'Was she upset about Joe?'

'She's fine,' said Evanne, who had decided she'd have to change the subject. 'How are Layla and Alex getting on? Has he learned anything new?'

'It's only a few days since you last saw him. He hasn't started walking around the room or singing ballads, if that's what you're asking.'

'Dad!'

'Sorry, pet. Alex is great. He's only flying it. Layla's in good form too. She's looking forward to her new job. We're all tip-top.' His face was eaten up by a big rictus grin.

Evanne knew her father well enough to know he was trying too hard.

Skype hadn't reached her mam and dad's world, so Martha had to rely on an old-fashioned phone call. She braced herself for regular warnings about the bill.

'Well?' her mother said. 'Is everything all right?'

'Oh, Mam, I'm so glad we met her. She told me all about what happened, and I told her all about our lives in Ireland. Evanne was great. You would've been proud of how grown-up she was. We talked for ages. And Rose sends her love to you and Dad.'

'Really?'

'She said that even though you've never met, she feels close to you. Oh, and she said she was very grateful. Wasn't that nice?'

'The poor woman, her life can't have been easy.' A sigh fluttered across the ocean. 'You'll have to give me the full story when you get home. I'd say this call is costing a fortune. Hold on there a moment, and I'll get your dad.' Her voice rose by several notches. 'Clem, come quickly, would you? It's Martha in America.'

Her father chatted about Rose until her mother butted in with a further caution about the price of transatlantic calls. 'One more thing,' he said. 'You did thank Rose for allowing us to have you, didn't you?'

Assuring him that she had, Martha felt a surge of affection for her parents. She would have to bring them a present. She didn't know what to buy, but she'd get Evanne on the case. Evanne was good at that sort of thing.

As she hung up, she realised something else. There were parts of her birth mother's story she would never discuss with Clem and Delia. She would never tell them how haunted Rose had looked while she described her time in Carrigbrack; how broken she'd appeared as she talked about Joe; and how clear it was that she hadn't forgiven her family.

Those were things they didn't need to know.

'Well, this is certainly . . . unusual,' said Brooke, as she leaned back in her chair. 'I have to tell you, Martha, we're all intrigued by your sudden appearance.'

Bobby gave his sister a sideways glance before turning to Martha. 'You've got to understand, until a few weeks ago we'd no idea you even existed. So, as great as it is to meet you, it's also kind of strange.'

'I promise you, I do understand,' said Martha. 'No doubt you got quite a land. Your parents did too. I'm sure they never expected me to get in touch.'

On the other side of the lounge, Rose gave an eager smile. 'But we're delighted that you did.'

'What intrigues me,' said Brooke, 'is why you decided to track Mom down now. You're what – forty-five? Why this sudden interest in your natural mother?'

Martha, with help from Evanne, did her best to explain.

Bobby was fascinated by Evanne's determination to find Rose. 'Aren't you the regular Nancy Drew?' he said to his niece.

'That's what Mum said. She's a terror for comparing people to characters in books. When I was little, she was always joking, calling me Laura Ingalls or Beth March. Or, when I was being a pain, she called me Veruca Salt. We even had a cat called Hermione Granger.'

Bobby laughed. 'I reckon your mom and I have quite a bit in common. We're both in the education business for starters.'

'That's right,' said Martha, grateful for an opportunity to deflect attention onto the rest of the family. 'What is it that you teach?'

'I teach third grade – eight- and nine-year-olds – so I guess I teach anything and everything. And then there are days when just keeping control is a challenge, and I don't teach anything at all.'

'Don't listen to him,' said Rose. 'He's a wonderful teacher.'

'I think Mom might be slightly biased.'

As she scrutinised her half-brother, Martha saw the family likeness. Fair-haired and blue-eyed, with a habit of tilting forward as he spoke, there was a certain Irishness about him. Brooke was a different proposition. Her Irish side was well buried. This was not a woman who watched *Riverdance* DVDs or read Maeve Binchy novels. With her sharp cream blazer, golden bob and brittle demeanour, it was easy to imagine her as a character in an American novel: a novel written by Candace Bushnell, with Gwyneth Paltrow taking the starring role in the film.

Mitch looked on. Save for offering the occasional word of encouragement or support to his wife, he said little. Martha couldn't imagine that he was always so quiet and she wondered about the dynamics of their relationship. After all, for decades he'd been the custodian of her secret. Was he genuinely happy that the truth was spilling out now?

She turned to Brooke. 'Rose said you work in public relations?'

'Sort of. I'm a communications specialist with an investment management company, so I deal with clients and influencers as well as with the media. And, of course, even how we define media is changing. Social media strategy is now a key part of the role.'

'I hope you understood all of that,' chipped in Bobby, 'because I'm never sure that I do.'

'Don't be taken in by my brother's simpleton act,' said Brooke, with a bow of her sleek head. 'There's a brain in there somewhere.'

'I worked in PR briefly when I left college,' offered Martha. 'I was useless. I couldn't take any of the clients seriously. It was all bending and scraping and treating mediocre businessmen like they'd patented a cure for cancer.'

'If you'd stuck it out past entry level, you would've been fine. The junior phase can be tough, but you need to persevere.'

'To be honest, I'm happy with what I ended up doing. It suits me better. I'm very fond of the library.'

'Such an important job,' said Rose, her smile even more eager than before.

'And you have two children, is that right?' asked Martha.

'You've certainly been doing your homework,' replied Brooke. 'Yes, two boys. Daniel is eight and Matt is six. Mom was hoping I'd produce a granddaughter, but you've stepped into the breach.'

Evanne giggled.

'Oh, Brooke,' said Rose. 'Ignore her, Martha, dear. She's being deliberately provocative.'

'She's good at that,' added Bobby.

'Why don't you tell us more about yourself, Martha?' said Brooke. 'You live in Dublin now but grew up in a small town, right?'

'Templemorris,' she replied. 'I've spent most of my life in Dublin, though. And Evanne's a real Dublin girl. I don't think small-town life would suit her.'

'The way Mom described Ireland it sounded – if you don't mind me saying so – pretty damn awful. Nothing but religion and poverty. Is that what it was like in Templemorris?'

'Gosh, not really. I mean, we didn't have much when I was growing up but we weren't poor or anything. A lot has changed too. I think Rose would find it quite different now. Not, obviously, that I'd blame her for having a jaundiced view of the place.'

'Templemorris is still kind of old-school,' said Evanne. 'Not much happens, so when people finish school they leave. They all head off to Australia and Canada. Oh, and the old people are forever going to Mass, even during the week.'

'Are they very religious?' asked Brooke, with the air of a woman whose worst suspicions had been confirmed.

Evanne scrunched up her mouth while she thought. 'No, I reckon it just gives them something to do. They can hang around afterwards and discuss the weather – and who died. Nan and Granddad are at their happiest when they're talking about funerals.'

Conscious that they were making her home town sound like an outpost of the 1950s, Martha attempted to lighten the atmosphere. 'Ah, now, we're being unfair. Templemorris has come on a lot. These days, there's even a place where you can get your nails done.'

Brooke chose not to get the joke. 'Having a manicure – is that considered modern?'

'I'm only messing. Mind you, my mother would view it as unnecessarily self-indulgent.'

'For real?' said Brooke.

The conversation stalled and, for a full minute, they sat in silence. Outside, the dusk was closing in.

'Here we are, sitting in the dark,' declared Mitch, as he rose and switched on two of the antique lamps.

Anxious to reignite the conversation, Martha turned to Rose. 'Maybe you might come and visit us sometime? And you too, Mitch, of course. And Bobby and Brooke. We'd love to show you around.'

'You never know,' said Rose, her smile faltering. 'Unfortunately, my memories of Ireland aren't the happiest. Going back there never appealed to me.'

Martha chided herself for being so insensitive. 'Sorry, I didn't think.'

'You've nothing to apologise for, Martha, dear. Perhaps I will visit one day. What's in the past can't hurt me.'

Martha watched Evanne stalk up and down, her arms jutting backwards at a comical angle.

'She wants to get a tan on the back of her arms and legs,' she explained to Cat. 'A proper even tan, like a tennis player at Wimbledon.'

Cat stretched out her legs and wiggled her toes. 'Being a teenager is a complicated business, and no mistake.'

'Just you wait until you have three.'

In front of them, a green wooden building with a red canopy offered fried clams, scallops and shrimp. On one side, fortune-tellers and tattoo artists plied their trades. On the other, a surprisingly calm Atlantic Ocean stretched out towards Ireland. They'd come to Cape Cod for the day to escape the city heat – and to draw breath.

'So,' said Cat, 'how bad was it?'

'I wouldn't say it was a disaster,' said Martha. 'It's not as though we had an actual argument. It was just very, very awkward. The whole time we were there, I felt like Brooke was looking down her nose at me. I was trapped in one of those situations where everything I said sounded wrong. Bobby kept stepping in to change the subject or to say something friendly, and Rose was overcompensating too. She kept praising Evanne and me, like she was saying to Brooke, "Look at them, they're not so bad."'

'Take it from somebody who was twenty-eight when she discovered she had two extra sisters, this can't be easy for Brooke or Bobby.'

'I appreciate that – and that's why I was doubly touched by Bobby's kindness. But Brooke was borderline hostile, and now I don't know what to do.'

'Maybe you shouldn't do anything. Leave her be, and she'll come to accept you. For all you know, she might be sniffy with everybody. Judging by how you described her, she sounds like one of those women who go to the supermarket to sneer at other people's groceries.'

'I can see her doing that, all right,' said Martha, with a reluctant laugh. 'I was wondering if I should get her number from Rose and give her a call.'

'Honestly, I wouldn't press it. When are you seeing Rose again?'

'Tomorrow. We're going for dinner. She asked if you'd like to come too.'

'I most certainly would,' said Cat. 'I'm only dying to meet them all.'

'It'll just be Rose and Mitch.'

'That's fine. Do you fancy an ice-cream? We've been in America for four days and we still haven't had an ice-cream. There must be a law against that.'

While Cat went to fetch three cones, Martha watched Evanne's funny walk. If Brooke's *froideur* had been the low point of the past few days, spending more time with Evanne had been an unexpected bonus. Next summer her daughter would be eighteen, and she'd probably be on one of those school leavers' holidays where everybody gets drunk and sunburned and does things they think will shock their parents. After that she'd be off to university for three or four years of wildness. Then she'd be thrust into the working world, and even if she enjoyed her job it would sometimes make her cranky and dispirited. She'd learn that mostly the world had no particular interest in her and she'd find this indifference hard to take. Occasionally, she'd become wistful for the comfort and certainty of school. Or maybe she wouldn't. Maybe Evanne would tackle life differently. But, one way or another, she'd be gone. 'Oh, for God's sake,' Martha said to herself. 'This is no time for getting maudlin. Enjoy what you've got for as long as you've got it.'

Cat returned with Evanne in tow. She handed Martha an overladen cone, strawberry ice-cream dribbling down the side. 'Eat up,' she said, 'before it melts away to nothing.'

'Give me a sec,' replied Martha. 'I heard my phone. I'd better see who it is.'

It was a text message. From Brooke. *I feel we should have a chat; just the two of us would be best. Can you meet me for a coffee in the morning?*

Martha passed the phone to Cat.

'Now I see what you mean,' said her friend. 'All joking apart, what sort of person uses a semicolon in a text message?'

# CHAPTER 29

Martha arrived five minutes early to find Brooke picking through a fruit salad and drinking black coffee. They had arranged to meet in a hotel not far from Brooke's office. The surrounding buildings were tall, with opaque windows and heavy doors. Banks, Martha assumed. Although she'd arrived via a warren of dark streets, the hotel café had a glass roof, and the room was splashed with sunlight. The light felt like a positive omen. Martha warned herself not to expect too much. Nevertheless, she hoped they could take a step forward.

For a couple of minutes, they engaged in jumpy small talk. Martha spoke about Evanne and Cat's plans to take a bus tour of the city. Brooke listed a few of her favourite spots. Then, without warning, she unveiled her statement of intent. This meeting wasn't about reaching out or becoming friends. It was about putting up barriers.

'You see,' said Brooke, 'I've got this feeling you have me pegged as the jealous daughter, the bitchy one who doesn't want to share her family with the poor outsider from Ireland.'

Martha's coffee scalded her throat. 'Please, that's—'

'That's not how it is, though. It's Mom I'm thinking of here. You don't know her, and you haven't seen how depressed she gets. I always assumed her dark moods were a genetic quirk. Now it's clear she's been suffering all these years because of what was done to her in Ireland. Those months have dogged her entire life. And the more I think about it, the more certain I am that your reappearance is not good news for her.'

'I don't know that you can—'

'Like I said, I can't see how you coming along, stirring up bad memories, will help her.'

Martha had read about sons and daughters who resented the emergence of an adopted sibling, and Brooke's reaction sounded like a textbook example. Given what Rose had been through, it came as no shock that she'd suffered from depression. It would be more of a surprise to hear that she'd sailed on without a scar. She told herself not to get rattled. 'Listen, I appreciate what you're saying. I hate to think of Rose being depressed, but why would I want to make life difficult for her? Until I began my search, I had no idea how much finding her would mean to me. Plainly, she wanted to meet me too. Otherwise, she would've ignored my letter. She didn't have to reply, you know.'

Although Brooke's jaw loosened, she said nothing.

Martha continued, 'So I'm sorry if you don't agree, but as far as I can see, your mother is thrilled we found her. Look at the fuss she makes of Evanne.'

'She's a good-hearted woman. I would be stunned if she wasn't kind to a teenage girl. But that's not the point. I don't think you appreciate how fragile she is. Like, inviting her to Ireland? Seriously, what was that about?'

'I was trying to be friendly, that's all. And I can't see that it did any harm. You're being too sensitive. Take my adoptive mother. She looks as delicate as a pressed flower. But let me tell you, she's tough.'

'Well, let me tell *you*. Mom's not. What were you planning for her – a misery tour? A trip around some orphanages. A convent or two, maybe.'

Her anger gathering pace, it occurred to Martha that she wasn't the only one whose stereotypes were out of date. 'I'm not going to bother responding to that. I would never in a million years try to defend what was done to your – to our mother. The way Rose was treated in Carrigbrack was shameful. And she wasn't alone. Some of what went on in those homes was unforgivable. The cover-up was appalling too. It still is.'

'I'm glad you admit that Mom was badly treated.'

'For pity's sake, why would I defend what happened? After all, I'm the one who was taken from her mother. I'm the one who grew up wondering who she was and where she came from. But we're talking about the events of more than forty years ago. I mean, what was happening back then in Boston? Wasn't there an almighty row about racial segregation in schools?'

'That was a complex situation. I'll bet that whatever you've heard is wrong.'

'I won't say that everything you've heard about Ireland is wrong, but I'm sure some of it is.' Martha paused. This was like arguing with Dermot. You started off talking about one thing, and before you knew it, you'd veered off on a poisonous tangent. She needed to defuse the situation before it degenerated into an out-and-out slanging match. Already people were staring at them. 'Jesus, I can't believe we're having such a stupid argument. What happened happened. It's not my fault.'

'I didn't say it was,' said Brooke. She appeared to crackle, like anyone who dared to touch her would come away with an electric shock.

'Besides, it's not as if Rose's family didn't play their part. It was her own mother and father who sent her to Carrigbrack. At least with families in Ireland, you could argue that they were in thrall to the Catholic Church. From what Rose has told me, that wasn't the case with her parents. I'm not saying religion didn't play a role, but it sounds like what mattered most was hiding the baby they saw as an embarrassment. And now here I am, their living, breathing nightmare.'

'Of course I'm appalled by their behaviour. They've got a lot to answer for.'

'At least life turned out well for me. I was raised by a great family. Not everybody was that lucky.'

'I wouldn't be too certain of that,' said Brooke, a chill in her voice.

'What do you mean?'

'I wouldn't be so cock-sure you have a great family.'

'I don't follow you,' said Martha. 'You don't know anything about my parents.'

'How do you think you ended up with them?'

'They applied to adopt a baby and they got me.'

'I think you'll find it was a little shadier than that.'

'What are you getting at?' asked Martha, properly perplexed now.

'It's bound to come out sooner or later.'

'What?'

'You weren't given away to some Irish stranger,' said Brooke. 'You were given to a cousin. The woman who adopted you – Delia, is it? She's Mom's cousin.'

# CHAPTER 30

It couldn't be true. The thought was too awful. Too grotesque. Her parents would have told her. They wouldn't have spent forty-five years pretending her background was a mystery. Would they?

But what if it was true? As she walked leaden-legged towards Boston Common, as she found a bench, as she slouched forward, her head in her hands, Martha kept asking that question. What if it wasn't happenstance that had brought her to Templemorris but design? What if, all those years ago, Delia had been approached by relatives from America? And what if, in return for a much-wanted baby, she had gone along with their plan?

It pained Martha to admit it, but everything Brooke had said rang true. She'd been too confident, she'd provided too much detail, for her story to be a lie. Sister Agnes was the intermediary, she'd said. The nun was related to both Delia and Rose. Rose had been sworn to secrecy. She'd promised not to interfere. Until Martha had tracked her down, she'd kept her word.

Having unburdened herself, Brooke had sat

there, her mouth in a straight line, her face aglow with silent victory.

'I don't believe you,' Martha had said. She'd wanted to say more, but the words crumbled in her mouth. She rose too quickly and, with a clatter, her chair tipped over. A woman at the next table gasped.

'Is there a problem, Ma'am?' a waiter asked.

But Martha was gone. Seized by an almost primitive urge to flee, she dashed down the stairs and out the door.

Now, here she was, on a park bench in the stifling heat, sweat collecting along her hairline, bile rising in her throat. Three days earlier, she'd thought her mystery was solved. How wrong she'd been. She could see now why Delia had been cagey and tense. She could see why Clem had warned her about upsetting her mother, why both parents had asked Una to intercede. They'd been trying to derail Martha's search. What they hadn't counted on was Evanne's tenacity and Winnie Lafferty's memory.

That wasn't all. She reached into her bag and removed Rose's first letter. Although she'd known that something wasn't quite right, only now could she put her finger on it. *It's a source of solace to me that you found a good and loving home*, Rose had written. How did she know what sort of home her child had grown up in? Martha hadn't told her.

Other episodes came back to her. Obviously, she couldn't recall the precise words, but she remembered the day she'd run out of Miss Casey's class. The day her mother had cautioned her against looking for her birth parents. 'Sometimes people pull at one thread,' her mam had said, 'and other threads unravel.' They ended up being sorry they hadn't let matters rest. That evening was imprinted on Martha's brain. The more she thought about it, the more she remembered other similar warnings. She'd always dismissed them as normal. Understandable. Delia wanting to protect her.

Delia. So they were flesh and blood, after all. A cousin, Brooke had said, but not how close a cousin. Pain was building in Martha's head. She would have to buy a bottle of water, take some painkillers. Then she might be able to think properly. She looked up. All around her, life trundled on. A crescent of tourists consulted a map; a boy windmilled his arms against a wasp; a squirrel scurried up a tree. The tang of sun cream and the sweaty smell of fried onions hung in the air. On the other side of the Common, the golden dome of the State House reflected the blazing sun.

She received a message from Evanne. They were in Fenway Park, her daughter said, and even though they knew nothing about baseball, it was really cool. Like something from the movies. *Still tied up here*, Martha replied. *Enjoy yourselves xxx*

Her fingers felt thick and awkward, like they belonged to somebody else. Pins and needles ran up and down her arms.

Fresh questions crept into her head. Did Una

know? What about other members of her mam and dad's families? Martha needed to talk to her mother and father. And she needed to talk to Rose.

'I didn't plan on telling her,' Brooke was saying. 'She was irritating me and it slipped out.'

'I don't care,' said Rose. 'I don't give a rat's what you did or didn't plan. How could you do this to me? I trusted you. I told you something. I asked you to keep it to yourself. And what did you do? The first opportunity you got, you betrayed me. You just couldn't stop yourself.'

Rose saw tears in her daughter's eyes. For once, she felt no sympathy. They were probably tears of self-pity when what she should be feeling was remorse.

Brooke had arrived in Amber Street ten minutes before, her face bloodless, panic in her voice. 'I've done something stupid,' she'd said. Rose, who had no idea she'd been talking to Martha, assumed she was referring to her marriage or to one of the boys or a problem at work. She felt a rush of sympathy. It soon evaporated.

Rose did another loop of the kitchen. From the start, she'd regretted telling Brooke and Bobby that she was related to Delia Sheeran. She'd done so only because of their strong reaction to her story. She'd expected them to be outraged by what had happened in 1968. The problem was, they'd also been appalled by her decision to hide the truth. To get them back on side, she'd provided another crumb of information. 'That was what I was up against,' she'd said. 'It was a family conspiracy, and there was nothing I could do.'

'Sit down, Mom. Please,' said Brooke, who was slumped at the table.

Rose did another circuit. 'Why didn't you bring Martha with you?'

'Because she'd disappeared.'

'For heaven's sake, Brooke. Why did you allow her to go?'

'I couldn't stop her. She was moving so quickly, she sent a chair flying across the room. She created quite a scene.'

'You can hardly blame her. You should've followed her.'

'By the time I'd settled the bill, and assured the waiter that everything was fine, she'd vanished. I did try to find her but . . .'

At last Rose sat down. The implications of her daughter's outburst were percolating through her brain. There was every danger that as they spoke Martha was on the phone to Ireland, demanding to know why Clem and Delia hadn't told her the truth.

'Have you any idea what you've done?' she said to Brooke.

'I told you,' said her daughter, a tear snaking down one cheek. 'I told you I didn't mean any harm.'

How strange was it to see Brooke – controlled, assured Brooke – like this.

'Do quit crying,' said Rose. 'It isn't helping. I'm

going to call Martha. I can only pray she hasn't done anything drastic.'

'Do you want me to—'

'What I want is for you to leave me in peace while I try to sort this out.'

Rose rubbed her knuckles against her forehead. For the first time, she feared that Mitch was right. Maybe Brooke wasn't the only one who'd lost control.

# CHAPTER 31

Evanne and Cat were in Cambridge, sitting beside the Charles River, eating ice-cream. In front of them, rowers were gliding through the water. Behind them was Harvard, all red brick and ivy, bookshops and bicycles. Evanne felt like a visitor in an unreal world.

Cat sighed. 'What you've got to do now is get seven A grades in your Leaving Cert, and all this could be yours. I can picture you at Harvard.'

'I think we both know that's never going to happen,' said Evanne.

'Ah, come on, don't disappoint me. You've even got local digs. Rose could put you up in her spare room.'

'Rose's house is miles away. Anyway, I'm definitely not the Harvard type.'

Cat gave her cone a thoughtful lick. 'You've got to aim high. That was the problem with the way your mam and I were brought up. Aiming high was considered vulgar. Or for boys.'

Seeing an opportunity, Evanne asked a question. 'Are you ever going to tell me why the two of you fell out?'

'You'll have to ask Martha.'

'Was it something to do with Dad?'

'No. Now stop fishing.' She turned to Evanne. 'Why do you think it was anything to do with Dermot?'

'I don't know. It's just . . . he's all funny at the moment. I don't think he's getting on with Layla. She's miserable too. Like, I know having a baby is meant to be stressful and everything, but they don't seem to enjoy Alex at all. It's not like they don't love him, more like they're frightened of him.' She crunched the last of her cone. 'I'm supposed to be going on holidays with them soon, and straight up, I'd rather a week of chemistry classes.'

'As bad as that, huh? Where are you off to?'

'West Cork. I bet it'll piss rain the whole time too.' She looked at Cat. 'And please don't give me the spiel about how when you were my age, you were grateful for a day trip to Quilty. I get enough of that from Mum.'

'Actually, when we were your age, we'd just finished the Leaving Cert. We both had terrible summer jobs, and then we thumbed around Ireland.'

'Your parents let you hitch lifts?'

'Mine did. I don't know that Delia and Clem fully understood what was going on. They were very protective of your mum.'

'It always sounds to me like she had tons of freedom – far more than she's ever given to me.'

'But those were different times,' said Cat, putting on an old-woman voice

'Yeah, right. Nothing bad ever happened back in the good old nineteen eighties. Guys were content to hold your hand, and nobody drank anything stronger than 7 Up. Oh, and drugs hadn't been invented.'

Cat laughed. 'That's not *quite* how I remember it.' She looked at her watch. 'Speaking of Martha, shouldn't we have heard from her by now? She'd love it up here. It's bookshop heaven. Do you want to send her a text or whatever it is you young people do?'

'I did. I sent her a picture of Harvard Square, only she never got back to me.'

Cat frowned. 'I hope Brooke didn't upset her. I'll give her a buzz.'

Evanne watched while Cat dug out her phone and got to her feet. For the next couple of minutes she listened to one side of an odd conversation.

'Take a deep breath,' said Cat, 'and tell me exactly what happened.' Whatever her mum said mustn't have made sense because Cat shook her head. 'I can't help you, Martha, if you won't tell me what happened.' There was a gap before Cat asked something about a loud noise. Then she said, 'Why are you going there?'

There was another silence followed by 'Christ,' followed by 'She might be lying,' followed by 'Don't worry, we'll find you.'

When the call ended, Cat sat down again. She

draped an arm around Evanne. 'You know the way you said that Rose's house was a good distance from here?' Her voice was gentle.

'Uh-huh, it's on the other side of the city. What's wrong?'

'Do you know how to get there?'

Evanne nodded. 'Tell me what's wrong.'

'I'll tell you on the way.'

By the time Martha reached Amber Street, she was exhausted and bedraggled. Rose must have seen her coming for she was already at the door. 'Thank God you're here,' she said. 'Come in. Please, come in. You shouldn't have trekked all this way. I would have found you. Look at you, you're—'

'In an awful state. I got the train and then I ran the rest of the way but . . .' She found she couldn't complete the sentence. During the journey, her initial anger had waned. It had been replaced by . . . Actually, she wasn't sure what had replaced it. All she knew was that, despite the heat of the day, she felt cold, so cold she could have been running naked through a shower of sleet. All of her limbs were heavy, and her head continued to thump. She kept thinking about what Brooke had said and about everything she'd learned that week: Carrigbrack and Joe and her mother and father and . . . She'd learned too much.

'I'm no medical expert but I think this might be shock. Shall I call a doctor?' asked Rose.

‘God, no,’ replied Martha. ‘Cat and Evanne will be here soon.’ She realised this didn’t make sense. Cat and Evanne weren’t going to cure her dizziness. *Oh, get a grip, Martha*, she thought. *What sort of idiot falls apart like this?* ‘I’ll be grand. I want to hear your explanation.’ She tried to judge Rose’s response but found she couldn’t focus.

‘And you will, but you need to sit down. Shall I fetch you some water? Or tea? Tea would be good.’

Although she couldn’t hear Rose properly – why was her voice so distorted? – Martha found herself agreeing. She also found the floor was rising up to meet her. Next she knew, Rose was yanking her by the arm towards the sofa. ‘I really should get the doctor,’ she was saying.

‘No,’ said Martha, who couldn’t stop trembling.

‘At least let me see what I can do to try and halt that shivering.’

Rose returned with a soft beige blanket. For two or three minutes, they sat in silence. Martha took a deep breath. Then another. And another. Rose got to her feet but quickly sat down again, as if she was at a loss as to what to do with herself.

Eventually Martha spoke. ‘Perhaps we could have that tea now.’

When Rose came back again, cups and saucers clanking on a tray, Martha was calm. ‘The sun,’ she said. ‘It got the better of me.’

‘That and the shock.’

‘Yeah, that too.’ For some reason, she attempted

a smile. 'I was like a Victorian heroine having a fit of the vapours.'

'I was frantic with worry,' said Rose, as she poured their tea. 'I tried calling, only you didn't answer.'

'I wanted to see you in person.' She lifted her cup. 'I did speak to Cat, by the way. That may have been a mistake. She's with Evanne. I think they're both on their way here.'

'So you said.'

'Sorry, I'm still a wee bit confused. What Brooke told me . . . It's the truth?'

Rose gave an almost imperceptible nod. 'You haven't spoken to your mom and dad?'

Martha explained that she'd been about to call them, but had decided to speak to Rose first. 'This,' she said, 'is not how I pictured our reunion.'

'You and me both. You do understand that it wasn't my place to tell you?'

'I do, I suppose. But you've got to tell me everything now.'

Rose blew across her tea. 'Are you sure you're ready?'

'I've got to know.'

As far as the basic facts were concerned, Rose's story deviated little from Brooke's. She did, however, promise to fill in the detail.

'You'll have to bear with me on this,' she said, 'and I don't know that your head's in any condition to handle the complexities of a family tree. I'll draw a diagram for you if you like.'

'Just tell me,' said Martha. Now the shock was subsiding, her confusion was giving way to irritation. She gathered the blanket around her.

'Okay. My grandparents, my father's mother and father, were called James and Margaret Moroney. They lived in Killeniska in County Clare and had eight children. Among them were two girls, Constance and Nora. Constance became a nun, and took the name Agnes. Nora married a man called Arthur Devane—'

'Oh, Jesus.'

'—who lived in Templemorris. They had a daughter called—'

'Delia.'

'—who's my first cousin.'

'And my mother.'

'Yes.'

Martha touched her hair. It was tacky with sweat. Then she reached for her tea. She didn't think she'd be capable of swallowing, but it gave her something to do with her hands. She tried to visualise Nora, but she'd been only six or seven when her grandmother died. She remembered a small woman with a pinched face. A brown coat came to mind. A tartan shopping trolley. The smell of clove rock. A cabinet filled with knick-knacks from other people's holidays in Bundoran and the Isle of Man.

'So, to be clear about this,' she said, 'Delia isn't a distant relation. She's my aunt.'

'I think, technically speaking, she's my first

cousin . . . and your first cousin once removed. Una's your second cousin.'

The implications hit Martha like a double-decker bus. 'Have you always known, then? While I wondered and dreamed about you, have you always known where I was and what I was doing? Has all of this getting-to-know-you stuff been a charade?'

'No, I promise you, no. At first, I knew nothing. As far as I was concerned, yours was an adoption like any other.'

'So when did you find out?'

'When my father returned to Carrigbrack to bring me home to America, he was shocked by the state I was in. Looking back now, I can see that I was catatonic with grief. He wanted to reassure me that you would be looked after – so he told me about my cousin Delia who couldn't have a child. It turned out he'd even been to Templemorris to see you.'

'Good Lord.'

'Crazy, huh? Anyway, he made me promise never to pester your family or to make enquiries about you. Once you were gone, you were no longer my child.'

Martha had to fight the urge to get up and shake the woman sitting across from her. 'But you could've found me. At any time, you could've tracked me down.'

'Yes and no. You've got to remember that I didn't know your name. To me, you were still Josephine.

And I assumed that, if you were married, your last name would be different too.'

'You assumed wrong. Even when I was married, I was Martha Sheeran.'

Rose picked up her cup. 'The truth, unpleasant as it might sound, is this: when I returned to Boston, Ireland reverted to being a faraway place, a place where dark things happened. Joe was gone, and I . . . I genuinely believed I had to try to forget about you. I had to move on with my life.'

'Why should I believe you? For all I know, you might have been getting regular updates from Mam and Dad. "Dear Rose, Martha's doing well at school" or "Dear Rose, Martha's marriage has fallen asunder."'

'No.' Even though Rose's voice had risen only slightly, it seemed to fill the room. 'No. They never did. Ever.' She paused. 'I did write once, when Brooke and Bobby were kids. I guess I was feeling kind of low and I got to thinking about you. I didn't have a precise address. All the same, Clem and Delia must have got my letter.'

Martha waited.

'They didn't reply. They were right not to. I'd broken our agreement. Later, a sort of paralysis set in. I felt as though making any attempt to find out about you would bring my life tumbling down. You see, I'd given Mitch my word. "I won't go prying," I'd said. I felt fortunate to have him. Putting my marriage in jeopardy would have been stupid. Plus, and maybe this sounds lame, I was consoled by the knowledge that you were with family.'

'In more recent times, though, did you not want to know what I was doing, or whether I was married, or whether you had grandchildren? Were you not curious?'

'Oh, God, yes, but let's face it, Martha, I wasn't the only one who turned her back on the past. You could have come searching for me at any time. You chose not to.' Rose gave a vigorous shake of her head. 'Sorry, dear, that sounded harsh. I didn't mean to be harsh. Please forgive me.'

''S okay,' said Martha, her voice just a squeak. She drained her tea. As she did, she recalled something Malachy McCracken had said. Nothing was too strange or unlikely, he'd told her. Compared to some of the tales he must have heard – rape, incest, cruelty, forged papers, faked deaths, babies spirited away in the night – Martha's story was all too believable. One family member had given another a dig-out. A well-placed relation had organised the paperwork. Knowing this didn't make the truth any more palatable. Not only was Rose a stranger, she felt she didn't really know Clem and Delia either. She would never have imagined them capable of such subterfuge.

Outside, a child squealed. What sounded like a van lumbered past. The time had come for Martha to shove aside her self-pity. Evanne would be here soon. She would expect her mother to be in control.

* * *

Mitch turned up first. Then, Bobby arrived. Finally, Cat and Evanne pitched up. All four were concerned, solicitous. If anything, they were too cloying for Martha. She wanted to shout, 'Just give me some space, would you?' She didn't, of course. She nodded and mumbled and smiled a pretend smile. After her earlier fire and fury, she was burned out. She needed time to decompress. She wanted to leave.

Evanne sent her an imploring look. 'But it might be ages before we see them again. We're going home tomorrow.'

Rose asked them not to go. 'You can have a lie-down, if you like,' she said to Martha. 'I'll fix us an early dinner. Please stay.'

That was what they did. They sat at the lacquered dining-room table and ate monkfish with salad, lemon mousse and strawberries. The meal was wonderful. Martha could tell that Rose had gone to a lot of trouble, yet she might as well have been eating sawdust and dirt. There was a hard lump in her throat and a larger one in her stomach. Every mouthful was difficult.

Afterwards, she was torn. Part of her wanted to spool forwards so she could have some time on her own; another part wanted to spool back to before Brooke's revelation. She peered around the table. What a ragged, jagged bunch they were. There was Evanne in cut-off denims and a vest top, her shoulders sunburned, her cheeks flushed from too much wine. Beside her, Rose was preternaturally calm. Perhaps she'd had pharmaceutical help. There was Bobby, eager as a sheepdog, anxious to prove that everything was under control. Mitch, on the other hand, appeared tired, tense. Cat flitted about, chatting to everybody, refilling glasses as if she was in her own home. And watching them, her summer dress crumpled, a blanket still draped over her shoulders, was Martha. The most befuddled of them all.

Cat sidled over to her. 'I like the new look,' she said, nodding at the blanket.

'Don't mock. I can see why old women used to get attached to their shawls. It's very comforting.'

'Ah, now, you don't look like a shawly. I was thinking more Stevie Nicks. Well, a cut-price Stevie Nicks.' Cat tilted her head towards the rest of the gathering. Evanne was showing Rose and Bobby something on her phone. 'They're grand people, you know. Bobby's a lovely fellow.'

'Shame his sister's such an uppity bitch.' Martha knew this was too simplistic. Right then, however, she felt entitled to see the world in black and white. Nuance and understanding would have to wait for another day. She fingered the edge of her blanket. 'Now you've had time to take it all on board, what do you think?'

'In a way, it reminds me of my own family's woes. There's that same sense of being hoodwinked, you know.'

'Don't I just.'

'Mind you,' continued Cat, 'with Dad, there were

reasons to suspect he was up to no good. But Clem and Delia? I wouldn't have put them down as the secretive kind. I think of all the conversations we've had about who your natural family might be, and I swear I never saw this coming.'

'That's two of us. When you found out about your father and his other family, what was it like? I mean, I remember you being upset. But mostly I remember your mam and how devastated she was.'

'It was awful. Honestly, it was such an almighty betrayal I could have kicked him into the middle of next week – only he was already in his coffin.'

'Does it still matter to you?'

'Yeah, it does. Like I told you before, I wish we'd never found out.' Cat hesitated. 'I know you mightn't see it right now, but this is different. Shocking and all as your news is, you can bet that Clem and Delia thought they were doing the right thing.'

'That doesn't stop me feeling duped, though. And I can't help thinking, if they were able to lie about something as big as this, what else have they lied about?'

'Nothing, probably. But . . . don't we all have our secrets?'

'I'll have to talk to them,' said Martha.

'Will you give them a ring?'

'Nah. I'll go down to Templemorris when we get home. I'll give Una a shout, though. I'd better tell her. That's if she doesn't already know.'

It was ten o'clock by the time they left, one of those uncomfortable partings where nobody knows what to do or say, where your arms feel stiff, and your words not quite right. As they stood on the porch, crickets sang.

Rose took Martha aside. 'About Brooke?'

'Uh-huh?'

'As maddening as she can be, I don't believe she set out to hurt you this morning.'

'She set out to warn me off. She said that having me around wasn't good for you.'

'She's wrong.'

'The thing is, Rose, even if she didn't plan on coming out with half of what she said, she did want to get rid of me.'

'I'll talk to her. The problem with Brooke is, she doesn't like life to be messy. If she can't control something, she has to shut it down. She's always been the same. I promise you, she's not a bad person.'

What could Martha do but agree? 'I'm sure she's not,' she said, as she forced a smile.

Rose squeezed her arm. 'None of us is.'

# CHAPTER 32

Evanne bounced up the stairs two at a time. It was insane how much she was looking forward to seeing Alex and Layla. Her mother had gone to Templemorris for the big showdown. For once Evanne was content to stay in Dublin. She'd no desire to listen to her nan and granddad trying to justify their trickery. All those years of lying! Pretending they didn't have a clue who Rose was, when they knew every little thing about her. Standing by while their daughter and granddaughter spent month after month searching and hoping. Evanne was relieved to get away from her mother too. Her mum had dug out her brave face and was doing her I'll-handle-this act when any fool could see she was absolutely shredded. On the plane home, she'd opened a copy of *Vanity Fair*, then stared at the same page for two hours. Either she was Shailene Woodley's biggest fan or she was super-upset.

In Evanne's humble opinion, Brooke had done them a favour. She might be a 'hatchet-faced shrew' (copyright Cat O'Dowd), but at least she'd told the truth. Evanne had pointed out that Cat hadn't actually met Brooke. Cat replied that she didn't need to, her photo was enough. To be honest, Evanne found her aunt kind of interesting. Brooke struck her as the sort of woman who kept her shoes in boxes with photos on the front. You couldn't imagine her getting blood on her knickers or neglecting her bikini line.

When they were back home in Dolmen Crescent, her mum had allowed herself to get upset. She called Una, who became all emotional too. 'You never knew?' her mother kept saying. 'You genuinely never knew?' Then she'd started talking about them being cousins as well as sisters. It truly was beyond weird. Imagine, Evanne and Una were blood relations after all. Second cousins, once removed, according to her mum. 'I still don't like chemistry,' Evanne replied. That gave them both a much-needed laugh.

Evanne leaned on the buzzer. After the second try, she realised that nobody was at home. Thankfully, she had her own key. Her dad had said he'd collect her later, but she'd wanted to give them a surprise. He was at work, while Layla and Alex must have gone for a walk.

She'd found time to buy some presents for her brother, including a Red Sox T-shirt and a tiny pair of Converse. Evanne was looking forward to dressing him up in his Boston finery and taking a picture for her Instagram. She was amazed by how much she was enjoying Alex. Before the summer holidays, she'd made the mistake of saying this to Miss McGovern, the career guidance teacher. Miss McGovern asked if she'd considered childcare as a career. That was not good: the woman was an Olympic-level snob who viewed childcare as a job for the slightly slow. She was only interested in girls who wanted to study medicine or law. Express a desire to do anything else, and she'd stare at you like you'd shaved off your hair or had your face tattooed. Actually, Evanne had decided what she wanted to do, and it wasn't childcare. Neither was it something requiring seven squillion As. She had a feeling her choice wouldn't go down well at home, but that was a battle for another day.

The apartment was looking less higgledy-piggledy than usual. Somebody had been tidying. This, she reckoned, was a positive sign. Life must be getting back to normal. After ten minutes of waiting, she rang Layla. When there was no answer, she went to make coffee. The kitchen wasn't just tidy, it was bare. All of Alex's baby paraphernalia must have been put away. She opened the fridge to find that apart from a carton of milk it, too, was bare. The milk was two days out of date. Layla must be at the shops. Evanne gave her another call. Again she didn't pick up.

She'd bought Layla a present from Boston. It was only small – a lipstick from Sephora – but it was something. Evanne reckoned the colour, a glossy, cheerful pink, would suit her.

Bored, she decided to go for a ramble around

the apartment. She could lay out Alex's new gear so it would be ready for him to try. When she entered her little brother's room, she got a shock: most of his belongings were missing. Oh, his cot was still in place, but his teddies weren't there. Neither was his special blanket. There were no nappies on top of the dresser. Nor was there any sign of his changing mat. She pulled open a drawer. Although it wasn't totally empty, it was far from full. That wasn't all. The room didn't smell right. It didn't smell of Alex.

Next door in her dad and Layla's room, the first thing Evanne noticed was the unmade bed. Then her eyes swept over the dressing table and the chest of drawers. Aside from a handful of change and a solitary moisturiser, there was nothing to see. Where was Layla's stuff? Where were her cleansers, her serums, her balms? Where was her stand of earrings? Her box of bracelets? In a panic, Evanne ran over to the wardrobe. Normally it was crammed to overflowing with Layla's gear, every last stitch smelling of Miss Dior. She tugged at the door so hard it almost flew off its hinges. She saw what she expected to see: nothing. Well, nothing apart from an unbroken row of dark suits. And the smell? Unless you counted a slight whiff of dry-cleaning fluid, there was no smell.

'Were you ever going to say anything?'

They were sitting at the kitchen table. Martha couldn't look either parent in the eye. Instead she focused on her father's corrugated white hair and her mother's helmet of steel.

The question hung between them. Eventually, her mam answered: 'We didn't think we'd need to. We didn't think you'd ever find out.'

Martha breathed in. 'Just to be clear about this, everything Rose said is true?'

'Yes,' said her dad. 'Obviously we're not familiar with everything that happened in Boston or in Carrigbrack. But, yes, that nun, Sister Agnes, arranged your adoption. And, yes, we knew that your natural mother was Delia's American cousin.'

Another deep breath. 'All I can say is, you're both far better actors than I gave you credit for. For as long as I can remember, you've been saying, "Sure we haven't a clue where you came from." Not only that: you told me that if I went searching I mightn't like what I found. "Leave well enough alone," you said. And all the while you were lying.'

Her mother began, 'Now—'

But Martha wouldn't be interrupted: 'You know what the mad thing is, Mam? Cat used to joke about me looking more like you than Una does. "Are you certain you're not related?" she used to say. She didn't know how close to the truth she was.'

Her mother blanched. 'It wasn't our place to tell you about Rose. In fact, we swore we wouldn't. And we kept our side of the deal.'

'Don't go blaming Rose.'

'I'm not blaming anybody. I'm telling you how it was.'

'Did you know she was coerced into giving me up? That she was bundled onto a plane and forced to live in that Carrigbrack place? And that my birth father was told she'd lost their baby? The way she was treated, the way both of them were treated, was scandalous. Scandalous.'

'Please, Martha,' said her father, 'be reasonable. You can't go blaming us for that. Of course we didn't know the full story. You've got to understand, we were so happy to get you, so grateful. It never occurred to us that Rose was anything other than satisfied with the arrangement. And as for your natural father? We knew hardly anything about him.'

'You knew later, though. She says she wrote to you, only you didn't reply.'

'That's right,' said her mam. 'It was an odd letter. I don't think she was in the full of her health, poor woman.'

'What do you mean?'

'Well, she—'

Clem intervened: 'She wanted to take you back. She said you belonged with her in America. Like your mother says, we didn't reckon she was thinking clearly.'

'Did you consider doing what she asked?' said Martha. 'After all, by then you had Una.'

Delia's face curdled. 'Oh, Martha, for the love of God, do you really think you meant that little to us? You were our daughter. You were eleven years old, your own little person. Our Martha, one minute all serious, the next as giddy as a goose. We loved you. We could never have let you go. Never ever. I thought you'd understand that.' She began to sob, her shoulders rising and falling.

'I'll get a handkerchief,' said Clem.

'I'm sorry, Mam,' said Martha. 'I never meant to suggest you didn't love me. It's just . . . This is all very difficult, you know.'

Her dad returned. Her mother dabbed at her face with the hankie. Her tears had stopped, but she remained hunched over, bent like a sapling in a force-ten gale.

'What I don't get,' said Martha, 'is why you gave me some information. Like, you let me know my original name. You didn't have to do that.'

'I suppose,' replied her father, 'we felt that if we didn't give you some help, we would alienate you or make you suspicious. Anyway, we didn't think you could possibly find your natural mother. She was in America. It was hard enough for people to trace their birth parents in this country, not to mind looking overseas.'

She nodded. 'And the paperwork you showed me from the shoebox? Was that forged?'

'No. Everything was provided by Agnes. She made sure we went through all the usual formalities.' Her mother sniffled. 'She was a demon for paperwork and the like. I hope you know there was nothing illegal about your adoption. It was just . . .'

'Slightly irregular,' said her father.

'And Sister Agnes? She's not still around, is she?'

'She's dead these thirty years. Some sort of cancer, if memory serves me well. We went to her funeral.'

'What about Rose's father, Ed Moroney?' asked Martha. 'Is it true he came to see me?'

'It is,' said her mam. 'You were only with us two or three weeks, and this American man arrived at the door. He introduced himself as my uncle Edward. When we got talking, you could tell he was from Ireland originally, but he'd been in America since before I was born. I was petrified. We both were. We were certain he was going to take you away again.'

'As I recall, he was a nice man,' added Clem. 'He sat in the front room with you on his lap, drinking tea, saying how glad he was that his granddaughter had found a good home. We relaxed then.'

'He showed us some pictures of the family,' said Delia, picking up the baton again. 'His wife was very beautiful.'

'By the sound of things, she was also an unmitigated cow,' said Martha. 'What puzzles me is how you've managed to sit out the past few months, knowing that I was getting closer to finding Rose . . . and then knowing I was going to meet her. Were you not worried the truth would come out?'

'I don't know,' said her mother, as she blotted her face again. 'We did talk about it but we assumed that the people in America . . . they would want a secret to remain a secret.'

Martha hesitated. She had another question to ask. She turned to her mother, finally looking her in the eye. 'You know the way you've always defended the mother-and-baby homes? Is that because a member of your own family, this Sister Agnes, was part of the system?'

She watched her mam's mouth twist. 'That, if you don't mind me saying so, is a touch simplistic. Maybe it did colour my judgement. I can't say.' Her tone was prickly. Clearly, this was not a place she wanted to go.

Her dad closed his eyes tightly so that the wrinkles fanned out across his face. 'How is she? Rose, I mean. From what you say, she's had a comfortable life.'

'As far as money's concerned, yes, she has.'

He opened his eyes. 'But the loss of your natural father . . . did that affect her, do you think?'

'I think everything affected her.'

'What do you mean?'

'I'm no expert, but from what I can gather, Rose never got on with her mother. She did trust her father, though, and, from the way she told it, being let down by him – being betrayed by him – has blighted her life.'

Another flurry of tears rained down her mother's cheeks.

Some time passed before Delia got to her feet. Her face was the colour of cold porridge. 'Have you had your dinner?'

Martha pushed her hair back from her face. 'I

ate on the way down,' she lied. 'I'll see you later. I'm going down the town to meet a friend.'

Nancy was on the phone and she wasn't happy.

'What did I say to you, Rose? "Reopening old wounds isn't a good idea," I said. And I was right. Not that saying so gives me any pleasure.'

Rose found that nowadays most people in her circle placed a premium on diplomacy. Their words were carefully calibrated: you had to read their tone. Her sister had no such constraints. If nothing else you had to give her marks for honesty. 'You've heard about Brooke's tantrum, then?' she said.

'It's hardly fair to call it that.'

'That was what it sounded like to me.'

'Brooke called me because she was concerned about you.'

Childish as it might be, when Rose was talking to Nancy she felt an instinctive need to be difficult. She decided to feign satisfaction with how everything had played out. 'At least it's all out in the open now. That can only be a good thing.'

'Please tell me you're joking,' replied Nancy.

'Nope. To begin with, I was furious with Brooke. Now I've had time to reflect, I reckon it's only right that Martha knows the truth.'

'I hope this is all going to end here.'

'That depends on what you mean. If you mean am I going to keep on seeing my daughter and granddaughter, then let me tell you that I am.'

'I can't think how Mitch must feel.'

'Mitch is fine, but then, unlike the rest of my family, he's always been supportive.'

Nancy's laugh was ragged, angry. 'That's as cruel as it's untrue, Rose. We all did our best to get you back on your feet. It's a shame you can't bring yourself to acknowledge it. If you want my opinion, you need to keep contact with this Irish family to a minimum. You don't know how complicated everything could get.'

That morning in the supermarket Rose had heard two girls having an argument. One had come out with a line that had taken her fancy. This, she reckoned, was her opportunity to put it to use. 'You know what, Nancy?' she said. 'As far as your opinion is concerned, I have zero fucks to give.'

She didn't wait to hear her sister's reply.

# CHAPTER 33

'Martha, if you were anyone else, I'd want you on the show.' Paudie put on his television voice. 'The search for her mother. One woman's remarkable story.'

'Ah, stop it, Paudie, would you? I didn't come out to be made fun of.'

'I'm not making fun. Honest to God, I'm not. In fairness, it is one hell of a story.' He took a gulp of his pint. 'I'd say it's the biggest story in Templemorris since Cat's old fellow's second family was uncovered.'

'Seriously, I'm warning you. I don't want a word of this around the town. Mam and Dad would be mortified.'

'You do have some sympathy for them, then?'

'I wouldn't go that far. What I don't want is to make matters worse. You should've seen the two of them, sitting at the table, faces on them as long as Lent. You'd swear I was the one who'd been lying. They were so . . . exasperating.'

'Sorry,' he said, 'I didn't mean to be flippant, and don't worry about me talking out of turn. I'm not home too often. It's only when the show's on a break that I get to enjoy the delights of Fennessy's Lounge.'

'Nah, you're grand. The last few days have been so crazy it's good to sit back and . . . I won't say laugh about it all. It's too raw for that. But it's good to try and relax, at least.'

'What did Dermot say?' asked Paudie.

'He was stunned. He can't imagine how Mam and Dad held onto a secret for so long. "Clem and Delia?" he kept saying, like there was something stuck in his throat. "They don't seem the types."'

He patted his knees. 'Another drink?'

'Please.' Martha was beginning to unfurl, her muscles unclenching, her mood lightening. At the same time, she was preparing herself for the conversation they'd both been avoiding since the night Evanne had tracked down Rose.

She watched Paudie go to the bar. Or, to be more precise, she watched the rest of the pub watch Paudie go to the bar. Many of the women stared at him, while the men adopted a studied indifference, as if they were saying, 'Don't have any ideas about yourself, son. Your sister has children with three different men, and your uncle has a conviction for drunk and disorderly.' She'd been surprised to receive his text, and doubly surprised to hear he was in Templemorris. She'd have to tell Cat they'd gone for a drink. Otherwise the local bush telegraph would do the job. She pictured Cat giving her the parental look, the one that said, 'We're very disappointed in you, Martha.' She shivered.

'I couldn't tell you the last time I was in Fennessy's on a Friday night,' she said, when Paudie returned. She peered around, taking in the new cornicing and mirrors, the leather seats and polished tables. 'They've given it a facelift. Mind you, there's still a whiff of the nineteen eighties about the place.'

'Show me the small town that doesn't have a whiff of the nineteen eighties about it,' said Paudie.

'Fair point. It's quiet enough for a Friday, not that I'm complaining.'

'I gather that these days the young people go to the Templemorris Tavern.'

'I don't think I know it.'

'It was Mossy Sullivan's in our day. The new owner tarted it up. Serves craft beer and tapas, apparently.'

'Craft beer?' said Martha. 'In Templemorris? Where do they think they are – Brooklyn?'

'My thoughts exactly. The next we know, they'll be carrying yoga mats and going to mindfulness classes.'

For a minute or two, they were quiet. Both knew what was coming but neither was willing to start the conversation. Around them, Friday night was cranking into life. A woman squawked with laughter. A man bellowed good-natured abuse at a friend. A couple gave their beer glasses a celebratory clink.

'So . . .' said Martha.

'So . . .' said Paudie.

'What I wanted to say was . . .'

'It's okay. You don't have to say anything. Not

unless you want to.' He rested a hand on her arm. 'Listen, Martha, you did what you thought you had to do. I wish you'd told me you were pregnant, but I can understand why you didn't. I'd behaved like a complete gobshite, and you didn't trust me.' He exhaled. 'After all this time, what can either of us say? But, if what you want is forgiveness, I forgive you.'

'Thanks.'

'Oh, and I hope you can forgive me for being such an awful eejit.'

'Yes, I do. Of course I do.' She studied her drink. 'I only wish we'd had this conversation years ago.'

'Me too. And I wish we'd stayed friends.'

Martha nodded, yet she knew that was something she could never have done. You didn't stay friends with someone you loved. It wasn't possible. If you'd loved a person, some part of you always remembered.

'After all,' he said, 'us old folks have to stick together.'

'Speak for yourself.'

'Ah, you know what I mean. I don't care what anybody says: the generations are different. You can be friends, you can have a laugh together, but unless you're family, it's like . . . you don't have the same reference points. You spend too much time at cross purposes.'

Martha resisted the temptation to say that she'd seen him in the paper with his current girlfriend. Like most of her predecessors, she definitely wasn't of his generation. She was closer to Evanne's.

'It's like Live Aid,' he said.

'You've lost me, Paudie.'

'Imagine not remembering Live Aid.'

'Remind me again, that was . . .?'

'1985.'

'I guess, then, that if you were born after about 1978, there's not much chance you'd recall Live Aid, no. I remember watching it in Cat's house. We wanted to be Madonna. Or, at the very least, we wanted her earrings. Oh, and we all cried when the sad video came on, the one showing the famine.'

'"Drive".'

'Come again?'

'That was the song. The Cars, "Drive".' He sang a line. Several people turned around in surprise, but he seemed not to notice. 'And the Troubles. Imagine not remembering the Troubles. All that misery on the news, all those funerals.'

'And all those reports ending with the line, "The deceased's family have pleaded for no retaliation." Gosh, that brings me back – and not in a good way.'

'You see,' said Paudie, 'there's no two ways about it. If you've been around longer, your world is different. Not better or worse, just different.'

'I suppose,' she said, wondering what had prompted this introspection.

'Still, getting older does have its merits. Some of the nonsense becomes less important. I mean, the relentless need to know what's cool – and to let it be known that you know what's cool. What's that about?'

It struck Martha that they were getting enmeshed in one of those do-you-remember-when-we-were-young conversations, and that this one had a particularly sharp edge. More than that, it contained a certain melancholy. Perhaps more melancholy than she could handle tonight. She decided it was her turn to go to the bar.

Fennessy's was filling up, and she had to wait for her order. At one point she turned around to see two teenage girls taking selfies with Paudie. How bizarre they looked.

'I see you met your fan club,' she said, as she handed him another pint.

'You know what they said? "My mother loves you. You and Daniel O'Donnell." The cheek of them. "I'll have you know, girls," I said, "you're talking to a man who once had a pint with Noel Gallagher."'

She couldn't stop herself laughing.

'Ah, I don't mind, really. It's when the young ones go on about their granny being a fan that you know you're on the slide.'

Martha drank some more wine. She was, she feared, reaching her limit, but there was something else she wanted to ask. 'You know,' she said, 'when you first met Dermot and you realised he was married to me, what did you think?'

'I thought, *You're punching above your weight there, man.*'

'Right. And your sensible answer is . . .?'

'Not a word of a lie, that's exactly what I thought. Like, Dermot's a friend of mine but even now . . . Well, he's a bit of an accountant, if you get my drift.'

'Hmm,' said Martha. 'Take it from me, librarians tend to be wary of occupational stereotypes. I'm sure there are lots of wild accountants.'

'I'm sure you're right, but old Dermo was never one of them. That's good, by the way. You don't want a wild man looking after your career. You want a man who thinks about work all the time. You were always too – I don't know – too lively for him. Too independent-minded.'

Martha didn't know if this tallied with how she saw herself. All the same, far worse had been said to her, so she was happy to accept the compliment. 'Thanks.'

Paudie's smile, tentative at first, ballooned into an all-out beam. 'I have to say, you're looking well. Did you change your hair or something?'

'I was given a makeover by a seventeen-year-old.' Martha opened her palms to the ceiling in what she hoped was an appealing gesture, and the two of them laughed.

'Well, well, well,' said a rasping voice, 'is this an intimate reunion of the class of 'eighty-six, or can anyone join in?'

'Tina Bennis,' said Paudie, 'as I live and breathe.'

'I've been Tina Coote for twenty-five years, as well you know. Move over in the bed, there, Martha, and let me sit down.' She shimmied in.

'Isn't this like old times?' said Paudie.
'Isn't it just,' said Martha.

Rose wrote two letters. The first, to Winnie Lafferty, was many years overdue. 'I've never forgotten your generosity,' she said. 'You were kind to me when you didn't have to be, and I hope life has been kind to you.' She also explained how Winnie had been instrumental in pointing Martha and Evanne in her direction. The second letter was harder to write. She apologised to Clem and Delia Sheeran for the way Martha's story had come bursting out. 'You have been wonderful parents to her,' she wrote, 'and I pray that you understand what happened.'

A third letter needed to be written, but that was someone else's job.

'A letter?' said Brooke. 'Fine. Give me her email address and I'll send her a few lines.'

'No, not an email,' replied Rose, trying to keep the irritation from her voice. 'A proper, old-fashioned letter in an envelope. And "a few lines" won't do.'

'What do you want me to say?'

'First off, you need to apologise. You also need to explain that when you blurted out all that stuff about Martha's family, you weren't trying to drive her away. You were . . . oh, I don't know . . . you were still in a state of shock. And you've got to tell her she's welcome here at any time.'

'What if she's not?'

'Excuse me?' said Rose, digging her nails into the kitchen table.

'I'm sorry, Mom, but let's be honest. All she's done is cause upset.'

'I think you'll find, Brooke, that the only upset has been caused by you.'

'All right, hands up, I didn't handle the situation too well, but I've already apologised for that. I've also had to put up with Bobby treating me like the Wicked Witch of the West. You've got to admit, her sudden arrival has turned everything upside down. I mean, look at you. It's plain you're not sleeping.'

Brooke was right about that. A good night's sleep was hard to come by. No matter what Rose tried, she woke at four a.m., her nerves on fire, her brain too busy.

'Listen, Brooke, I appreciate your concern, but Martha and Evanne weren't here to upset me. Meeting them, getting to know them, is important to me in ways I don't think you can understand. Now, I don't expect you and Martha to become best friends or anything, but I do want you to welcome the two of them into the family. Okay?'

'Okay,' said Brooke, the word embedded in a sigh. She reached out a hand to pat her mother's arm. 'Take care of yourself.'

'I will.' Rose gave what she hoped was a confident smile. 'I wonder how they're all getting on in Ireland now that Martha knows the full story. That can't be easy either.'

Although she didn't say it, couldn't say it, Rose believed there was one upside to Brooke's outburst. The disclosures about her family had stopped

Martha asking questions about the Moroneys and the Brennans. The questions would come, though. She was certain of it.

It was a good job Evanne hadn't been relying on her dad for a lift. He didn't call until seven and then he had the nerve to complain that she hadn't waited for him.

'I was planning on surprising Layla,' she said, 'only I'm the one who got the surprise. Where are they?'

'Ah,' said her dad. 'They've gone away for a . . . rest. Why don't we talk about that when I get home?'

'Why don't we talk about it now?'

'Later, Evanne. All right?' And he was gone.

Another three-quarters of an hour went by before she heard his key in the lock. By then she was in a state, angry and worried in equal measure. She'd called Serena, who said she was making a big fuss about nothing and that it was Friday night and she should be out trying to find a sex life rather than stressing about a pair of old people who were well able to look after themselves. It was Evanne's turn to hang up. In response, Serena sent her a one-line text: *You know I speak the truth xxx*

'Right, then,' she said to her dad, as she paced the sitting room. 'What's the story?'

'The story is I'm starving, and there isn't a bite of food in the place. Do you fancy going out?'

'No.'

'Let's get a takeaway, then. You can choose, but I've heard the new Thai place is—'

'Why didn't you tell me that Alex and Layla had gone away?'

'I didn't think you'd come round here on your own. I was going to tell you when I picked you up.'

Evanne dug her hands into the pockets of her blue hoodie. 'But you knew I'd be dying to see Alex. I've got presents for him and everything.'

Her father attempted a smile. 'I thought you'd be looking forward to seeing your old man too.'

'Where are they?'

'Sit down, would you, Evanne?' he said, as he folded himself into the sofa. 'All this tramping up and down is making me uneasy.'

She did as he asked. 'So?'

'Layla's gone to stay with her mother in Fourmilecross. She was feeling a bit down, so we both figured it made sense. I'm up to ninety with work and—'

'When'll they be back?'

'I'm not entirely sure. Layla needs a break with her mother, and the country air won't do the little chap any harm either.'

'Does this mean we won't be going to Cork?' asked Evanne.

'Aren't you just back from one holiday?'

'That's not an answer.'

Her father rubbed his eyes. 'No, we probably won't be going to Cork.'

'Why don't we give Layla a ring? I tried earlier

but she must have been busy or something. She can put Alex on the phone too, let him gurgle his hellos.'

'We'll give her a call over the weekend.'

'Uh, *hello*? Do you not want to talk to her tonight? And what about Alex – your son? Remember him? Small fellow? Likes a good cry and a bottle of warm milk?'

The muscles in her father's neck stiffened. 'Sweet Jesus, Evanne, can you stop it with the bloody questions? I said we'd call over the weekend. Now, I want a bite to eat and I want it in peace. Okay?'

Evanne was knocked off her stride. Her father never got annoyed with her about stuff like that, only about schoolwork and such. 'Sorry,' she said. 'I'm sorry.' But she wasn't. She was confused.

'No, I'm sorry,' he said. 'I shouldn't have shouted, pet. You didn't deserve that.' He went to hug her.

She squirmed away. 'They're not coming back,' she said. 'Are they?'

# CHAPTER 34

Saturday morning saw Martha slumped at the kitchen table, staring at a plate of burned toast and wishing she could lay her hands on some heavy-duty painkillers. The rattling and creaking in her poor head needed codeine, not her mother's wishy-washy pills. Her mam had gone to a meeting of one of her many committees. Her dad was in the garden, slaying slugs and weeds. On the radio, a man was reading the death notices. Before she left, Delia had given her daughter a tight-faced appraisal. 'You were out very late,' she'd said. Martha fought the urge to remind her that she was forty-five. If she was eighty-five, her mam would behave the same way. She'd also come close to saying that a shade more contrition on their part would do her parents no harm, but she wasn't able for a row. Not this morning.

She looked at her watch. Ten thirty. She'd better give Evanne a shout to let her know she'd be back that evening.

Her thoughts returned to the previous night. Paudie forgave her. She forgave him. So that was it.

And yet.

Now that they'd made their peace, she wondered if he would ghost out of her life again. She'd enjoyed the evening. Or, rather, she'd enjoyed it until Tina had arrived. Paudie and Tina had spent the rest of the night wallowing in memories of their glory days, when he'd been the captain of every team and she'd received twenty-two Valentine cards. At one point, they'd even reminisced about the field behind the graveyard. Martha had sat there, a rigid smile on her face, pretending she'd been one of the cool crowd. It was frightening to think that the three had known each other for forty years, since their first day in Our Lady of Perpetual Succour National School. Even then, Tina had been a pest, the girl who'd snaffled all the good crayons and cheated at skipping.

'Stop it,' Martha said to herself. 'You've got far more important matters to think about than Tina bloody Coote.' Tina was like politicians who misquoted poetry or people who claimed they read only 'serious' books: an irritant but, in the grand scheme of things, a minor one.

A small pile of newspapers sat at the end of the table waiting to go into the recycling bin. A quick look showed that not much had happened while she'd been in America. The biggest story was the threatened cancellation of a string of Garth Brooks concerts. Government ministers were urged to try to avert this looming catastrophe. In her mind's eye, Martha saw Brooke cringing with horror at a country where such things could make the headlines.

*Oh, yes, Brooke,* she thought, *we're a funny lot.* Otherwise, the papers contained the usual fare: feuding criminals, gruesome court cases, preening celebrities. At the bottom of the heap was the previous Sunday's *Herald.*

'Oh,' said Martha, when she saw the front page. 'Oh, hell.' There she was, a vision of youth in a deep green slip-dress: Sara Richardson, Paudie's girlfriend. Or, rather, Paudie's former girlfriend. *The Perils of Dating a Middle-aged Man,* blared the blurb: *Read Sara's hilarious and thought-provoking column.* Martha flipped to page eleven. In a full-page article, the young columnist described what it was like to date a man who'd passed his prime. Torture, apparently. That the name Paudie Carmody was never mentioned was neither here nor there. Everybody would know whom she was talking about.

From his inability to appreciate any music made after the turn of the millennium to his fondness for custard-laden desserts, Paudie's list of offences was long.

> It's not like I have any animosity towards older people [Sara had written]. Older people are interesting. It's the suffocating dreariness of the middle-aged that appals me.

She'd met some of his friends and they were equally awful. Why, she asked, were they sentimental for a past that had patently been dreadful?

Why were they willing to tolerate mediocrity? Why did they allow their lives to become safe and soft? And were these failings universal or part of a peculiarly Irish disease?

Towards the end there was one especially wounding paragraph:

> What truly upset me, the columnist wrote, was his attitude towards the young women of today. Our experiences are deemed less important than those of older women because, and I quote, 'If you'd been around forty or fifty years ago, then you'd really have had cause for complaint.'

Oh, it was crass. It was wrongheaded. But in the depths of an argument, Martha could hear Paudie saying it. Let's face it, everybody came out with daft opinions from time to time. That didn't mean they deserved to be dismantled in a Sunday tabloid. Still, the fairness of the article was irrelevant. That one paragraph had the capacity to damage Paudie's reputation. And his career. Now Martha saw the previous night's ramblings about Live Aid in a new light. She wished he'd said something.

She was stewing over what to do, her head continuing to throb, when her father pottered in. 'I'd have a cup of tea if you were making one,' he said.

'Would you now?'

'Ah, go on, pet.'

Martha filled the kettle. Depriving him of tea was unlikely to soothe her anger. Her anger was on another plane.

'Don't be too rough on us,' he said, as he pulled out a chair.

'Actually, I'm impressed by how reasonable I'm being.'

'You know what I meant to ask you? Did you find out anything else about your birth father, Joe?'

'Joe Brennan,' said Martha. 'No. I'd planned on doing some digging . . . only I got side-tracked.'

'I know the poor fellow's in his grave, but are you thinking of looking for his family?'

'Yeah, that's what I'd like to do. At the minute, I feel like part of the picture's missing.'

She wondered how easy it would be to trace Joe's relations. She'd have to ask Rose. After all, the Brennans didn't know that Joe had had a daughter. There was something else too. Joe wasn't just Martha's biological father. It was clear that Rose had loved him with all the tenderness and ferocity of a first love. And that he had loved her back. Martha wanted to hear more about their story.

For half a moment, as the bus pulled out of the station, Evanne asked herself if she was doing the right thing. Was there a simpler way of getting a proper answer? No, she decided, there wasn't. Between her dad's stonewalling, and Layla's refusal to answer her phone, it was impossible to get the truth. She would have to go to Fourmilecross. Layla couldn't ignore her then. There was one snag: Evanne had only the vaguest idea of where Fourmilecross actually was. 'The arse end of nowhere, and then on another bit,' her father always said. Some googling told her that the nearest town of any size was Westport. She'd assess her options from there.

Her dad didn't know about her journey west. He'd gone to the office. After that he was attending an awards lunch ('a bunch of privileged people giving prizes to another bunch of privileged people'). It would be late afternoon by the time he got home. With any luck, Evanne would be in Layla-land by then. She had been due to go shopping with Serena, and her friend wasn't pleased. 'You know what?' she'd said. 'You are totally tragic.'

Patiently, Evanne had explained the importance of her task. 'I've no time for Hollister or Penneys, not while my family's falling apart.'

'Exaggeration, much?' said Serena.

'Why don't you come with me?'

'To bogger country? I don't think so.'

'Serena!'

'I'm playing with you. I'd only be in the way. Say hello to Layla and Alex for me.'

To be fair, when Evanne's mum and dad had split up, Serena had been brilliant. That had been the grimmest time, her parents constantly fault-finding and bickering until full-scale war broke out over some nonsense or other. For ages, she'd thought they'd sort it out. If only her father was a bit less high-handed and her mother a bit less hippie-dippy, they might have done too. In the end, she took her friend's advice. According to Serena, her parents were like girls who insisted on dating losers or existing on grapefruit and Marlboro Lights. They refused to see sense, so no matter how dumb their behaviour, you had to let them get on with it. Besides, Evanne had been only fourteen then, not old enough to intervene. Perhaps if it was all happening now, she'd react differently.

The journey wasn't too bad. The worst part was people's insistence on wedging themselves in beside her even though there were plenty of empty seats. Her first companion gobbled her way through a family pack of liquorice allsorts in less than twenty minutes. While Evanne tried not to stress about calories (two hundred in a hot chocolate, three in a grape), the woman must have eaten an entire day's allocation in one go. Gross. Next up was an acne-strewn guy who kept asking why she was on her own and whether she was running away from home. Her final companion was a man in a squeaky leather jacket who looked her up and down, then fell asleep with his mouth open.

Evanne clamped on her headphones and stared out the window. With Hozier as her soundtrack, she thought about Alex, Layla and her dad. She thought about Rose too. What a shame the revelations about Clem and Delia had prevented them finding out more about the Moroney family – and about Joe. She tried to picture what Rose's life had been like before she got pregnant. Her relationship with Joe sounded so romantic. It was difficult to imagine anything that exciting happening now. Had her mother ever had such a passionate relationship? she wondered. Probably not. She'd had adventures, though, like hitching around the country with Cat. Evanne's life was short on adventure. The problem was, both her parents treated her like she was fresh out of the pram. Serena had a theory about this: she said they were overprotective because they were ravaged with guilt over their separation. 'That generation?' she said. 'When they were growing up, they were bombarded with religion and now they feel guilty about everything.' Evanne reckoned this would make her mother roar with laughter. Then again, maybe her mum protested too much.

From the depths of her backpack, she heard her phone ringing. Her mother, no doubt. Evanne would return the call later when she had something to say. She also needed to work out what she'd say to Layla. Flecks of rain were gathering on the windows. Hopefully, it wouldn't get any heavier.

It was only when the bus arrived in Westport that she appreciated the full awkwardness of getting to Fourmilecross. There was no bus, not on a Saturday. Everybody she asked shook their heads, as if to say, 'What would you want to go *there* for?' Then they told her she'd need a lift. As to where she might find that lift, they couldn't say. By now, the rain was staining the pavement and the sky looked worryingly dark.

There was only one thing for it: she'd have to stick out her thumb and hope for the best.

'Run that by me again, Dermot. What do you mean you've lost her?'

'I mean what I said. Evanne has disappeared on me, and I thought she might be with you.'

Martha was on the outskirts of Dublin, only fifteen minutes or so from home, but she decided she'd better pull in. She came to a halt outside a small row of shops. 'Have you tried ringing her?'

'Of course I have. I've rung a hundred times, but she's not answering. Have you been talking to her?'

'No, same story. I assumed she was doing something with yourself and Layla. Maybe she told Layla where she was going.'

'She wouldn't have done that,' said Dermot, a little too quickly.

Martha watched the rain pouring down the windscreen. If anything, her hangover had got worse. She couldn't wait to have a bath and go to bed. She'd left Templemorris without saying goodbye to her mother. Now that she thought about it, she shouldn't have made tea for her father either. It was too conciliatory a gesture. Just then, however, she didn't know how to behave. She wanted to think about her parents. She wanted to think about Paudie. And she wanted some peace. Besides, she doubted Evanne had gone far. 'I hate to say this, but she is seventeen. Is it really that big a deal if she goes missing for a few hours?'

There was a pause, followed by a *tsk*-ing sound, followed by another pause.

'What happened?' asked Martha.

'We had a small disagreement, nothing major. She was asking a lot of questions, and I told her to ease off for a while.'

'I see. What was bothering her?'

'Something and nothing.'

'I see,' she repeated, hoping to coax out more information. When Dermot didn't oblige, she suggested he call Serena.

'I rang her mother, who gave me Serena's number. She claimed she hadn't seen Evanne . . . but I'm not sure I believe her. She's a poor liar.'

Martha thought for a moment. She was starting to feel bad now. Dermot wouldn't have called her unless he was genuinely worried, and it was unlike Evanne to go missing. 'She can't have gone very far in this weather. It's foul. And she was looking forward to spending the weekend with Alex . . . and yourself and Layla, of course.'

'Ah,' said Dermot. 'That might be the problem.'

'Do you know what?' said Martha. 'I think it's time you told me what's going on.'

# CHAPTER 35

Evanne was drenched. Sopping. Water ran down her face, and her clothes were heavy with rain. Why hadn't she brought an umbrella? Why had she worn such silly clothes? She was in her favourite denim shorts, the ones with the long pockets. Kylie Jenner had worn a similar pair on her Instagram. Mind you, Kylie had never hitched a lift to Fourmilecross in the teeming rain. And Evanne's shoes? Her beautiful silver ballet flats were ruined. When she moved, they made a soft sucking sound, and the silver paint was peeling onto her feet. She had jeans and runners in her bag, but she could hardly change at the side of the road. Every now and again she heard her phone trilling and buzzing. Chances were it was Serena sending pictures of her new clothes.

Few cars passed, and the one driver who stopped told her his destination was only a mile or two away. 'I'd be more harm to you than help,' he said, 'and that's the truth. You'd want to get in out of that rain, though. I'd say it's down for the evening.'

This was the last thing Evanne wanted to hear.

It was five o'clock already. The journey to America had been quicker. She was about to walk back into Westport when another car, a battered black model, pulled in. Telling herself not to get her hopes up, she squelched over.

'Fourmilecross?' said the driver. 'I'm heading that way, right enough. Hop in.'

'I'm sort of damp.'

'You'd want to get out of those clothes,' said the man, a stick-thin guy with white hair and dark eyebrows. Evanne must have looked like she was about to hop right back out again because he quickly added, 'You're all right. I don't mean now.' He gave a gasping laugh, and they were on their way.

Before long they were in the true countryside with barely a house to be seen. If anything there were more ruined cottages than modern ones. In places, the narrow road was bordered by grey stone walls. Bogland stretched into the silvery distance. Bleak as it was, Evanne had the feeling that on a better day it would be beautiful.

Her saviour introduced himself as Tom Kilcoyne. 'A Dublin girl, am I right?' he said.

'Is it that obvious?'

'Let's just say, if you were a local lassie, you'd be better prepared for the elements. Where exactly is it you're going to in Fourmilecross? We don't get many visitors. Apart from the Germans, that is. They're great for the scenery, the Germans.'

'I don't know the exact address, but I'm looking for the Fogartys. Layla Fogarty and . . .'

She tried to remember Layla's mum's name. They'd met once, shortly after Alex was born. She was a tall woman with wings of chocolate-coloured hair. To the best of Evanne's recollection, Layla's dad had died when she was a teenager. She had two sisters: one in New Zealand, the other in Dubai.

'Geraldine Fogarty,' said Tom. 'I know Geraldine well. I'll drop you to the house.'

'You don't have to,' said Evanne. 'Wherever suits you would be fine.'

'Not at all. I couldn't be letting you get any wetter. How is it you know Layla, if you don't mind me asking?'

'She's . . .' What was Layla? A friend? A relation? 'She's going out with my father.'

'So the baby's your brother? He's a grand little chap, isn't he?'

'He is,' said Evanne, wondering how Tom had met Alex.

They said nothing for the next mile or two. Considering the state of the road, Tom's driving was ultra-speedy. Evanne wished he'd slow down but didn't like to ask. She peered out the window. Unfortunately, the rain was heavier than ever, and it was impossible to see very much. Rose had spoken about her mother, Grace, being from Mayo. She might have grown up around here. Imagine going from such an isolated place to a big American city. That must have been tough. Not that Evanne would ever have sympathy for Grace. She didn't know whether she believed in

Heaven and Hell, but if Hell did exist she hoped a particularly hot corner had been reserved for Rose's mother.

'Almost there now,' said Tom, who continued to bomb along. No wonder his car was so wrecked-looking.

Evanne found it hard to fathom that they were almost anywhere. Then, in the near distance, she spotted a cluster of four or five white bungalows. She remembered how, on childhood country drives, her dad would always moan about something he called 'bungalow blitz'. 'Typical Dublin snobbery,' her mum would reply. 'The west of Ireland's not a gated reservation, you know.'

Tom pulled up beside the first bungalow. 'Here we are,' he said. 'Do I get the idea they're not expecting you?'

'It's supposed to be a surprise.' Evanne was nervous. What if Layla wasn't happy to see her?

'Grand. I'll say hello. As I'm here, like.'

They were hardly out of the car before Layla appeared at the front door. She was carrying Alex, who was tugging at her hair. 'Hello, Father Tom,' she said. 'Evanne, uh . . . hello. What are you doing here? Did your dad send you?'

*Father Tom?* thought Evanne. *This guy was a priest?*

'I found Evanne outside Westport,' he said. 'She was doing her best to get washed away.'

Now that she was here, Evanne couldn't find the right words. 'I . . .'

‘Ba ba ba ba ba,’ said Alex.

Layla’s mother arrived at the door.

‘How are you doing, Geraldine?’ asked Father Tom.

‘Ba ba ba ba ba,’ repeated Alex.

‘You’d better come in out of that rain,’ said Layla.

‘Thanks,’ replied the priest. ‘But I think I’ll leave ye to it.’

Geraldine insisted that before Evanne did anything else she needed to get changed.

‘The state of you,’ she said. ‘You’ll be lucky not to get pneumonia.’

Evanne did look a state. When she caught a glimpse of herself in the bathroom mirror, she was mortified. Her hair hung in sodden hanks, and her mascara had washed right down her cheeks. ‘Waterproof, my arse,’ she said.

Evanne wasn’t great at guessing the ages of old people, but she reckoned Layla’s mother was in her fifties. She had the air of a woman who wouldn’t put up with much messing. While drying her hair, Evanne searched for a way of explaining her sudden appearance on the Fogartys’ doorstep. She figured she’d have to tell the truth. She wanted to know if Layla and Alex had left for good. Simple as that.

Layla was in the kitchen, giving Alex a bottle. Geraldine, who was engaged in general fussing, asked how Evanne had come across Father Tom.

She explained, then asked if he was the parish priest.

'The poor man looks after several parishes,' said Geraldine. 'There was talk of us getting a young fellow from the Philippines to give him a hand, but nothing came of it. Not, it has to be said, that many folks bother with Mass, these days. Bouncy-castle Catholics, I call them. They turn up for baptisms and communions, and that's about the height of it.'

'And who's to blame for that?' replied her daughter. 'For decades weren't people bowing and curtsying before those priests? And what were they doing only attacking children and locking up young girls?'

'Now, now, they weren't all at that carry-on. There were good priests then and there are good priests now.'

Layla winked at Evanne. 'Father Tom is Mam's boyfriend.'

Her mother snorted. 'Don't listen to her silliness. I take it you'll be staying for your dinner, Evanne?'

'Ma-am!' said Layla. 'Of course she will. Where else would she go?'

'Sure I don't know the girl's plans.'

Layla rolled her eyes. 'You're welcome to stay the night, sweetie. Alex is only delighted to see his sister, aren't you?'

Alex squealed his approval.

Evanne wondered what she'd got herself into. She did notice, though, that Layla was looking lots better. She was almost back to her glossy self. She was far more at ease with Alex too. She actually seemed to be enjoying him. 'I've got some presents for Alex in my backpack,' she said. 'They're about the only things that didn't get wet. And I bought something for you, only I think I left it in Dublin.'

'Don't worry about that,' said Layla. 'We're only dying to hear about America, aren't we, Mam?'

While they drank tea from blue-and-white-striped mugs and Geraldine made dinner, Evanne told them about her trip. She wasn't sure whether she should tell them about Rose being related to Delia. Eventually she decided to go for it.

Layla was agog. She asked a million questions. In fact, she asked so many questions that Evanne suspected she was trying to delay discussion of her own situation. After all, she'd always been sceptical about the hunt for Rose. By now, Evanne was holding her half-brother. She kissed his dark feathery hair. 'He smells great.'

Layla smiled. 'You wouldn't say that if you had to change his manky old nappies.'

Geraldine's head swivelled around. 'Don't be mean about him. He's a little smasher.'

'First grandchild,' said Layla. 'Mam thinks the sun shines out of his tiny backside.'

For ten minutes, they discussed Alex's feeding, sleeping and general superiority to all other four-month-olds. All the while, the tension ratcheted up. It seemed to Evanne that one of the hallmarks of adulthood was the ability to talk for hours without ever saying what you wanted to say. Finally, after some aimless chit-chat about the scenery around Fourmilecross, she decided she'd have to plunge on in.

'So,' she said, 'I guess you're wondering why I'm here. It's just . . . when I got back I thought you'd be there, but you weren't. And Dad was behaving like Dad. He wouldn't tell me anything. I kept calling, only you never answered. And what I wanted to know was: you haven't left, have you?'

'Pffft,' said Geraldine. 'What you need to do is talk to your father about his behaviour. He's the one with questions to answer.'

Layla sent her mother a cool look. 'I don't know what to say. I—'

'I got such a massive fright when I saw all your clothes were gone and your make-up and everything. Dad said you'd be back soon, but that's not how it looked to me.'

'I'm afraid I left in a wee bit of a tear. I gathered up all my belongings and threw them into the car. There was barely any room left for poor Alex.' Layla tipped forward and stroked one of the baby's chubby legs. 'Was there, sweetheart?'

'Ba, ba, ba,' he replied.

Evanne waited for Layla to continue. The breeze pressed against the orange-and-yellow curtains. Her grandmother Delia's kitchen curtains were almost identical. She was, she realised, holding her breath.

'Go on, pet,' said Geraldine. 'The girl's come all this way. She deserves an explanation.'

Layla gave the baby another tickle. 'You probably

guessed that your dad and me . . . Well, things hadn't been great for a while. I thought that having Alex would bring us together, and I really was delighted to be pregnant . . . only it became such a palaver. I did one interview. Then a couple of magazines asked if I'd do something with them, so I did. Then more asked and, hey presto, I was a one-woman pregnancy circus. But I wasn't enjoying any of it, and the more hassled I got, the more of a bitch I became.' She shook her head. 'Honestly, so much bullshit.'

Geraldine released a series of tuts.

'Sorry, Mam, but it's true.'

'Those interviews drove my mum mental,' said Evanne. 'She pretended they didn't, but I could see the truth on her face.'

'I'm not surprised. Take it from me, genuinely happy people don't broadcast their happiness. They just get on with whatever it is that makes them happy. Anyway, tedious and all as that was, it was only a sideshow. After Alex was born, I was tired and frazzled and your dad didn't understand. He was at work all the time, so how could he? He'd come home expecting me to be full of the joys of motherhood, only I felt so low. Then I lost my job, and everything got worse until . . .' Layla swallowed whatever she'd been about to say. 'Not that I'd be without this guy for a second.' She blew a kiss to the baby. 'What would I do without you?'

'Squeee,' he said.

'I know it sounds stupid,' said Evanne, 'but I was worried that you didn't want Alex.'

'Oh, Evanne, of course I do. How could any sane person not want him? He's a little dote. I was worn out, that's all. I suppose I was kind of depressed too.' She gave a tiny smile. 'But I'm on the mend.'

'Have you split up with my dad?'

'I don't know.'

Geraldine, who was leaning against the counter, a tea towel draped over one arm, butted in: 'It wouldn't hurt your father to get into his car and come up here.'

'He says he's very busy,' replied Evanne, 'and that Layla won't reply to his calls.'

'He's that, all right. Very busy drinking with other women.'

'Your potatoes are about to boil over, Mam,' said Layla.

Evanne's throat tightened. 'If you stay here, I'll never see you – or Alex.'

Layla threw back her head and laughed. 'Evanne, sweetie, have you taken leave of your senses? Live in Fourmilecross? You've got to be kidding. There isn't a job to be had, and Mam's probably the youngest person in the village. Don't worry, we'll be back in Dublin soon. I'm starting my new job in September, remember?'

'Believe you me,' said Geraldine, from behind a wall of steam, 'I wouldn't want her here either. She'd have me in the madhouse. I'd keep Alex, though.'

Evanne wanted to ask about her dad drinking with other women, but that would have to wait. 'I'm so happy you're coming back to Dublin. I was scared I wouldn't see either of you again.'

'You can relax. Alex wouldn't abandon his big sister.' Layla squeezed Evanne's knee. 'By the way, is that your phone that's been chirping away for the past few minutes?'

'It's likely to be my dad – or my mum.'

'Do they know where you are?'

'No,' said Evanne, who noticed a sour pong wafting towards her face.

'Oh, crap. Dermot's probably having a nervous breakdown as we speak or calling the guards.'

'Alex needs changing.'

'Let me worry about that. Go and call your father before he sets the police on your trail.'

# CHAPTER 36

One minute Rose was all keyed up, the next she was as listless as an August Sunday. That's what lack of sleep did to you. If she could just get a proper eight hours, she would find her way back to an even keel. But how could she sleep when her head was crammed with thoughts? As wonderful as meeting Martha had been, it had also rekindled uncomfortable memories. Her daughter's presence had forced Rose to think about the past.

The unfinished past.

Now, as she lay awake, she thought about the girls she'd known in Carrigbrack: about Dolores, who'd hidden in the closet, and Florence, who'd been forced to stay long after her baby was gone. She thought about the timid girls and the gutsy ones. The girls who'd been keen to start anew and the ones who'd wept for the children they weren't allowed to keep. What had happened to them? Did they still carry around the shame they'd been told they must feel? Or had they been able to slough it off? Were many reunited with their stolen children? Or had they tried to forget? Every day another memory ambushed her. She thought of her father and mother, long dead now. She thought of Joe.

Rose instructed herself to keep going. One foot in front of the other. One day after the next. She had recovered before and would do so again. How ridiculous was it to slide into depression when what she'd craved had been given to her? Her elder daughter was back in her life. What, though, if she wasn't? What if Brooke had driven her away? What if their relationship ended as suddenly as it had begun? These were destructive thoughts; Rose knew that. Martha would return. She would return because she still had questions about Joe.

The previous day, Rose had driven to Southie. She'd walked along Broadway, now an unlikely cocktail of old-style Irish bars and gourmet coffee shops, nail salons and social-service offices. Liquor stores had been replaced by upscale restaurants. Construction-site billboards promised luxury apartments with 'head-turning architecture' and 'unparalleled amenities'. The old neighbourhood was gone. For a while she stood there, immersed in her memories. Eventually a policeman approached her. 'Ma'am, are you okay?' he asked. She must have looked like a confused old lady.

Perhaps she was a confused old lady.

Rose remembered one of the shrinks she'd seen in the early eighties, a relentlessly positive man called Stephen Maxwell. He'd been the first to mention post-traumatic stress disorder. What a fraud she'd felt. She'd read about PTSD. Men who'd been to Vietnam suffered from it. Men who'd witnessed atrocities; who'd committed atrocities. Men who sat near Park Street station with pints of whiskey in brown-paper bags. Men who begged for quarters. Nice suburban housewives with loving husbands didn't suffer from such afflictions. She told herself that Carrigbrack wasn't to blame; that her depression was her own fault; that her head was defective, the wires all tangled and disconnected.

It took many sessions with Dr Maxwell for Rose to accept that his diagnosis was accurate. Most sufferers didn't end up as public casualties, he told her. They found ways to carry their pain, but that didn't make it any less potent. She saw him now, urging her to confront the roots of her unhappiness. 'A toxic brew of religion and respectability,' she'd said. 'That's what's to blame for my troubles.' They'd both laughed. The black humour of the psychiatrist's office.

Over the years there had been numerous doctors, myriad therapies, truckloads of pills. She'd come to realise that there was no cure. The weight of the past would always be there.

Like everybody, Rose had her ways of coping. She was grateful for the good things in her life. She had Mitch. She had her garden and her house, her children and grandchildren. She'd taught herself to appreciate small pleasures, like clean linen, the smell of rain or a really good book. She liked to go to the Museum of Fine Arts or the Isabella

Stewart Gardner Museum. Where was more soothing than a gallery? Even the people who congregated in the MFA, the women with their special rolling walk and the men with their learned nods, had a calming effect on her. She would stand in front of her favourite painting, Signac's *Pink Cloud*, hypnotised by its dabs and swirls, until a cough or some exaggerated foot-shuffling told her it was time to move on.

At the moment, though, none of her tricks were working. Mitch, who had cautioned against replying to Martha, didn't say, 'I told you so.' He didn't have to. His every gesture revealed his feelings.

When Bobby arrived, Rose was in the back garden, soaking up the stillness. She hadn't seen him since the night of Martha and Evanne's departure. For a while, they sat together in silence. She sensed that something was on his mind.

'Do you ever see the gang you were friendly with before you went to Ireland?' he asked.

'No, my parents kept saying I had to begin afresh, and that's what I tried to do. Of course, back in those days we were still in touch with my mom's family. They're scattered all over the place now, so we don't have too much contact. My cousin Teresa got married and moved to Chicago. We exchange Christmas cards and such, but I couldn't tell you the last time I saw her.' A dart of pain hit Rose's right eye. Lack of sleep always made her head ache. 'Where's all this coming from?'

'Nowhere in particular, just idle curiosity. It's a funny one, isn't it? Both you and Dad are Irish, but we're not really part of that world.'

'You'll have to take up Martha's invitation and go visiting. She'd be delighted to see you, I'm sure, especially after the business with Brooke.'

Bobby was gazing at her as if she was being deliberately obtuse. 'That's not what I meant. I meant the Irish world in Boston. Like, we know plenty of Irish people, but you never sent us to step-dancing classes or anything like that.'

Rose spluttered out a laugh. 'You should be thankful for small mercies. I can't imagine your sister in one of those curly wigs. She would've sued me for crimes against style.'

Her son smiled, and she thought she'd defused the situation. She was wrong.

'Brennan,' he said, voicing the name like it was exotic. 'Joe Brennan. Do you ever think about him?'

She couldn't stop herself flinching. The movement was tiny, but Bobby saw it.

'I'm sorry, Mom. That was tactless. You don't need me wading in with dumb questions.'

Rose looked away. The sun had been covered by a gauze of cloud. Maybe the weather was about to break. The garden could do with some rain. Her roses were looking a little scrappy, and the grass was starting to burn. She urged herself to focus, to act appropriately. 'Oh, Bobby, that was such a long time ago. It feels like a different lifetime. I find it's best not to dwell on these things.'

'I hear what you're saying.' He hesitated. 'There was a guy called Brennan in some of my classes at BU. A good guy, as I recall.'

Rose felt more energy drain from her body. 'It's a very common name.'

'I guess, but if Martha has cousins or any sort of close family on Joe's side, she might like to meet them. Or maybe they'd like to meet her.'

'You've got to be practical, honey. They don't know anything about her. You can't say how they'd react. And, let's face it, we've already had enough upheaval.'

'I guess,' repeated Bobby, but his face was glazed with doubt.

To Martha's relief, Cat wasn't overly interested in her night out with Paudie. Nor did she ask many questions about Clem and Delia. What exercised her was the Dermot and Layla situation.

'Is he having an affair with this Justine Winstanley woman?' she asked.

'Do you know, I don't think he is. But he'd promised Layla he'd be home early so she could go out with a friend. Instead he went drinking with Justine—'

'—who'd already taken Layla's job.'

'Hmm. I can understand why she stalked out and went home to her mam. I'd do the same. Well, now that I think of it, I wouldn't because Mam would tell me to go straight on back to him . . . but you know what I mean.'

'Have they split up, then?'

'Evanne doesn't know. Or if she does, she's not saying. She has to go outside to call me for fear either Layla or Geraldine is eavesdropping. The phone reception is dreadful too.'

'I'm beginning to think she's abandoned you. Is she ever going to come home again?'

'What do you mean?' asked Martha, her voice too high, too fast.

'Oh, Martha,' said Cat. 'What are you like? I'm only messing with you. Of course I don't think Evanne's abandoned you.' She raised her voice. 'Go easy there, Jake, pet. Weeds have feelings too.'

Cat's garden, where they were trying to top-up their Boston tans, was an extravaganza of dandelions and bindweed. Jake was running and jumping in the undergrowth.

'She says she'll be back in a couple of days,' replied Martha. 'I called Geraldine, and she insists she's happy to have her.'

'Sheesh, that must have been awkward.'

'To the power of ten.' Martha raised her face to the sun. 'Part of me is paranoid about how much Evanne enjoys being with Layla. Alex is her half-brother, though, and Layla's his mother, so what can I do? Anyway, despite the lack of shopping centres, she's having a great old time. Layla suspects her mam's carrying on with the parish priest, and they're trying to catch her out.'

'Far be it from me to tell Dermot what to do, but would he not go up and sort things out?

Anyone would think he doesn't want to see his son.'

'Of course he does, only he's still in a sulk. He's convinced Layla overreacted. And it doesn't help that Geraldine has him pegged as a complete lowlife. I've a feeling he's scared of her.'

Personally, Martha thought Dermot's behaviour was foolish, especially when his relationship was already in a parlous state. She did wonder whether he wanted to reconcile with Layla. Almost a year had passed since he'd voiced his blithe assumptions about marriage. A lot had changed since then.

'I like the sound of Geraldine,' said Cat.

Martha reckoned the time had come to tell Cat about the unsettling conversation she'd had with Dermot.

'Eeew! The cheek of him. Why are you only telling me about this now?'

'We weren't talking, remember?'

'Will I ever forget? Dermot's memory must be failing him, though. I can't believe he wittered on about how happy you used to be.'

'Once upon a time we were.'

Cat took off her sunglasses and squinted at Martha. 'Here, you're not considering—'

'Lord, no. I can promise you that's never going to happen.'

Somewhere Martha had crossed a line. She realised that she'd spent too much time picking over the carcass of her marriage and indulging in self-pity. She would never forget the good times. How

Dermot had lifted her out of her post-Paudie stupor. How wonderful he'd been with Evanne. How surprisingly skilful he was in bed. But the prospect of a reunion simply didn't interest her. She didn't regret her marriage but attempting to rekindle it would be a mistake. Although it had taken a long time, she was ready to leave Dermot behind. The one issue she did wish to discuss with him was extra tuition for Evanne. As soon as their daughter returned to Dublin, they would have to sit down and talk it all through.

'You know what I meant to tell you?' she said. 'I got a letter from Brooke.'

'I hope you checked it for anthrax.'

'Believe it or not, it's very friendly. Rose must have dictated it.'

Cat was rubbing sun cream onto her arms. She passed the bottle to Martha. 'And what's the story with your parents?'

'We're better off not talking to each other. They're doing the old if-we-pretend-everything's-grand-it-will-be act. If I go down there, there's a danger I'll kill them.'

'You won't get any more nights out with Paudie and Tina in Fennessy's, so,' said Cat. 'I'd love to have seen the three of you.' To Jake's alarm, she threw her arms into the air and started singing about partying like it was 1986.

'Stop it now,' said Martha, through her laughter.

'Did you drink Malibu and pineapple – and smoke a few roll-ups?'

'God, yeah. And I wore my leopardskin leggings and put half a can of Elnett in my hair.'

'Lovely. Was Paudie all morose about the mauling he received from the young one?'

'I only found out about it afterwards. How did you . . .?'

'Richie's brother emailed him the article. He says it's the talk of Templemorris. Everybody knows it's about Paudie. As you can imagine, there's a good deal of sniggering.'

'Aren't people very cruel?'

Cat crossed her arms. 'Martha, a word to the wise: we're not going to fall out over that man again, but please don't go soft on him. Paudie got what he deserved.'

# CHAPTER 37

They shouldn't have bothered with the damn dinner party. Rose had said she didn't feel up to it, but Mitch had wheedled and cajoled until she'd caved in. Now, here she was, sitting beside a man who'd probably bored his own mother. Ron Spellacy was one of those guys whose lack of knowledge doesn't prevent them having a view on everything. Immigration, Islam, traffic snarl-ups on the I-93: you name it, he had it covered. And his opinions were voiced in a tone that said, 'If you really understood, you wouldn't argue.' He was like a host on a low-rent radio talk show: empires might rise and fall but he would sail on, secure in his ignorance.

For a while, Rose zoned out. She was good at that. She allowed her mind to drift so that she felt as if she was hovering over the gathering. When she zoned back in again, she couldn't believe that Ron was still talking about climate change, his tone becoming ever more hectoring, his face more florid. Rose had no particular views on the subject. Nor did she have any specialist knowledge. She was willing to bet that Ron didn't either. She didn't know why the other guests were humouring him. It was possible to be too polite.

'Have you ever known a moment's self-doubt?' she asked.

'Excuse me?' he replied, with a twitch of his substantial nose.

'I was wondering, has there ever been even an instant when you've said to yourself, "Hey, maybe, I don't have all the facts here. Maybe, just maybe, there's another way of looking at this."'

Ron's reaction was hilarious. His eyes popped like a cartoon character's, and his wife – Bitsy or Mitsy or some such – got all affronted on his behalf. 'Well, I never,' she said. 'Such rudeness.'

Mitch became apologetic in that pay-no-attention-to-my-wife, she's-not-quite-sane way of his.

Their host, an underfed, over-filled lady called Evelyn Bamford, laughed a tinkling laugh before flashing Rose a look of pure loathing. Then she started yammering on about some local political scandal or other. As an effort at distraction, it was pretty lame.

Rose felt a laugh rising up from her chest and had to suppress it. The truth was that she got a buzz from Ron's tetchiness. The amateur psychiatrist in her wondered if this was because her behaviour would have infuriated her mother. Nearly half a century later, was she still trying to score points?

They left early. Mitch didn't say anything. He didn't need to. In a classic Mitch manoeuvre, he was biding his time, waiting for her to apologise. Rose reckoned he was overdoing the annoyance. It wasn't as though her remarks had been *that* outrageous.

When, after three or four miles, she still hadn't apologised, he broke his silence. 'You know, Rose, you might find Ron Spellacy tedious, but his companies do a lot of business with us. Would it have killed you to stay civil?'

'I didn't want to be there,' she said. 'I told you that.'

'Don't act like a child. It's not fair.'

Rose looked at Mitch's hands. Even in the semi-dark she could see how tightly he was gripping the steering wheel. He really was flustered. Her resolve withered. 'You're right,' she said. 'I'm not being fair. I should have . . . Oh, I don't know what I should have done. I'm sorry.'

'The thing is,' said Mitch, 'if we went out again tomorrow night, you'd do exactly the same. You know I've always believed that you were treated badly. And, against my better judgement, I agreed to let Martha into our lives. I've done everything I can to be supportive, but this can't go on.'

'Please, Mitch. I'm not that bad.'

'Yes, you are, and you've got to the stage where you can't see how unreasonable you're being. Even before you'd said a word to Ron, you were sitting there with this vacant look on your face, as though everything and everyone was beneath you. And I've been reluctant to mention this, but Nancy called me in a snit about something you said to her. We both know she's a royal pain in the ass, but there's no point in making her worse.'

'You'll have to cut me some slack. I'm not at my best right now.'

'Do something about it, then. Go back to therapy or do whatever you have to do, but please stop taking your own problems out on the rest of us.'

*Your own problems*. The words hit Rose – *wham* – like a blow to the back of the skull. Mitch was right. They were her problems and she wasn't handling them well. She felt as if every person she met was looking for something, as if they would take her oxygen if they could. When she went out, everybody seemed to be clipping her heels or invading her space. She couldn't bear crowds or standing in line. She'd find herself inwardly shouting, 'Just move, would you? Just goddamn move.' Even the most mundane tasks were impossibly hard. She'd start something, then lethargy would take hold and she'd have to stop. As for talking to neighbours and friends? Rose would rather dance on a bed of razor blades.

In two days' time her youngest grandchild, Matt, would celebrate his seventh birthday. She still hadn't found the energy to buy him a present, and just the thought of his party made her feel unwell. She'd been distant with Martha and rude to Brooke. And then there was Evanne. Her granddaughter had sent a lengthy email about a madcap trip she'd taken across Ireland in search of her father's partner. She'd even included photographs of County Mayo, beautiful pictures of empty land and endless sky. The email was funny and sweet and it deserved a proper response. Rose knew what she'd like to write. Don't change, she wanted to say. Don't become jaded. Don't turn in on yourself. Don't be afraid. She supposed some people would consider this advice hokey or simplistic, but it was how she felt. Perhaps she was talking to her seventeen-year-old self. The problem was, the torpor in her brain and body kept holding her back, and the email remained unwritten. She felt as if she was lumbering around with a sack of stones on her shoulders. If she wasn't careful, the weight would tip her over.

And always at the back of her mind, niggling and prodding, was the extent to which she was responsible for her own suffering. Deep down, down where she didn't want to go, Rose knew she'd made bad decisions. No, not just bad decisions. She'd made damaging decisions.

She realised that Mitch was talking again. 'Will you do that for me?' he asked.

'Sorry?'

He breathed out too heavily, a sure sign he was trying to control his irritation. 'I was asking if you'd go back to your therapist.'

'I will,' she promised.

'This is like old times,' said Dermot, from the middle of the sofa.

'Why?' asked Evanne. 'Are you and Mum going to start shouting at each other?'

'You know what I mean. I mean the three of us together in this house, having a family conversation.'

She grinned and punched his arm. 'Relax, Dad. I'm only joking.'

'God, Evanne, you're a hoot,' he said.

Martha blew across the top of her coffee. Dermot was looking distracted, she thought. There was a false jauntiness about him too. He kept displaying what Cat called his 'TV chef smile', a smile so stiff it couldn't possibly be sincere. Although Layla had returned to Dublin, she was staying with a friend. Whether this arrangement was likely to change, Martha didn't know. Neither did she want to ask. She'd spent more than enough time pondering her ex-husband's relationship. It was time she focused on her own problems. She still hadn't figured out how to handle her parents, while Rose was sounding all weird and forgetful.

A civilised conversation about Evanne's future, that was what they were there for this evening. Everything else could wait.

She'd been hoping that Dermot would start the conversation. Unfortunately, the blank look on his face suggested the task was hers. She examined her fingertips.

'So, love,' she said to Evanne, 'you don't need us to tell you that this is an important year. And what we were thinking, your dad and I, was that a little extra tuition might be helpful. Just in maths, say. And chemistry.' Martha laughed, a nervy, fluttery laugh that even she found annoying.

'You want me to get grinds?' asked Evanne.

'Yes,' said Dermot. 'I know you're not fond of either subject, but, like the politicians always say, we are where we are. A few months of hard work, and it will all be over.' A flash of the TV chef smile. 'Then you'll be off to university to study something you really care about.'

'That's what I've been meaning to tell you. I've found what I want to do.'

'That's great news,' said Martha, feeling a spark of hope. If Evanne had a course to aim for, she was more likely to knuckle down and do the extra work. 'Which college are you thinking of?'

'Actually, I'm thinking of none of them. None of the ones you're familiar with, anyway. I've decided I want to be a beautician and make-up artist. Some of the courses are brilliant. I've been looking them up online. I'll show you, if you like. You wouldn't believe how many options are available. Like, I can learn about massage too – and all about diet and nutrition.'

Martha sent Dermot a look of distress. Again, she wanted him to say something. Again, he let her down. She was hunting for the right formula of words. Was there a diplomatic way of saying, 'Over my dead body'?

'Surely you want to go to university, Evanne. School's a pain, but college is completely different.

And make-up . . . well, it's more like a hobby, isn't it?'

'No, it's not. It's a massive business. It's what I love, so why shouldn't I make a career out of it? And, as an added bonus, I won't have to go through a head-wrecking year. I'll do my exams but I won't be under the same pressure.'

'Ah,' said Martha. 'That's what I thought. You're picking this because you're worried about failing your exams.'

'No, Mum. I guarantee you, even if I was in line for fifty A1s, I'd want to do exactly the same thing. My mind's made up.'

Martha persevered: 'Honestly, pet, you shouldn't let the pressure get to you. I failed an exam the year before I did my Leaving Cert. I might even have failed two. Then I got my act together and achieved what I wanted to achieve.'

'That's just it. You did what you wanted to do. You wanted to go to college to study . . . whatever it was you studied. And you got there.'

'That's not what I'm saying. I'm saying that you can still get the grades to do a decent university course.'

'And I'm saying that's not what I want.' Evanne spoke in staccato bursts, as if she was addressing the slowest child in an extremely slow class.

'And I'm telling you that you're making a mistake.'

'Your mother's right,' said Dermot. 'Go to college first. Then, if you still want to do this beauty lark, we'll support you. Education is never wasted.'

Evanne got to her feet. 'Why can't you respect my choice?' She waved a hand towards her mother. 'You were happy enough to accept my help when you wanted to give yourself a makeover. You know that's where my talent lies.'

'It's not that simple, Evanne.'

'Why not? What's wrong with what I want to do?'

'What's wrong is . . .' Martha instructed herself to stay calm. 'What's wrong is that you'd be part of a world where all that matters is a woman's appearance.'

'That's completely over the top. All I want is the freedom to do what makes me happy.'

'I hear you, only I'm concerned that what you're talking about is, well . . . not very serious.'

'Oh, please. Do you have to be such a snob?'

Martha didn't believe that Evanne's use of the S-word was an accident. Her daughter knew it would wound her. She hated snobbery. 'That's not fair, love. You've got to understand where I'm coming from . . .' she looked at Dermot '. . . where we're both coming from. For a long time, women had to fight to go to college. Families thought that education was wasted on them.'

'I'm well aware of that. You can spare me the sermonising.'

'I'm not sermonising, and in case you think I'm referring to the dark ages, I'm talking about my own life. My mother didn't want me to go to university. She thought it was a waste of time and money. She wasn't much better with Una. One of

Una's teachers had to take Mam aside and explain how clever her daughter was.'

All these years later, Martha still wasn't totally sure why her mother had been so set in her ways. For a long time, she'd feared it was because Delia hadn't wanted anyone to think the Sheerans were getting uppity. In the 1980s, having notions above your station was regarded as a serious offence, guaranteed to provoke an outbreak of disapproving nods and whispers. Now, she believed the true reason was more poignant. She believed Delia had been frightened of losing her girls.

'Yeah, well,' said Evanne, folding her arms across her chest, 'everybody knows Una's a genius. But perhaps Nan was right about you.'

'What's that supposed to mean?'

'It's not like going to college made you any more broadminded. You reckon you're so different from Nan, don't you? Did it never occur to you that you're exactly the same? You have one set idea about what girls should do, and you refuse to listen to anybody who disagrees.'

'That's—'

'You think there's only one way to do things – and that's your way.'

'Now, Evanne,' said Dermot, 'just because you disagree, there's no call for that sort of talk. Your mother only wants what's best for you. We both do.'

'You know what, Dad? You might be better off concentrating on your own life rather than interfering in mine.'

'That's enough,' said Martha, her words twanging with anger. 'We were trying to have a grown-up conversation but—'

'No, you weren't. You were trying to force me into doing what you want. It's my life we're talking about. Remember? Not yours.'

If you asked Martha, Evanne was the one who took after Delia. She was incapable of tamping down her anger. When a line came into her head, no matter how caustic, she had to come on out with it.

'All right,' she said, 'we'll have to return to this when we've all calmed down.'

'Yeah, whatever,' replied Evanne. 'But don't expect me to change my mind.'

'Straight up, Serena, you'd think I'd announced I was off to be a jihadi bride or something. The faces on them.'

Evanne's friend clucked with sympathy, then took another swig of her gin and tonic. 'My old pair aren't any better, you know. My dad read this piece in the paper about some guy who taught himself Russian and got an A1 in the Leaving Cert. "Why don't you do something like that?" he said to me. "Because I'm not a total nerd from Planet Nerdville," I said.'

Evanne picked a slice of pepperoni from her pizza. 'Still, I'll bet if you really, really wanted to do something, they'd support you. They wouldn't say, "Oh, no. I insist you do things my way and have a majorly crap life."'

'I suppose.'

Evanne knew she was ranting. She didn't care. True, she hadn't expected her mother to say, 'Grand so. How much does it cost, and when do you start?' But neither had she expected such overwhelming opposition. As for her dad? He'd been worse than useless. At least her mother had been engaged, she'd been listening. He just came out with platitudes like, 'Education is never wasted' and, 'We only want what's best for you.' Pah-thetic!

How lucky was she that Serena's parents and little brother had gone to Wexford for the weekend? The two had ordered pizza and were laying waste to Tilly's gin. They'd considered going into town, but that could wait for another night. Serena had split up with Josh so they were looking forward to getting glammed up and having some wild times. But, no, silly Evanne! Getting glammed up was a heinous crime. As for making your living from improving other people's looks? You might as well deal smack or sell children into slavery.

One thing was for sure: Evanne wouldn't waste any more time stressing about her mum and dad and their miserable lives. How decent had she been? Tracking down Rose and convincing Cat to come to Boston and listening to her mum moan about her parents. Not to mention hiking across the country in monsoon rain to find her dad's other family. The one he'd mislaid because he'd been too busy looking after the careers of a tribe of nonentities. That she'd wanted to do all of these things was beside the point. She'd been endlessly patient and accommodating. And what thanks did she get? Nothing, only a deluge of sarcastic remarks and condescending looks.

'If you ask me,' she said, 'my folks are determined to make my life as rubbish as their own.'

Serena gave her a thoughtful look. 'That's kind of harsh.'

'No, it's not. Take my mum: she wants me to do what she did whether I like it or not. Whether it suits me or not. She's acting like everything's about her, like I've managed to make myself good at something just to spite her. Why can't she allow me to live my own life?'

'Because running somebody else's life is far easier than managing your own.'

'Yeah, but—'

'I mean, take the pair of us. Aren't we forever going on about what some of the idiots at school should be doing?'

'But the solutions to their problems always seem so obvious.'

'That's my point. We're all experts on other people's lives.'

That Serena spoke the truth didn't dilute Evanne's anger. Why couldn't her mother let go a little? Why couldn't she understand that Evanne needed to make her own decisions? Rose would understand, she was sure. But Rose had stopped replying to her emails. Oh, why did everything have to be so bloody complicated?

She sank the last of her G&T with a noisy gulp and raised her glass. Serena poured another hefty measure of gin. The ice made that lovely cracking sound.

'To our own lives,' said Evanne, as they clinked their glasses together.

# CHAPTER 38

This was not a date. Whatever it was, it was not a date. Martha said this to herself as she put on the silky summer dress she'd bought for her American trip. She repeated it as she put on her best strappy sandals. The fine weather might end tomorrow, and then the poor sandals would spend another year decaying at the back of the wardrobe. It would be a crime not to wear them. Finally, she pulled on a navy jacket she'd had since the Ark had hit dry ground. Okay, it was her favourite jacket, but it definitely wasn't something you'd wear on a date.

Evanne had sent a text to say she was spending another night at Serena's house. Martha decided to let her. She hated falling out with her daughter.

Life with a seventeen-year-old was a conveyor belt of worries. What did she worry about? What *didn't* she worry about? She fretted about drink, drugs and bullying; anorexia, bulimia and self-harm ('Cutting?' she'd said to Cat. 'Was that even a thing when we were growing up?'). She worried about rape culture, online shaming, revenge porn and all of the new phrases and phenomena she didn't quite understand. Mostly, though, her worries were the age-old ones: men who wouldn't take no for an answer, casual sex, pregnancy, and the nagging feeling that Evanne would drift into a life that didn't make her happy. Seriously, was there anything as scary as a teenage girl?

Martha wanted her daughter to have the things she'd wanted for herself but hadn't known how to pursue. A great education. Time in a foreign university. Travel. Like a fool, she hadn't foreseen that Evanne would have different ambitions; that she would look at her mother and say, 'I don't want to be like you.' Now that Martha had been presented with the truth, she didn't know how to feel or what to do.

Briefly, she wondered if this interest in make-up and beauty was due to Layla's influence. But, no, that wasn't fair to either of them. Evanne knew her own mind.

When Paudie had called and suggested dinner, she'd almost said no. She'd planned on rereading an Anne Tyler book, *Breathing Lessons*. (She'd been rereading all of Rose's favourite authors.) Then she'd thought, *Well, why the hell not?* She was a free woman after all.

Sometimes Martha wondered why tourists bothered with Dublin. She'd look at her adopted home and everything would appear shabby and worn. At other times, she was knocked sideways by the city's beauty. This was one of those evenings. The city centre glowed in the late-summer light.

The faces streaming past, the youngsters milling around: everybody looked unusually appealing, as if they'd been gathered up from some far-off land of gorgeous people and beamed in for the night. The place had a vibrancy that made her feel she could be anywhere in the world.

Her thoughts slipped back to a time when she'd known every pub and café, every cinema and night-club. Now entire streets were a mystery. She needed to escape from the suburbs more often.

Paudie was at the restaurant before her, the first time she'd known him to be early. She smiled, but as she sat down she was struck by a leg-wobbling, stomach-flipping sensation. *What am I doing here?*

'It's only just occurred to me,' he said, 'that this place mightn't suit you. I hope you're okay with Nepalese food.'

'To tell you the truth,' said Martha, feeling horrifyingly unsophisticated, 'I don't think I've ever had it.'

'Not to mind. It's like Indian, only better. I'm sure you'll love it.'

'Sounds good to me. I always wanted to go to that part of the world.'

Martha had only one memento from her time with Paudie: the 1991 Aeroflot timetable. Periodically she thumbed through its faded pages, searching for the flights that had captivated her on that long-ago day in Moscow. That the Soviet Union had fallen apart before the timetable had run its course only added to the book's appeal. There was, she remembered, a flight from Shannon to Kathmandu via Moscow and Delhi. Alas, Dermot had been less than enthusiastic about the prospect of a trip to India and Nepal. Promises of temples, lakes and mountains had left him cold. 'Why go on holiday to get ill?' was his definitive word on the subject.

From the other side of his menu, Paudie sent her a frown. 'You said you always wanted to go to Asia. Why the past tense?'

'I'm hardly likely to go there now. Those trips are for young people.'

'Ah, Martha, if you're going to act all middle-aged on me, I'm going home.'

He put down the menu and pretended to rise from his chair. Despite his game-playing, Martha wondered if she'd detected a slight wince when he'd said 'middle-aged'.

'I was in Kathmandu a few years back,' he said. 'It's like Galway, with mountains. Lots of blokes with scraggly beards and women with hairy legs.'

'Trust you to come out with something like that.'

'I'm only trying to get a rise out of you.'

'Anyway,' she said, 'you're a fine one to talk. A month ago you were ready to claim your pension and bus pass.'

'I've rebounded.'

'I'm glad to hear it.'

Something in Martha's tone must have told him that she knew about the Sara Richardson debacle. He leaned back in his chair and sighed. 'If I've learned one lesson, it's this: falling out with someone who writes a popular newspaper column is not a good idea.'

'Ah.'

'I take it you've seen the article?'

'Well—'

'Come on, Martha. If you haven't, you must be the only person in Ireland.'

'Yeah, I read it. I thought it was pretty nasty, but—'

'I hope you're not going to give me any lines about today's paper being tomorrow's chip wrapper. Everything's on the damn internet now. Not only does the article live on, all the lame-brained Facebook comments do too. I've been called every kind of misogynist and Neanderthal. And, worse, all the really sexist lads have adopted me as their martyr.' He looked around the room. 'Our fellow diners are probably wondering what such a fine-looking woman is doing with that boring bastard, Paudie Carmody.'

'It will be forgotten.'

'I know,' he said, his voice weary. 'And I suppose I had it coming. I mean, twenty-six, what was I thinking? I wouldn't mind if the two of us had anything in common, but we're talking about someone who brings bottled water and hand sanitiser if she travels further than Kildare. I dread to imagine what she would've made of Templemorris.'

On cue, a woman with ramrod-straight auburn hair and clown-like eyebrows swayed over. She tipped her head towards Paudie. 'Good to see you with someone your own age.'

Martha bristled. Forget Templemorris. Sometimes Ireland was a small town. 'We're friends, actually,' she said.

'Whatever,' replied the woman, as she waltzed away.

'The cheek of some people. I don't know how you put up with idiots like that.'

'Let her be,' said Paudie. 'I've heard worse.'

Martha noticed that their waiter was hovering. This was good. She didn't want to get mired in a conversation about Paudie's love life. The restaurant was full now, the overlapping conversations creating a satisfying babble. *Don't over-analyse*, she thought. *Just enjoy the meal.*

And she did. They ate Nepali dumplings and prawn curry and had one of those old-friends discussions where everything slots into place. You repeat the old lines. You adopt your old persona. It was like muscle memory. Except there was more to it than that. The flirtation that had been stymied by Tina's arrival returned. The banter was a little too personal, the glances a little too affectionate. Old friends didn't smile at each other in such a goofy way.

They talked about Rose.

'I can tell she's not in great form,' said Martha. 'I feel like I need to see her again so we can get used to each other. We need to do some normal mother-and-daughter things without any pressure or drama. Oh, and the more I think about him, the more I want to find out about my birth father. If nothing else, I'd like to visit his grave.'

Paudie reckoned she should return to Boston as soon as she got the chance. 'Isn't the autumn supposed to be beautiful over there?'

'It's not as simple as that. Leaving money – and work – aside, Evanne will be back at school.'

'Can't you go by yourself?'

'And put up with the wrath of a teenager? I don't think so. I'm already in big trouble.' She told him about their spat.

'No offence,' he said, as he broke off a piece of naan bread, 'but I thought you were going to tell me something awful. I mean, say Evanne had taken up with some guy who looks like the final picture in a "Faces of Meth" poster, or say she'd stopped eating, then, yeah, I could understand you being worked up. But this? Is this really bad news?'

'It's just not what I'd expected.'

'It sounds to me like she has her heart set on becoming a make-up artist, and if it's what she's good at, where's the harm?'

'I know . . . only I had other plans for her.'

'Your mam probably had other plans for you.'

'You're beginning to sound like Evanne.'

'I've been called a lot of names recently, but that's the first time I've been compared to a teenage girl.'

Martha speared a prawn. 'She's with her friend,

Serena, tonight, and when I was walking down Grafton Street I half expected to bump into them.'

'No doubt they're having a wild old time somewhere.'

'Don't get me going. She's seventeen, and I have to let her out sometimes but then all I do is worry. I can't sleep until I hear her key in the door. And when she stays with Serena, I'm a fright altogether. I remember one Saturday morning there was a story on the radio news about a young girl dying in a city-centre nightclub, and I was frantic. I rang Evanne. She was asleep and, needless to say, she didn't thank me for the call.' Martha took a mouthful of wine. 'Give Ruán a few years, and you'll find out what it's like . . . although I don't think boys stir up quite the same anxiety.'

'I've heard they're worse. Anyway, when you think about it, we did plenty of stupid things at that age and we're still standing.'

'At that age?'

'All right – and at every other age too.'

Paudie told her that his son was due to visit the following week. 'I'll have to take him to see Mam and Dad. It's been more than a year since they last saw him, and I'm starting to get the are-you-ashamed-of-us-down-here routine.' He paused. 'How are things with your own parents?'

'They keep calling me, and I keep avoiding them. I'm still flailing around. It's like . . . I went to America to find out more about myself, but all the trip did was make everything murkier.'

He leaned in and stroked her fingers. 'That's why you've got to go back.'

The taxi driver was listening to one of those radio stations where Steely Dan are still on the playlist and the DJs sound like they're suffering from laryngitis. Martha and Paudie held hands. For a short time, they pretended they were going to his house to continue their conversation.

They kissed in the hall and on the stairs. A tingling feeling drifted from Martha's throat to her chest and beyond. Her skin buzzed. Memories reignited. *Say what you like about Paudie*, she thought, *he always was a great kisser.*

For a moment, she questioned what she was doing. This was a man who'd been publicly spurned by a younger lover. His ego was in need of a boost. He was using her. She should do the sensible thing and go home. They could meet again when she'd had time to think this through.

On the other hand . . . this was also a man who'd had lots of sex with lots of different partners. She'd had a moderate amount of married sex and then . . . nothing. Three years of nothing. Maybe she was using him.

They kissed again, and the moment passed. She felt wonderfully lightheaded. She felt untethered.

'So then,' said Paudie.

Martha tried to catch her breath. 'So then.'

'Will you stay?'

'I've always had a weakness for old men.'

'*Et tu, Martha*?' he said, but his smile was a mile wide.

They kissed some more.

If she was making a mistake, so be it. She'd made plenty of others, and she'd survived.

# CHAPTER 39

Rose took Mitch's advice. Actually, she went further. She told her psychiatrist everything. Save for her husband, this was the first time anyone had heard the full story. Of the seven other people who'd always known, four were dead. The surviving three – Nancy, Ray and Ed junior – would never speak.

Dr Scott Woodford was an ascetically thin man with a high forehead and a forensic gaze. He appeared to be in his mid-forties but could have been ten years older. To Rose, everybody looked disconcertingly young.

When she'd finished her story, she sat in his bright, Spartan office and felt the tears stream down her cheeks. How many times had she heard it said that shrinks were latter-day priests, their offices replacing the confessional? For the first time, the comparison seemed accurate. Or partially accurate. Rose would like to say she felt better but she didn't. Dr Woodford couldn't absolve her of her sins. She remembered her parting words to Martha. 'Brooke's not a bad person,' she'd said.

'None of us is.' She wondered if Martha had considered this odd.

'What I did was shameful,' she said.

'You were very young,' replied Dr Woodford.

Rose rubbed the scar on her left hand, the small white line a permanent reminder of her time in Carrigbrack. 'It was shameful then. It's shameful now.'

'You were young, Rose. And you were ill.'

Her shoulders began to shake and, within seconds, she was sobbing like a lost child. The psychiatrist passed her a wad of tissues from a large box in the centre of his desk.

Rose had cried when she'd first met Martha and Evanne, but not like this. Not with huge hot tears and whimpering. The last time she'd wept in such a messy way had been at her brother Kevin's funeral. Dear, dear Kevin. He had always been the best of them. When his coffin was lowered into the ground, she'd been devoured by grief. Her oldest ally was gone. If only he'd lived long enough to meet Martha.

'Do you think,' Dr Woodford asked eventually, 'that if you came clean to everybody involved, it would help?'

'I can't do that.'

'Okay,' he replied, his tone making it clear he didn't agree. 'But what you *can* do is forgive yourself.'

'It's too late,' said Rose, throwing another sodden tissue into the wastepaper basket.

'Is it?' he asked. 'Is it really?'

# CHAPTER 40

The drizzle was wrapping itself around Martha, creeping inside her jacket and frizzing her hair. 'A grand soft day,' her dad would say. He had a knack of seeing good in everything. The rain would be hopping off the ground, and he'd say something about the garden being in need of a sup of water. The frost would be a foot thick, and he'd claim it was great weather for killing off germs. Now that she thought about it, one of her mother's favourite sayings would be more appropriate. 'Any fool can bring an umbrella on a wet day,' her mam liked to say, 'but the wise person carries it every day.' Martha had no excuse. The sky had been filling in for hours, yet still she'd set off without an umbrella.

She hadn't heard many of her parents' expressions lately. Apart from the occasional strained telephone conversation, they weren't talking. Even when they did speak, they didn't address their differences. Their conversations were brisk, brittle. Once or twice, Martha found herself thawing. Then the truth came hurtling back. *They'd known. They'd always known. Yet they'd said nothing.* And when she'd confronted them, the best they could come up with was a half-hearted apology and a stream of self-justification.

The same thing happened when she thought fondly of them, like she'd done just now. The thoughts were pushed away by the knowledge that they'd lied to her.

Evanne wasn't saying very much either. She sat in her room with her headphones on or she went out. Meals were eaten in silence. The quiet put Martha on edge. 'I preferred you in venting mode,' she'd said to her daughter. 'Throw a good old strop, would you? And then we can talk. I still think you're wrong, but we've got to talk.' Evanne had just shrugged, and Martha had come as close as she probably ever would to a full-on when-I-was-your-age rant.

As if the stand-off with Evanne wasn't difficult enough, Dermot had gone from being a lukewarm supporter of Martha's position to deciding that their daughter had a point. 'I had another chat with her,' he'd said, 'and she really is enthusiastic about those beauty courses. And, you know, she's such a determined girl. Look at how she made her way to Fourmilecross. Not to mention how she found Rose. Maybe we should have faith in her judgement.'

Martha had put up a fight. 'I thought you wanted her to be some sort of scientist, like Una,' she said.

'If Evanne can't hack Leaving Cert chemistry, I doubt she'll ever trouble the Nobel Prize committee,' he replied.

She was wasting her breath. Dermot's head was elsewhere. How she cursed him and his change of heart, and how she cursed Evanne for playing divide and conquer. If Dermot decided to pay for the beauty course, Martha's objections were futile.

Then there was Rose. Martha had emailed her twice without reply. She'd called and left a message. Again, she'd received no reply. A whispering unease took hold, her head invaded by an army of buts, maybes and what-ifs. What if Rose was having second thoughts about their reunion? What if Brooke had persuaded her mother to cut off communication? One friendly letter wasn't enough to persuade Martha that her half-sister was trustworthy.

Once, she would have found escape at work. Libraries were calm, gentle places. Or, at least, that was how they were supposed to be. Martha's branch had turned into a repository of madness. That afternoon she'd had to contend with two teenage boys shaping up for a fist fight in Young Adult, a girl throwing up in Large Print and an elderly man spitting abuse because his Lee Child novel was missing ten pages. In short, it had been one lousy day. That was why she was on her way to Cat's house. She needed a cup of tea, a friendly face and half an hour of grown-up conversation. Usually, Martha enjoyed the walk, but tonight wasn't just wet, it was cold. The sky was an ugly tobacco colour, the suburban streets were deserted, and a light glowed from almost every house.

She would have liked to speak to Paudie, but he was in Templemorris with Ruán. He did send frequent texts. In the last one, he'd suggested dinner on Saturday night. It would be his final free Saturday before the chat show came back for the new season. If she went, she supposed she'd have to call it a date. Oh, what did she mean, '*if* she went'? Obviously she would go.

Their night together had been fun. Not too embarrassing or fumbly either. *Here I am again*, she thought, *downplaying what it meant to me*. Hand on heart, the night had been great. She'd felt like a woman released from jail. Of course she'd dashed to the bathroom in the morning, desperate to detangle her hair, remove the mascara from under her eyes and rub toothpaste onto her teeth. Mind you, she'd behaved no differently twenty years earlier when she'd been young and unlined. What a waste of time that had been.

Five days on, she was as confused as she'd been at twenty-three. Were they a couple now? That was what his texts suggested. What, though, if all he wanted was some no-strings-attached sex until another shiny young thing passed his way? The sex had been fantastic for her, but was it enough for him? Martha's repertoire was fairly limited. Who knew what Paudie was used to? She hated herself for thinking, *Why is he bothering with me?* Yet the thought kept slithering in. As she squelched along, she remonstrated with herself. She didn't have time for teenage angst. She was the mother of a teenager. Her behaviour was silly. Pah-thetic, as Evanne might say (if she was talking to her). What she needed to do was take charge of the situation. Yes, she wanted to see Paudie again. But she didn't want to be messed around.

She'd had enough of that.

Cat put on her listening face. She dug her teeth into her bottom lip. Then she tilted her head. Finally, she spoke. 'Don't get annoyed, but I'm with Evanne.'

'Oh?' said Martha, running a hand through her damp hair.

'From what I can see, she's far more together than we were at that age. Good luck to her, I say.'

'But—'

'Let's be honest here, Martha. Why did we go to college? We went because it was a passport out of Templemorris. Three years of partying and going to the cinema in the afternoon, lectures an optional extra.'

'Speak for yourself.'

Cat nibbled at a biscuit. 'Well, that's how I remember it. Which is not to say we didn't learn a few things along the way. But it sounds to me like Evanne has a clear idea of what she wants.' Another nibble. 'I only hope my crowd have that much sense. What does Dermot think?'

'Dermot?' said Martha, finding it impossible to keep the annoyance from her voice. 'At the start, he agreed with me, only then he went away and became all Dermot-like. “It’s a growth industry,” he keeps saying, like he’s talking about computer parts or something. “Yeah,” I said. “A growth industry built on convincing women they’re not good enough.” Then he told me I needed to get over my “student feminism”. Oh, it’s like old times.’

‘Do you think he might be sorting things out with Layla?’

‘I don’t know. I’d ask Evanne, only she’s taken a vow of silence.’ Martha sipped her tea. ‘Do you honestly think she’s doing the right thing?’

‘What you seem to be forgetting,’ said Cat, ‘is that I was brought up by a hairdresser. I remember when I was nine or ten, I used to sit on the stairs and watch women parading in to Mam, all dowdy and downcast. An hour later, those same women would bounce out again, and I’d see them sneaking a glance in the hall mirror. My mother had given them a lift. Now, if you compare that to what I do – flogging overpriced hotels and rip-off bank accounts and all sorts of other crap – I’m convinced Mam had the more worthwhile job. So I hear what you’re saying and, believe me, I wish girls weren’t so obsessive about their looks, but I also think you’ve got to trust your daughter.’

‘I do trust her, only . . .’

Cat fixed Martha with a firm look. ‘I’m going to say something else and the chances are . . .’

She inhaled sharply. 'The chances are . . . you're not going to like it.'

'Go on.'

'You can't relive your life through Evanne.'

'That's not . . .' Martha stopped. She wanted to rail against Cat's last comment. She wanted to say it was unfair. But how could she when it was true?

'And before you point this out,' continued Cat, 'I know it's easy for me to say, "You've got to let her go." When Hope reaches Evanne's age, I might view everything differently.' She slurped her tea. 'It's mad, really, isn't it? When we were teenagers, we were told to expect nothing. Now they're told to expect everything, and I'm not sure which is worse.'

'I understand,' said Martha, who was floundering. Her head was filled with objections to Evanne's choice, but to voice them now would be to risk criticising Cat's mam. And there was nobody dead or alive whom Cat loved more.

Her friend was giving her a questioning look.

'There's more, isn't there?'

'Why do you say that?' asked Martha.

'Because I know you. You came out without an umbrella, which tells me that your mind is elsewhere. And you're sitting here with that Dolly Daydream look on your face. Now it could be that you're just het up about Evanne, but I reckon there's something else going on.'

'We-ell . . .'

'I'm not going to like this, am I?'

'Perhaps not. We're not going to fall out, though, are we?'

'Do your worst,' said Cat.

After her session with Dr Woodford, Rose was exhausted. Exhausted and conflicted. Although he'd avoided telling her what to do, he clearly believed she should revisit old decisions. Didn't he appreciate how tough that would be? Back and forth she swung: one minute seeing wisdom in his suggestion, the next dismissing it as madness.

When Mitch asked how she'd got on with the psychiatrist, she hadn't known what to say. She was too listless to give an honest account of the session. Besides, what if her husband reckoned she'd said too much?

'I had difficulty opening up,' she said. 'But we had a chat, and I'll go back next week.'

Mitch kissed her head and told her she was doing the right thing.

The lump that had taken up home at the base of her throat became even harder. It was a good job she didn't believe in Hell because her sins were stacking up like empty bottles at a party.

Although Dr Woodford had given her some sleeping pills, when she did drop off, the dreams that awaited her were grim. The previous night she'd dreamed she lived in Dublin with Martha and Evanne. Sister Agnes came calling, and they tried to run away. Rose had woken with a shout, her nightgown soaked with sweat, her legs feeling like she'd climbed a mountain.

Not for the first time, it occurred to her that the line between sanity and meltdown was razor thin. There was every chance she knew people who suffered like her. People who were beaten down and worn out. People who had demons they couldn't defeat and stories they never told. Sometimes, though, Rose passed a person in the street and she knew. Something about their eyes or their walk gave them away, their pain as evident as if they were bleeding or limping. She wanted to approach them, to say, 'Me too.' But she never did.

That afternoon was a fine one, and she planned on spending an hour or two in the garden. Some weeding might help her to relax. First, she needed to check her phone. She'd heard the ping of a text message. She could cope with texts. They were short and uncomplicated. Phone calls and emails were another matter. Voice messages and emails from Martha and Evanne had been piling up. What must they think of her?

The text was from Bobby. *Can I come over? I need to talk.*

Rose prodded out a reply. *Very busy here. Why don't you tell me what you need to talk about?*

*Because I've found something and I want to show it to you.*

*Can it wait?*

*No!*

*What's with the mystery?*

*No mystery. I just need to talk to you. See you in thirty minutes.*

Rose didn't know what Bobby was talking about, but she doubted his news was good. Oh, why couldn't everybody leave her alone? The muscles in her legs started to dance. She slumped into a kitchen chair, closed her eyes and tried not to think.

Martha knocked on Evanne's door. If she was brave enough to tell Cat about her night with Paudie, she was brave enough to make peace with a seventeen-year-old.

'Come in,' said a bored-sounding voice.

Evanne was sprawled on the bed, tapping at her iPad. Martha noticed that she'd added some new pictures to her collection. Her daughter's room was decorated with images of places she wanted to visit. The New York skyline was there, as were Sydney Harbour Bridge and the pink city of Jaipur. Martha's favourite picture was of people drinking wine outside a Paris café: some were talking; others were reading; all had a slightly crumpled elegance. She thought of Evanne's gallery as the technicolour version of her Aeroflot timetable.

'So,' she said, 'everybody seems to think I should trust your judgement. In fact, one or two people have suggested I might've been unfair to you.'

Evanne sat up and drew her knees in close to her chest. 'I see.'

'And maybe they have a point. Maybe I was too quick to say no.'

'Oh.'

'Now, if I'm being honest, I'd rather you did something else. But, like you pointed out, it's not my life. Perhaps I am more like Mam than I care to admit.'

A glimmer of a smile passed across Evanne's face. 'So . . .?'

'How's about we do a deal? I'll support your decision to do beauty and make-up, but only if you promise that you'll still try your hardest at school. I want you to get the best Leaving Cert you can. At the risk of sounding like your father, education is never wasted.'

The smile broadened. 'That's what I want too. I swear it is.'

'Do we have a deal, then?'

Evanne straightened her legs. Then she reached out and shook her mother's hand, as if she'd just sold her a second-hand car. 'We do. Thanks, Mum. That's . . . that's brilliant.'

Relief washed over Martha. Even though she'd meant everything she'd said, she wasn't so much embracing her daughter's decision as acknowledging it. She could hold out – but at what cost? Between her parents and Rose, Cat and Paudie, nothing was straightforward at the moment. Being at odds with Evanne was more than she could handle. She thought of herself at seventeen: straining to get out into the world, excited one minute, scared the next. Then she thought of Rose, exiled in Carrigbrack. She wanted Evanne to have good memories.

'I take it you're talking to me again?' she said.

'Sorry for being a bitch,' replied Evanne.

'You're forgiven. Oh, and one other thing.'

'Yeah?'

'I'm not a snob.'

Evanne giggled. 'Okay, all allegations of snobbery are withdrawn.' She paused. 'Just so you know, I'm minding Alex on Saturday night. Layla's going out with Dad.'

'Ah, interesting. What's the story?'

'Your guess is as good as mine, but I'm not going to get involved. They'll have to sort themselves out.'

'A wise move.'

'You've really got to meet Alex, though. Like, he is my half-brother and everything. And I promise you'd be super-crazy about him.'

'One day, love. Not yet, though, huh? Some things need time.' Martha hesitated. 'Speaking of which, I've got something else to tell you.' She had decided to tell Evanne about Paudie. A heavily censored version, obviously. To paraphrase Cat, you had to be careful with the truth.

'Oh?'

'It's about why I fell out with Cat. What happened was . . . I met up with an old boyfriend, a guy I went out with before I knew your dad. It was only a drink or two, but she was put out.'

'Why so?'

'When we broke up – and you've got to remember we're talking about more than twenty years ago – I was in a bad way. She didn't want to see me getting hurt again.'

'But it was only a drink, right?'

'It was, but I met him again last weekend.'

'When I was with Serena?'

'Mmm.'

'You dark horse, you.'

Martha smiled. 'Anyway, I'll be seeing him on Saturday. Not that it's a big deal or anything. I mean, I wasn't even sure I should tell you, but then . . . I can't expect you to be open with me if I'm not honest with you, can I?'

Even as she spoke, Martha was conscious of a reversal in the natural order of things. By rights, the daughter should be telling the mother that she'd met a guy but wasn't sure if he was a keeper.

'Does Cat know?' asked Evanne.

'I told her this evening.'

'And?'

'She's still talking to me, anyway.'

Cat had been surprisingly calm. 'I can't pretend I'm happy,' she'd said, 'but you're a big grown-up now, and I'm not able for another row.' When Martha was leaving, the two had hugged as though one of them was setting off for war. 'Please, take care of yourself,' Cat had said.

Evanne played with her hair. 'So, this unnamed

man, he's not some type of scumbag or something, is he?'

'Lord, no.'

'Will I get to have a look at him?'

'You already know what he looks like.' Martha felt her face becoming warm. 'I was at school with him. It's, ahm, Paudie Carmody.'

Evanne's mouth rounded into a small *o*. 'You're not serious?'

'I am, actually.'

'Wow! Just wow. Wait until Serena hears about this. She will *die* with jealousy. Like, big-time jealousy.'

'Please, love. What I've told you is to go no further than this room. I don't know what's going to happen between us, and I'd like to keep everything low-key.'

'Oo-kaaay,' said Evanne.

'Seriously, you've got to promise me you won't say a word to anybody, including your dad.'

'All right.' Evanne's eyes glinted. 'You'll have to keep me sweet, so.'

Martha laughed. 'You cheeky pup. Would a hot chocolate be enough to keep you onside?'

'It'd be a good start.'

As Martha rose from the bed, the doorbell rang. There was a brief pause, and then it chimed again. She looked at her watch. 'You're not expecting anybody, are you?'

'Nope.'

'Somebody must be lost. I'll go and see who

they're looking for.' Another ding-dong. 'Hold your horses, I'm coming,' she said, as she trotted down the stairs.

Martha opened the door to see a tall woman in a black jacket. The way she held herself, her air of sophistication, made it clear she lived abroad. Beside her stood a smaller, older woman, her mouth set in a sombre line, her eyes pink-rimmed.

'Ahm, Mam? Una?' said Martha, her voice squeaky with surprise. 'Is something wrong?'

'Aren't you going to invite us in?' asked her sister.

'Of course I am. Come in, come in. Sorry, I'm a bit . . . Well, you don't normally turn up like this. I mean, it's ten o'clock at night. Why didn't you call to say you were coming?'

'You won't speak to me when I do ring,' replied her mother, as she stepped out of her shoes. 'Take off your boots there, Una, for fear you dirty Martha's lovely carpet.'

Una's eyes rose to the heavens, but she did as she was told. 'We need to talk,' she said.

# CHAPTER 41

It was easy to underestimate Bobby. Rose blamed his looks. He had the sort of face that said 'good-natured, not too serious'. Throw in his helpful attitude and slow smile, and a stranger could be forgiven for dismissing him as lacking in substance.

His mother should have known better. She should have remembered that his breezy appearance masked a seam of determination.

Truth to tell, Rose had been so preoccupied by the whirlpool in her own head that she'd given scant thought to Bobby's interest in the Brennans. Two or three weeks had passed since he'd last asked about Joe's family and, like a fool, she'd assumed he had abandoned any thoughts of tracking them down. If anything, Rose had worried that Martha or Evanne would go hunting. In particular, she'd fretted about her granddaughter's single-mindedness. But she'd always known that in replying to Martha's letter she was taking a gamble. And she'd always known that the real story wouldn't be too difficult to unearth.

Now, as they sat at the kitchen table, she had

the sense that Bobby had done just that. Since his arrival five minutes before, he'd been brusque to the point of rudeness. Most of Rose's observations and questions had been met with a nod or a grimace. He was closing in on her like a bird of prey gliding on a jet of warm air.

Finally, he reached into his jacket pocket, removed three pieces of A4 paper and unfolded them. The top sheet showed a black-and-white photograph of a man in his sixties. He was wearing a dark jacket and an open-necked shirt. His thin face was lifted by an enthusiastic smile.

'I did an internet search and came across this,' said Bobby. 'To begin with I wasn't sure. *Nah,* I thought, *the name's similar, only it doesn't quite tally. Anyway, it couldn't be. It couldn't be.*' He stared at Rose, his blue gaze steady. 'But I kept looking at that picture. I couldn't stop looking.'

Rose peeped at the sheets of paper her son had placed in the middle of the table. She was familiar with their contents. She'd read them the previous year when the article first appeared in the paper. Back before Bobby knew about Martha. Before he knew about Joe. She'd kept a copy of the piece in her underwear drawer.

'Aren't you going to read it?' he asked.

'In a minute.' Rose's words were hesitant. 'I've seen it before. Your father came across it and showed it to me.' A drum beat started in her head.

'I see. So that is . . .?'

She was cornered. There was no plausible excuse. How could she even start to explain?

'Yes,' she said. 'That's him.'

'I don't understand,' said Bobby.

The drumming became louder, more frenetic. 'His sister always called him that. His mom too. On account of his father's name also being Joe. I guess at some point he must have adopted it.'

Bobby shook his head. 'It's not the name that bothers me. It's everything else.'

Rose picked up the sheets of paper and ran her eyes over the familiar words.

**A life devoted to second chances**

Call JP Brennan a hero, and he'll most likely laugh at you. But to many in the city's drugs-ravaged communities that's what he is. This month, Brennan will mark forty years working in the drugs and addiction services. When he began, Boston was gripped by a heroin epidemic. In the eighties cocaine became the big issue. Now he has to cope with the resurgence in opiate addiction.

For the past two decades, the sixty-four-year-old has overseen a number of the city's substance-abuse programs. But he started his working life as an addiction counselor and he tries to have as much contact as possible with addicts and their families.

'The day you realize you only ever meet other guys in suits is the day you ought to give up,' he says. 'You need to talk to people, to see their desperation, to hear their stories. And you need to tell them that their life matters. Otherwise, what's the point?'

It's an attitude that impresses former addicts like Samantha Cleary. She says Brennan's supportive but no-nonsense approach helped to wean her away from heroin addiction.

'I was at rock bottom,' she recalls. 'Living on the streets, shooting hundreds of dollars into my arm. JP assured me that I could get clean, and that if I did, I'd get my kids back. He told me that when I was ready to give up, the support would be there. Without his help I'd be in prison. Or in the cemetery.'

Today, Cleary, whose smart-suited appearance belies her years of drug abuse, is herself training to be a counselor.

Another former addict, Gabriel Johnson, says Brennan kept repeating a simple message until he started to believe it. 'He used to tell me that just because I'd made some bad choices, I didn't have to be defined by them for the rest of my days,' he says. The forty-two-year-old has been clean for eight years.

Brennan, who was born and raised in

South Boston, could also have drifted into a life of trouble. He had a hardscrabble youth. 'Eventful' is the word he chooses. A scar over his left eye is a testament to those years. 'A fight over a girl,' he jokes.

He was fortunate that a high-school teacher spotted his potential and encouraged him to apply to college. The teenage Brennan thought he knew better, but two years working at 'this and that' convinced him that without an education he would never achieve his ambitions. Eventually, he secured a scholarship and went to college.

'You've got to believe in second chances,' he says.

It's a maxim he still lives and works by. He reckons that most people, no matter how serious their addiction, are capable of turning their lives around. 'If I didn't believe that, I wouldn't belong in this job. But you've also got to know where to draw the line. Addicts don't just hurt themselves. They hurt their families and their communities. Most of all they hurt their children.'

According to the latest figures, more than one thousand people in Massachusetts have died from heroin or other opiates this year. Brennan sees every death as a failure. He also believes the issue doesn't receive sufficient political priority. Many times he's crossed swords with politicians. Back in the eighties, he occupied the office of a state senator because he didn't believe the politician was taking the crack problem seriously enough.

'There was me and three women, all mothers of kids with serious addictions,' he recalls. 'We sat on his desk and refused to move until he had a proper conversation with us. I don't think the poor guy knew what hit him.'

Next year Brennan will retire. He jokes that it's a day his wife, Sofia, is dreading. Ask him what he plans on doing, and you'll get a smile.

'We have three sons and six grandkids,' he says. 'So I'm hoping I'll see a bit more of them. But I have other plans too. Just because I won't be on the payroll doesn't mean I can't get involved.

'I hope I can still make a difference.'

Rose placed the article back on the table. For several minutes, neither she nor Bobby spoke. When she looked up she realised her son was staring at her as if she was a stranger. She turned away.

'Why?' he said.

# CHAPTER 42

*Boston, April 1969*

The bedroom was filled with glittery spring light. Rose flipped the pillow over to the cool side and pulled the blankets over her head. She preferred the dark. She longed for wet, murky days. When the weather was bad she wasn't under pressure to be out there, doing something. Every day, her mother tried to get her to run one errand or other: 'Go to the grocery store'; 'Take this cake to Mrs Grady'; 'Fetch your father's best suit from the laundry.' Every day, Rose said no. She'd been home for a month and sometimes she reckoned that life had been easier in Carrigbrack. She'd had less time to think.

She felt bad about staying in her room. She felt bad about everything. A parrot sat on her shoulder, reminding her of her failures. She had sworn she'd bring her baby home. And she'd failed. Her heart ached – an actual, physical ache – for her daughter. Rose's father said Josephine's new family were kind people. Decent. He claimed not to know if they'd changed her name. Rose didn't believe him, but what did it matter? Her little girl was three thousand miles away.

She wanted to see Joe, only she was too scared. Did he know they'd had a daughter? Would he forgive Rose for allowing her to be taken away? Her family never mentioned him. She wondered if he was still at home. The only way to find out was to go and see, except just brushing her teeth or putting on her clothes was hard. Getting to Joe's place would require more energy than she possessed. The previous week she'd tried to spend an hour downtown. Her mother had insisted. 'Come on,' she'd said. 'It'll help to buck you up.' Before long, Rose had become overpowered by the faces and the noise. She'd ended up sitting on the sidewalk, crying and shivering. Her mom, her embarrassment almost palpable, reminded Rose that many people had coped with far more. She told her to think of all the women losing husbands and boyfriends in Vietnam, or the women who had to cope when their men returned all disconnected and strange. 'You don't see them behaving like little girls, indulging in crying jags on the street,' she said.

Rose's mother was right. Her behaviour was pathetic. She couldn't help it, though. She honestly couldn't. She attempted to explain this, but the right words eluded her. Talking to people was difficult. Neither did she want anybody to see her. She couldn't get dressed up because she didn't feel pretty enough. It would be wrong to try to gild her gaunt face and scrawny limbs. As for her hair, it was long enough to tie back now, but fluffy wisps kept escaping. She felt like a freak. She *was* a freak.

Kevin had tried to coax her into going out. They could go to the movies, he said. Or they could try a walk along the beach. Sunlight would help a little, he was sure. If she wanted, they could talk about Josephine, but they didn't have to. 'The Rose I know would want to talk about those nuns,' he said. 'She'd want to rip them apart.'

Why didn't her brother understand? She wasn't that Rose any more.

Sometimes, she heard her parents arguing. Mostly, they had the same circular conversation, but once her dad claimed they'd done the wrong thing. They should never have sent her to Ireland, he said. 'I hope you're not blaming me,' her mother replied. 'Anyway, what was the alternative? She'll just have to start behaving like a grown-up.' Then her mom began to cry. That Grace's tears were probably for herself didn't matter. Rose listened to the muffled sobs and was overcome with shame.

The one person with the ability to stir her from her stupor was Nancy. Her sister's power was akin to that of the electric fence that bordered part of the grounds in Carrigbrack. One burst of Nancy's adenoidal voice, and Rose's body snapped to attention. No doubt at their mother's prompting, Nancy asked Rose to be a bridesmaid at her wedding.

Rose said no. She didn't want to wear a long frilly dress. She didn't want to go to the wedding, period. Well-meaning relations, who thought she'd been helping her dad's aunt, would ask about Ireland, and she wasn't sure she'd be capable of lying.

'One day acting like a normal person won't kill you,' said Nancy.

'I tell you what,' replied Rose. 'Why don't I pitch up and tell the truth? What a lark that would be. I'd say Theo's family would *love* to hear all about Carrigbrack.'

Nancy went into meltdown, and Rose was summoned by her parents. They sat at the kitchen table: Rose on one side, Ed and Grace on the other, like a two-person firing squad. Her father looked tired, her mother wrung out.

'This can't go on,' said her mom. 'Sooner or later, you'll have to go out and face the world again.'

'You're only eighteen,' added her dad. 'You can return to school in the fall and begin again like nothing has happened. We know that you're upset about Josephine but, honestly, Rosie, you've got to let all that go. You need to get back in touch with your school friends and let them know you're home. Perhaps you'll even meet a nice young man . . . someone who'll take you out of yourself.'

Her dad's smile was so false it made Rose's face hurt. 'What I need is to see Joe,' she said.

'You can't do that,' said her mother.

'Why not?'

Rose noticed her dad sliding his eyes towards her mom, as if to say, 'Go on.'

Grace exhaled. 'Before Christmas I went to see him, and I told him you'd lost the baby.'

Rose gasped. 'Why did you do that?'

'Please, Rose, for once in your life would you use the brain that God gave you? I was protecting your interests. You don't want to be shackled to that guy. You don't want him thinking he has some connection to you.'

'We *are* connected. We'll always be connected. I had his baby.'

Her mother and father exchanged another glance. Then Grace dipped into her purse and pulled out a small newspaper cutting. She handed it to her daughter. Rose's hand shook as she read the brief notice announcing the sudden and tragic death of Joseph Timothy Brennan of South Boston, beloved son of Paul and Nesta.

'I don't get this,' she said. 'That's not my Joe.'

'But it could be,' replied her mother. 'He could have been the Joe Brennan who was killed in a car wreck.'

Her father explained that when they'd first seen the obituary back in January, they'd assumed it was Rose's Joe. They'd quickly realised their mistake, but then they'd decided that was how they *should* think of him. To all intents and purposes, he was dead. Gone from their lives.

'And that's how you ought to think too,' added her mother.

Rose couldn't stop herself. 'Are you out of your fucking minds? First you tell Joe that his baby died. Then you try and convince yourself that the guy himself is dead.'

Her mother winced. 'I'm sure they didn't tolerate that sort of language in Ireland. I can't tell you what to think, but I have a feeling you'll come to see the sense in what we're saying. It hasn't escaped my attention that you've been home for a month, yet you've made no attempt to contact him. Mind you,' she added, with a sniff, 'he hasn't made any attempt to find you either.'

Rose didn't know what to say. She rubbed her potato-peeling scar, which had turned a livid purple.

'We've managed to keep your secret,' her father said. 'And we've done that by staying quiet.'

Silence was not just the best policy, her parents maintained. It was the only policy. One ill-considered word and the truth would escape, the ripples would spread, and Rose's reputation would be for ever soiled. 'It's 1969,' Rose wanted to reply. 'The world doesn't work like that any more.' Then she thought of Carrigbrack. She remembered how scared some of the other girls had been. They didn't care what happened so long as nobody knew about their pregnancy. People judge you, they said. They would keep on judging. Your life would be destroyed. Was Boston so different? Rose wondered. She needed to digest what her parents had said. The problem was, her head was lined with lead. Her eyes were gritty, her thoughts sluggish. She would go back to bed and try to think it all through.

Another week went by. There were times when Rose felt as if the walls were moving in towards her, as if all she had to do was wait and the room would run out of air. Gradually, though, she was working on herself. She had to go and see the boy who'd loved her and who'd wanted to marry her. Her mother had told him a terrible lie, and Rose needed to put that right.

Finally, on a sun-splattered Saturday afternoon, she left the house. Nobody asked any questions. Presumably they were just relieved to see her up and about. As she walked, her mind played with her. It told her she was making a mistake. Her feet knew better, however, and they took her to the station. She was going to be reunited with Joe. She would have to be calm and clear about what had happened, and she would have to apologise for her family. The Moroneys had behaved like a bunch of goons. On the train, her urge to see Joe, to touch him, became more powerful. Nobody touched her any more. It was like they feared she would break and they wouldn't be able to clear up the mess. They wanted to insulate themselves from her sorrow.

She decided to go to Bree's apartment. Joe's sister would know where to find him. He might even be there. With every step, Rose became more nervous but also more excited. She tucked her hair behind her ears, focused on her breathing and knocked. For a minute or so, nobody answered. She gave another small tap. The door opened with a wheezy sigh, and . . . and there he was. His hair was a little longer, his shoulders a little broader, but otherwise he was the same. Well, almost the same. There was a mark over his left eye. Her brothers' work, she assumed. Her stomach turned over.

Joe squinted. 'Oh, my God. Rose!'

'Yes,' she said, 'it's me.'

'I thought you were gone for good. I . . . I can't believe you're back.'

'Yep, here I am. Back,' she replied, not knowing what else to say. *Please touch me*, she thought. *Please put your arms around me and say it's good to see me.*

'Back,' he repeated. 'Your mother and your brothers . . .'

'I'm so sorry about Ray and Ed. I didn't get the chance to talk to you before I had to go away. What they did was awful. I wouldn't blame you if you were upset with me. And as for my mother . . . Maybe I could come in and have a glass of water? We can sit down and I'll explain.'

Rose took a step forward and, as she did, she heard a woman's voice.

'Who is it, Joe?' the voice asked.

For a couple of seconds, Rose thought it was Bree. Then a girl appeared. A blonde girl in a tight pink sweater. She had mussed-up hair and bare feet. She was not beautiful, yet beautiful, if that made sense. Her hair was too yellow and her eyes were too far apart, but she glistened with life. Rose felt all the more drab.

'Rose, this is Lois,' he said. 'Lois, this is my old friend Rose.'

Pain snapped across Rose's forehead, and her body went limp. How dumb had she been? How disgustingly dumb and naive? She'd disappeared for almost a year yet she'd imagined that Joe would be sitting here waiting for her.

'Hi, Lois, nice to meet you,' she said, her voice all skittery. 'Anyway, Joe, like I say, I was in the neighbourhood so I thought I'd drop by and say hello. But you've got company and . . . I don't want to interrupt. Give my love to Bree, would you? And to Davey and the girls.' She hesitated. 'I guess . . . I guess I'll see you around.'

Before he could reply, Rose was gone. She ran back down the steps and tore up the street as though fleeing from a fire. After about two hundred yards, she stopped to gather her breath. It was then that she heard the *slap slap slap* of running feet.

'Rose, wait up,' shouted Joe.

She turned around, and for a while they stood there, each as still as stone.

'You didn't write,' he said. 'I thought you'd tell me where you were. I thought I'd hear something from you, even if it was just "So long, buddy."'

'I'm sorry,' she said. How could she explain that

she'd been in a place where writing was forbidden? 'Everything got too complicated.'

His mouth opened as if he was about to speak, but no words came.

'I swear,' continued Rose, 'I thought about you all the time. Not a day passed that I didn't wonder what you were doing. I really am sorry.'

Joe reached out and folded his arms around her. She inhaled his familiar soapy smell and willed herself not to cry.

'No. I'm sorry,' he said, his words tickling her ear. 'I'm sorry about everything. I thought you were gone for good.' They pulled apart and he smoothed a finger down one cheek. 'That aunt in Ireland didn't feed you, huh?'

She tried to smile. 'I'll be back to normal soon, I hope.'

'It's just . . . when you didn't get in touch . . . Well, I'm with Lois now, you know? You'd like Lois. She's fun. And she's smart, like you.'

Rose waited for him to say something about their baby. Or his marriage proposal – shouldn't he mention that? Voices were chattering in her head.

*You've got to tell him*, one voice said.

*Don't tell him*, said another. *He doesn't need to know. It's not like he can ever meet her.*

*Tell him. You love him. You want to be with him.*

*Don't tell him. That's all over now. He doesn't love you.*

*Tell him.*

*Don't tell him.*

She looked into his grey eyes. The power was his. If he said something, if he asked about the baby, she'd tell him the truth.

He remained quiet.

'I'd better get moving,' she said. 'Lois will be wondering where you've got to.'

After what felt like an age, Joe replied: 'You're right, I should go back.' He touched her cheek again. 'Take care of yourself, Rose. I hope everything works out for you.'

'Thanks.' She swallowed. 'And, Joe?'

'Yeah?'

'I truly am sorry about my family. And I wish all the best for you as well. You know that, don't you?'

He nodded.

Rose watched him walk away. She felt exposed, as if her skin had been ripped off. She'd felt the same when she'd lost Josephine. She thought of Lois waiting in the apartment. Funny, smart Lois. A year ago that had been her. But she'd been a different person then.

# CHAPTER 43

*August 2014*

Bobby asked a stream of questions. So many questions, voiced in such rapid-fire succession, that Rose felt as if they were bouncing off the walls and zinging around the room. He stalked the floor, pausing occasionally to look at her.

She kept on answering. Her mouth was flannel-dry and there was a quiver in her voice, but the words continued to spill out. She supposed that since her conversation with Dr Woodford she'd been preparing herself for this.

'So what happened when Joe walked away and you went back home?' he asked.

'I took up where I'd left off. Mostly I stayed in my room. When I did go out, I tried not to engage with people. I learned to do everything by rote. Looking back, I suppose I retreated into myself because it seemed like the safest thing to do.'

'Listen, Mom, I do have sympathy for you. Honestly I do. I can see why Lois upset you, and it was wrong of Joe not to mention the baby. But why didn't you give it a week or two? You could've returned then and spoken to him. Or, if that was too hard, why didn't you write to him? He deserved to know he had a daughter.'

Rose shifted in her chair. What her son said sounded reasonable, but back in 1969 everything had felt different. Over the years, she'd had ample opportunity to reflect. What if Lois hadn't been there? Would her life have taken a different course? No, she'd concluded, if it hadn't been Lois, it would have been somebody or something else. By the time Rose turned up on Bree's doorstep, Joe had moved on. He was no longer hers.

'He was nineteen, Bobby,' she said. 'And he'd found somebody else. Somebody as vibrant as him, not all worn and fragile like me. I asked myself if he needed to be saddled with the knowledge that he had a child . . . a child he could never meet.'

'If he never wanted to hear about her again, fair enough. But surely he was entitled to know she existed?'

'All I can say is, that wasn't how I saw it at the time. "You've got to struggle on," I said. "You've got to forget about Joe." I couldn't risk having contact with him. If I did, I'd be opened up again, and I wouldn't have had the strength for that.' Rose pulled at the ends of her hair. 'I . . . and I'm not saying this as an excuse . . . I was in a bad place. Everything seemed so desperate. I did consider taking my own life, only I couldn't have done that to Kevin or my dad or even to my mother.'

Bobby pinched the bridge of his nose. 'You were ill, I get that. By the sound of things, you'd had some sort of breakdown. What I don't get is why your family did nothing to help you.'

'People – respectable people – didn't talk about depression or breakdowns. If they did, they spoke in euphemisms: "She has a problem with her nerves," they'd say. Or "She's tired." My parents looked at me and thought, *She's young. She'll snap out of it*. Needless to say, my mom was the more zealous one. She got really irritated. But my dad also became impatient – and that hurt.'

As time went on, their words had worn her down. Rose had concluded that her mother was right: she was a malingerer. She'd thrown a fire blanket over her feelings and tried to get on with her life.

'Did you ever see a doctor?' asked Bobby.

'Not at the time. Anyway, just say my parents had consulted a doctor. It's likely I would have ended up in a psychiatric hospital. I'd already been through one institution, and look at the harm that had done. So, the way I saw it, I was better off on my own. Years later, your father insisted I got professional help and, well, I won't claim I conquered all my problems because that wouldn't be true . . . but I learned to cope. And I've been lucky. I have you and Brooke and,' her voice faltered, 'everything else.'

By now, Mitch was home. At Bobby's insistence, Rose had called him. He sat beside her, cradling a tumbler of whiskey. He looked part exasperated, part scared. To her relief, Brooke, Chris and the boys were in Ogunquit, taking a short vacation. She couldn't have handled her daughter. Not today.

Outside the sun was setting. Soon it would dip behind the trees, leaving them in darkness. Right then, however, time seemed irrelevant. Rose knew she wouldn't sleep. She had too much to consider. Bobby was talking again, his words slipping past her ears. She was remembering what it was like to be eighteen, nineteen, twenty. Her memories were in washed-out colour, like a 1960s Polaroid.

'I'm sorry?' she said eventually.

Bobby released a noisy sigh. 'What I said was . . . I know it was never going to be easy, but you've had four decades, Mom. More than half a lifetime. At any stage, you could've found Joe and told him what he was entitled to know. Instead, you seem to have gone along with your mother's lunatic scheme. You pretended the poor guy was dead.'

'I'm sure it must sound terrible, but . . .' How could she explain that effectively this was what she and Mitch had decided to do? On the night she'd confessed to her future husband, she'd also agreed to forget about Joe and her daughter. 'I won't compete with a memory,' Mitch had said. She'd felt so unbelievably lucky that someone so good and kind and desirable had wanted her – difficult, damaged Rose – that she'd seized the opportunity. Carrigbrack had taught her about the power of kindness, and once she'd found it, she couldn't bear to let it go. Perhaps her parents had been right, she'd thought. Perhaps she could start afresh. But she'd been young. She hadn't realised that you can't just walk away from a memory.

Now she was casting about for the right words; for a way of explaining herself without sounding callous.

Mitch intervened: 'What you've got to appreciate, Bobby, is that your mother never expected to hear from Martha. Joe was consigned to the past. Whether he was dead or alive wasn't an issue until that letter arrived from Ireland.'

Although Rose welcomed her husband's support, what he said wasn't true. How often had she thought about Joe? Thousands upon thousands of times. Sometimes those thoughts were momentary. Sometimes they took hold and filled every corner of her mind.

Bobby was clenching and unclenching his hands. 'So you never saw Joe again?'

'Yes and no,' said Rose. 'I saw him once at the movies, but I'm sure he didn't see me. And there was another time – about a decade ago – I saw him on the street. But again he either didn't see me or he didn't recognise me.' The back of Rose's neck burned. That second sighting was no accident. She'd sought Joe out. At the last minute, her confidence had evaporated and she'd run away.

'And we've seen him in the papers,' added Mitch, 'talking about his job.'

'And on the TV. That incident they referred to in the article you gave me, the one where he occupied the senator's office? That was big news at the time.'

How well she remembered Joe's first appearance on the local news. He'd been in his late thirties then. Handsome. Articulate. Driven. She'd been so proud of him (although this had to remain hidden). So delighted that he'd fulfilled his ambition and found something worth doing. So heart-sore that she no longer knew him.

'And yet,' said Bobby, 'you told poor Martha that he was dead. Jesus Christ, Mom, that was unforgivable.'

'So tell me,' said Rose, 'what was the alternative?'

Bobby said nothing.

'You can't tell me because there wasn't one. I couldn't say to Martha, "Your father's alive and well and counselling heroin addicts. There's one small issue, though: he doesn't know you exist."'

Rose wasn't being straight. She could have levelled with Martha, just as she could have sought out Joe and confessed to him. She hadn't done so because of her pact with Mitch – and because she was frightened.

'But—' started her son.

'What you don't understand, Bobby, what you'll never understand, is how much I wanted to see her. She was stolen from me, and I needed to see her.'

Bobby found his voice. 'Yeah, only you don't

seem to appreciate what you've done. You've stolen her from Joe. I mean, reading that stuff from the paper . . . he sounds like a good guy. He ought to know about Martha, and she deserves to know about him.'

'It's too late for that,' said Mitch.

For the first time, Bobby sat down. 'No, it's not. Besides, if I was able to find out the truth, what's the betting Martha will do the same? Right now, she's probably preoccupied by the situation with her parents, but when her life settles down again, she'll start asking questions. Or, if she doesn't, Evanne will. What will they think then?'

'What are you suggesting?' asked Rose.

'I'm not suggesting anything. I'm *saying* that tomorrow we're going to pay Joe, or JP as we should probably call him, a visit.'

Mitch put down his glass. 'He mightn't be there any more. The paper said he was due to retire this year.'

'I called the office,' said Bobby. 'He's there, all right. He doesn't retire until December.'

'And what are you proposing we say to him?' asked Rose.

'We're going to tell him the truth: that he has a daughter and a granddaughter. Then you're going to call Martha and put her in the picture.'

'What if I'm not willing to do that?'

'Then I'll have to do it for you.'

* * *

In Dublin, Martha lay in bed, listening to the rain tip-tap against the window. With the moon hiding behind the clouds, the room was a fuzzy black. Beside her, her mother slept.

What a bizarre night it had been.

'She's had me driven demented,' Una had whispered, as the sisters puttered around the kitchen, making tea and hot chocolate. 'Honest to God, she was on the phone a hundred times a day. "Did you hear from Martha?" she kept asking. "Did she mention me or your dad?" I swear to you, Martha, the same woman wouldn't turn a hair if I disappeared on her.'

'You know that's not true. Anyway, I didn't disappear.'

'That's not the way she sees it. She says you haven't been home in ages and that you barely talk to them.'

'I was in Templemorris a month ago, Una. You can hardly blame me for needing a bit of space.'

'She says you left in a huff.'

'What did she expect me to do?' Martha's voice spiked with irritation. 'Say, "That's okay, Mam. Fire ahead. I don't mind being lied to"?'

'Ssh, she'll hear you.'

'No, she won't. Evanne's telling her about Fourmilecross. The poor woman will be comatose with boredom by the time we go back into the front room.'

'Mam adores Evanne,' said Una. 'She'd never get bored of her. Anyway, where was I?'

'You were explaining what the two of you are doing here.'

'Like I say, she kept on and on at me, so in the end I said, "I tell you what, we'll go and see Martha." I got a flight. Mam got a train. And here we are.'

Martha swirled boiling water around the teapot. (Her mother liked everything to be done properly. Tea wasn't tea unless you warmed the pot.) 'I can't believe you've gone to this much trouble.'

Una shrugged as if to say, 'Think nothing of it.'

'It's great to see you all the same,' continued Martha. 'Really great. As for Mam . . .'

'She's pretty cut up about everything, you know. Both of them are. Apparently, Dad considered coming up to Dublin too.'

'Good Lord, things must be serious.' Clem didn't like Dublin ('noisy, dirty place') and hadn't been to the capital in at least fifteen years.

Una smiled. 'For what it's worth, I don't think you being an actual, physical relation has ever been particularly important to Mam. And Dad's the same. They'd love you no matter what. You understand that, don't you?'

'I suppose I do, but the fact is, they had tons of opportunities to be straight with me, and they chose to continue lying.'

Una gave Evanne's hot chocolate an enthusiastic stir. 'Listen, I'm annoyed with them too. When you called to tell me the full story, I was raging. But you can't allow this stand-off to get out of control. I work with a fellow who fell out with his parents because he thought they'd insulted his wife. They ended up not talking for four years.'

'Ah, here, Una, that's not—'

'I'm not claiming that could ever happen in our family. More than a few months, and Mam would spontaneously combust. But there's a danger your differences will fester.'

'I hear you, only there's no point in me pretending I wasn't hurt when I was. I still am.'

'Come on,' said Una, picking up the tray of cups. 'We'd better go and have a talk.'

And so they did. For more than an hour, the four Sheeran women (technically speaking Evanne was a Waters, but in Martha's eyes she was a Sheeran too) thrashed out their differences. An unusually contrite Delia conceded she'd made a mess of things. She insisted, however, that the situation had been impossible.

'I'm not saying we should have told you about Rose right from the start. But when it became clear how determined you both were,' she nodded at Evanne, 'we should have had an honest discussion. I'm sorry we didn't.'

Martha could tell that this was hard for her mother. It was also clear that the tumult had taken its toll. The lines at the top of her nose had deepened into crevices, and there was a sheen of anxiety on her skin. What she said wasn't as important as the fact that she was there, in Martha's front room, saying it.

Martha heard herself sighing a deep sigh. 'I'm sure this hasn't been easy for you either, Mam. It's a mad situation, isn't it? I mean, how can things be wrong and right at the same time?'

'I don't follow you,' said her mother, wariness in her voice.

'What I'm trying to say is . . . I still believe Rose's parents were wrong to send her to Ireland. They should've allowed her to stay with Joe. And, who knows, if they'd been together, maybe he wouldn't have been killed. But, at the same time, I couldn't have asked for better parents than you and Dad.'

'Or grandparents,' added Evanne, still in high good humour after her mother's make-up capitulation.

'But,' said Martha, 'while we're on the subject, there's something else I need to say.' Although Una sent her an uneasy look, Martha wouldn't be deterred. 'You're entitled to your views about what happened back then, and I'm sure there were plenty of good nuns. But the way Rose was treated was plain wrong, and I'm convinced that if you spoke to her, you'd agree.'

'Maybe so,' said her mam, in a small voice. She smiled a wan sort of smile, and for a moment Martha feared she was going to cry. Instead she confined herself to some heartfelt tutting and sighing.

For a while, they sat in silence. Even though it was late, traffic continued to whip past, the cars making a skeetering sound as they ploughed through puddles. When the four spoke again, it was to indulge in family reminiscences. A few do-you-remember-whens always had the capacity to unite them. Martha supposed most families were the same. When the present was tricky, what could you do but seek refuge in the safe long-ago? Delia sat there chuckling and chipping in the odd memory of her own, but it was only when the conversation moved to the present day that she got to take aim at one of her favourite targets.

'I saw that latchico Paudie Carmody during the week,' she said. 'He was down the town with a child. His son, by the look of him. I presume he never bothered to marry the mother. Answer me this, what do women see in that fellow?'

Evanne's face was swallowed in a huge smirk, while Martha felt her cheeks turn pink. Una gave them both a questioning look. Thankfully, Delia didn't appear to notice.

'He must have hidden talents,' said Evanne. 'What would you say his appeal is, Mum?'

Martha could gladly – and justifiably – have throttled her. 'I haven't a clue,' she said. 'It would take a smarter woman than me to work that one out.'

Now, as she tried to sleep, Martha's mind churned, her head filling with everything, good and bad, that bound the Sheerans together: their rituals and rows, prejudices and traditions. It still rankled that her parents had hidden her identity. Yet she could no more cut ties with them than she could with Evanne. Oh, and there was another consideration, one that insisted on popping into her head no matter how many times she told it to go away. Her mam and dad wouldn't be around for ever. She didn't want to find herself in ten years' time thinking, *If only* . . .

By contrast, she realised, Rose remained a stranger. They shared DNA but little else. Paudie was right. Martha needed to see her birth mother again soon. First, though, they needed to talk.

She would call her tomorrow and she would keep on calling.

# CHAPTER 44

She wasn't eighteen; she was sixty-three. Sixty-three-year-old women didn't run away. They stood their ground and faced up to their responsibilities. That was what Rose kept telling herself. All the same, every time the car stopped she had to fight the urge to jump out and flee.

Bobby was driving. He'd made the appointment too. He'd called Joe's office, said he was the son of an old friend and needed to talk. After thirty minutes, Joe's assistant had got back to him. 'That will be no problem,' she'd said. 'Mr Brennan would be delighted to meet with you.' What Joe didn't know was that Rose would also be there. 'The poor guy probably thinks I'm an addict,' said Bobby.

They drove past a park, a swathe of Victorian row houses, a Home Depot and a U-Haul storage unit. The closer they got, the more jittery Rose became. She felt as if she'd been cut loose from her moorings, as if everything was out of control. Deep down, though, she also felt something surprising: a sliver of relief. For most of her life, she'd been pinned down by all the things she couldn't say. Now she was being released.

'You've got to tell Joe what you told me,' said Bobby. 'I'm not saying he won't be upset. He has every right to be upset. But if he appreciates how sick you were, it might help to explain.'

Rose went to reply, but all that came out was a croak. She cleared her throat with difficulty. 'Thanks,' she said. 'I will.'

She glanced at her son. Was she for ever diminished in his eyes? What about Brooke? How would she react? And what about Martha? And Evanne? Would they hate her? Would they cut off contact? While Mitch had supported her in Bobby's presence, he'd later lapsed into silence. She'd asked if he was okay. His response – a deep inhalation, the raising of his palms to the sky – hadn't been encouraging. The more time he had to think, the more unsettled he became. He'd left early for the office. 'Shall I call you later?' she'd said.

'No,' was his reply. 'We'll talk when I get home.'

As Rose and Bobby walked the final block, a cool wind rippled through the trees. The sky was the colour of wet concrete. Fall was on the way. She'd gone to some trouble over her appearance. She was wearing a cream top and pants and a favourite blue jacket. Her clothes were her chain mail, she supposed. Her way of telling herself and others that she could cope. Nevertheless, her old enemies, the chattering voices, had returned.

*You were young*, one said. *And you were suffocated by grief.*

*You could have been brave*, the other countered. *But you were a coward.*

*You were ill.*

*You were weak.*

*He might understand.*

*He'll never forgive you.*

Joe's office was in a six-storey brownbrick building. Addiction Services was on the top floor, the receptionist said, past Sexual Health and Infectious Diseases. If they got to Domestic Violence, they'd gone too far. Bobby took the lead.

'Here we are,' he said, coming to a stop in front of a glass-doored office.

'I need a minute to compose myself,' said Rose. Her knees had started trembling, as though they'd taken on a life of their own.

Before Bobby could reply, the door opened. Rose had expected an assistant or a secretary, some sort of buffer. Instead she found herself face to face with Joe.

The years fell away.

He looked younger than she'd expected. And healthier; fit, like he ran or climbed hills or something. For a few seconds, his eyes clouded with confusion. He looked at Rose, then at Bobby, and then again at Rose.

'No,' he said. 'Rose? Rose Moroney?'

'Yes,' she said softly. 'I'm Rose Collins now, but you knew me as Rose Moroney.'

'I wasn't expecting you'd . . . Your son spoke to my assistant . . . I thought . . .' He ran a hand through his pale grey hair.

At least he remembered her. Well, of course he remembered her. The scar over his left eye was a permanent reminder of Rose Moroney and her family.

'I'm sorry,' she said. 'I know you thought it'd just be Bobby.'

Joe or JP – she wasn't sure which to call him – composed himself. A smile broke across his face, and he took her hand. His handshake was vigorous, firm; the handshake of a man who was accustomed to greeting nervous strangers. 'Believe me,' she wanted to say, 'when you know why we're here, you'll be sorry you did that.' Instead she mumbled something about how amazing it was to see him. By then he was ushering them into his office.

'Well, I never,' he said, as he leaned back in his soft chair. Rose and Bobby were in similar chairs. Presumably the furnishings were like the handshake: designed to put visitors at their ease.

She tried to imagine what was passing through Joe's head. Her own brain was in chaos. For decades, the man in front of her had been a ghost. She'd trained herself to think of him as a non-person. And now she was sitting in his office, looking at posters, photographs, certificates and testimonials. If the walls could talk, they'd say, 'Good work happens here.'

She wanted to stare at him, to see what had

stayed the same and what had changed. His laugh certainly hadn't altered. It remained throaty, contagious. Again, she wanted to say, 'Stop. When you hear my story, you'll regret this.' They exchanged scraps of information. He'd been married to Sofia for thirty-five years. One of their sons was a social worker, one a carpenter, one a university administrator. He'd adopted the name JP to avoid being confused with his father, but some folks still called him Joe. He was happy to be called Joe. Bree and Davey had divorced in the 1970s. She'd remarried and moved to Florida. As they chatted, Rose could feel Bobby becoming restless. He fidgeted in his chair and picked at an imaginary hole in his jeans. She wanted to savour the moments before Joe knew the truth, but her son was anxious to move on.

Rose straightened her shoulders and smoothed back her hair. Then, with a brief nod in Bobby's direction, she began. 'I'm sure you're wondering why we've contacted you,' she said, 'and there really isn't an easy way to tell this story, so I'm going to dive on in.'

Although Joe gave her a quizzical look, he said nothing.

'I suppose,' she said, 'it begins on the day my parents discovered I was pregnant.'

At the start, Rose stumbled and meandered, including information that wasn't relevant. 'They're only words,' she told herself. 'You just need to find the right ones and put them in the right order.'

Gradually, she found her stride. She told Joe about Carrigbrack and Sister Agnes. She told him about giving birth. About the baby being taken away. About her anger and her grief.

'Hold on a minute,' he said. 'That can't be right. You lost the baby. Your mother told me you had a miscarriage.'

'My mother lied.'

'But you came to see me,' he said, his words clipped. 'I remember it. You were just back from Ireland. Why didn't you tell me the truth?'

She tried to explain. As she did, an image flashed into her head: her eighteen-year-old self, forlorn on a South Boston street, swiping at her tears. It was a long time ago, yet the memory was so potent, it could have been yesterday.

'Correct me if I've got this wrong,' he said, 'but you got spooked by Lois Green so you decided to screw me over? Seriously, Rose, it didn't matter where the baby ended up. I was entitled to know about her.' His hands cut through the air. 'We were going to get married, for God's sake. Or we were until you decided I wasn't good enough for you.'

'No,' replied Rose, her voice too loud. 'It was all far more complex than that. And I swear to you, Joe, I never, ever thought you weren't good enough.'

'Mom's family put an awful lot of pressure on her,' said Bobby. 'I mean, think about the way they shipped her off to that place in Ireland and took away her baby. It was unbelievable.'

'That's one way of putting it,' said Joe. 'You know, Rose, I've come across every kind of dysfunctional behaviour over the years, most of it explained by someone having a needle in their arm or a crack pipe in their mouth. But the Moroneys are in a league of their own. What's your family's excuse, huh?'

Not knowing how to answer, she resumed her story. The words were streaming out now. She told Joe about her marriage, her agreement with Mitch and about the letter arriving from Ireland. Finally, she revealed what she'd said to Martha.

His anguish became more obvious. His left eye twitched and sweat gathered over his upper lip. He rose and walked around the office, the movement so sudden his chair almost toppled over.

'So, let's be clear about this,' he said. 'If this guy here,' he gestured towards Bobby, 'hadn't dug out the truth, chances are I would never have known that Martha existed. Is that right?'

'Well—' began Rose.

'I would've gone to my grave not knowing I had a daughter. Oh, and from what you've told me, that's exactly where she thinks I am: in Blue Hill Cemetery turning into a mound of ashes and bones.'

'Mom is going to tell her,' said Bobby. 'When we leave here, she's going to call Ireland.'

'Is it not a bit late for that?' Joe hurled back. 'Or in your mother's warped world, will one phone call be enough to wipe out four decades of lying?'

'Listen,' Rose said, 'I'm not proud of what I've done. Of course I'm not. But all I can do is try to make amends.' She knew these were clichés, but arguing with someone you no longer know is hard, especially when right is on their side.

'Make amends?' said Joe, with a mocking laugh. 'After forty-five fucking years? You've got to be kidding me.' He paused. 'I need some air. I'll be back in ten minutes. Don't either of you go anywhere.'

After he'd left, Rose realised she was shaking. Every single solitary part of her had its own tremor. She let out a sound like that of a wounded animal. In truth, though, his reaction was no more ferocious than she had feared. At least he believed her. He hadn't dismissed her story as the deluded ramblings of a failing mind.

Bobby put a hand on her forearm. 'You've done the right thing, and you've got to keep on doing the right thing.'

When Joe returned, he was less agitated.

'Tell me about Martha,' he said, as he sat down. 'And about Evanne.'

Rose made a steeple shape with her still-shaking hands. She should have thought of this. She should have prepared a speech. Of course he was going to be curious about his daughter and grand-daughter. She took a deep breath. 'Martha's lovely, genuinely lovely. She's smart too. I wonder if she's lacking in confidence, though. If she's too anxious to please. Then again, I've only just got to know her, so I may have her all wrong. She's a bit of a dreamer, I think. She loves reading. But that's no surprise, given that she's a librarian. Did I mention that she's a librarian? Oh, and she looks like you. A lot like you.'

Rose showed him a photo on her cell phone. Martha and Evanne were sitting in her front room, Martha looking slightly frazzled, Evanne beaming like Miss Universe. 'I'm not sure if you can see the likeness here,' she said, 'but in the flesh, it's obvious.'

'I see it, all right,' said Joe, his voice thick. 'Oh, I can see it.' He closed his eyes and turned away, like he was trying not to cry.

'And Evanne,' said Rose, 'is a real bright spark. I'd say she can be trouble, though. She has a mind of her own, that girl.'

'She's funny too,' said Bobby. 'Both of them are.'

Joe turned back again and faced Rose. 'When can I meet them?' he said.

# CHAPTER 45

Martha picked up a cup and hurled it at the kitchen wall. It smashed with a satisfying *thwack*, and the remains of her coffee went dribbling down the magnolia paint.

'I am not the sort of person who throws crockery,' she said. Not that she knew who she was addressing. Evanne was at Serena's house, so she was on her own. Energy thrummed through her body. She wanted to stomp around the house smashing things up and tearing things down.

She'd just returned from work when Rose had called. For a second or two, Martha had been thrilled to hear her voice. 'Can you talk?' Rose had said. 'There's something I need to tell you.'

*Crash!* A plate shattered and fell. So Martha had been misled again. She'd been lied to by two mothers. Or had she been wilfully blind? Should she have guessed that Joe being dead was too convenient? Yes, she decided, she'd been a complete and total fool. She should have probed further. She should have prised out the real story. Come to think of it, that was what she would have done

– if the other bombshell hadn't got in the way. The bombshell from which she was still recovering. But shouldn't that first lie have made her even more alert? If you're mugged once, shouldn't you always be vigilant for footsteps behind your back?

'You've got to stop blaming yourself,' she said, as a second plate met a messy end. 'It's not your fault that your family are irredeemably screwed-up.'

Martha thought of her social worker's comments about the lies people were willing to tell. 'Well, Malachy McCracken,' she said, 'wait until you hear about this. This is definitely one for your list of fucked-up families and their fucked-up lies.'

She picked up another cup, a pleasingly weighty one. Then she paused and looked at the mess on the floor. What was she doing? She needed to find Evanne and tell her the news.

'No,' said Evanne. 'That's not possible.'

'Not only is it possible,' replied Martha, 'it's true.' She gave Evanne the newspaper article that Rose had guided her towards: *A life devoted to second chances*. 'Here he is.'

'Wowser,' said her daughter. 'You're the spitting image of him.'

'At least that's one thing Rose didn't lie about.'

Evanne read the newspaper profile, her face taut with concentration. When she looked up, her eyes were hard and shiny like blue marbles. 'Is it just me,' she said, 'or does Joe sound like someone you'd be proud to have in your family? Were Rose's parents stupid or what?'

'It's not just you,' said Martha. 'And, yes, they really were thick.'

'Imagine, he's only just found out about us. He could be telling his wife about us right now. He could be saying, "Sit down, honey, there's something we need to talk about."' Evanne had attempted a Boston accent. She'd sounded like a gangster from one of those films she was fond of watching.

Despite herself, Martha smiled. 'Does it change how you feel about Rose?'

'I don't know. I'll have to do some thinking. I suppose it explains why she hasn't been replying to my emails and such. She must've been having a difficult old time of it, what with this stuff going on in her head . . . and then Bobby saying, "Guess what? I know the truth."'

'She did mention your emails. She said to tell you she was sorry.'

Evanne nodded slowly. 'And you – how are you doing?'

'I keep telling myself that this shouldn't be as big a deal as the last shock. After all, it's not as though we've known Rose for very long.'

'True. But to pretend that someone's dead? That's a big deal in my book.'

Martha realised that in the space of two hours her rage had given way to sadness. The sadness had been joined by something else: an uncomfortable feeling that she couldn't dislodge, no matter how hard she tried. Earlier, when Rose had finished her story, Bobby had come on the line. 'Are you sorry you ever got involved with us?' he'd asked.

'No,' she'd replied, and it had been the honest answer. She had wanted the truth, and now she had it. All of it. The shame was that it was so intensely sad, and that Rose had perpetuated such an enormous lie.

'What are you going to do?' Evanne was asking. 'I presume you want to meet Joe or JP or . . . Now that I think of it, what should we call him?'

'I'm tempted to say we should call him Lazarus,' said Martha. 'And, yes, I do want to meet him, but I'm the same as you. I need to do some thinking.'

She should have told Evanne that Joe was insisting they meet. 'We'll pay your fare,' Rose had said. 'Please come.' Martha had explained that with the new school term about to start, Evanne would have to stay in Ireland. 'Come on your own, then,' replied Rose. But Martha couldn't go to Boston without her daughter, could she?

Evanne cocked her head. 'It's funny. A year ago, there was only you and Una. Then there was Bobby and Brooke. And now there's . . .?'

'Michael, Joel and Eric.'

'What a lot of family we've got.'

'And so many Americans.'

'Can I ask you another question?'

'Fire ahead,' said Martha.

'Why's there a big brown stain on the wall?'

* * *

'Good Lord almighty,' said her mam, 'are you joking me?'

'Nope,' said Martha. 'I kind of wish I was. Well, no, I don't. Of course I don't. I'm delighted that Joe's alive.'

'Clem! Clem!' shouted her mother. 'It's Martha on the phone. You won't believe what Rose has told her.'

Martha heard the swish of voices, then her dad asked, 'Is she all right?'

'Are you all right, pet?' echoed Delia.

'I'm fine, Mam.'

'I'm sorry now that Una and myself came back to Templemorris this morning. I'm sure you could do with a bit of company. Only with you at work and Evanne off somewhere with one of her friends, there didn't seem much point in us hanging around.'

'Is Una there?'

'She's up the town with a couple of her old friends, although what they've all got to say to each other I don't know.' Her mother's voice made it clear she didn't approve of this socialising. 'What does Dermot think?'

'I haven't told him yet.'

'I take it you'll be keeping him in the loop?'

'Don't worry, I'll give him a shout in a small while.' She could tell that her mother was torn: part pleased that they were first to hear the news, part anxious that Martha remain on good terms with her former husband. Not that her mam would use the word 'former'. Evanne's Fourmilecross story had convinced Delia that Dermot and Layla were no more. Martha expected the reconciliation hints to start soon.

The more things changed . . .

'Jesus wept,' said Cat. 'You can't be serious.'

'I am, you know.'

'Do you want me to come over?'

'Nah, you're grand. Evanne's talking to me again. Anyway, I'm okay. I'd forgotten about the therapeutic power of firing stuff against a wall.'

'Stuff?'

Martha explained.

'Well done,' said Cat. 'I did something similar when I found out about my dad's other family. There's a lot to be said for the mindless destruction of inanimate objects. What did Paudie say?'

'I haven't been talking to him.'

'Are you tired of him already?'

'As a matter of fact, we're having dinner tomorrow night. We can talk about it then. By the way, you would've died with laughter if you were here last night. Mam got stuck into him. "I don't know what women see in that fellow," she said.'

'Hold on a sec, what was Delia doing in Dublin?'

'Ah, hell, I'm sorry. With everything else going on, I forgot to mention that Mam turned up on the doorstep. She wanted to make peace. Una was here too.'

'Do you remember,' said Cat, 'when we used to complain that nothing happened any more?'

'So when are you planning on going to America?' asked Paudie, twirling linguine around his fork. They were in a restaurant close to his house, an Italian place with a relaxed atmosphere and a house white that went down like nectar.

'If I can get everything sorted, the week after next. I'm due time off work, and my boss isn't the worst of them, so I'm hoping the short notice won't be a problem.'

'And Evanne?'

'Doesn't know yet,' said Martha.

It was only on the walk to the restaurant that her thoughts had crystallised. If Joe wanted to see her, she should go as soon as possible. Two days ago, she'd thought the closest she would get to meeting him was standing beside his gravestone. Now he'd been resurrected. There would be other chances for him to meet Evanne.

Evanne was babysitting while Dermot and Layla were – or weren't – reunited. She'd sent Martha a text with a photo of Alex. The little fellow was grinning like the national bonny baby champion, his lone tooth on display. *Look who wants to say hello*, Evanne had written. Martha had to hand it to the girl: she didn't give up easily.

While she walked, she'd had the time and space to consider what Rose and her family had done. The air was clear, the way it always was after a couple of days of rain. Its sharpness aided her thinking. Not for the first time, she marvelled at Grace and Ed's cruelty. She marvelled, too, at Rose. There she was: a middle-class housewife with flawless manners and a perfect blow-dry, the very essence of respectability. Yet for decades she'd lugged around a pernicious secret. Oh, and less than two months earlier, she'd sat there, cool as you like, and told Martha that her natural father was dead. Neither could Martha leave Mitch out of the equation. The personification of the ever-so-slightly dull businessman, he'd encouraged his wife to live a complex lie.

On her journey, Martha passed street after street of pristine red brick, gleaming doors and well-tamed hedges. How conventional everything appeared. How mundane. And yet . . . who was to say what people were doing behind those glossy doors? They could be sitting around the dinner table like a Dublin incarnation of the Waltons or they could be passed out drunk on the kitchen floor. Her dad used to say you should be nice to people because you didn't know how they were suffering. But it wasn't just their troubles you didn't know. You knew nothing of their joys either; their ambitions or desires; their capacity to inflict pain or their ability to lie. Lives that appeared small might be immense. Lives dismissed as uneventful might be brimming with intrigue or emotion.

'Are you going to say it or will I?' she said to Paudie.

He ran a finger down the side of his glass. 'I won't pretend that I don't know what you're talking about. It's not the same, though, is it?'

'Some would say it is. When Rose first told me about Joe, I was beside myself with anger. Then I started thinking about my own life. So now everything I say is tempered by the knowledge of what I did.'

'We've been through this, Martha.'

She stared at her risotto. 'I know. It's . . . I suppose this is a reminder that just because you confront something, that doesn't mean it goes away. It's not like a TV programme where the truth comes out, the characters have a good old rant and everybody moves on, like nothing happened. People keep asking me if I can forgive Rose, and I want to say to them, "*Me?* How can I not?" Instead I hum and haw and dance around the question.'

Martha had imagined that once she told Paudie about the abortion, the episode would be consigned to history, but she'd kept something from him for a very long time, something he'd deserved to know. Could he really forget about that? She didn't want to say it might always come between them because that would imply a permanence to their relationship. She didn't even know if it was 'a relationship'. *Oh, great, Martha,* she thought. *Why don't you sit here obsessing and ruin a perfectly good night?*

Paudie moved his hand along the table so that

their fingertips touched. 'I saw your mother when I was in Templemorris. She really doesn't like me, does she?'

'Why do you ask?'

'Her face says it all. Ruán said to me, "Why did that woman give you a funny look?" I said, "Because thirty years ago I teased her daughter and made her cry."'

'She's loyal, is Mam. What did Ruán say?'

'Not a lot. He's a boy of few words. But I think it confirmed his suspicion that Templemorris is a strange sort of place. I was tempted to holler, "Evening, Mrs Sheeran. Did you know I've been keeping company with your daughter?"'

'Is that what we're doing?'

His hand covered hers. 'I've always liked you, Martha. You know that. Even when I was at school acting the bollocks, I liked you. You had this lovely calmness about you. Oh, and you wore very tight jeans.'

'Mam used to say they'd give me varicose veins.'

Paudie smiled.

'They didn't, by the way.'

'And you were a dreamer.'

'I still am, or so everybody complains.'

'Tuh,' he said. 'What's wrong with dreaming? I'm not sure I'm in favour of all this living-in-the-now business. Sometimes the now is a grim place. More dreaming, that's what I say.'

It was Martha's turn to smile.

'And then,' said Paudie, returning to their shared

history, 'when we did get together . . . I lost the run of myself, and things went . . . awry.'

For a man who spoke for a living, he was wonderfully inarticulate. 'That's one way of putting it,' she said.

'Then the next time I came across you, you were married to the man who keeps me on the straight and narrow, so that kind of put the kibosh on that. And now, all these years later . . . here we are.'

'Here we are,' repeated Martha, sounding, she was sure, slightly simple. She liked Paudie far too much. She knew that. He was flaky and unreliable. He was overly fond of flattery and the lure of twenty-six-year-olds. Her best friend disapproved of him. Her mother had nothing but disdain for him. And Martha liked him far too much.

'I'm still a bit of a fool,' he said.

'You're not alone in that.'

'You're anything but a fool, Martha.' He gave her hand a squeeze. 'You know the way it is: sometimes you don't realise how much you've missed someone until you see them again, and you find yourself thinking, *This. This is what I've been missing.*'

Warm feelings sloshed around inside her.

'I really enjoy being with you,' he said.

'And I enjoy being with you.'

'So, as I might have said if we were having a smooch at the community hall disco, will you go with me?'

'Go steady, like?'

Paudie's eyes crinkled in a way that had always made her dizzy. 'Yeah.'

'Do you sometimes feel,' she said, 'the same as you did back then? Like, just as clueless?'

'God, no. I was way more together back then.'

Martha did her best to look serious. 'Just so as we're clear here, this going steady, there'll be no messing?'

'I promise. Absolutely no messing.'

'All right, then,' she said. 'Going steady it is.'

# CHAPTER 46

She was in the air now.

Within the next few hours, Martha would be back in Boston. Rose had invited her daughter to come and stay, but the offer was politely declined. After everything that had happened, who could blame her for wanting to keep her distance? She would stay in a downtown hotel. Tomorrow they would both go to see Joe, a prospect that thrilled and terrified Rose in equal measure. In the meantime, she had to contend with another member of her family.

It had taken more than a week for the news to filter down to Nancy, but when it did, she'd decided that a face-to-face encounter was needed. The sisters rarely saw each other. Apart from the occasional stilted phone conversation, they kept contact to a minimum. Their relationship was long on resentment, short on understanding. After the zero-fucks phone call, Nancy had vanished in a sulk. Now, though, she was sitting on Rose's couch, looking as if she'd stepped out of an advertisement for ill-fitting beige synthetics. Then again, you could wrap Nancy in Chanel haute couture and she'd still manage to look like the final discount rail in Marshalls.

'It's all true,' said Rose. 'Everything you've heard.'

'That,' said Nancy, 'is what I tried to warn you about. When the letter first arrived from Ireland, I said, "That's trouble coming down the pike. You get involved with that girl and you'll lose control."' She squirmed, as if her underwear was too tight. 'But you insisted you knew better.'

'Martha,' said Rose. 'My daughter's name is Martha.' Other than this, she chose not to argue. After all, was there not some truth in what Nancy was saying? In replying to Martha's letter, hadn't Rose known that the full story might emerge? And, deep down, hadn't that been what she'd wanted? In her heart, hadn't she hoped that her daughter's arrival would lead to the end of the family charade? Oh, for months she'd continued to play the game. She'd lied to Martha and Evanne. She'd muddled on, the push and pull tipping her into a dark place. Then Bobby had discovered the truth, and when Rose's initial shock had subsided, she'd realised that something within her had loosened. She was where she wanted to be.

'I assume he wants to see her,' said Nancy.

'He does. In fact, she's on her way to Boston right now. We're meeting up tomorrow.'

'You know, for once I'm glad Mom and Dad are no longer with us. This would have been very difficult for them.'

Telling Martha had been hard. Her initial disbelief had been followed by anger. 'What's this problem you all have with the truth?' she'd asked Rose. The following morning she'd called back. 'I should have known there was more,' she said. 'There always seems to be more.' Evanne called too. Unusually, she said relatively little. Rose sensed that her granddaughter wanted to hear at least some of the story at first hand so she could go away and try to make sense of it all.

And Brooke? Oh, Brooke. It would have been easier if she'd been angry and abrasive. Instead, her head slumped into her hands and her voice became a low murmur. 'This is all so fucking awful,' she kept saying. 'What sort of people *are* we?' She'd returned the next evening with a bottle of cabernet. They'd drunk it together. Then they'd drunk another bottle. The drunker they got, the more maudlin they became, but it was a companionable sort of maudlin. Save for the occasional baffled look, Mitch avoided them.

'Who knows?' said Rose to Nancy. 'Maybe Mom would've had a change of heart. Joe turned out to be very respectable in the end.'

'I wouldn't go that far. If you ask me, most of those drugs counsellors should emote a little less and condemn a little more. Only the other week, Theo's sister had her purse snatched by a guy who was off his head on something or other.'

Rose stretched out her legs. 'Look at us, Nancy, bickering about the events of almost fifty years ago. Do we really want to keep fighting a war that began when we were teenagers?'

Nancy pressed her lips together, as if she was saying, 'Come on, Rose, this isn't how it goes. We have a routine here. You're supposed to get snippy with me.'

'I'm not saying we should be best friends,' continued Rose. 'That's never going to happen. But let's not carry on sniping about the past. Think about it: why should you care what I do? What happened was all about avoiding shame and—'

'It was about more than that. Okay, Mom was always looking over her shoulder at the neighbours, but she genuinely believed that if you became entangled with the Brennans your life would be ruined. And Dad was worried too. Whatever you might think, they weren't wilfully cruel.'

'I don't know what they were, Nance. What I do know is that Carrigbrack was a long time ago. And, whether you agree with me or not, I'm trying to do the right thing.'

'This isn't just about you,' replied Nancy, her face colouring beneath her powder. 'And don't look at me like I'm heartless. I do remember how Ireland affected you. God knows, I've often asked myself if Mom and Dad did the right thing.'

'They didn't,' said Rose, after a moment's pause. 'Please don't have any doubt about that.' She spoke softly. Her sister's admission had surprised her, and she didn't want to sound triumphant.

'You've got to consider other people's feelings,

though. I can't imagine what all of this is doing to Mitch. What does he think about Joe Brennan coming back into your life?'

'He's not back in my life and, given what I did to him, it's a miracle he's willing to talk to me at all.' She ran a hand through her hair. 'Jesus, I know none of this is ideal. I know Mitch is cut up about everything. Still, we'll get through it. We'll have to.'

Rose's husband was conflicted. He didn't have to say so. It was there on his face, in the twist in his mouth and the strain in his eyes. He was a good man. He hadn't wanted her to keep on suffering, but he hadn't wanted this mess either. There were days when she wondered if their marriage would ever be the same. And then there was the other question. Mitch hadn't asked it yet, but one day soon he would. *Would Rose have preferred a life with Joe?* Obviously her answer would be no. 'How can you even ask such a thing?' she would say. But the truth – the cold, stinging truth – was that she didn't know. Maybe what she'd had with Joe was no more than a teenage flirtation. Maybe they would never have formed a lasting bond. Or maybe they would still be together, with other children and grandchildren. Maybe they would have been happy. She would never know.

But she would always wonder.

'Ed and Ray were asking about you,' said Nancy. 'What'll I tell them?'

'Tell them everything's good, sort of topsy-turvy, but good.'

Rose could only imagine what her brothers made of developments. Right now, though, she didn't want to dwell on what others thought of her. She didn't want to feel the weight of their judgement.

She'd had enough of that.

# CHAPTER 47

Pauline Bennis had got it right. She'd said that when you first saw someone who looked just like you, the sensation was incomparable. Now Martha knew what she'd meant. There could have been a thousand people in the hotel lobby, and still she would have spotted him. With Rose, she'd had to search for the similarities; for the small things, like her ankles and her ears. Seeing Joe was like seeing herself.

All the same, she flicked a questioning look at Rose.

Her birth mother nodded.

For ten, twenty seconds, they stood and stared. Then Joe reached out and folded her into an embrace. His shirt and jacket were soft, his smell slightly old-fashioned. A soapy sort of smell, it reminded Martha of her other father back in Templemorris.

'My girl,' Joe kept saying. 'My girl.'

When they disentangled, they stared again. Martha felt as if every sound was amplified, as if she was breathing different air. There was a fast fluttering high up in her chest, a tingling along her arms. Her mind was doing cartwheels.

'We'd better sit down,' he said eventually. 'We're starting to turn into a public exhibit.'

Martha followed his gaze around the lobby. Yes, people were gawping at them.

Joe's mouth curved into a big bear hug of a smile. 'They'll be selling tickets in a minute.'

Martha smiled too. Not just at the comment, but at his voice. Evanne's impersonation hadn't been too far out. It was a gorgeous voice.

Rose hung back slightly, as if she wasn't sure whether she belonged, as if she was scared of intruding.

'Come on, Rosie,' said Joe. 'You too. Let's get a coffee.'

Martha wondered how much effort it took for him to be so cordial. By rights, he should be congested with anger, barely able to utter a civil word. How did he really feel about the woman who'd pretended he was dead? Martha would have to learn how to decode him, like she was learning to decode Rose. At first sight, the past few weeks had changed her. There was a chalkiness to her skin and new hollows beneath her eyes. Her walk was jaunty, though, and she held her head high. She was a complicated woman, was Rose Collins.

'And I gather you have a daughter?' said Joe, as the three drank their coffee.

'Yes. I wish she was here, only the school term has started and this is an important year for her. She sends her love, though, and she'll be with me next . . .' Martha allowed her voice to trail away.

Was it presumptuous to talk about a next time? She wished there was a handbook: *Meeting Your Birth Father When You'd Thought He Was Dead and He's Only Just Discovered You Exist.*

Mercifully, Joe didn't appear to notice her discomfort. 'She's what? Seventeen?'

'Mmm, and you know how it is – some days she acts like she's seven, and other days you'd swear she was forty-seven.'

'She's a smart young lady,' said Rose.

Martha tapped the side of her head. 'I almost forgot.' She reached into her bag and took out a wallet of photographs. 'I was planning on doing the modern thing and showing you the pictures on my phone, but they're so much better like this, aren't they?'

As Joe shuffled through the photos, he shook his head. 'Am I looking at Evanne?' he said. 'Or am I looking at Rose Moroney, *circa* 1968?'

For the first time, Martha worried that he might break down. 'Is this – all of this – very difficult for you?'

He blinked slowly. 'Truth to tell, I'm not sure I've taken it on board yet. But I will. I will.'

He passed the photos to Rose, and there they sat, heads bent like they were a regular couple admiring a grandchild. Although they didn't say very much, there were worlds of information in what they did say.

'I've never been to Ireland,' said Joe. 'Sofia's originally from Puerto Rico, and that's where we usually spend our vacations. But our son, Eric, was in Galway a few years back. It was wild, he said.'

'I might try going back,' said Rose. 'Next year, maybe.'

Martha couldn't help but imagine them as they'd been in 1968, before life had chipped away at them. They'd been kids back then. Good kids. Vibrant. Passionate. In love. Impulsive. Impatient. Ambitious.

She'd spent the bulk of her life thinking that Rose and Joe had abandoned her. That wasn't true. She'd thought that meeting them didn't matter to her. That wasn't true either. She'd worried that they'd reject her, disappoint her; that tracing them would be disloyal to Clem and Delia. Not true. Not true. Not true. The pity was that she hadn't found Rose and Joe years ago. Then again, maybe it was only now that she was ready. That all of them were ready.

She thought about what had been done to them, then pushed the thought away. There would be another time for that. She wanted to hold this moment.

'Tell me about Sofia and your sons,' she said to Joe.

'You have no idea how intrigued they are by you,' he said. 'They're dying to meet up – if that's what you want.'

'Oh, gosh, it's definitely what I want. I'd love to meet them. In fact, Evanne would kill me if I didn't.' She breathed in. 'It's all so . . .'

'Overwhelming,' said Rose.

'That's exactly what it is,' agreed Martha. 'Overwhelming.'

Afterwards, Martha and Rose went for a walk. They crossed Boston Common, each preoccupied by her own thoughts. Mostly Martha thought about Joe, but her mind flicked back to Dublin too. Evanne would have finished school by now. She'd expect a call. Martha also needed to ring her parents. And Cat. And Paudie.

What a scene she'd left behind at Dublin Airport. Cat had insisted on giving her a lift, but as Martha checked in, who had turned up only Paudie, his smile as wide as O'Connell Bridge. With US Immigration and all the other palaver to clear, she'd just had time for a hurried goodbye. As she'd stood in the security queue, she'd watched the two go for coffee. They were . . . well, friendly might be stretching it, but they weren't openly hostile. When Martha returned to Dublin, she'd have a word with Dermot. According to Evanne, he and Layla were making progress but continued to live apart. A small part of her worried how he'd react to her news. She didn't want him to think that Paudie was a revenge relationship; an elaborate up-yours. That being said, she'd have to be a saint not to take some pleasure from surprising him, and sainthood was not an honour she was ever likely to claim.

They were walking more briskly now, into the

Public Garden, past the pond and the swan boats, Beacon Hill to their right, clusters of tourists all around. Up ahead, a jumble of tall buildings glinted in the sun. The light was different here on the Atlantic's western shore, sharper somehow. American light. Martha was struck by how little she knew about this city, but she was part of its story, and it was part of hers.

She took Rose's hand. 'Are you all right?'

'Uh-huh. What about you?'

Martha recalled another day like this, exactly a year before, summer's warmth on the wane, the first puffs of autumn in the air. She remembered leaving Dermot's office, swaddled in loneliness. Yet all along her life had been waiting for her. She had two mothers, two fathers, a daughter, a sister, a half-sister, four half-brothers, a friend.

And she had the promise of more.

She smiled at Rose. 'I'm good,' she said.